Available
from Katy Regnery

a modern fairytale

The Vixen and the Vet
Never Let You Go
Ginger's Heart (coming soon!)
Don't Speak (coming soon!)

THE BLUEBERRY LANE SERIES

THE ENGLISH BROTHERS

Breaking Up with Barrett
Falling for Fitz
Anyone but Alex
Seduced by Stratton
Wild about Weston
Kiss Me Kate

THE WINSLOW BROTHERS

Bidding on Brooks
Proposing to Preston

ALSO

Frosted, a novella
Playing for Love at Deep Haven
The Wedding Date, a Kindle Worlds novella

Never Let *You* Go

*****

KATY REGNERY

Cover by Marianne Nowicki
Developmental Editing by Tessa Shapcott
Copy and Line Editing by First Person Editing Services
Formatting by Cookie Lynn Publishing Services

Please visit my website at www.katyregnery.com
First Edition: June 2015
Katy Regnery
Never Let You Go : a novel / by Katy Regnery – 1st ed.
ISBN: 978-1514171400

For Gretl, who was nothing like Cutter.
My grief started this journey.

We miss your gentle spirit.

ESCAPE

Holden

"Get up, Holden!" she hissed at him, one dirty hand waving wildly in his face. His eyes were level with her bare feet, which were filthy and scratched, bright red blood oozing through a layer of dust and mud splatter.

Holden could hear them coming, getting closer and closer with every labored breath he took, but his legs burned and his feet were torn to pieces.

Griselda reached down, grabbing a handful of his hair and jerking his head up. "I mean it. Now!"

He pushed himself up out of the muddy puddle that had tripped him, and reached for her hand.

"Run!" she demanded, setting off at a clip, pulling him down the rugged dirt road, the tail of one amber braid whipping into his forehead as they made their way closer to the safety of the high corn. "I know you hurt, Holden. I hurt too, but don't stop!"

Tears rolled down his cheeks as his shorter legs worked twice as hard to keep up with her.

"G-G-Gris," he sobbed, staring at the dirty, ripped, yellow

and white gingham dress that covered her back. "M-m-my ankle's twisted."

"Don't think about it. Keep running," she said, without looking back, her grip on his hand unmerciful. "We're almost there."

From behind them, Holden heard the Man's voice. "Dang cornfields! Don't let them make it through the rows, or we'll lose them, Cutter!"

The words were loud and slurred, and the baying of the meanest hound on earth answered his master's command.

"You hear that?" Gris gasped between pants. "Faster, Holden!"

Amazingly, she sped up, dragging him along behind her, running as fast as her thirteen year old legs could carry her. Holden's feet barely set down long enough between steps to register the sharp prickles of the spurge weed as they sped barefoot across the field.

"Through the cornfields and across the river. Through the cornfields and across the river."

He heard her whispering it under her breath like a mantra, and though Holden couldn't feel his legs anymore, he wouldn't let her down. Somehow his feet kept moving, despite the pain.

Fight through it, he thought. *Fight, damn it!*

With a yank and a whoosh, she steered them into the nearest row of corn, the hot green stalks batting them in the face as the dead brown leaves below sliced into their bare legs and feet like blades.

Holden whimpered from the sharp cuts but kept the sound as quiet as possible, lest she hear him. His fingers were numb from Gris's iron grip on them, and his wrist ached from the way she jerked his hand as she pulled him along. He looked down at his feet and saw a blur of brown below. He had no idea if they'd make it, but he knew one thing for sure: he wouldn't have had a chance without her.

"Th-th-thank God you're so d-d-dang stubborn."

"Almost there," she said, risking a quick look behind her, and even managing a small, encouraging smile at her friend.

Holden wanted to offer one to her in return, but his lip had been split last night and it hurt too much to smile.

"You get 'em, Cutter!"

The Man's voice was getting closer, and they were only halfway through the cornfield. Cutter barked his pleasure, and the sound vibrated through Holden's thin body like a beating.

"Not today, Cutter," growled Gris, darting to her right and crossing two rows before heading left toward the river again.

"Th-th-think we'll make it, Gris?"

"Keep running," she panted. "We're almost there."

He finally heard the rush of water, and when he looked up, just beyond Gris, he saw it—

the banks of the Shenandoah.

"Remember, Holden. Don't look back, no matter what. Our feet are smaller than his. Stone to stone. I jump, you jump. We get halfway across, he won't follow."

We get halfway across, we still might die, thought Holden, looking at the way the water rushed white over the rocks in the middle, painfully aware that he didn't know how to swim.

"I hear you thinking, Holden Croft," she said, her words choppy and short since she was so out of breath, "but it hasn't rained in nine days. That's why today. That's why *now*."

They finally rushed through the end of the row, their feet alighting on the softer grass that ran along the banks of the river. Not having eaten since yesterday morning, Holden was light-headed and dizzy, and he didn't know how he'd keep his balance if they couldn't stop to rest for a second. As they reached the water's edge, Gris, who must have been as dizzy as he, dropped his hand and leaned over, placing her hands on her bony knees to catch her breath.

Cutter's baleful howl drew closer, and Holden looked up to

see the stalks shaking about twenty yards back, the Man's rifle tip poking up over the golden tassels. When Holden turned his head, Gris's sky-blue eyes captured his.

"This is it. You ready?"

Holden looked at wide stretch of river. Gris was right that the water didn't look as deep as the other time they'd seen it, almost three years ago, but it didn't look safe either. Rocks jutted up from the bottom, sharp and ragged, and water whooshed white over some of the stones in the middle.

Gris took his hands, her keen eyes darting back and forth between his. "Stone to stone. I jump, you jump."

Holden whipped his neck to see Cutter bound out of the corn, emitting a proud wail when he caught sight of the two children huddled together by the shore's edge.

"Now!" screamed Gris.

Pulling Holden's hand, she stepped forward with a splash and Holden followed, the cold water both shocking and soothing on his shredded feet. She dropped his hand so she'd be able to maintain her balance, and started hopping from rock to rock. Holden stared at her feet, just as he had all the times they'd practiced in the damp, dark cellar. As she leaped, the water cleaned her feet, until they were shiny and white, with deep scratches and gouges. Hop, steady. Leap, stop.

If she looked behind to confirm he was following, he didn't know it, his eyes were so fixated on her feet. His heart thundered in his chest, knowing that at any moment Cutter could leap into the water, or the Man could grab the back of Holden's threadbare gray T-shirt and yank him back to shore, away from Gris.

From behind, Holden heard a loud splash, like how it would sound if a pair of men's boots hit the water at the same time, but Cutter didn't sound as close. His barks went back and forth across the riverbank, where he must have been pacing and howling, reluctant to follow his master into the cold, rushing water.

"Ruth!" the Man called to Griselda. "Ya stop right now, gal, or I'm a'set to lash s'many stripes in yer back, it'll take the devil hisself to stop me."

The Man's breath wasn't so far away now. Not close enough to smell, but like a dragon's from the fairy stories Gris told, it was burning and hateful and roaring and low, filling Holden's ears with dread. He fought the temptation to turn around, to look at the monster behind him, but he heard Gris's voice in his head: *Don't look back, no matter what. Our feet are small. Stone to stone. I jump, you jump.*

He hazarded a glance up, and Gris was getting to the middle now, but consumed with her progress, she wasn't looking back anymore. The distance between them was widening little by little as Holden struggled to keep up with her.

"And you, ya godforsaken half-wit, I'll club yer head in and finish the job the devil started, Seth."

Holden clenched his fists at his side as he heard a loud splash followed by some angry cussing.

We get halfway across, he won't follow.

Hop, steady. Leap, stop. Hop, steady. The water rushed around the rocks now, making them more slippery than they'd been closer to the shore, and Holden's breath caught as he almost slid off a mossy one, compensating by tilting his body back, then forward, to find his balance.

"You still with me, Holden?" Gris yelled.

"I'm still—"

The butt of the Man's rifle rammed against Holden's ear with a sharp, shocking thwack that made the side of his face explode in pain and sent him sailing off the rock and into the river. Disoriented, with stars bursting behind his eyes, he heard Griselda scream "Holden!" over the sound of the water sluicing between them.

The Man stood waist-deep in the rushing water, holding the

neck of Holden's shirt bunched up in his hand. With one yank, he dragged him up out of the water and onto a nearby rock like a rag doll.

"I got'ya now, dummy . . ."

Holden coughed and gurgled, crouched on the rock in defeat, the front of his shirt almost strangling him from the Man's hold on it. It took strength he didn't have to raise his head and find Gris's stricken face about ten feet ahead. She hopped back one rock closer, her eyes desperate as she looked from Holden to the Man, back and forth, her face crumbling in agony as she understood her choice.

"Oh, Holden," she sobbed.

"Ya'll come on along, now, gal. Ya'ain't leavin' him all on his now. Are ya?"

Holden could hear Cutter's victory wail from the shore as the Man's hand twisted and tightened on Holden's shirt, almost cutting off his oxygen supply.

"You leave him be! Let him go!" she demanded in a shaking, furious voice, small hands fisted by her sides. She flicked her devastated blue eyes to Holden before looking back up at the Man.

"Fuck. You," he drawled. "Ya'll come on along, Ruth. *Now!*"

Holden shook his head back and forth, faster and faster, his throat chafing against the tightness of the fabric around his neck, as his eyes locked on hers. He felt the hot, wet, humiliating tears trail down his cheeks, but he kept his jaw firm and square, his lips tight, his eyes burning with thanks and regret and love.

Ask me if I'm whole . . . Ask me . . .

"G-G-Gris," he sputtered. Then, mustering the last bit of strength in his small body, pushing through a haze of tears and terror and exhaustion, he bellowed, "R-r-r-r-uuuuuun!"

Thwack!

And then there was only darkness.

CHAPTER 1

Ten years later

Griselda

"No, Jonah. I can't do that. I won't."

"Don't you love me, baby?"

Griselda shifted her glance from the windshield to her boyfriend's handsome profile, running her eyes over his thick, chestnut hair, aquiline nose, and pouty lips. He caught her staring and winked at her playfully before turning his glance back to the road.

"I—I care about you, sure," she hedged.

He clucked at her, shaking his head as his knuckles tightened on the wheel. "Didn't ask if you *cared* about me, Zelda. Asked if you *loved* me."

She heard the warning in his voice and subtly crossed her fingers in her lap. "'Course I love you. But what does loving you have to do with it?"

"You know? Sometimes I think you like to play stupid just to piss me off." He picked up the Snapple bottle in his lap, pressing it to his mouth, and she watched a stream of dark brown spit shoot to the bottom of the glass. When he turned to her, some brown spittle on his bottom lip made it glisten. "If you *love* someone, you want to make them happy."

"By doing something we both know is wrong?"

"Wrong?" He clucked again, backhanding his mouth to wipe it clean. "Now, honey, the only thing *wrong* is the way you're looking at this."

"How's that, Jonah? How is me stealing from my employer *right*?"

"Because then you and me can join our friends for a sweet little weekend getaway. And your Jo-Jo will be happy. And happy is always right."

Griselda shook her head, angling her body away from his and leaning her elbow on the window. She knew very little about happiness, but Jonah's version of it didn't agree with her.

"You like Shawn and Tina," he cajoled.

She ignored him.

"A few beers? A good time?"

. . . that would likely end up with Jonah and Shawn, his friend from the cable company where he worked, getting stinking drunk and shooting beer cans off rocks like rednecks until the sun came up.

"Didn't even tell you where we're headed yet," he said, poking her thigh just a little too hard to be playful.

Looking askance, she gave him a bored, annoyed look.

"Makes me want to smack your mouth when you look at me all ugly like that, Zelda."

She flinched before forcing a small, brittle smile.

"That's my girl," he said, spitting into the bottle again. "Shawn knows a guy who owns luxury cabins a couple of hours from here. Somewhere out in Pennsylvania. Said he'd rent one to us."

"Whereabouts?"

"Naw, that's not right. Not Pennsylvania. Uh, West Virginia, I think."

Griselda's breath hitched, but Jonah was staring out the windshield and didn't notice.

"Always so much goddamned traffic in the goddamned city," he griped, merging into the thick D.C. traffic as they crossed the bridge into the quaint neighborhood of Georgetown. One modest benefit of dating Jonah was that he drove her to work every morning, which meant she didn't have to take the bus anymore. "Why can't you work for a family closer to home?"

"Money's better in the city. Where in West Virginia?" she asked, trying to calm the fierce thumping of her heart by taking a long, deep breath.

Jonah's eyes darted back and forth, looking for an opening in the stream of cars before finally turning. His voice was distracted. "I don't—uh, it's by a river, I think."

Her fingers trembled in her lap as she scrambled to remember the names of them, praying it wasn't the same one that she visited over and over again in her dreams, in her nightmares.

"The Cacapon?"

"Naw, that wasn't it."

"One of the Forks?"

"Naw."

"The Cheat?"

"You making that up, baby?" His eyes darted to hers, narrowed in accusation.

"No," she said, shaking her head. "There's a river called the Cheat in West Virginia. Honest."

"Well, that wasn't it, anyway."

"The . . ." She clenched her jaw hard before spitting out the words, "The Shenandoah?"

He pulled up in front of Senator McClellan's townhouse and turned to her. "Look at you, all booky-booky smart and shit. Yeah. The Shenandoah River. That's the one."

Griselda took another deep breath and nodded, looking down at her lap, her brain short-circuiting as she flashed back to the last time she'd felt the waters of the Shenandoah against her skin. She shuddered, trying to force the thought from her mind, but she couldn't. The shock of hearing the river's name had already conjured the image of Holden's wet, filthy face, his hair plastered to his head, his eyelashes dripping with water, his terrified gray eyes that somehow managed to tell her how much he loved her, even though she . . . she—

Jonah grabbed her chin a little harder than necessary and dropped his lips to hers, kissing her forcefully, bruisingly. When he pulled back, his eyes were narrow again.

"You know I hate it when you space out."

"Sorry, Jonah," she said. "Got lost in thought."

"If I ever thought you was thinking about another man, I'd—"

She shook her head. "There's no one but you."

He smirked, kissing her again, still hard, but not quite as angry, and it shamed her that the bitter taste of his mouth was so comforting. "Now tell me you'll do it."

"Do it?"

"The money. Take a bracelet or something. I'll fence it. She'll never notice."

"She might. I could lose my job."

"Now, baby, you're really pissin' me off," he said, his fingers tightening on her chin, over the scar there, pinching into her skin painfully.

Griselda reached up and covered his fingers with hers, rubbing them softly to soothe him. "Couldn't we wait until next weekend instead? I get paid next Friday—"

"No." His fingers, which had gentled, tensed again. "Shawn already fixed it. I want to go tomorrow, and he needs a hundred and fifty for our share. It's *luxury* cabins, Zel. Luxury ain't cheap."

"Tomorrow? I don't know if I can go tomorrow. I might have to work this weekend or—"

His thumb shifted slightly, digging into the soft flesh under her jawbone, and she winced.

"You don't have to work. She always tells you in advance. Now, you listen to me, Zelda. You're stealing a ring or bracelet that Mrs. Hoity-Toity will never notice, you're giving it to me when I pick you up at seven, and we're going to West Virginia with Shawn and Tina bright and early tomorrow morning."

His voice was low and menacing, and the painful pressure of his thumb made her teeth clench and her breath catch. It hurt, but she welcomed it, refusing to linger on how sick and twisted that made her. Pain was the only thing that stopped her from seeing those frightened gray eyes.

"Got it, baby?"

Griselda nodded once, and Jonah grinned, relaxing his fingers and leaning forward to kiss her gently. His lips touched down on hers with tenderness, nipping softly, licking the seam of her lips open and seeking her tongue with his. The mint and tobacco taste of him filled her nostrils, turning her stomach. She stopped breathing through her nose, holding her breath, and felt light-headed when he finally released her mouth.

When he drew back, his eyes were dark and possessive. They spelled it out for her in no uncertain terms: *You might be leaving me right now, but you're not free. You're trapped with me, whether you like it or not.*

She took a deep breath, staring back at him, wondering if he'd kiss her one more time, and hating herself that she wanted him to.

"Run along, now," he said, gesturing to the townhouse with a flick of his head, dismissing her.

Run. The word reverberated in her head as she opened her door and slammed it shut, any trace of disappointment supplanted with a panicky burst of painful mental images. She walked up the stairs to the glossy black door with a shiny brass knocker. Taking the house key from her purse, she turned the lock and stepped inside.

The thing is? Griselda had run, all right, but she'd never actually gotten away.

***

"Zelda? Is Prudence down for her nap?" asked Sabrina McClellan, entering the kitchen where Griselda was loading a colorful plastic cup and cereal bowl into the dishwasher.

"Yes, Mrs. McClellan. She's sleeping."

"Wonderful." Griselda's boss leaned her elbows on the black marble kitchen island, sipping coffee from a clear glass mug and giving her employee a warm smile. "You're so good with her."

"She's easy."

"Coming from the system, you must feel like taking care of only one is simple."

"Yes, ma'am," said Griselda. Mrs. McClellan's casual reference to Griselda's years in foster care made her uncomfortable, as it always did, though she knew no harm was intended.

All three post-Holden foster care homes she'd lived in before her eighteenth birthday had sheltered more than four kids each, and the care of the younger children had always been left to the older girls, like Griselda. She'd never resented it. She felt bad for the little ones, entering the system at four or five with no memories of a normal childhood. In that way, they were just like Griselda.

She closed the dishwasher door and turned the dial, wiping down the countertop with a dish towel before turning to Mrs. McClellan. Noting that her boss's coffee was half finished, Griselda picked up the warm pot from the hot plate and refreshed it.

"Why, thank you." Her employer looked up from the *Washington Post* and smiled distractedly before dropping her eyes again.

At thirty-three years old, Sabrina McClellan was just ten years older than Griselda, but their lives were a world apart. The daughter of a venture capitalist who'd made a killing in the nineties, Sabrina Bell had attended a posh college in Newport where she'd met her husband, Royston McClellan, a hotshot pre-law student attending Brown University. They'd married right out of college, but waited on starting a family until Roy had been elected to the Senate. Little Prudence was almost four.

Three days a week Sabrina worked at a nonprofit organization, Nannies on Ninth, that placed young adults from the foster care system in child care positions all over D.C. It was how they'd met, in fact. Griselda's third foster mother, who wasn't the best or worst of the bunch, had once offhandedly remarked that Griselda was the only foster child she'd ever had who took her child care responsibilities seriously. Short on compliments in her life, Griselda had treasured the words, and they'd led her to Nannies on Ninth after her high school graduation, at the recommendation of her guidance counselor.

She'd never forget the day she walked into the bright, clean storefront with a small play area in the front to keep children occupied as their mothers filled out applications seeking child care help. Griselda had been nervous that day, but she'd used her modest spending money to purchase a simple blue skirt and white blouse, like businesswomen wore on TV, and she'd pulled her honey-blonde hair into a simple bun, hoping to look older.

Her efforts paid off. Sabrina McClellan, who was eight months pregnant at the time, hired Griselda that day and paid her to help set up the nursery, prewash onesies and baby clothes, and run errands until she gave birth to Prudence Anne, the prettiest baby Griselda had ever seen.

Griselda had been with the McClellans for four years, and Prudence owned as much of her shredded heart as anyone could.

"Have you given any more thought to those courses we discussed?" asked Mrs. McClellan, still staring down at her newspaper.

After overhearing Griselda make up a fairy tale for Prudence one night before bed, Mrs. McClellan had commented that Griselda might have some talent as a writer and asked if she had ever considered attending college.

"I've never heard that story," she'd told Griselda, her eyes alight with wonder as Griselda closed the nursery door and stepped into the upstairs hallway. "It was charming! Who wrote it?"

"Oh," said Griselda, her face coloring a little. "N-no one wrote it. I like making them up sometimes. For Pru."

"Well, it was wonderful," Mrs. McClellan gushed, tilting her head to the side as though seeing Griselda in a new light. "Hidden talents."

A few days later, on Friday evening, as Griselda prepared to leave, Mrs. McClellan stopped her in the front vestibule, holding a yellow envelope in one hand and a glass of wine in the other.

"Did you know, Zelda, that there are over twenty colleges and universities in D.C. alone?"

"No, ma'am," she answered, wondering if Jonah was already outside waiting for her. She got a perverse pleasure out of making him wait, even though it pissed him off—even though it also meant he'd grab her arm roughly or kiss her too forcefully as punishment. It was a fair price for the small victory of displeasing him.

Mrs. McClellan held out the envelope, and Griselda peeked inside, surprised to find it full of college brochures.

"Many of them have writing courses for promising storytellers." She flashed her elegant smile before shrugging playfully. "Take a look for me?"

Griselda tamped down the quick bolt of pride she felt in the compliment. Not only was college a luxury she couldn't afford, there was no way she'd actually get in. Colleges weren't exactly lining up to recruit girls like Griselda. "That's really nice of you, but I don't have the money for—"

"There are loads of scholarships out there," said Mrs. McClellan, waving her hand dismissively as she took a sip of wine. "Take a look. Then let's talk. Okay?"

"Okay," Griselda had answered, rushing to wrap her scarf around her neck and hurry to meet Jonah before he beeped the horn.

That was six months ago, and although she'd fantasized more than once about the possibility of college, she hadn't allowed herself to look at the brochures. Her savings were designated for something else. Something important and nonnegotiable. She needed to work, and college would eat away at her working time. Work meant money, and money was needed for Griselda's only shot at redemption. The formula was simple, and deviating from it unthinkable.

Have you given any more thought to those courses we discussed?

"No, ma'am," she said softly, worried about her boss's disapproval.

"I overheard you telling Pru another story last night. I really do think you have talent, Zelda."

"Thank you, Mrs. McClellan."

"Will you give it some more thought?" she asked with a light smile, and Griselda nodded, wondering what it would be like to go to college, to learn how to write her stories on a computer, maybe even to make a living like that someday— writing stories and selling them.

She doused her hopeful thoughts quickly, trading them for a cold dose of reality. She *had* a plan, and it didn't include college.

Work, money, redemption.

"Well, I'm off," said Mrs. McClellan, throwing a windbreaker over her gym clothes and grabbing her purse from

the kitchen desk where she managed the household accounts.
"I'll be at the gym, then the club for lunch, then I'll stop by N-on-N for a few hours this afternoon. Back by five. Pru's laundry is ready for folding, and I bought Gruyère so you could make her a grilled cheese. No TV, Zelda. She watches too much as it is. Call if you need me."

"Have a good day, Mrs. McClellan."

"You too!"

Once the door clicked shut, Griselda leaned back against the counter, closing her eyes in the silence of the tidy kitchen. After a moment of peace, she poured herself a cup of coffee, hooked the baby monitor to the belt of her jeans, and went outside to the small but beautiful garden patio behind the townhouse. Griselda was lucky that Prudence had held on to her morning naptime later than other children. It wouldn't be long before she gave it up and Griselda wouldn't have this little break to herself anymore, and although Griselda should spend the time folding the laundry, she allowed herself a rare moment of quiet reflection instead.

Except that there was a problem with quiet reflection—her mind turned to something unpleasant immediately: Jonah's demand that she steal something from the McClellans.

It was good that he still believed they'd need to steal to come up with $150 quickly. It meant he hadn't discovered that she'd amassed a small, but respectable, sum in her private savings account.

When she went to work for the McClellans, they'd offered her the option of direct deposit twice monthly and asked for her account numbers and distribution. A laughable question, since Griselda didn't even have one account. She'd gone to the bank closest to the McClellans' house, and a well-meaning banker had advised her to set up two accounts: one for savings and one for checking. Though she funneled only twenty percent of her earnings into her savings account, she rarely touched it, and it now held several thousand dollars, earmarked for one very specific use. The rest—almost every dime—went toward her rent, utilities, and living expenses, aka, supporting Jonah.

Heading back inside, Griselda made her way upstairs. Quietly opening the pair of elegant French doors that led to the McClellans' bedroom suite, she crept across the room, her bare feet sinking into the plush cream-colored carpet. Stopping at Mrs. McClellan's dressing table, she ran her fingers gingerly over a pair of gold hoop earrings and a matching bangle bracelet. They were undoubtedly real and would likely fetch more than the $150 Jonah required.

Drawing her hand away, she walked back across the room, closing the French doors behind her. She wouldn't repay the McClellans' kindness by stealing from them. Griselda had lived through many frightening and unsavory situations, and she was many things as a result, but she wasn't a thief. Not then, and not now.

Which left her no other choice. Today, after she took Prudence to the park, she'd have to stop by the bank and withdraw $150 from her savings account. She pulled her bottom lip into her mouth and bit it hard enough to taste blood. Touching that money went against everything in her heart, but she couldn't think of another way. Later, when Jonah picked her up, she'd tell him she'd stolen the earrings and bracelet and fenced them on her lunch break. He'd buy that story. He'd be relieved not to have to do it himself.

She headed back downstairs and picked up the coffee cup she'd left on the kitchen counter, resting her bruised chin on her palm and swallowing the lump in her throat as she mulled over their weekend plans, and recalled the first—and only—time she'd ever visited West Virginia.

July 4, 2001

Griselda

Sandwiched in the back of the musty station wagon between her foster sister, Marisol, and the new kid, Holden, ten-year-old Griselda Schroeder could feel the sweat dripping from her neck, down her back, and into her butt crack. On the other side of Marisol sat Billy, who was fourteen, and had been living with the Fillmans longer than anyone else. Saying that Griselda hated Billy would be like sheep saying they hated wolves. Sure, they hated them, but they were terrified of them too.

When sixteen-year-old Marisol had moved in with them a year ago, it had been an unexpected blessing because she had, more or less, taken younger Griselda under her wing, calling her "lil' sis," braiding her hair, and showing Griselda how to wear makeup. Bigger than Billy and just as mean when she wanted to be, Marisol wasn't someone the boy wanted to mess with. It had become more challenging for him to torment Griselda, though he still found ways to hurt and humiliate her. After all, Marisol was old enough to have an afternoon job—she simply wasn't around all the time.

Holden had joined the mix three days ago, arriving at the Fillmans' house with a black eye, split lip, and lots of attitude. Ten years old, just like her, he was smaller than Griselda, but scrappy, and very quiet his first day. She'd quickly discovered the reason: he stuttered. Badly.

On Holden's first evening with the Fillmans, after checking that the coast was clear, Griselda had run to the shared bathroom in the upstairs hallway to brush her teeth only to find Billy and Holden getting into it. Billy, Holden's new roommate, had stolen an Orioles ball cap out of the younger boy's meager duffel bag, and was taunting Holden, holding it out of reach above his head. Holden jumped up several times, trying to reclaim the hat, but the third time, Billy punched him in the stomach with his free hand, and Holden fell to the floor, clutching at his belly.

Looking up at Billy with furious, churning eyes, Holden demanded, "G-g-give it t-t-to m-me!"

Billy froze for a moment, staring down at Holden in shock before a loud guffawing laugh made him double up.

"Holy shit!" he panted through loud, jagged laughter. "You're a retard!"

Still spying on them from her spot in the hallway, Griselda felt helpless for Holden and furious with Billy, so she watched with a certain amount of satisfaction when Holden's eyes widened with anger. He leaped to his feet and drew back both fists, pummeling every square inch of Billy's body that he could reach. The fight turned vicious as the boys knocked over a table, which crashed to the floor, and within minutes Mrs. Fillman was pulling them away from each other. Once separated, she let Billy go and smacked Holden's face. Hard.

"We ain't had no trouble before you got here!" she yelled, clamping Holden's ear in a painful grip. "Say you're sorry to Billy."

Holden's mouth was a firm, tight, white line as he stared back at Billy, who bled from his lip, but he gave Holden a superior, expectant smirk. Griselda was captivated, riveted by Holden's face as he stared back at Billy. His eyes were narrow and defiant, his nostrils flaring with every breath, his small fists balled by his sides. Mrs. Fillman yanked on his ear, and he flinched momentarily before clearing his expression to neutral.

"Say it, or I'll call your social worker and have you removed."

Holden continued to stare back at Billy, who crossed his arms over his chest, his smile fading. This smaller, younger boy had held his own in a way that Billy grudgingly respected, and finally Billy sighed, turning away from Holden and Mrs. Fillman.

"He's sort of a dummy, Miz Fillman. He don't talk right."

Mrs. Fillman, who fancied handsome Billy and had become attached to him during the six years they'd lived together, jerked Holden's ear again. "Look at me."

Holden finally dropped Billy's eyes and turned to look up at Mrs. Fillman.

"You start trouble again, you're outta here. Clear?"

Holden stared back at her for a long, tense moment before finally nodding. Mrs. Fillman let go of Holden's ear and placed her hands on her beefy hips, over her stained housedress, and grinned at Billy with yellowed teeth.

"Don't forget we're takin' all of you to that park in West Virginia on Sunday," she said, her voice changing from imperious to wheedling and needy. "A special outin' on a river. Not all foster kids got such good foster parents, you know."

"Can't wait," Billy answered, jerking back as Mrs. Fillman reached forward to tousle his hair, but giving her a forced smile to make up for recoiling.

"And you best not start any trouble," she said, turning to Holden, her stubby finger a millimeter from his nose. "Ya get what ya get, and ya don't get upset."

He nodded at her again. Curtly. Without speaking.

As Mrs. Fillman left the room, she muttered, "Great. Another weirdo." Catching sight of Griselda, she pursed her lips with general annoyance before heading back downstairs.

As Holden watched his foster mother go, his eyes suddenly shifted to Griselda, easily, casually, as though he'd known she was there all along. And then, in an act of bravado that shocked her ten-year-old heart, he winked at her, one side of his lips twitching up in the barest semblance of a smile.

She hadn't gathered her courage to talk to Holden since then. At dinner, Holden had sat across from her two nights in a row, staring at her steadily, and Griselda found herself sneaking peeks at him, wondering about him, curious as to where he'd ultimately fit in with all of them, and hoping, though she'd never admit it, that he could be a friend. More than anything—more than anything else in the entire world—Griselda longed for a friend.

She glanced at him beside her in the car, looking at his dark blond hair, a little too long and curling up at the ends. His eye was still bruised, but his lip had healed a little over the past three days.

He turned to her slowly, casually—just as he had when she was standing in the hallway—and without saying a word, he raised an eyebrow, that lip quirking up again just a little. Caught, Griselda's heart sped up. She shook her head with a jerk and looked down at her lap. Folding her sweaty hands, she promised herself not to look at him again.

He pushed his upper arm back just a little until it was pressed against the back of the vinyl seat, and flush with hers. Over the next few minutes their sweat combined until they were stuck to each other, but Griselda wouldn't dream of moving her arm in a million, zillion years. It felt too good to be touched gently, too nice for words. Her heart thrummed with gratitude, and she clasped her fingers together tighter in her lap.

Looking straight ahead out the window, she saw the large blue, green, and yellow sign that read "Welcome to West Virginia.

CHAPTER 2

"Careful, baby," called Griselda from the park bench, watching Prudence make her way up the slide for the fourth or fifth time. Griselda's best friend, Maya, sat beside her while her charge, Niall, who was the same age as Prudence, kept Prudence company.

"Okay, Zelda," said Prudence, giving Griselda a gap-toothed grin before continuing her ascent.

"So, you're going? To West Virginia?" asked Maya, wrinkling her nose. "I don't get you."

"What's to get? He set up a weekend getaway, and he wants me to go."

"But you clearly don't *want* to. I mean, come on, Z. West Virginia? Of all places?"

Griselda sighed. "I didn't have much say in the matter. Anyway, it'll be fine."

"'Fine.' You love the word *fine*. Just remember, I know you, girl. I've known you a long time."

In addition to living with Maya for a year and a half at her second post-Holden foster home, they'd attended the same high school from freshman year until senior year, which was unusual for kids in the system. When you moved homes, you often had to switch schools, but Griselda had been moved to a foster home in the same school district. Friends for almost a decade, Maya was the closest thing Griselda had to family, but even Maya didn't know everything. Nobody knew everything except for Holden.

"I *know* you, but I don't *get* you," continued Maya, shaking her headful of brown braids, the colorful beads on the ends clicking with the movement.

"Yeah, well. No use rocking the boat."

"Not unless you want to get smacked."

Griselda shot Maya a look, telling her friend to shut up.

"You don't think I can see those fresh bruises on your chin? And news flash, Zelda . . . you're wearing long sleeves in the middle of June. Shit. I seen it all a million times before, starting with my mama. I just don't understand why you put up with it."

Because someone who did what I did doesn't deserve better.

Griselda hated this particular conversation, but she knew from experience that the best way to hurry it up was just to remain silent.

"You're beautiful, Z—"

Griselda scoffed loudly, rolling her eyes, her fingers reaching up to trace the scar on her chin.

"Not to mention, you're flush," continued Maya, referring to Griselda's secret stash. "Get your own place. Tell Jonah to take a hike. Find someone who treats you nice."

I don't get to have nice. Not until I know that Holden has nice too.

She cleared her throat. "I don't touch that money, and you know it."

"Yeah. But I don't know why. What're you saving it for if not to make a better life for yourself?"

A better life for herself? Theoretically, there were probably many ways her life could be improved, but only three that really mattered: find Holden, help Holden, be with Holden again.

Griselda made $640 a week with the McClellans, which worked out to $33,280 per year, $6,000 of which went back to Uncle Sam. That left $21,824 for living expenses and $5,456 a year that went into her savings account for Holden. The first year, she'd spent several thousand dollars on a private detective, but the money had run out quickly and the detective, whose business had been shut down a few months after Griselda gave him a check, hadn't found out much. He'd discovered that the Man who held them, Caleb Foster, was born in 1961. At the time of Griselda's and Holden's abduction, he'd been forty years old and the last surviving member of his family, outliving his parents and a younger brother and sister, both of whom had been tragically killed in an accident in the seventies.

Despite her efforts to research Caleb Foster on the library computer at the Laurel Public Library, she'd never found very much. There were thousands of Google hits when she searched his name, but none of the profiles jibed with what little she knew about him. And when she searched "Holden Croft," she found nothing beyond the news of their abduction. No hits. Not one. Which always made her grief intense and painful because it made her wonder if Holden was dead, how he died, and when. Had he been frightened? Alone? Was he thinking about her in his final moments?

Staying hopeful that Holden was still alive was the most gut-wrenching and exhausting challenge of Griselda's sorry life. But she could not—she *would* not—give up on him until she knew for sure that he was dead. Until then, she would keep looking . . . because she *owed* him, because once upon a sweet and terrible time, she'd *loved* him, and he'd loved her in return.

Internet research had finally led her to the Browne & Castle Agency in New York City, one of the best private detective firms in the country, and rather than throwing away any more money on scams, Griselda had decided to book their services as soon as she was able. The catch? The retainer was

$5,000 up front, which she had, but the per-hour expenses ranged from $40 to $100. If Caleb Foster had driven Holden all over the country, it could take weeks or months to track down their trail and what had eventually happened to them. Griselda figured she'd need about $20,000 before she could retain Browne & Castle's services, and right now she was more than $5,000 short. So she worked. And she waited. And she hoped that next year she'd have enough money to find Holden, to help him, to spend whatever she had to make up for leaving him behind . . . or at least find out what had happened to him.

In the meantime, giving Jonah $100 here and there hurt her heart, because every dime she gave to Jonah was another hour further away from finding Holden, the only human being whom she knew—beyond any shadow of doubt—had ever truly loved her.

Taking a deep breath, Griselda gave Maya, who was still waiting for an answer, a sidelong glance. "Honey, if it ain't your tail . . ."

". . . don't wag it," finished Maya, quoting their foster mother, Kendra, with whom they'd lived for the first two years of high school. "Damn, but she loved saying that."

"Yes, she did."

"You deserve so much better than Jonah."

No, thought Griselda. *No, I don't.*

"Why, Zelda? Why stay with him?"

Because I should have gone back with Holden and I didn't. Because we were supposed to make it together, but one of us got dragged back to hell. Because life is only bearable when it's more bad than good.

And, her heart added in a guilty whisper, *because when Jonah shuts up and falls asleep, his arms are warm and solid around me, and sometimes I can trick myself into believing he's someone else.*

"Forget I asked," said Maya, sighing heavily. "Ain't my

tail."

Griselda nodded, watching Prudence run from the slide back to the ladder. "Jonah's not always mean, you know."

"Yeah, sometimes he sleeps."

"He can be sweet to me sometimes."

"He's mean enough, often enough. A little sweet don't make a difference," said Maya, suddenly sitting up straighter and tsking. "Niall, don't you grab that child's braids. You leave her be, now." She turned back to Griselda. "Most days I don't know if I'm grateful that you got me this job or not."

"You're grateful."

Griselda paused, thinking how much better this weekend would be if Maya and her boyfriend, Terrence, were in tow. She had nothing against Jonah's friend Shawn, and his girlfriend, Tina, had been pretty nice the one time Griselda had met her. But still, they were practically strangers.

"Can't you and Jonah be friends?" she asked.

"Not going to happen, Zelda. He and me is like oil and water—hell, oil and a *match*." Maya chuckled, shaking her head. "I'd belt him good if he came after me the way he gives it to you."

You'd lose, thought Griselda, and her upper arm throbbed where it was covered with the black-and-blue imprints of his fingers. She'd exchanged pleasantries with the cashier at ShopRite last night, and the minute they got back in his truck, Jonah had grabbed her arm and accused her of flirting.

Still staring straight ahead at the kids, Maya's voice was soft when she asked, "You ever gonna tell me, Zelda? What happened to you? I mean, besides the old news reports I can read on the internet?"

Griselda turned to her friend, and Maya faced her, her chocolate-brown skin satiny in the sunshine and her deep brown eyes profoundly sympathetic.

It had taken Griselda a half a day of hiking through woods

barefoot before she made it to a highway at dusk. An older lady picked her up, chastising her soundly about the dangers of hitchhiking before dropping her off in front of the Charles Town sheriff's office. Griselda ran into the building like a maniac, delivering her entire story to the first person she saw and ending with the demand, "Please! You've got to *find* him!"

The sergeant working the front desk had stared at her for a moment before calling a female officer to escort Griselda to a small interview room. They found a sandwich in the kitchen, half a sleeve of Oreos, and two cans of pop, which they placed in front of her, and someone rustled up a blanket, which the officer placed carefully around Griselda's shoulders. Although she was starving, Griselda wouldn't eat until she had shared every bit of information that she possibly could: the names of her foster parents, how she and Holden had been taken, the general location where they'd been held captive, and how she'd escaped. She begged them to race to the Man's house, and only when the officer assured Griselda that two cars were en route did she lay her head on the metal table before her, weeping with fear and relief and exhaustion.

How tempting it was to tell Maya the whole story. It would be like stepping off the side of a pool into warm water, free-falling, sinking into the compassion of a friend, then drowning as she faced the awful truth of what had happened.

Her breath was ragged as she inhaled deeply.

"No, Maya."

Griselda pushed off the bench and fixed a smile on her face as she walked over to the slide.

"Time for lunch, baby," she called to Prudence. "Playtime's over."

***

"You know where my fishing pole's at, Zelda?" Jonah asked, peeking his head into the bedroom.

Griselda looked up from where she sat on the edge of the

bed and shook her head before turning back to the TV.

"Aw, baby. Can't you try to crack a smile? We ain't had a vacation in months."

Actually, they'd never had a vacation. Not in the year they'd been living together. They met when the cable company sent Jonah to her apartment block to check on a faulty connection. He'd buzzed her apartment instead of the super's, and even though—or maybe because—she suspected he was so mean, they'd started dating that night. He'd been rough the first time they had sex, and she hadn't liked it, but then he'd held on to her as he fell asleep, and it felt so nice, she didn't ask him to leave. Mostly, she hated him for his meanness, and she hated herself for liking the moments he was gentle.

To Maya's point, Griselda wouldn't let herself be with someone kind and decent. That would mean that while Holden's life was likely a living hell, she was pursuing a happiness that she didn't deserve. Being with Jonah made her pay mightily for every embrace, every kind touch. She couldn't relax or let her guard down. Whatever tenderness she received from him was balanced by his meanness, which was the only reason she allowed it.

Sometimes, when she went days without a kind word or touch from Jonah, she almost likened her time with him to doing penance. Penance was a matter of choice for the transgressor, wasn't it? It was punishment for the wages of sin. It felt good to do penance, even though punishment hurt by nature, because it moved her life closer to redemption.

But tonight? With a weekend in West Virginia bearing down on her? She just didn't have the energy for his abuse.

"Maybe I should stay home, Jonah. I just don't think I'm—
"

He crossed the room in a flash, standing before her with his hands on his hips. "You don't want to spend time with me and our friends?"

She leaned back on her hands to look up at him, crossing one finger over the other. "I do. Of course I do."

"Then what's the problem?"

She scrambled to think up a plausible explanation for not wanting to go to West Virginia. "Wouldn't it be nice to go away together? Just you and me?"

"Sounds boring as fuck," he said, pulling a mashed-up pouch out of his back pocket, opening it up, and pinching a wad of brown tobacco between his fingers.

She looked up at him, feeling her eyes flash with a rare show of hurt.

"I don't know why we're together," she mumbled, despising him. Despising herself more.

Tucking the tobacco between his bottom lip and teeth, he grinned at her like a shit-eating baboon. "Because you're sweet, Zelda. You take care of me. Hell, you suck cock better than any girl I ever met."

Much like Billy, her tormentor of old, Jonah was a bully. The only child of older and deeply devoted parents, he'd steamrollered them for most of his childhood and adolescence, from what Griselda could piece together. He'd been in trouble for petty crimes once or twice—defacing property and drunk and disorderly conduct, the stories of which he shared with pride—but his parents had always arranged for good lawyers, and Jonah had never served any time.

Griselda had never met his mother and father—they'd passed away two years before she met Jonah—but when she met him, he'd just blown through the life savings they'd left him, and their house, on which he'd failed to pay two years' worth of taxes, was being repossessed by the bank. He was very handsome and kept himself in good shape. His jokes were crude, which his friends from the cable company liked, and she had to admit that he could be charming, even though he was also self-centered and mean if he didn't get his way. But when his hands weren't slapping or grabbing her, they could be gentle and warm. And when he clasped her against his chest in the middle of the night, she could close her eyes and pretend it wasn't him, lulled to sleep by the soothing whisper of his warm breath against her neck.

Refusing to rise to the bait, she lowered her head and took it, accepting his ugly words and feeling just as dirty as he'd intended. She looked down at her knobby knees, barely covered by her oversize T-shirt.

"Why do you make me say things like that to you?" he asked. "I tell you what . . . you're contrary today, Zelda. Mrs. Hoity-Toity rubbing off on you?"

She didn't answer. She clenched her jaw, knowing what was coming.

He grabbed a handful of her hair and yanked her head up. "I asked you a question."

"I'm just tired." She sighed, staring into his mean green eyes. He'd hit her if she didn't tell him what he wanted to hear, and she wasn't in the mood for extra pain tonight. Anticipating the trip to West Virginia was painful enough. "I-I'm looking forward to tomorrow."

"That's better." He nodded at her, smiling, easing his grip. "I feel better now. Don't *you* feel better?"

She nodded once, forcing her lips to tilt up.

Jonah's hands reached for his belt, the sound of the jangling buckle making her blood run cold as it always did. "You're so beautiful, baby. You know what I said before? It was a compliment. You're the best, baby. I mean it. The best. How about you—"

Her stomach rolled just as his phone rang. Wincing with disappointment, Jonah zipped up his fly and took his phone out of his back pocket. His expression brightened immediately. "Shawn! We all set for tomorrow, cocksucker?"

Griselda watched as Jonah pivoted and exited the room

without another glance. Taking a deep, ragged breath, she lay back on the bed, tears welling in her eyes as she stared up at the ceiling fan rotating slowly over her head.

***

"Baby, I'm sorry if I made you mad before. I shouldn't be crude to you."

Griselda's eyes fluttered open, and she was surprised to find herself in bed, under the covers, the TV off, the lights out. She'd fallen asleep staring at the fan, and Jonah had tucked her in. Now he held her gently from behind, whispering into her ear tenderly.

"I'm crazy about you, Zelda. Sometimes I feel like I'd die without you."

She concentrated on the way it felt to be held and tried to block his voice and words out of her ears.

"Don't you want to go to West Virginia, baby? You ever been there before?"

She swallowed the lump in her throat. She'd been dreaming about Holden again, as she did almost every night, and she wiggled her feet under the covers. She could almost feel the dry soil of West Virginia seeping between her toes. They'd been watching the mother deer and her fawn, speckled with spring freckles. *Sh-sh-she's awful pretty, huh, Gris?*

Her head pounded, and she clenched her eyes shut. "It'll be fine."

"I'm so horny," Jonah murmured, hardening against her backside. "I want you, Zelda."

"Shouldn't we get some sleep?"

"Won't take but a minute."

He pulled down her panties just enough for access, pushed her back forward a little, grabbed her hips, and thrust into her unprepared body from behind without permission or warning. She clenched her teeth and closed her eyes as he grunted with every thrust, kneading her soft skin to the point of pain. After

37

several minutes, he cried out, his forehead falling into the back of her neck as his grasping fingers relaxed. She felt him come inside her, pulsing hot and wet, as he whispered, "So good. So good. So good, Zelda."

He pulled out of her and rolled onto his back. Not a moment later, the rumble of his snores filled the room.

I didn't answer you, she thought to herself, his semen dripping onto the sheets as she rolled onto her back and wrapped her arms around her chest.

No, I don't want to go to West Virginia.

Yes, I've been there before.

July 4, 2001

Griselda

Mr. Fillman pulled into a Yogi Bear Campground, but it turned out the Fillmans hadn't made a reservation in advance and all the campsites were taken on account of the holiday. The gate attendant had advised them that a spell down the road they'd find the county campground. "Not as nice," she said, looking at their rusty, outdated station wagon and sniffing like something smelled bad, "but they might have space."

"A spell down the road" had turned into a journey of several more miles, with Mrs. Fillman's cigarette smoke wafting into the backseat and the hot air blowing in from the windows. They passed a country market on their left, which had a rickety, peeling billboard that informed them that the "Shenandoah Camp-It" was a mile and a half up ahead.

And despite the discomfort of sitting four across in the hot backseat, Griselda felt a momentary pang of sadness, because when the car stopped, Holden would get out of the car, removing his arm from where it still pressed up against hers. She gave herself a moment to mourn that loss in advance, then tried to raise her spirits. This was the first foster family that had ever taken Griselda on any kind of excursion, and she felt a little bit excited. Yes, there would still be stale bologna and cheese sandwiches for lunch that Marisol had packed that morning, but they'd be eating them somewhere new. And though Griselda couldn't swim, she imagined the water clear and cool on her feet and legs. Under her lemon-yellow gingham sundress she wore a faded, pink one-piece bathing suit that Mrs. Fillman had found in the left-behind pile, used by one of her previous charges. Griselda didn't care that it had been someone else's or that it was faded and old. Today it was hers.

Mr. Fillman pulled into the parking lot, and Griselda strained her neck to look out Holden's window. It was more parked-up than the Yogi Bear gate attendant had led them to expect, with cars of all shapes and sizes sandwiched into neat spaces, and up ahead, on the green strip of grass by the river, she saw families on blankets, little kids in bathing suits, and the odd dog on a leash. Loud rock music blared from a car speaker, and Griselda could smell hot dogs on a grill. She felt an unfamiliar burst of hope. This felt like a party, like something normal and fun, and she couldn't help the expectant smile that spread across her face.

Still leaning over Holden, she felt his eyes on her and turned to look at him. He wasn't staring at the parking lot, or families, or children with brightly colored inner tubes around their waists. He was staring at Griselda and smiling that one-sided grin that she was beginning to like so much.

She giggled, smiling back at him, and whispered, "It looks fun!"

His smile widened, evening out a little, but he didn't respond. He just nodded.

"I'm working on my tan all afternoon," said Marisol with a loud sigh.

"You'll help me set up the lunch first," said Mrs. Fillman, stubbing out her cigarette in the car ashtray, which overflowed with butts and ash.

"Why can't Billy help?" Marisol whined. "Or the kids?"

Mrs. Fillman turned around and fixed Marisol with a narrow-eyed scowl. "One, don't back-talk. Two, oldest girl helps with meals. Those are the rules."

Marisol looked down at her lap, muttering, "Fine," as Billy chuckled beside her.

"I think *I'll* work on my tan," he said, elbowing Marisol in the side.

"Oh, Billy," said Mrs. Fillman. "A tan wouldn't make you one jot more handsome."

Griselda noticed Mrs. Fillman's eyes in the rearview mirror, the way they softened on Billy's face, staring at him like she'd never get her fill of looking. Shifting her eyes over Marisol's bent head to look at Billy, Griselda saw him turn away from their foster mother's gaze, his nostrils flaring and jaw tight.

"I guess Billy and Holder could help me unload the car," said Mr. Fillman.

"Holden," said Griselda softly.

"What's that?" Mr. Fillman asked.

"Holden," said Griselda again. "Not Holder."

"Right you are," said Mr. Fillman absently, cutting the engine and opening his car door.

The four children followed, piling out of the car, and Griselda took a deep breath of warm, fresh air. Even from the parking lot she could hear the rush of the river, and her toes ached to feel the blessed coolness.

Mr. Fillman stood by the car, stretching his scrawny arms over his head as he looked out at the river, then turned to his wife, who was taking a cooler out of the trunk. "Sadie, you still got those cousins that live around here?"

"Jim and Melody? Guess so. If they ain't dead yet."

"Maybe you should call 'em. Ask 'em to bring a cooler of beer and come set a while."

Mrs. Fillman muttered something about no-good relatives, handing Griselda a folding chair, and waved her hand toward the grassy patch by the river.

Fifteen minutes later, they had an old sheet spread out on the grass, with two chairs set up for the adults, and Mrs. Fillman asked Marisol to open the cooler. The stink of rotten bologna and turned mayonnaise made Griselda's stomach flip over.

"Aw, hell," said Mrs. Fillman, staring daggers at Marisol. "Are you so stupid you forgot to cover the sandwiches with ice? They been baking in that trunk for two hours!"

Marisol stared at the sandwiches, grimacing. "Sorry, Miz Fillman."

"Worthless. Just as worthless as your crackhead mama. I don't know why I even try."

Marisol bent her head, staring down at the cooler and closing it slowly.

Standing up and putting her hands on her wide hips, Mrs. Fillman looked at her husband, then at Billy. "You two men got any ideas? I'm hungry, and there ain't no lunch now, thanks to crack baby here."

"Was a store a ways back," said Billy.

"We drive to the store, we lose our parking spot," said Mr. Fillman, taking a seat in one of the two chairs and kicking off his black shoes but leaving his black socks on.

"Then someone ought to walk it. Someone who made the mistake in the first place," said Mrs. Fillman, staring down at Marisol, who still knelt on the blanket with her head bent over the closed cooler.

Griselda thought of all the nights Marisol had brushed her hair, braiding it distractedly as she told Griselda her dreams of being a hairdresser one day. She thought of all the times that Marisol had stepped in when Billy was pinching her or tormenting her. All Marisol wanted was to sit in the sun today. Well, Griselda could help make that dream come true.

"I'll go, Miz Fillman," she volunteered. "I don't mind the

walk."

"Huh," her foster mother huffed, turning to look at Griselda with a mix of annoyance and surprise. "You'll go, huh?"

"Yes, ma'am," she said. The store was only a mile and a half back. That wasn't too far away. She could make it there and back in an hour and still have the whole afternoon to dip her feet in the Shenandoah.

Marisol looked up at Griselda, her eyes bright with tears, and mouthed, *Thanks, kid.*

Griselda nodded at her friend before turning back to the Fillmans. Mr. Fillman's aluminum chair creaked as he shifted to free his wallet from his pocket. The five-dollar bill he handed Griselda was wrinkled, warm, and limp.

"Loaf of bread, bologna, cheese," instructed Mrs. Fillman. "You got extra, get some mayonnaise. You got that?"

"Bologna again?" complained Mr. Fillman, tenting a piece of newspaper over his face.

"Ya get what ya get, and ya don't get upset," snapped Mrs. Fillman before turning back to Griselda expectantly.

"Bread, bologna, and cheese," she confirmed. "Mayo if possible."

"*Mayo if possible,*" mimicked Mrs. Fillman, whisking her hand at Griselda. "Go, then. Don't dawdle."

"I'll, uh, g-g-go too."

Griselda turned to where Holden was standing just behind her. She was surprised to hear his voice, surprised he'd spoken up, surprised he wanted to go.

"Fine," said Mrs. Fillman, settling her considerable girth down on the blanket beside Billy, who was staring at three teenage girls sunbathing nearby. She put her hand on Billy's bare thigh and said, "Hurry up. Mr. Fillman's gonna be hungry after his nap."

"Yes, ma'am," said Griselda, her eyes lingering on Mrs.

Fillman's hand for an extra beat before turning to walk away, with Holden by her side.

CHAPTER 3

With the windows down in the back of Shawn's Ford Escape so that Tina's nails could dry, Griselda wasn't expected to make conversation with her, which was a relief. Tina seemed nice enough, but with every mile, they headed deeper into West Virginia, and Griselda's dread multiplied. Her stomach wouldn't settle, and her fingers trembled if she wasn't tightly clasping them her lap. Making small talk would have been excruciating if not impossible. Trying to find a bit of peace, she leaned her elbow on the windowsill, keeping her eyes closed and letting the warm wind buffet her face.

Try as she might, however, she couldn't think about anything but her sad history with this corner of the world and finally succumbed to her memories. How hopeful she'd been when she'd walked into the Charles Town sheriff's office ten years ago. How hopeful. How stupid.

By the time the police arrived at the Man's house, Holden and the Man were long gone, but Griselda hadn't known that terrible fact quite yet. She'd watched with relief as the police put out an APB on Holden Croft, two cop cars tearing out of the parking lot headed for the Man's house. Her aching feet and legs had screamed in pain as she rolled her chair forward and reached for the Oreos, savoring the first bite after three solid years of gruel and raw produce.

The Fillmans had been removed from the foster care system after losing two charges over state boundaries, so Griselda was taken to the first of three foster families back in Washington, D.C.. That's where she met her new roommate, Maya, who immediately reminded Griselda of Marisol.

Over the next three or four days, she was enrolled in a nearby junior high school and interviewed by the police many times about Holden and the Man, but the visits quickly stopped. A few days later, she found out why.

Her new social worker visited her a week after the escape and shared the devastating news—when the police got to the Man's house, it had been abandoned. No Man. No boy. Just a dog shot through the head and buried in a shallow grave on the front lawn.

"Cutter," she gasped, trembling as she wondered if the same gun had been used on Holden.

The Charles Town police searched the area for a full week but came up dry—there was no trace of Holden or the Man, who, Griselda learned for the first time, was named Caleb Foster. The social worker asked if Griselda had any idea where they may have gone, but she didn't. Other than the barn, garden, and cellar, she and Holden hadn't been allowed anywhere else, certainly not in the main house. And in the three years she and Holden had lived there, they hadn't left the farm once. She knew almost nothing about him. She had no idea where he'd go. She only knew that she had to get back to his house and try to figure it out.

That night she made her first attempt to run away, stupidly hitchhiking at the end of her foster mother's street and being picked up by the police on suspicion of solicitation. Her foster mother locked her in her bedroom at night after that, and Griselda didn't tried to run away again. But when the next spring rolled around, she longed for Holden with a fierceness that left her breathless and weak every morning. She ran away the second time that June and got a little farther, but a well-meaning trucker radioed in her location, and again the police picked her up. She was transferred to another foster home. Again the lockdown, again the defeat. The following June, she tried again, but when she was picked up outside of Leesburg, her social worker told her she'd go to juvie if she tried it again. They also switched her to the worst and strictest of her three foster homes, separating her from Maya. At this house, she shared a bedroom with two other girls who had also tried to run. There were bars on the windows, and they were locked in every night with a dead bolt.

The threat of juvie didn't scare Griselda. It just inspired her to be smarter. That year she didn't run. That year she smartened up and came up with a plan: Earn trust. Get a job. Make money. Buy clothes. Dye your hair. Take the bus back to West Virginia. Figure out what happened to Holden.

Holden. Holden. Holden. Holden.

When August rolled around, right before senior year, she put her plan into action. She'd saved up $200 from her summer job at Wendy's, which meant she had enough to take the bus from D.C. all the way to Harpers Ferry, West Virginia.

Her plan worked too. No one bothered a young woman wearing a baseball cap and minding her business on an early morning bus. She made it to Harpers Ferry in two and a half hours, hefted her pack on her back, and walked west on Route 340 toward Charles Town. Seven miles and three hours later, she stopped at a diner, where she bought a tuna sandwich and got her bearings. It was another four-hour walk down Kabletown Road to the vicinity of Caleb Foster's farm. By the time she got there, the sun was much lower in the sky.

As she walked up the dusty path from the road, she could tell the place hadn't been lived in for years. The grass was high and unkempt, and the paint on the house and the barn was peeling worse than it had been three years ago. But even more than that, there was a dead feeling to the place: no animals, no people, no fear, no hope, no life. Empty. Like a vacuum.

As she approached the abandoned house, Griselda could see that several windows were broken and the porch sagged in the corner where Caleb Foster used to sit on a stool in the shade reading Leviticus and Deuteronomy aloud, over and over again, in a booming, terrifying voice, as Griselda and Holden tended to the garden in the hot sun for hours on end.

He hath uncovered his sister's nakedness; he shall bear his iniquity . . . Cursed be he that lieth with his sister . . .

She hated that she knew the words by heart. She hated that they ran through her mind on autopilot as she stared at the porch. She hated that her mind would never be free of them.

Auction notices were stapled to the front door and the two porch pillars, and the warm afternoon breeze made them flap lightly. At the base of the pillars were two long, rusted metal chains, the ends hidden somewhere under the porch. Griselda didn't need to see the ends of the chains to know what was there. Her ankle twitched in remembrance of the tight metal cuff she'd been forced to wear on gardening days—a cuff that kept her tethered to the porch.

A shiver ran through her as she looked to the little garden plot where she'd first told Holden about her plan for escape. It was nothing but dead, dusty earth now, though she could still make out the several dozen rows they'd painstakingly created and tended together. She could almost hear the metallic jingle of the long, long chains that had almost sounded musical in the very beginning. Like Christmas bells with every step they took. Like the hope of being rescued.

"Oh, Holden," she sobbed, sinking to the lowest porch step, her legs weary and her eyes burning. "Holden, I'm so sorry."

What had she expected to find here? Sixteen-year-old Holden waiting for her? Freckled, tall, and healthy, smiling at her in hello? Stupid girl. They'd told her he was gone, and he was. Gone. And it was such a long way to come only to find nothing.

She flicked her glance to the back of the house, picturing the storm cellar doors in her mind. Caleb Foster would hold their chains in one hand and open each exterior door at the end of the day, when they were forced back into the dark hole. The old, sturdy doors would creak and growl, and he'd unlock their ankles right before they made their descent down the crumbling cement steps. After locking Griselda in her room, he'd leave— for a while, at least, if not until morning—slamming the two doors above their heads, and turning his key in the padlock.

Dare she revisit the site of so much pain?

Although she had no wish to be reminded of the darkest moments of her childhood, the strange contradiction of Griselda's life was that the darkest times were also some of the best and brightest because Holden had inhabited those dark moments with her. Like a match light in the blackness, like hope in the midst of deep, desperate despair, he had been her only joy, and her prevailing source of comfort, strength, and spirit. She fought hard not to forget him. Even when it hurt so badly she ached and throbbed, and her regret was so overwhelming she thought it might be better to die, she still *fought* to remember the thousand nights in Caleb Foster's cellar. She fought not to forget the sound of Holden's voice, the color of his eyes, the touch of his fingers on her face, his breath against her skin. She only went on living because it was possible he was still living too.

Pulled toward the rickety storm doors, she was surprised to find the padlock and chain gone. Looking around, she found them, the chain like a rusty-colored snake, rotting in the long grass beside the cellar where she'd thrown it after picking the lock that morning three years ago.

And it told her something that the police wouldn't have known: Holden hadn't been locked back in. Holden and Caleb

Foster had left immediately. In fact, they were probably long gone before Griselda ever even arrived in Charles Town.

She took a deep breath, trying to calm her racing heart, and pulled up one rotted wooden door, then the other. Taking a quick look at the waning sun, dread weighing down her movements, she slowly descended the stairs.

As she reached the bottom step, Griselda took in a deep breath, letting her eyes adjust to the dim light filtering in from the open doors behind her. It smelled achingly familiar, like mildew and earth, and she swallowed the lump in her throat as she stepped forward into the small, low-ceilinged room. Her foot knocked into something that clattered a short way across the packed dirt floor, and, realizing it was Holden's tin porridge bowl, a small sob-like sound rose from deep in her throat. She leaned down and picked it up, fingering the edges, holding it against her chest like a talisman.

To her left stood the old iron cot with the thin brown-striped mattress where Holden had slept. Stepping gingerly across the room, still clutching the bowl, she stood beside it as tears streamed down her face. She pulled the bed away from the wall just a little, and there, scratched into the wall so lightly that the Man would never notice, were the letters *H+G*.

***

"Holden, tell me about your mama and daddy," she whispered into the stark, cold silence.

Though she could feel his chest push lightly into hers, his every breath warming her neck every five seconds or so, she couldn't see a thing. It was blacker than black at night, a darkness so consuming and pitch you might think the whole world had disappeared.

They were both very tired after a long day of gardening with the Man's beady eyes watching their every move. They'd learned quickly that if Holden's arm should brush Griselda's, or her gaze should linger on Holden for too long, it meant a beating. Depending on the Man's mood, one that could knock you out for hours, or just leave you in a world of pain for the rest of the day. The first time, it had taken weeks for Holden's bruised ribs to heal. And Griselda still bore the mark on her chin where the man had split her face open a few days later. It hadn't healed very pretty. When she ran her fingers over it, she could feel the uneven, bumpy scar that she'd probably have forever.

Griselda concentrated on Holden's breathing, on the warm, comforting pressure of his arm slung over her hip. Her eyes were heavy, and it was warmer with Holden than it was in her own bed, but she knew better than to succumb to exhaustion and fall asleep together. If that ever happened, the Man would surely kill them.

Holden's breath caught. "D-d-did you hear that?"

Griselda stopped breathing, and her whole body tensed, ready to roll off Holden's bed to the floor and crawl a short way to the paneled wall that separated their rooms. Two months into their captivity, Holden had discovered a loose panel in the wall, and Griselda had become adept at rolling, crawling, pushing aside the loose panel without a peep, and returning to her room. So far, the Man had never discovered them together, and it had been their saving grace over the past two years to find comfort holding each other every night before bed.

She heard a low whimper on the other side of the door at the top of the stairs.

"Cutter," whispered Griselda, listening for the sound of his claws clicking back across the floor upstairs. Once they heard them receding, they both exhaled in relief. It wasn't the Man, about to come downstairs to administer "lessons."

Holden squeezed Griselda closer to him and took a deep breath before saying the words softly, the same words he said every night. "M-m-my mother's name was C-Cordelia, but my father called her C-Cory."

"And your daddy . . ."

". . . w-w-was named Will."

"Cory and Will Croft."

"Th-that's right."

"And one day, I'll be Griselda Croft," she said, moving on quickly because she heard the tears in his voice.

"Yep. You and me. W-w-we got to stay together."

"Holden," she said, shifting her body on the lumpy, dirty mattress to face him. She couldn't see him, but she felt his breath against her lips. "When you take your time, you don't stutter so bad."

"S-s-stammer," he corrected her for the thousandth time.

She tucked her head under his chin, snuggling a little closer, as he adjusted the arm draped over her waist, his fingers curling under her body as her chest pushed up against his. Resting her forehead in the curve of his neck, she closed her eyes for a moment and breathed in deeply, bypassing the smells of dirt and mildew, and finding Holden—warm skin and sweet boy and sunshine. She'd turned twelve a month ago, and she knew beyond any shadow of a doubt that she wanted that smell to whisk her to sleep every night for the rest of her life. Someday they wouldn't have to say goodnight and part. Someday Holden would belong to her, in every possible way.

"Holden?"

"Y-y-yeah, Gris?"

"I'll figure out a way. I promise you I will. It'll be summer in a few more months, and I'll figure out a way to get us out of here."

"I know you will," he said, but his voice was defeated.

"Don't give up, Holden."

"I won't." His fingers slipped out from under her as his lips pressed against her hair for several long minutes. "N-n-now, go to bed, Gris. D-d-don't fall as-sleep here."

She clenched her jaw, and her eyes burned with almost

unbearable sorrow, the same way they did every night at this dreaded moment.

"Keep your fingers over the letters," she said softly, pulling away from the warmth of his body, glad that the darkness hid her weak tears.

"I will," he said, turning toward the wall, and though it was so dark she couldn't see her own hand, she knew the exact spot he was touching as he fell asleep.

She moved soundlessly through the panel and climbed into her own bed on the other side of the wall, pressing her fingers to the identical, carefully carved letters until she finally fell asleep.

***

Tears covered Griselda's face as she backed away from the little bed, the power of her memories making her head pound and swim at the same time. The yawning grief she felt every day from Holden's loss was almost paralyzing in its intensity here, where they'd spent so much time together. She turned to face the room and noticed the man's tools still neatly hanging on pegs over his tool bench. It occurred to her that she could pick up any one of those tools—a hammer, a screwdriver, a saw, anything— and end her pitiful sixteen-year-old life right now.

It was tempting to die here, where she'd experienced the best and worst moments of her life. Chances were good that Holden was already dead, and that meant if she killed herself, she'd be reunited with him. She stepped toward the workbench, but her own words stopped her.

Don't give up, Holden.

The whisper ricocheted through the dead, quiet space like she'd said them aloud.

I won't.

Still clutching Holden's bowl, she turned sharply away from the tools and ascended the concrete steps into the twilight of early evening. She shut the cellar doors with a loud thump, then turned her back on the dark, dingy space where she'd been imprisoned until the day she made it across the Shenandoah alone.

As the sun set, she made her way back up to Charles Town on foot, arriving long after dark and checking into a motel that would accept cash up front from a teenager.

Weary and hopeless, she drew a bath, stripped, and stepped into it.

That was when the unavoidable truth assaulted her: Holden was gone.

Three years ago, they'd told her he was gone, but she'd never really believed it. It was almost like she was sure Holden was hiding somewhere in that horror show of a cellar and the moment she appeared, he'd reveal himself, gray eyes soft with relief and love, opening his arms to her and burying his lips in her amber hair.

But now she'd seen the abandoned farm with her own eyes. He was gone, whisked into the night with a monster for company, and Griselda wept there in the motel bathtub, wondering whether he was dead or alive, if he was still scrappy, if he still stammered, if he ever thought of her, and if he hated her for abandoning him. Her heart clutched and wheezed and begged for death at the thought of his hate for her, but she had already made the decision to live.

Her strength was sapped. Her spirit was shattered. Her hope was gone. But she'd told him not to give up. She'd *demanded* that he not give up. And until she knew—with her eyes and her ears and her heart and her soul—that he was dead and gone from this earth, she had no choice. She wouldn't give up either. Whatever strength, spirit, or hope was left in her wasted body belonged to Holden. There was nothing left, even, for herself.

The pain and emptiness had been so profound, in fact, that she knew living was the best punishment of all. To live aching and broken was exactly what she deserved. She had promised to save him, and the only person she'd saved was herself.

Shawn's SUV went over a bump, and Griselda gasped, jolted from her memories, then shivered as desperation lingered.

"Too much wind, honey?" asked Tina, offering a kind smile and asking Jonah to turn up the music.

"It's fine," Griselda said, blinking her tears away before turning her glance back to the window.

They were almost at Harpers Ferry now, and from there it would be a quick thirty-minute drive south to the cabin they were renting on the river. She'd checked a map, and from the cabin, it was less than twenty minutes to Caleb Foster's farm. The place that her body had escaped. The place where she'd left her heart in darkness with a gray-eyed, sweet-smelling boy.

July 4, 2001

Griselda

    The country route didn't have a sidewalk, but there was a scrubby patch of brown grass by the side of the road just wide enough that Holden and Griselda could walk side by side. They turned out of the campground and headed in the direction of the country store they'd passed in the car.

    "Why'd you volunteer to come with me?" she asked, watching her worn-out sneakers get more dust-covered with every step she took.

    Holden shrugged. "S-s-sat a long time in the, uh, c-c-car."

    "Yeah. It was cramped."

    The sun was burning the back of her neck, and she felt a large drop of sweat start by her ear and trickle down her throat.

    "Hot out today," she said.

    "Uh-huh."

    "You don't say much."

    "N-n-nor would you if you s-s-stammered."

    "I thought it was stutter."

    "S-s-stammer."

    "Huh. Do you *mind* talking?"

    "N-n-not to you."

    Her cheeks flushed with pleasure. It was rare for Griselda

to feel special or important, and Holden's words felt precious to her. She wanted more.

"Why me? I ain't special."

"You're, uh, n-n-not mean."

"How do you know?" she asked, turning to look at him with a grin. "Maybe I act all nice, then attack."

"N-n-no. I *get* people. You aren't mean . . . and you're r-r-real p-p-pretty."

Pretty? Pretty! A stranger to compliments, she turned her face to this one, like a sunflower worshipping the sun.

"Thanks."

"It's true."

"Hey, you just talked without stuttering," she said, beaming at him.

"It's b-b-better when I'm not uncomfortable."

"So," she asked, wondering more about this boy who'd held his own against Billy and seemed to have a soft spot for her. "Where were you before the Fillmans'?"

"D-d-different foster family."

"Didn't work out?"

"Th-th-they were drunks."

Griselda nodded. Her previous foster parents had had substance abuse problems as well. She always thought it was strange that she was removed from her mother's apartment just to go to a new home with similar problems. When her social worker visited without notice and observed the situation, Griselda had been moved to the Fillmans'.

"They hit you, huh?"

Holden's hand moved instinctively to his eye, which was a little less purple now, and a little more greenish-yellow. He didn't answer, just kicked the dirt with his next step, raising a cloud of light brown dust.

"Your parents in jail?" she asked.

His eyes whipped to hers, fierce, angry. "N-n-no. Absollutely n-n-not!"

"Oh," she said, feeling sorry that she'd asked a question that made his stammer so much worse. "Only asked 'cause my mama's probably in jail. Maybe. I don't know. I ain't seen her in five years. When my grandma died, there was no one else, so I had my first placement."

Holden was silent for a long time. "M-m-mine are dead."

"I'm sorry," said Griselda.

Holden didn't answer, but he didn't kick the dirt again either, and they walked along in silence for a few minutes. Griselda's neck, arms, and legs prickled from the mix of sweat and dust, and she sighed, wondering why she'd volunteered to make this walk on a ninety-degree day. She guessed they were about halfway to the store, but it was hellish hot, and damn, but they'd have to walk back carrying the extra weight of the food.

She was so mired in her own thoughts, feeling so sorry for herself, that it startled her when a battered red pickup truck suddenly slowed down and stopped just ahead of them on the side of the road. She paused for a moment before continuing her walk, moving slowly toward the truck. She flicked a nervous glance at Holden as a man got out of the driver's side and turned to them.

"Been lookin' for you two."

"Us?" Griselda looked at his unfamiliar red truck and caught a glimpse of a puppy scratching excitedly at the back window. Griselda felt her eyes light up, and she looked at Holden to see if he was seeing what she was seeing. "A puppy!"

Holden's face was grim and tight, his eyes staring at the approaching man, who stopped before them with his hands on his hips. He wore denim overalls and a flannel shirt that had seen better days, and his brow was glistening with sweat. His hair and beard were shaggy and unkempt, probably brown once, but pretty gray now.

"Come on 'long, now," said the man. "Parents sent me to

come git ya."

"The Fillmans?" asked Griselda, wrinkling her forehead.

"Fosters," the Man muttered.

"Oh," said Griselda. Their foster parents. Well, that made sense. Sort of. Then she remembered Mr. Fillman asking Mrs. Fillman about some relations who lived nearby. "You the cousin?"

"Brother," he said.

Huh. Well, if Mrs. Fillman had cousins in the areas, maybe she had a brother too. That made sense, didn't it?

Griselda looked up at him: his eyebrows were bushy and his lips taut with disapproval or annoyance. He looked angry and a little scary, frankly, but she'd expect a relation of Mrs. Fillman's to look a little scary. And, she reasoned, if he *wasn't* sent to pick them up by Mrs. Fillman, how would he know the Fillmans were her foster parents?

But Holden still held back, his face cautious. His expression made her pause. She should verify the man's identity again before getting in his truck.

"You say you know our foster parents?"

"Fosters, yeah. Now, quit playin' games. Ain't got time for it. Need to git you two 'uns back," he said, gesturing to the passenger door of the truck.

Griselda moved around the truck toward the door, with Holden following silently behind her, then stopped.

"But we didn't get the bread and bologna yet," she called to the man.

"Got plenty to eat," he replied impatiently.

Sadie, you still got those cousins that live around here? Ask 'em to bring a cooler of beer and come set a while.

Mr. Fillman's words circled in her head, and Griselda cut her eyes to the back of the truck, where she spied a large, beat-up red cooler bungee-corded in the back.

Looking at Griselda over the hood of the truck, the man

narrowed his eyes. "Day's wastin', gal. Now *git* in the danged truck."

Griselda looked up at the puppy. He whined, leaping up against the window and running his little paws against the glass like mad.

"Your puppy's real cute," she said.

"Yeah, well."

"Can she sit in my lap on the drive?"

"He. Cutter." The man shrugged. "I guess."

Griselda turned to Holden and shrugged, then reached for the door handle.

Holden grabbed her arm, leaning close to her ear, but keeping an eye on Mrs. Fillman's brother. "I d-d-don't l-l-like it. She d-d-didn't say anyth-th-thing, uh, about a b-b-brother p-p-picking us up."

"You really want to walk all the way to the store, spend Mr. Fillman's money, and walk all the way back just to get a beating because we wasted the money and sassed her brother?"

"We d-d-don't really know, uh, w-w-who he is."

Griselda turned back to the man. "Mister, you said our foster parents sent you, right?"

"Dang it. What've I said already, ya half-wit? Fosters. Right. An' they'll beat ya good if'n ya keep wastin' their time. An' mine!" He yanked his door open and got into the driver's seat, slamming it loudly and starting the engine.

"See?" she said, pulling her bottom lip between her teeth. "I don't want a beating. I just want to stick my feet in the river . . . and pet that puppy."

"G-G-Gris, n-n-no," he said, still drawing back as she reached for the door handle again.

"Then don't come with me." She reached into her pocket and took out the five-dollar bill, handing it to Holden as Mrs. Fillman's brother blasted the horn. "Go get the food. Waste their money. But you'll get the beating, not me."

She opened the door and stepped forward, but he grasped her shoulder. "D-d-don't. P-p-please."

"Holden, he knows our foster parents. And you heard Miz Fillman. She said she had family in the area. And he has a puppy, for God's sake. Somebody with a puppy ain't gonna hurt us. I'm going."

She hefted herself into the cab of the truck, and the puppy leaped into her lap, licking her face with joy. When she looked down at Holden, his lips were pursed and his chest rose and fell quickly. He was shaking his head slowly.

As she reached for the door handle to shut the door and leave him behind, he suddenly knocked her hand away and lifted himself up into the truck, shoving her over a little to sit beside her. As the truck started moving, the puppy shifted from Griselda to Holden, licking his cheek with glee, and Griselda giggled. But Holden didn't even seem to notice the puppy. He was staring into Griselda's eyes like he knew a terrible secret, and even though she didn't completely understand why, it frightened her, and her giggled faded.

He lifted his eyes to the man, who stared straight ahead at the road, and Griselda suddenly realized he hadn't made a U-turn. He was driving away from the campground, not returning to it.

"Took ya long 'nough, Seth," said the Man. "An' Ruth? Ya ever make me wait like that agin, I'll strip the skin off'n yer back."

CHAPTER 4

Griselda

"This is the life!" exclaimed Jonah, falling onto the bed in their room and pillowing his hands under his head. "Come and lay down here with me."

He raised his hand, and Griselda looked at him, taking a deep breath before lying down beside him. It was a nice enough place—new wood, a plush sofa and fieldstone fireplace in the living room, a plush comforter on the bed. Plus, she and Jonah had their own bathroom attached to their room, and it had a little bottle of shampoo and conditioner, just like at a nice motel.

Jonah had opened one of two small windows after putting their duffel bags on top of a dresser. "We can hear the river, baby. Nice, huh? That one-fifty went to good use, right?"

"Yeah."

She lay back now against the wing of his bent elbow, listening to the Shenandoah, her memories so sharp and painful she wondered how she would get through the next two days. She bit the side of her cheek until she tasted blood, and her fingers, clenched tightly by her side, slowly unfurled.

"Oh, and hey! At that gas station where we filled up? Shawn overheard two guys talking about some fight club thing tonight going on outside of Charles Town. Out in the sticks."

"Fight club?"

"Yeah, some real hillbilly shit out in a field. Two guys get in a ring of hay bales by a cornfield and beat the shit out of each other for an hour. When one doesn't get up, it's over. No rules. It's pretty ugly stuff."

Griselda winced. After a childhood filled with beatings—from her mother, various foster parents, and Caleb Foster—she wasn't especially anxious to go watch two adults beat each other silly.

"I'm not going to that," she said softly.

"Hell yes you are. Local flavor, baby."

Griselda turned onto her side, facing him. "Jonah, I don't want to see that. You know how I feel about blood."

"You and Tina can stand way back from the ring and talk about your girl shit. Me and Shawn want some fun. I'm not coming all the way back here after dinner just to bring your sorry ass home. Jesus, that's why we're here! To have fun!" Jonah shifted onto his side, propped up on his elbow, staring at her. He traced the scar that ran from the base of her chin to the bottom of her lip. His voice was low and his eyes were mean when he added, "You'll go, Zelda."

She took a deep breath and nodded, opening her mouth as his finger increased its pressure on her lips. As she sucked on him, he leaned forward to press his forehead to hers.

"That's my girl," he said, the hint of an edge in his voice as he reached for her hip. "Oh, and by the way . . . You are *my* girl, aren't you?"

Her hands were trapped between them, but she managed to cross one finger over the other. "Mm-hm."

"Right. So, I've been meaning to ask . . . Who the fuck is *Holden*?"

The name shot through her like a shotgun bullet, ripping through the soft spots and gouging an ugly hole that hurt like hell. Her eyes whipped open. Her teeth bit down.

"Fuck, Zelda!" he said, snatching his finger out of her mouth.

"Sorry," she said, working to suck in enough air to fill her suddenly depleted lungs.

"Should be. You said his name in your sleep last night," said Jonah, eyes narrow and fingers digging into her flesh. "Who the fuck is he?"

Never, not once in the year she'd been with Jonah, had this happened. She didn't utter Holden's name aloud, and hadn't since the day she'd sobbed on the porch step at Caleb Foster's abandoned farm seven years ago. She buried that beloved name so deeply that her lips understood it was taboo to utter, even when she was unconscious. It must have been the impending trip that had brought it to the surface last night, falling asleep remembering his thin arm around her, his lips pressed against her hair, his fingers touching their bound initials on the wall. *Holden.* His name was sacred to her, and hearing it fall from Jonah's lips was blasphemy, was profane and disgusting in her ears.

Her heart picked up, racing in a different way than usual, and she recognized it immediately as a sensation she had almost forgotten: fury. It rose up within her, boiling and spitting like the lava inside a volcano waiting to erupt. And she realized something else: right now, right this minute, no part of her was frightened of Jonah.

Who the fuck is he?

"No one," she said, her voice holding a warning as she leaned back from Jonah's face.

"Must be someone. You never say 'Jonah' in your sleep." Jonah's fingers twisted on her hip to pinch her skin, and his voice took on a taunting quality. "Tell me who he is, this . . . *Holden.*"

Griselda's anger roiled and swelled as she stared back at Jonah with a bold, fearless rage that she had never shown him before.

C-c-calm down, Gris. C-c-calm down.

"Stop saying his name," she ground out, reaching for his wrist and pulling his fingers off her hip with surprising strength. She shifted away so that she wasn't touching him, rolled onto her back, and stared up at the ceiling.

Jonah snickered low with surprise, then stopped abruptly. "Well, lookee here. Sweet little bootlicker Zelda actually has some claws underneath all that soft fur." He straddled her hips, grabbed her chin hard, and forced her to face him. "You think you can tell me what to do? I'll fucking stop when I'm good and ready to stop, bitch. Holden . . . Holden . . . Holden . . . Who is he? Are you fucking him?"

She saw white. White behind her eyes. White in front of them. White where Jonah's face had loomed over hers a moment before. White, hot, savage, vicious anger. She didn't give a shit if he abused her, hit her, fucked her, used her. But Griselda had one line. One. And Jonah had just crossed it.

"Stop saying his name!"

Bracing her hands on the quilt and leaning her head back as far as it would go into the softness of the pillow, she used her neck like a slingshot, shooting up into a sitting position and nailing Jonah's nose with her forehead. As he cried out in pain, she twisted her body and leaped off the bed. She stood beside it with her hands on her hips, staring at Jonah, who was grasping his bloody nose with both hands.

"What the *fuck*, Zelda?!" He leaned his face over his lap as drops of blood splattered on his white nylon gym shorts. "*Bat. Shit. Crazy!*"

"I asked you nicely," she growled softly through clenched teeth, then opened the door and walked out of the bedroom and into the great room of the cabin. She stood in the middle of the room catching her breath.

"Hey, Zel," said Tina from the open-plan kitchen to her

left. "I'm making mojitos . . . you want?"

Griselda turned into the kitchen, picked up the open bottle of rum, and upended it against her lips. Her throat chugged greedily for several seconds before she lowered the bottle onto the counter with a bang. Backhanding her lips, she shook her head at Tina.

"No, thanks."

Then she beelined for the door, walked through it, and slammed it shut behind her.

***

The upstairs door slammed shut, and she heard the latch click. Griselda's shoulders sagged with relief because the sound of the latch meant safety . . . for a little while, at least. It meant that she and Holden were alone in the cellar, probably—hopefully—until morning.

Pushing the panel aside, she crawled across the floor. She could just make out his huddled form under the tool bench in the corner of the room, aided by the dim twilight filtering in through the seam of the cellar doors.

"Holden," she said, wincing as she knelt before him, cradling his cheeks. "Your eye's already swelling shut. Why'd you do that, Holden? Why? Don't ever do that again. Don't ever."

"I h-h-hate it when he c-c-calls you R-R-Ruth. You're n-n-not evil. You're n-not!" whispered Holden in a rush, jerking his head out of her grasp and letting his neck droop forward. She'd seen the tears brightening his eyes, and since he'd turned thirteen, he'd gotten uncomfortable letting her see him cry, so she didn't try to pull his head back up to look at her. He kept his head bowed, resting on his knees, which he still held tightly, protectively, against his chest. "D-d-don't look at it. You hate blood."

She shifted to his side and sat down next to him against the stone wall under the table, her hip flush with his, her legs straight out.

"Why'd you do it?"

"I told you," he said, resting his forehead on his knees, which muddled his voice. "Its', uh, n- n-not your name."

"You know why he calls us Ruth and Seth."

Griselda and Holden had pieced together the story of the Man's younger sister and brother, Ruth and Seth, who had been twins. From what they could gather, the siblings had been involved in a relationship with each other that made Ruth "a dirty temptress" and Seth "weak for the flesh." As far as they could tell, the Man had abducted Holden and Griselda because he thought they were his long-lost sister and brother, and he was hell-bent on reforming them . . . this time.

"This time" because—reading between the lines of his rants, which were unpredictable but frequent—Griselda was fairly certain the Man had eventually killed Ruth and Seth for their sins. She and Holden were terrified that he would one day decide to reenact that part of history.

Holden looked up at her, the tracks of tears snaking down his dirty face. "He's c-c-crazy."

"I don't mind it, Holden," she said, laying her head tentatively on his shoulder, relieved when she felt the gentle pressure of his cheek resting against her hair. "It doesn't matter if he calls me Ruth."

"I mind. You're not R-R-Ruth. You're not d-d-dirty. You're b-b-beautiful." Holden was silent for a long time before sitting up straight and turning to her, his brows creased and his lips tight. "Someday he's g-g-gonna k-k-kill us like he did them."

"I won't let that happen," she whispered fiercely. "I promise you. I'll find a way for us to escape."

She touched his hair, grateful when he let her.

"But you gotta stop talking back. You gotta stop fighting back," Griselda sniffled. "He's so much bigger. He's gonna break you."

Holden turned to her, scowling, his discolored jaw clenched as snot collected under his nose, mixing with blood and dirt.

"You ask me if I'm wh-wh-whole or br-br-broken, G-G-Griselda. G-g-go on and ask me. Ask me!" he demanded, his bruised eyes bright and shiny with unshed tears.

She would not cry. She had no right. If he could bear it, she could bear it. But her voice caught as she asked him, "Are you whole or broken?"

"I'm whole," he said, swiping at his nose and holding her blue eyes with his gray ones in the sparse and dying twilight. "I'm wh-whole because I'm with you."

***

I'm whole. I'm whole because I'm with you.

Griselda found a footpath not far from the cabin and walked alone for a good hour down the shoreline of the Shenandoah and back. She guessed that she wasn't too far from the place where she'd crossed ten years ago this month, leaving Holden—bloodied, battered, exhausted, and terrified—utterly alone with Caleb Foster.

Hot tears blurred her vision as she stared out at the water— the same water that had separated them, ripped them apart, split them into something partial, something incomplete, something that would never be whole and would always be broken.

"Holden," she whispered, stifling a sob as tears rolled down her cheeks. "Oh God, Holden, what happened to you?"

Her only answer was the rush of the water, an early-summer afternoon breeze, and the lament of her weary heart. The river held no answers, just as it hadn't been a solution a decade ago. It had betrayed them. She turned sharply away from the Shenandoah, heading back to the cabin.

She returned to find Jonah, Shawn, and Tina sitting on the front deck, laughing and talking over an empty pitcher of mojitos. As she approached, she noticed the dried blood crusted just inside Jonah's nose, though he'd changed his shirt and shorts. His eyes narrowed, but he smiled at her. "Got rid of whatever crawled up your ass?"

Tina, who sat between the men, her cheeks red and wearing a broad, glossy smile, slapped him playfully on the arm. "She didn't get you on purpose, hot stuff."

"That's right, she didn't. Did you, Zelda?"

Griselda crossed her fingers in her pocket. "I sat up too fast. It was just an accident."

"We were thinking of trying a local dive for dinner on the way up to Charles Town," said Shawn. "There's a place west of here on 340 called—"

"Rosie's," said Griselda, sitting down in the open chair across from Tina.

"That's right," said Shawn. "You know it?"

She shook her head quickly, maybe too quickly for Jonah's shrewd eyes, which cut to her, searching her face.

She made up a quick excuse. "Saw an advertisement for it somewhere. Probably while I was out walking."

The truth was that Caleb Foster had frequented Rosie's, often coming home drunk and angry, stomping down the cellar steps to exact his punishment on her and Holden. She'd never been to Rosie's, but the name was burned in her brain.

"They're supposed to have good barbecue," said Tina. "You like barbecue, honey?"

"Sure."

"And then we're going to that fight," said Jonah, challenging Griselda to argue with him.

"Fine," she answered, leveling her eyes to his.

Something critical had shifted between them since she head-butted him, and she wasn't sure of what it meant now and what it would mean later. Jonah knew that she'd clocked him on purpose, and he'd never gotten an answer to the question he

69

asked her about Holden's identity. She sensed he was spoiling for a fight with her, but that he was also confused by the sudden change in her behavior. In the year they'd been together, she'd never raised a hand to him, rarely argued with him, and put up with almost everything he dished out without complaint. She could feel him looking at her with new eyes, like he was trying to figure her out, like he wasn't sure exactly who she was anymore.

He took a deep breath, and his lips tilted up in a lazy smile of victory before he looked away from her.

"Boys hitting boys. Ain't they got nothing better to do?" asked Tina. "I'll stand back with you, okay, Zelda? We don't have to watch."

Griselda gave her a weak smile and nodded. "Sounds like a plan."

Several hours later, after Jonah and Shawn had spent the afternoon fishing and Griselda had spent it suntanning and flipping through magazines with Tina on the porch, they headed off to Rosie's.

As they walked in, Griselda was surprised to discover that everything she'd always assumed about Rosie's turned out not to be true. She'd pictured Caleb Foster's Rosie's as something dark and evil, a place ripped from the pages of Old Testament iniquities. It wasn't.

It looked like a barn from the outside, and the walls inside were wooden and old, but festive white lights roped around the room, old-fashioned lighted beer signs blinked cheerfully, and she heard the sound of cue balls knocking together from somewhere in the back. They were greeted by an older woman dressed in Western-style boots and wearing her hair in gray braids. She led them to a roomy wooden booth, where she handed out greasy menus and told them what beers were on tap.

Griselda shifted slightly in her seat, her eyes zeroing in on a lonely stool at the end of the bar. She tried to imagine Caleb

Foster here, slamming back shots of whiskey before returning to the farm late at night, his boots loud and heavy on the basement stairs, breaking through the darkness and mercy of sleep, as buckets of hot water and pungent bleach slopped onto the dirt floor.

Get up! Filthy heathen. Get up! Get up and scrub this floor now! Scrub! Scrub the sin away! "And if a man shall take his sister, his father's daughter . . ."

She forced herself to shut off his voice in her head and swallowed the bile in her throat, looking up as Shawn slid into the booth beside Tina and gave her a quick kiss on the cheek before picking up his menu.

"So the bartender didn't know anything about the fight, but that guy over there?" Shawn gestured to a man sitting alone at the bar with his back to them. "He overheard me asking and said we could follow him. Said it would take about half an hour to get there."

"Good work," said Jonah, raising his hand to high-five his friend.

"Said we could place bets with his son too," said Shawn.

"What do you say, Zelda?" asked Jonah. "Ready to win some green?"

Or lose some, she almost muttered but bit her tongue. Jonah hadn't hit her or picked a fight when he returned to the cabin after fishing. In fact, as they'd gotten ready to go out, he kissed her on the back of the neck and said something about how her getting so pissed off had been a turn-on for him.

"I like you sweet," he said, biting her ear and shoving her facedown on the bed. "But fuck if I don't like you spicy too, baby. Didn't know you had it in you."

All things equal, the weekend would go faster and smoother if she kept the peace. Despite her flash of temper this afternoon, she had no further reserves of spirit to waste. As long as Jonah didn't mention Holden's name again, she was ready to let things return to the status quo. She leaned into him, and he put his arm around her shoulder, pulling her up against him as they ordered dinner.

It didn't take long for them to finish off baskets of barbecue and fries and to polish off three pitchers of beer. To Griselda's surprise, she had loosened up and was even enjoying herself a little. Tina was in high spirits and did a good job of keeping the conversation moving, deflecting obnoxious comments by smoothing them over and asking questions that managed to be provocative and funny. They were all red-faced and smiley when the man from the bar stopped by their table, flicking his chin to Shawn.

"Y'all ready to go?"

He was about fifty years old, with salt-and-pepper hair and a straggly beard that came to a point right above his T-shirt–covered chest. Griselda looked up at him, giving him a bland smile. She was about to look away when his eyes locked on hers, widening in recognition. He leaned forward a little bit, narrowing his eyes and examining her face.

"How do I know you?"

Griselda stared back at him but didn't recognize him at all. Not a bit. For a moment, she wondered if she could have somehow met him during her three-year stay at Caleb Foster's farm, but the Man had been careful. She and Holden had lived in secret; she didn't recall ever meeting anyone during that time.

"I—I don't—"

"Hey!" said Jonah. "What the fuck?"

The man checked out Jonah's arm draped possessively across Griselda's shoulder and shook his head. "Sorry. She—uh, your girlfriend reminds me of someone."

"Someone hot who doesn't belong to you?"

"Didn't mean to offend, son."

"Hey, Jo," said Shawn. "Quint here said he'd take us to the fight. Let's all be friends."

"I don't like guys lookin' at Zelda."

"She's a beautiful girl, Jonah," said Tina, winking at him as she stood up, dusting her hands on her jeans. "Can't blame a man for admiring her, honey."

Jonah nudged Griselda, who stood up so he could get out of the booth. He stood a good three inches taller than the older man and crossed his arms over his broad chest when he asked, "Who's fighting tonight?"

"Two local guys. One by the name of Eli," answered Quint, indifferent to Jonah's peacocking, and picking up a fry from an abandoned basket on the table. He glanced at Griselda again, chewing slowly as his eyes searched her face. "Other one's called Seth."

Griselda's mouth dropped open, and her breath hitched and held, burning her lungs. She reached for the table to steady herself, digging her fingernails into the soft oilcloth table cover and gasping for a breath.

Quint took another fry but didn't drop Griselda's eyes, clearly interested in her reaction. He spoke distractedly to the others, "Grudge match. Seth won last time."

"Seth," she murmured, staring back into his bluish-gray eyes.

"Yeah," said Quint, nodding slowly.

She swayed lightly, and Jonah put his arm around her, pulling her close.

"You have too much to drink, baby?"

Griselda took another deep breath and shook her head before looking back up at Quint.

He cocked his head to the side, furrowing his brows as he stared at her. His voice was thoughtful when he asked, "How the hell do I know you?"

"You don't," she answered, dropping his eyes. Her heart thundered painfully, and she turned back to Jonah, leaning her forehead on his chest.

"You're being weird and freaking her out, man," said Jonah in warning. "You don't know her. She don't know you. Quit fucking staring at her or—"

"Okay, okay, okay," said Shawn, positioning himself between Jonah and Quint.

Tina quickly laced her arms through Quint's and Shawn's elbows and moved them toward the door together, asking Quint cheerful questions about the match.

Seth.

A name that equaled heartbreak.

Seth.

It echoed and circled in Griselda's head in an endless circuit as fuzzy images of Holden's face filled her mind and her knees buckled, making her stumble on the way to the door.

Jonah tightened his arm around her. "Damn, baby, didn't look like you drank that much. You drunk? Or is that old bastard upsetting you?"

"Just a head rush," she managed. "I'll be fine."

The fresh air of the cool June evening was a welcome relief to her burning cheeks and helped relieve some of the buzzing in her head. As the parking lot gravel crunched under her sandals, she reminded herself that there were plenty of people named Seth in the world. It wasn't exactly an uncommon name.

But it wasn't exactly common either.

It isn't him. It can't be.

He'd never go by that name.

Never, ever.

She took another deep breath as they reached Shawn's car, and straightened up a little.

Besides, if Holden was alive and well in West Virginia, wouldn't he have come looking for her by now?

It's not him. His name isn't Seth.

It wasn't him. It was just that being here—so close to where she'd known him, so close to where she'd lost him—and hearing that name, was messing with her head.

She climbed into the backseat, and Jonah pulled her close to his side.

It isn't him, she told herself again. *His name isn't Seth.*

CHAPTER 5

Seth

Seth sat in the cab of his truck, winding the white surgical tape carefully through his fingers, then around his knuckles, while Garth Brooks sang "To Make You Feel My Love" on the CD player. Technically, it was a Bob Dylan song, but the Garth Brooks version had been playing on the radio the night Seth had his first fight, a few years ago. He hadn't expected to win. He'd been told he'd still make a hundred dollars just for showing up, but his rage was so wild and overwhelming after listening to the song, he'd beaten his opponent to a pulp. That night he'd been offered the chance to fight in a local fight club once or twice a month, and he made it a rule to listen to the song before every fight. It made him ache. It tormented him so bad, the moment the song was over all he wanted to do was hurt someone just as much as he was hurting inside. It was a relief to hit and be hit.

He clenched his jaw as the song played on repeat for the second time, watching the white tape go round and round his fingers as ragged snapshots flashed through his mind: a filthy yellow and white dress, honey-blonde braids falling over her shoulders, the tassels resting just above the softness of her budding breasts. Bony, scratched-up legs. Small, torn-up feet that fought for balance on a slippery rock a few feet away as the raging water rushed between them.

The last words she'd uttered on this earth had been for him, pleading with Caleb to let him go. He hadn't. Crazy fucker had knocked him out cold, and then he'd put a bullet through Gris, through the sweetest, strongest, bravest girl who'd ever lived.

***

Holden came to sobbing her name while his head pounded with pain from the two hits he'd taken to the temple at the river. "G-G-Gris? G-G-Gris?"

"You mean Ruth," the Man spat, offering him a tin cup of water. Holden sat up slowly on the porch floor, looking up at Caleb's bloody shirt and scrambling backward until he was flush against the clapboard wall of the farmhouse. Panting and trembling with fear, he stared up at the monster before him.

Caleb set the cup on the edge of the porch and jerked his head to a fresh mound of dirt in the front yard. Holden followed the movement with horrified eyes.

"Ruth's dead, little brother, an' you can thank me for puttin' an end to her evil ways. She ain't never comin' back to torment you with her wickedness. We're headin' west. West. Fact, that's who we are now: Caleb an' Seth West. Now shut up 'bout Ruth, or I'll smack yer mouth off yer head. She's gone. Good riddance. We ain't never talkin' 'bout her agin an' glory be for redemption!"

As Caleb walked to the red truck parked in front of the house and hefted a box into the flatbed, Holden turned his head to the side and vomited the meager contents of his stomach onto the porch floor beside him.

The mound of earth was a grave.

She was dead. Griselda was dead.

Holden had loved her, and she'd been killed trying to save him.

His blood rushed like a waterfall through his ears, his breathing fast and erratic as his small hands curled into fists.

"N-n-nooooooo!" he screamed. "G-G-Gris!"

He jumped up, leaping off the porch and running toward her grave, but Caleb caught him around the waist before he reached the pile of overturned earth about the size of a curled-up thirteen-year-old girl.

"P-P-Please . . . p-p-please . . . Oh G-G-God, p-p-please! G-G-Griiiiiis!"

"I warned ya, boy."

He felt the impact of Caleb's fist against his cheek, but the darkness that followed was merciful.

When he woke up, it was dark outside, and Holden was strapped into the passenger seat of the old truck, Caleb driving beside him.

"Good. Yer up. We'll stop for supper soon."

Holden's head pounded like a hammer on an anvil. He clenched his eyes shut, then blinked twice, the red taillights before him streaking like blood against the black of the highway. It took him several minutes to process what had happened earlier in the day—he and Gris had tried to escape after Caleb left for church, but Caleb must have gotten home early and tracked them to the cornfields. He'd captured Holden in the Shenandoah, and Holden had told Gris to run . . .

Caleb had knocked out Holden, shot Gris, and buried her in the front yard before leaving West Virginia for good.

"Oh n-n-no," he sobbed, turning to look out the window. "No. N-n-n-o-o. N-n-n-no."

"Quit that cryin', dummy. Can't hardly understand yer words as it is."

Holden took a deep breath and spoke as carefully as he could. "W-w-why did you k-k-kill her?"

"That gal was pure evil."

"She w-w-wasn't."

"I knew her better'n you, I guess. It was happenin' all over agin. Right afore m'very eyes."

"W-w-what was?"

"Lust!" he bellowed. "Lust, damnation, an' hellfire!"

Holden gasped and cringed as Caleb banged the steering wheel with fury once, twice, three, four, five times. Over and over again, until Holden lost count, until Caleb finally yelled, "Ya got redemption, boy! Drop to yer ever-lovin' knees!"

Holden cowered in the corner of the passenger seat, as far to the side as he could, pressed up against the door.

"Ya don't have to die for yer sins no more! Ya can live on in the blessed light of redemption! Through her blood I've made ya whole!"

(Are you whole or broken, Holden?)

"Now . . . No. Talkin'. 'Bout. Ruth. No. More!"

(I'm broken, Gris. I'm finally broken.)

There is some pain in your life that, when you experience it, you're shocked to the core that it doesn't kill you. It feels like it should kill you, like your heart should stop beating and your lungs should stop breathing and your eyes should stop seeing. Everything should just . . . stop. With pain that profound and regret that unfathomable, it should be impossible for your body to stay alive.

Holden turned slowly toward the window, staring at the reflection of his face, a study in misery, in desolation, in surrender.

The real horror of that truck ride was that Holden's body had survived, that he had to keep living with the knowledge that Gris had died trying to save him, trying to free them both, and that now he was completely alone. As they sped west into the dark night, his heart kept beating, his lungs kept breathing, his burning eyes kept seeing. He tucked the memories of his beloved girl deep, deep, deep into the most secret recesses of his heart, closed the door, and buried the key as surely as his beautiful girl lay buried in a fresh grave in West Virginia.

His body stayed alive, but Holden Croft died with Griselda

Schroeder on that river.

Inside he was dead.

Inside he didn't care what happened to him anymore.

Inside he surrendered to darkness and to Caleb Foster.

And the body that remained—that, for a long time, did very little but beat, breathe, and see—became Seth West.

***

He didn't know how long the song had played on repeat, but the knock on his window made him jump. His eyes flashed open, and his fingers fisted, ready for battle. As he turned to see his friend and co-worker, Clinton, knocking on the glass, pantomiming that Seth should roll down the window, he relaxed, pausing the song.

With one hand he gave Clinton the finger as he rolled down the window with the other.

"Sorry, man," said Clinton. "You're in the zone, huh?"

"What do you want?"

"The bets are good tonight. Your take's going to be strong. Folks love a grudge match."

"You seen Eli?"

"Yeah," said Clinton, spitting on the ground.

"Drunk?"

"Didn't look it."

Seth flinched, and his nostrils flared. Fighting a drunk was always easier than fighting someone sober.

"He's a mean fucker, Seth."

"Yeah."

"Gemma coming?"

Seth looked out the window at the trucks rolling onto the field about a quarter mile down the hill from where he'd parked his truck. He shook his head. "Asked her not to."

Clinton pursed his lips. "Since when does she listen to you?"

"Fuck," sighed Seth. "True 'nough. You seen her here?"

"Naw. Just busting your balls."

"Bust 'em later," said Seth in a low voice, not in the mood for teasing.

"Got it."

"So, what else? You here to give a pep talk?"

Clinton stared at Seth for an extra beat before dropping his eyes and shaking his head.

"Spit it out, Clinton."

"I heard a rumor he's got a knife."

"W-weapons aren't allowed."

"He's pissed at you, Seth. Says you cheated last time."

Seth clenched his jaw. "I didn't cheat."

"Fair enough. Forget I said anything." Clinton turned to go.

"Clinton!" called Seth. Clinton turned around, and Seth nodded at him. "Thanks."

"Good luck," said Clinton before continuing back toward the field.

Seth stared until his friend blended into the darkness, watching as more and more trucks pulled in and parked in the field below, the energy amping up with every new arrival. Someone had a truck radio on pretty loud, and there was some whooping and hollering making its way back up to the hill. Half the spectators would be drunk by the time the fight started. That was fine, as long as they stayed away from the ring. Once Seth started fighting, he didn't stop until he was knocked out, and he hit anything—*anything*—that got in his way.

He leaned forward and pressed Play again.

***

"Seth West, please report to the principal's office. Seth West, to the principal."

Seth stared up at the speaker over the blackboard, flicking questioning eyes to his English teacher.

"Seth, go to the office, please."

Without saying a word, Seth slid out of his desk and loped up the aisle, ignoring the batted eyes from the girls on either side of him. When he got to the office, the principal, an older lady who'd always resembled a sparrow to Seth, small and birdlike, closed her office door behind him.

"Won't you sit?" she asked, her voice soft and serious.

Seth sat down across from her.

"I'm so sorry, Seth. I'm so very sorry to have to tell you this."

He stared at her, his face purposely blank.

"It seems your—your older brother passed away this afternoon. He was . . . well, he was hit by a car crossing the street. The doctors did everything possible, but . . ."

Her blue eyes were gentle as she stared back at him helplessly. Blue eyes bothered Seth a lot more than brown. Blue eyes reminded him of Gris, and he preferred not to think about her. He felt her in his gut, all the time, like you'd feel a heavy stone resting in the bottom of your stomach. She was always, always with him, but there was a difference between feeling her constant presence and thinking about her. He lived with the former; he hated the latter.

"That all?" he asked, looking around her office for the last time.

This school had been a shitty experience, mostly, with obnoxious kids who'd had far more schooling than him. The one bright spot was that a speech therapist had worked with him for the past couple of years twice a week after school. She'd taught Seth to limit his phrasing, make soft contact with beginning consonants and use one breath for each short sentence. Always having hated his stammer, he'd taken her advice to heart and practiced religiously. As a result, he barely stammered at all anymore unless he was upset. Of course, he had nothing to say, which made it easier.

"Seth," she gasped. "Your brother is dead."

"Wasn't my brother."

"But . . . But, he—"

"Wasn't my brother."

"Oh. Oh my goodness. You may be in shock. I can ask the nurse to—"

Seth stood up, pushing the chair back under the lip of her desk, and walked out of her office without another word. He walked the two miles to the twenty-five-foot trailer he shared with Caleb, unlocked the door, and stepped inside. Walking purposefully to the back bedroom, he opened the overhead compartment above the bed and removed a metal cash box. Feeling around for the tiny key taped to the back of the shelf, he opened it and took out the money that was inside. He counted it carefully: $662. Shoving the bills in his pocket, he pivoted, opening another overhead compartment and taking out a beat-up brown cardboard boot box.

Turning back into the kitchen, he took the truck keys off the nail by the door and headed outside.

He pointed the truck east.

He never once looked back.

***

The song finished playing again, and as the opening bars restarted, Seth reached forward and flipped down the visor. The small mirror lit up, and he stared at himself.

Dead gray eyes stared back at him, cold and stony. His dark brown lashes were long and slightly curled at the ends like star points, offsetting his eyes with a soft, innocent quality that confused people momentarily as they reconciled his eyes with their setting. His cheekbones were high and cut, but crisscrossed with white scars from the many open gashes that had healed over the years. Same with his forehead and lips, which had been split, by both Caleb and other fighters, more times than he could count. His nose, which hadn't been straight since he was a kid, was crooked and slightly thicker than average, due to it having been broken several times. He had it set once at the hospital, two years ago, because he was having trouble sleeping, but fight club had ensured it had been broken again since then. His jaw was covered with a light brown scruff that, combined with the hardness of his face, gave him the appearance of a man six or seven years older than his twenty-three.

Despite these imperfections—or maybe because of them— he was still a good-looking man. He knew this because of the way women looked at him, and he wasn't ashamed to admit he wasn't above accepting their offers and invitations. His heart had died ten years ago, gasping and bleeding to death on a rock in the middle of the Shenandoah River, but his body could still feel and give pleasure. There was only one woman he'd ever loved, and when he was having sex, if he clenched his eyes tightly and blocked out the smell and voice of the woman beneath him, he could almost trick his mind into believing it was her. And for just a moment, for a split second, he could swear that she was returned to him.

Gemma had learned to shower first and shut up in his bed, not because he'd ever told her anything about his past, but because his commitment to her pleasure was unmatched when she came to him clean and quiet. The problem was, lately, that Gemma, whom Seth had been fucking for several months, kept talking about moving into his one-bedroom apartment. That he was considering her request was so fucked-up he could barely get his head around it.

His thoughts were sidetracked by the two portable stadium lights that suddenly flashed bright white, plugged into a generator on the bed of one of the trucks. They instantly lit up the empty square surrounded by hay bales. He sighed. He had about five minutes.

Listening to the words of the song, his heart raced with anticipation as he loosened the strong, high, rigid barriers around his memories. His breath caught, and his fingers trembled as he leaned his head against the back of the seat, closed his eyes, and

84

let himself find her face, the only sliver of light in the dark, murky depths of his mind.

I could hold you for a million years to make you feel my love.

***

Gris made life bearable.

So bearable that, while Holden lived in constant fear of beatings, there were some days he thought he'd die if he was ever separated from her, even if it meant his freedom.

He knew that part of him should hate her for getting in the goddamned truck, and for a little while—for the first few weeks—he had. He'd refused to speak to her, despite her efforts to reach out to him. He'd purposely gotten her in trouble a couple of times, watching with terror and guilt as she was beaten in front of him. He'd shunned her attempts at friendship, listening as she cried in the darkness on the other side of the paneled wall.

But over time, faced with the reality of his life, he'd warmed up to her. She lived in the darker half of the basement, accessible only through a padlocked door or broken wall panel, and sometimes when the Man forgot to bring down two porridge bowls, Holden heard her crying softly from hunger.

Gradually he came to realize that it wasn't her fault that he was here—he'd followed her into the cab of the truck of his own free will, after all—and his heart gravitated toward her bit by bit, until a solid friendship formed between them. And lately, a few weeks after his twelfth birthday, his feelings for her had blossomed into something deeper entirely. Trapped together in a life of hard work; erratic food, drink, and sleep; regular beatings; and no comforts, they'd forged a tight bond, and Holden knew—beyond any shadow of doubt—Gris kept him alive.

When they were out in the garden together under the hot sun, after the Man had finally dozed off in the shade, she'd whisper long, made-up stories, her lips sometimes tilting up just a little as she got to "the good part." When her blue eyes lit on him, bright and soft, it made things happen to him that he couldn't explain.

It made him feel strong and weak, happy and terrified, excited and guilty. It made strange and new things happen to his body that felt good, but wrong, somehow, even though he couldn't help them. It made him try harder to remember his parents. It made him desperate to review what little he knew about men and women being together. It made him want to learn more about those things with her.

He'd lived with her for twenty months now, and she was as much a part of him as his family had been long ago. More, even. Gris was his whole world.

The lock clicked shut at the top of the stairs, and his heart raced with anticipation, knowing that his favorite part of the day was coming. He was a prisoner in a filthy, dark, dank cellar, and yet when the basement door clicked shut and he heard the panel slide to the side as she crawled out from her black hole, his heart hammered with nothing but love for her.

"Holden?"

"Yeah?"

"You still up?"

"Yeah."

"Can I get in bed with you?"

Goose bumps rose across his skin, and his breathing hitched. For almost as long as they'd lived in the Man's basement, Gris had crawled into bed with him at night, lying beside him until it was time for them to separate to sleep. Asking his permission was new. And it made him feel different. It made their relationship feel different somehow—in a good way, in an exciting way—like she acknowledged the subtle changes he was noticing too.

"'C-c-course," he whispered, moving closer to the wall, as

his body flushed with heat and he folded his sweaty palms over his pounding chest.

The mattress depressed just a little as she lay down beside him. And suddenly, he could feel the warmth of her, the softness of her bare arm pressed against his.

"Holden?"

"Yeah, Gris?"

"I'm sorry. I'm sorry we're here. I'm so dang sorry I took that ride."

This was a familiar refrain, and no matter how often he told her she could stop apologizing, she still did. He took a deep breath and sighed. "I kn-kn-know."

"Do you still hate me? Ever? Even a little?"

"N-n-not anymore. You know that."

"But you did? You hated me?" She rolled onto her side, facing him.

He clenched his jaw, staring up at the darkness. He loved her too much now to admit how much he'd hated her then. He wanted to forget he'd ever felt anything but love for her. Shifting to his side to mirror her, he placed a trembling hand on her hip and pressed his forehead gently against hers.

"Don't ever hate me again," she whispered, her warm breath fanning his lips. "Promise."

He swallowed, his heart bursting with love for her, his soul swearing that he would never, ever love anyone as deeply as he loved her.

"I won't ever hate you again. I p-p-promise, Gris."

***

Go to the ends of the earth for you . . . to make you feel my love.

Seth reached forward and turned off the CD player.

He yanked up the sleeve of his unbuttoned flannel shirt and stared at the tattoo on his forearm for a long, hard minute before jerking the shirt back down.

It was time to hurt someone.

CHAPTER 6

Griselda

The very last thing Griselda wanted to do was attend a fistfight. She was emotionally exhausted, both from revisiting the place where she'd known so much heartache, but also from her earlier scrape with Jonah. And the way Quint had stared at her, almost insisting that he knew her, had really creeped her out. All she wanted to do was head back to the cabin, wrap herself up in blankets, and escape into sleep and dreams.

That said, sitting in the back of Shawn's SUV with Jonah's arm protectively around her shoulders, leaning into the solid warmth of his body, she couldn't force herself to put up a fight. It was just too comfortable, and she was just too weak.

"Hey, Zel," said Tina, turning in her seat to catch Griselda's eyes as Jonah and Shawn trash-talked about who would lose more money tonight, "I meant what I said before. I don't like blood either. Let's find a comfy place to sit down and pretend we're at a barbecue or something." She reached down, then shot Griselda a smile as she showed her a bottle of Wild Vines Tropical Fruit Chardonnay. "Picked it up at the gas station next to the restaurant."

Griselda couldn't help rewarding that sort of ingenuity with a grin. "Cheap and sweet?"

"Just like me, honey," said Tina, giggling.

"You ain't cheap," argued Shawn, reaching over to place his hand on her thigh. "But you are sweet."

"Eyes on the road," said Tina.

"Later?" asked Shawn, grinning at her hopefully.

"Oh, you know it, baby."

Jonah squeezed Griselda's shoulder, holding an empty Coke bottle over her head and spitting into it so it almost looked like he was filling it back up with soda.

"How come you never talk to me like that?"

Griselda snuggled deeper into his chest, breathing in the familiar smell of tobacco and soap.

"Guess I like playing hard to get."

"Well, I hate to tell you, but I already got you, baby. You're mine."

Her body wanted to stiffen on instinct, but she took a deep breath and forced herself to stay limber. *I'm not yours.*

He must have decided to drop it, because he kicked Shawn's seat as they turned down a country road and started bouncing along.

"Shawn, you cocksucker, you gonna loan me a Benjamin?"

"Whaddaya, think, dickhead?"

"I think I'm betting on that dude Seth. He sounds badass."

Though she'd already convinced herself that she had no connection to the Seth who was fighting tonight, a shiver went down her spine to hear the name spill from Jonah's mouth. It wasn't the sacrilege of him taunting her with the name Holden, as he had earlier, but she still didn't like it.

Shawn was still following Quint's truck when they jostled into an open field at the end of the dirt road. The sound of heavy metal music grew louder and louder the closer they got to the center of the field.

A good fifty trucks were parked in neatish rows, with small groups of men hanging out by the tailgates, drinking beer, smoking, and spitting. Two large, tall, stadium lights suddenly lit up the entire field as Shawn parked the SUV, and they piled out of the car.

Holding Jonah's hand as they picked their way through the maze of trucks, Griselda didn't notice many other women, but here and there she caught the eyes of another girl, mostly leaning up against her man, smoking cigarettes, and narrowing her eyes as Griselda and Tina passed by.

The energy was wired and angry, and Griselda huddled next to Jonah as Quint led them closer to the ring of bales, where the crowd got thicker. She noticed, however, that several men moved aside to allow Quint to pass, greeting him by name, with a semblance of respect, like he was someone. As it turned out, he was. He and his son, Clinton, were the bookies of the event.

"What took you so long, Pop?" asked a sandy-haired, younger version of Quint, who was flush against the hay bales, in what could be considered the first row of viewing. He held a notebook in his hand and was furiously writing down bets.

"Met up with these college boys at Rosie's."

Clinton flashed his eyes at Jonah and Shawn, taking in their polo shirts and cargo shorts with a look just short of disdain. "College boys, huh? I see you brought your women. Did you bring your wallets?"

Neither Jonah nor Shawn had attended college, but working at the cable company in D.C. allowed them both a lifestyle that would have seemed luxurious to a lot of the folks on this field, thought Griselda, taking in Clinton's ripped, too-tight Metallica T-shirt and worn-out work boots. As she checked out the tattoo of a daisy between his thumb and forefinger, she felt his eyes land on her and linger.

"Hey," he said. "Where do I know you from?"

"Aw, fuck," said Jonah. "Here we go again."

Shawn snickered, taking the bottle of Wild Vines out of Tina's hand and taking a swig.

"She's real familiar-lookin', huh?" asked Quint, looking at his son, then back at Griselda.

"Yeah," said Clinton, softly, thoughtfully, like he was working hard to place her. "You from around here?"

"No," said Griselda, the hairs on the back of her neck standing up.

Clinton narrowed his eyes, leaning closer to her, but Jonah reached out and placed a palm on the other man's chest. "Close enough, dude."

Clinton's eyes changed course, looking down at Jonah's hand lazily before shifting his glance back up to Jonah's face. "I ain't as big as Seth or Eli, but if you don't remove your fucking hand from my person, I will remove it for you."

Jonah searched Clinton's face for a second before grinning and dropping his hand. "Man's got a right to protect his woman."

"Which is why you ain't on the ground," said Clinton, looking back at Griselda for a moment before shaking his head like he just didn't have the mind power to figure out the mystery of his connection to her.

Griselda was disgusted by Jonah's dick measuring and creeped-out again by Quint and his son. Damn, but why did these men seem to know her? She racked her brain, trying to remember if Caleb Foster had ever taken photos of her and Holden, but she couldn't remember any such occurrence. Then she remembered something else, and her mouth dropped open as she looked down at the ground in shame.

Of course.

All along the country road where she and Holden had been taken, there had been missing children signs posted by the local police. She'd seen one on a bulletin board at the Charles Town sheriff's office when she finally showed up there. If this father and son had lived in this area all their lives, they'd likely seen a picture of Griselda as a ten-year-old child, posted at the local post office, in a bar or bank, at the Laundromat. Everywhere. It was why she looked familiar, but they weren't able to place her. It was why they kept narrowing their eyes, wanting to see her slightly differently and, though they didn't realize it, slightly younger. It made her belly turn over.

She took a deep breath to settle her stomach, but the close smells of chaw, smoke, booze, and men's sweat infused her nostrils. Clapping her hand over her lips, she threw up into her mouth, hunching over in case a little escaped. Desperate not to embarrass herself, she swallowed the regurgitated fries and beer, and looked up at Tina just in time for the other woman to understand what was about to happen. She grabbed Griselda's arm, pulling her away from Jonah.

"What the hell?" said Jonah, grabbing her other arm and yanking her back against him.

"She's about to get sick, Jonah! Jesus! Let go!"

Griselda looked up at Jonah just as her stomach lurched again, and he cringed as her shoulders hunched and cheeks filled. "Yeah, okay. Sorry. Can you help her out, Tina? I think the fight's about to start."

"What do you think I was trying to do?"

It was the angriest Griselda had seen good-natured Tina yet, but she was grateful as Tina led her away from Jonah and Shawn, back through the crowd. She stumbled over the uneven ground, but if she could just get away from the crowd, away from Quint and Clinton, and get a few deep, clean breaths, she'd be okay. She was sure of it.

Tina dropped Griselda's wrist and put her arm around her shoulder, leading her toward a solo hay bale on a little hill, almost hidden in shadow, about twenty feet from the parking area. From here they had a partial view of the ring if they stayed seated, but if they stood up, they could make out most of the fight area. At any rate, they could rest here and rejoin Jonah and Shawn as soon as the fight was over. When Griselda was seated,

Tina shoved the bottle of fruity wine onto her lap.

"Wish I could offer you a mint or some water, honey, but this is all I have."

Griselda took the bottle gratefully, holding it between her thighs as she took several deep, shaky breaths. The smells of gasoline and smoke were strong here, but more palatable somehow, and she was finally able to fill her lungs and her stomach settled.

"Thanks," she said, exhaling slowly. "I owe you one."

"No problem," said Tina, sitting down beside her. "Puke and sandals don't mix."

Griselda chuckled softly, nodding.

"You know?" Tina continued, taking a cigarette out of her purse and lighting it. "I try to see the good in everyone, but your boyfriend holds on a little tight, doesn't he?"

Griselda shrugged, opened the bottle of Wild Vines, and touched the rim to her lips. It was obnoxiously sweet, but it was better than the almost-puke taste she was presently enjoying. She took a swig, hoping it would stay down, and feeling grateful when it did.

"But," continued Tina, her cheerful voice back now, "maybe it was a stroke of luck, you feelin' sick, because I was *not* excited to see those two fools beat each other's faces in, and your tummy kinda set us free. So, thanks, upset tummy."

She giggled, knocking her knee into Griselda's.

Griselda was just about to offer Tina the bottle when the roar of the crowd suddenly distracted her. Standing up, the wine bottle bumping limply against her leg, she looked over the hundreds of heads, three men thick, around the ring, to see a lone figure walking down the far hill across the field from them. When he got to the bottom, he threw his flannel shirt to the ground and stepped into the ring.

***

Seth

Striding purposefully down the hill, he ignored the catcalls and heckling, focused intently on the brightly lit oval in front of him. Just before he got there, he pulled off his shirt and threw it down, giving a menacing look to the people crowded around the ring. They shuffled aside quickly, some of them slapping him on the back and wishing him luck as he stepped over the bales.

He scanned the ring for Quint and Clinton, his guard up, because the fight would start the second his opponent set foot in the fight area.

There were very few rules at fight club:

1. Once you're both in the ring, the fight is on.
2. No weapons.
3. When you can't get up, you've lost.

He finally found Clinton, standing ringside beside his father, who was talking with a couple of college boys Seth didn't recognize. Fucking tourists? Looked like it. Probably came up to fish or hunt and somehow ended up here.

As Seth stalked the ring, the crowd quieted to an excited buzz. At the opposite end of the oval from where Seth had entered, the crowd parted so that Eli could jump over the bales, stirring up a cloud of dust as his bare feet landed in the ring.

Fuck, he's big.

Seth was fairly certain that Eli had done nothing but weight train in the three months since he'd lost to Seth. His pecs bulged, and his arms were thick and solid as he pulled his T-shirt off and threw it back into the crowd.

But Seth had something Eli didn't have: a god-awful fury that turned hatred into fuel.

Seth rushed his opponent, flying across the ring in a rage, imagining Caleb's face staring back at him.

Girls like Ruth are evil . . .

Seth threw a two-punch combination, hitting Eli hard in the face then clocking him in the chin before Eli could get his bearings. His face whipped to the side and then up, causing him to stumble back, but he shook his head and roared to life, coming at Seth like a bull and slamming him in the stomach. Seth gasped from the pain, the air knocked out of his lungs, but he caught Eli's neck in a headlock and twisted savagely until Eli jerked back, out of Seth's grip.

The crowd was wild tonight, taunting and screaming, but Seth didn't need their energy to feed his wrath—it was a living, breathing, fiery thing that demanded vengeance.

. . . and filthy creatures. Impure and deceitful . . .

Seth jabbed at Eli, then threw all his strength into a right hook that slammed into the side of Eli's head, making him lurch backward. Seth swept his leg, pummeling Eli's face as they fell to the ground together. Suddenly Eli rolled, flipping over on top of Seth. He took a fistful of Seth's hair in his hand, lifting his face and smashing his fist into Seth's nose . . . cheek . . . cheek again. Seth opened his mouth, and the next time Eli's fist landed, he clamped down with his teeth, tearing a chunk of flesh from Eli's hand and making him scream before recoiling.

. . . and an abomination.

Seth jolted up, spitting blood and flesh to the dirt, and launched his body onto Eli's back. Grabbing Eli's arm, Seth twisted it at an almost-impossible angle, then held it against Eli's back while he grunted and groaned beneath Seth. Eli grappled at the dirt with his free hand, finally managing to grab a handful and somehow throw it back into Seth's face.

Wilt thou also destroy the righteous . . .

Momentarily blinded, Seth dropped Eli's arm, and Eli bucked Seth off his back, rising to all fours. Seth, on all fours across from Eli, had raised his hand to wipe his eyes when he felt a fierce punch to his temple. His knees collapsed, and his chest hit the ground hard. Eli rolled him over, straddling his chest with his considerable girth and landed two more punches on Seth's face, the crack of bone alerting Seth to the likelihood of another cheek fracture.

. . . with the wicked?

He grunted from the pain, sliding his arms through the backs of Eli's sweaty knees and pinching him hard under the thigh. Eli shrieked with surprise, garnering a loud laugh from the bystanders, and Seth used the advantage to wriggle out from underneath him.

Are you whole or broken, Holden?

Scooting back on his ass, his face on fire and blood blurring his vision, Seth drew his leg back, then shoved it forward, catching Eli in the center of the chest and knocking the wind out of him as he fell back. Seth crawled the short way to Eli, punching him hard in the balls before straddling his chest. Eli groaned with pain, his body trying unsuccessfully to jackknife as Seth whaled on his face indiscriminately with his fists, over and over and over again, until his knuckles were covered with blood, slick and slimy, and he heard the wet choke of Eli trying to gasp for breath.

I'm broken, Gris. I'm finally broken.

"Seth! Seth! It's done! Seth! Stop! It's over!"

Through a feverish haze of vicious anger, he heard Clinton's voice directly above him. His fists stilled, and he leaned back, sucking down a raspy boatload of air and staring up at the starry sky.

Over?

No way.

It'll never be over.

Struggling to his feet, Seth swayed, staring down at his opponent, whose face looked like a mask—misshapen and covered with a thick slick of reddish-black blood. Sliding his glance to Eli's chest, he noted that it still swelled and fell with breath, so he wasn't dead.

Clinton put his hand on Seth's arm, and Seth turned to him. Through one swollen eye and one blurry from blood, he looked at his friend.

"It's done, Seth. You win."

Clinton held up Seth's arm, and the crowd went wild, chanting, screaming, cheering, and jumping into the ring to celebrate.

"Good," mumbled Seth.

He shook off Clinton and started across the ring toward Quint, who beamed back at him, his triumphant fists in the air. But Seth was suddenly distracted. Behind Quint—just behind him and to the side—he saw long, strawberry-blonde hair. The girl's back was to Seth, but her hair fell past her shoulders, in soft, beautiful waves. The amber color was painfully familiar, and he dropped his eyes to her tight waist and the gentle swell of her hips in blue jeans. Sliding his eyes slowly back up her body, he noticed that her hands were on her hips, and it appeared as though she was yelling at the taller of the two college boys because her posture was rigid and the boy was laughing at her. She shook her head before turning away from the guy next to Quint, giving him her back as a gesture of anger, and pivoting to face the ring.

And suddenly all of the air—every last particle of oxygen—was sucked out of that field.

Unable to breathe, frozen in place, Seth's eyes widened, and his whole body started to tremble. He tried to blink because—*holy fuck!*—this had to be a hallucination or a head injury, or maybe he was dead and this was heaven. Because standing there beside Quint, arms crossed angrily over her chest, was a girl who was the spitting image of Griselda. She was ten years older, but her amber hair flowed free around her shoulders, and her blue eyes flashed with an expression so familiar it made his heart race and ache at the same time.

The college boy put his hand on her shoulder, turning her around partway with a jerk so that her profile faced Seth, and he felt it again, like a shot to the gut: she was familiar. She was so goddamned familiar, he felt like this was a trick, or he was in a movie, or like maybe that hit to his cheek had somehow fucked up his brain. Because—*oh my God*—this girl looked so much like Gris, he could almost believe it was . . . and there wasn't a force on earth that could have stopped him from moving closer.

Plowing through well-wishers, he pushed his way across the ring as he kept his eyes glued on the girl, who was arguing furiously with the college boy now. She was so distracted, he had a perfect view of her profile as he drew closer, and his knees buckled in an awe that was so huge it frightened him. Weak and shocked, confused and crazy, he still staggered forward, examining her features with every step closer.

It can't be her.

She's dead.

You're hallucinating.

When he was about ten feet away, the college boy shifted his eyes to Seth, and after a moment, her neck twisted to see what her boyfriend was looking at. Her lips parted, her eyes locking on Seth's. She cringed, searching his face as her blue eyes widened in revulsion, not recognition. If Eli's face looked like burger, there was a good chance his did too. She didn't recognize him, but fuck if he didn't recognize her.

Gris. It's you.

"Is it you?" he rasped, his heart thundering, his lungs barely able to fill, and his head increasingly whirling.

Like the sweetest sweet dream, or the most delusional insanity, she stood before him once again, resurrected from the dead. His Gris. Dead and yet alive. Was it possible? Was it possible that she had somehow survived? Dug herself out of that grave and survived?

No. Dead people do not come back to life.

I'm seein' dead people. I've gone crazy, he thought, laughing to himself, which hurt like fuck. Even with the same-colored hair and similar blue eyes, it couldn't be Gris. She was dead. He'd seen the grave. He'd visited it again the same day he returned to West Virginia, and there wasn't a trace of her body left, ravaged by wild animals and dragged away in the night. She was gone. Gone, gone, gone. And yet . . . and yet, if he could just get a little closer to this girl, maybe he could reach for her, look into her eyes . . . just to make certain.

He shook his head violently, blood and spit flying in both directions as he tried to block out the congratulations and cheering, forcibly pushing away someone who got in his path. When he was about five feet away, he swiped at his eyes with the back of his hand, then looked back at her, his chest constricting and his heart stopping as he dropped his eyes, half afraid, to her chin. And there, in the crease under her lip, was a two-inch scar.

His eyes jerked back up to hers, and his heart thundered in his ears, blocking out the noise of the crowd around him. Feeling her name on his tongue for the first time in ten years, it bubbled up from a lost and almost-forgotten place.

The knife pierced his side a first, second, and third time, *whoosh, whoosh, whoosh,* and he felt the slices—the sharp, foreign pain of blade to flesh—but still he didn't stop.

Without dropping her eyes, he pushed someone else out of his path, shrugging off someone who tried to put an arm around his shoulders. *Whoosh* again, as a fourth stab cut through his skin, making him twist slightly and gasp in pain. But still he wouldn't release her eyes. He couldn't let her go. It was impossible that she was alive, and yet somehow . . . he flicked his eyes to the scar again for reassurance, and there it was.

He was almost there. Two more steps and he'd be over the bales. He'd reach out his hands and fall into her arms. Bracing one foot on the hay bale before him, he gathered his strength to step over. Quint was yelling something, leaning toward Seth and yelling something, but Seth used all his draining strength to stay focused on her.

"G-G-Gris?" he sobbed, and her eyes widened, just before her face was suddenly whipped sharply to the side. Her body seemed to go limp, falling into the man she'd been fighting with, and Seth screamed, "G-G-Griiiiiiiiiis!"

Lurching forward, he was reaching for her when a blow to the back of his head knocked him out cold. His unconscious body fell, slumping over the hay bales between them, soaking the pale yellow strands with his blood.

CHAPTER 7

Griselda

It was pitch-dark, like every other night, but it was getting cold again. Griselda guessed that it was late September or early October, which meant that they'd been living in the Man's cellar for a year and three months. A couple more months and she'd be twelve.

The Man had come down an hour before, giving them each a bowl of watery oatmeal, which they ate on a bench as he read from the Bible. As soon as they were finished eating, he'd locked Griselda back in her room. She'd listened for his feet going back up the basement stairs, for the closing of the door, for the turn of the lock. About thirty minutes later, she heard the engine of his truck as he pulled out of the driveway.

For now—for the next couple of hours—there would be peace, but chances were, he'd be back with a vengeance later, whiskey on his breath, two pails of hot water and bleach in his hands as he demanded that they scrub the cellar floor until dawn.

Idle hands are the devil's playground! And you are the devil's child, Ruth!

Her cracked hands ached from gardening all day, and she wished they had more than chainsaw bar oil to soften them and heal the cracks. She thought of taking a little and rubbing it into her hands, but there was only half a container left, and they were lucky they'd found it among the things on his tool bench. Don't waste it, she thought. Better to wait until tomorrow. By tomorrow, after her hands had essentially soaked in bleach all night, they'd be on fire.

She crawled through the panel and sat on the floor by Holden's bed, leaning her shoulders against the rusted metal bed frame behind her.

"Hey," he said softly.

"Hey."

"W-w-want to lie down?"

"Nah," she said, staying on the floor.

Sometimes when she got in bed next to Holden, she felt so warm and so safe for a little while she could almost trick herself into believing they weren't being held captive in a cellar. It hurt all the more when she had to go back to her own bed.

Holden rolled as close as possible to the edge, near her head, so that when he exhaled, she could feel the warmth of his breath on her ear, and it made her shiver in a good way.

"T-t-tell me a story, Gris."

"A story?"

"Yeah. You f-f-finished that one about the city cat and the c-c-country mouse today."

"And you're already wanting another?" she teased, letting her eyes flutter closed as he breathed in, then out.

"P-p-please, Gris."

"Okay," she said, relenting, as she always did, and smiling into the darkness because it felt good to be needed. "A story. About what?"

"How about a happy ending?"

"Mmm," she sighed. "A happy ending. Those are your favorite, Holden."

"Sure are."

"Okay. Let me think for a minute."

She thought about the fairy tales she'd read before the Man had kidnapped them and locked them in his cellar, letting different characters and story themes mesh together until they became something original.

"Once upon a time, there was a princess. Princess . . ."

"Griselda?" offered Holden, who, she noticed, rarely stammered when she was telling stories, almost like he forgot to for a while.

"No, silly. I'm not a princess. Princess . . . Sunshine. Princess Sunshine was the most beautiful girl in the kingdom. She had hair so white it shined like silver, and eyes so blue they were like a summer sky. Her heart was warm and true, and it belonged to Prince . . ."

"Holden."

She giggled. "Nope. Prince . . . Twilight."

"T-twilight?"

"Yes. She's the bright sun. and he's the quiet end of day."

She knew Holden was smiling at the back of her head, even though she couldn't see his face, and she smiled too.

"Anyway, there was an evil princess who was jealous of Princess Sunshine. She was Sunshine's sister, called Princess Stormcloud, with jet-black hair and dark gray eyes, and she was in love with Prince Twilight too."

"B-b-but he loved Sunshine."

"He did," said Griselda.

"One night, Princess Stormcloud put poison in Princess Sunshine's soda goblet, and when Princess Sunshine drank it, she fell off her chair and looked dead."

"B-b-but was she?"

"She sure looked like it."

"Then what?"

"Princess Stormcloud dragged her sister to a shed and locked her inside. Princess Stormcloud told the whole kingdom

that her stupid sister who she always hated was dead. And Prince Twilight was supersad when he heard the news. But he wasn't like a crybaby sad. He was angry sad."

"A fighter," said Holden, with respect.

"Uh-huh. A fighter," confirmed Griselda, grinning. "So he had to go see what had happened for himself and maybe kill Princess Stormcloud for revenge. He rode his horse up to the castle, and Princess Stormcloud did her makeup all perfect so she was real pretty, but he could see her cold and false heart and demanded to see her dead sister. Princess Stormcloud felt mad about that and offered him some soda from Princess Sunshine's goblet."

"He didn't drink it!"

"He did. He was tired from riding that horse all afternoon."

"And then?"

"He fell over too. So Princess Stormcloud decided to drag him out to the shed too, until she could figure out what to do with the two dead people on her property. Meanwhile, Princess Sunshine and Prince Twilight were dumped in the shed, but the way Princess Stormcloud had dragged them there, they were dead face-to-face."

"This one's sad, Gris," said Holden, propping himself up on his elbow.

"Don't you have any faith in me?"

"I guess," he said, lying back down again.

"So that night, the kingdom had its one hundredth earthquake, and nobody knew it, but that was a special earthquake for two reasons: one, it released a whole bunch of fairy pixie dust that could bring two special people back to life, but only if they kissed; and two, the earthquake jostled Princess Sunshine and Prince Twilight enough that their lips pressed together in that shed. And guess what?"

"They came back from the, uh, the d-d-dead?"

"Yep! They came back from the dead! Prince Twilight broke down the door of that shed and picked up Princess Sunshine off the dirt floor, and they walked outside. And even though there was some damage from the earthquake, it was still their kingdom, so they hired people to fix stuff."

"And P-P-Princess Stormcloud?"

"The same fairy pixie dust that brought the prince and princess back to life sent her to the everlasting fires of hell," she said, borrowing one of the phrases the Man used every day.

"Good."

"And she never bothered nobody again."

"The end," said Holden.

"The end."

"G-g-good one, Gris."

She leaned her head back against the mattress, and the top of her head brushed into his chest. After a moment, she felt one of his hands drop to her head, moving gently across her hair, following the woven lines of one of her braids.

"That's so nice," she murmured, closing her eyes, and he did it again, more confidently this time. Griselda wiggled backward a little, twisting her neck until her cheek lay against the mattress.

His hand moved back to her crown, his warm, rough fingers caressing her forehead before drawing back, over her scalp to the braid, which he followed to her neck, his fingers lingering on her skin for a moment before lighting back to her crown once again.

***

The sun in her eyes was blinding as she blinked to open them. She bolted upright, scrambling against the headboard of the bed, disoriented and confused. Hugging her knees to her chest, she looked down to see Jonah snoring beside her. She was wearing a T-shirt and panties, but she had no memory of coming home, getting changed for bed, going to sleep. She had no memory except . . .

Except the fighter in the ring last night, staring at her, stumbling toward her. He was her last memory. The eyes in his swollen, bruised, and bloody face had locked on hers as he staggered across the ring, and she couldn't force herself to look away, no matter how strange it felt. He kept moving toward her, as though fascinated, as though transfixed. And then, just as he got close enough to reach out to her . . . darkness.

She took a deep breath, turning to look down at Jonah again, and realized that her head was throbbing with pain. Wincing, she slid her hand into her hair and felt a welt the size of a golf ball.

"What the hell?"

"You took an elbow to the head," mumbled Jonah, eyes slitted open, looking up at her.

"An . . . an elbow?"

"Mm-hm."

"What happened?"

"That big fucker who lost the fight had a knife, apparently. He got the winner—um, Seth? Yeah, he got Seth two or three times in the gut from behind before sucker punching him in the back of the head. Dude was headed toward us across the ring. Quint saw it happen and jumped his ass over the ring to grab the knife from the other guy, and you caught Quint's elbow in the head."

"Quint elbowed me in the head?"

Jonah yawned. "Yeah."

"Then what?"

"Well, you and Seth were both knocked out cold, and that's when the whole fucking place explodes. I mean, crazy shit. Everyone from one town hitting everyone from the other town. Just an all-out ugly brawl. Um, so . . . oh yeah, so Quint and Clinton dragged Seth back to their truck. The cuts didn't look too deep, but he was bleeding all over the place and shit, and I was carrying you over my shoulder. Quint put an old horse blanket down in the back of the truck, and Shawn helped them get Seth lying down back there, and I put you down next to him for five minutes 'cause Quint had a few beers left over, and we thought you would wake up. But you didn't, so Shawn helped me get you in his car, and I think they took Seth to a clinic or something to be sure he was okay. I knew you'd be fine. You're tough, Zelda."

It was strange having an entire chunk of her life retold to her. She had almost no memory of anything Jonah described . . . but her dream came back to her suddenly. She jumped out of bed and looked in the mirror, and there, on the crown of her head were bloody fingerprints, as if the injured fighter had run his fingers over her hair.

"How'd I get blood in my hair?"

Jonah sat up, scrubbing his hands over his sleepy face and shrugging. "I don't know. Probably brushed up against Seth when you fell . . . or maybe when we put you next to him in the back of the truck for a few minutes."

She sat on the edge of the bed and wished she had some Advil. "What happened to him?"

"Seth?" Jonah shook his head. "Fuck if I know. He needed a few stitches. Pretty sure of that." He swung his legs over the side of the bed. "I'm taking a shower. Want to join me?"

She shook her head, covering the welt with her palm. "Not right now."

He nodded, circling the bed and closing the bathroom door behind him.

Griselda's memories of last night, after leaving Rosie's, were not great. Like many children who'd suffered cumulative physical abuse, the three years of regular, sustained trauma at Caleb Foster's hands meant that her memory was not top-notch. Add another concussion like last night's to the pile and it meant a significant blackout.

Not totally sure why she felt such a strong need to remember the events of last night in better detail, she concentrated hard, trying to put together what had happened after leaving Rosie's.

She remembered sitting beside Jonah in Shawn's car and driving out to the field. She remembered parking the car and walking to the hay bales, but her stomach turned over when she realized that Quint and Clinton were probably recognizing her from abduction posters. Coupled with her distress over the fighter's name and Jonah almost getting into it with Clinton, she'd let Tina guide her away from the ring. They'd found a hay bale on its own a little way away from the roar of the crowd and sat down together, drinking much-too-sweet wine and talking about what asses men could be.

When the fight began, some real rowdiness followed, and she remembered two guys approaching her and Tina. They got a little fresh, offering the girls whiskey before the smaller one reached out and groped Tina's chest. She hauled off and smacked him, and he smacked her back. Griselda stood up quickly, kicked the bigger one in the balls as a distraction, grabbed Tina's arm, and ran back to Jonah and Shawn. As soon as she found them, she lit into Jonah, screaming about what had happened and insisting that they leave immediately.

Just about then, the crowd around the ring exploded. The fight was already over. Jonah, who was half laughing about not being able to hear her, pissed her off, and she gave him her back.

That's when she saw him: the fighter. Seth.

He was bare-chested, covered with sinew of muscle, maybe thirty years old, with a torso and arms covered with tattoos, and a thick head of light brown hair. His face was barely human, covered in blood, his lips puffy and bloody, one eye swollen shut, the other narrow and slitted as blood ran from a gash in his forehead. His nose appeared broken, but it was hard to tell behind the blood. His wounds were so grotesque, she gasped and stared as he approached her. But once his eyes locked on hers, she found it impossible to look away. She didn't know him, didn't recognize him, and yet she felt an incredible connection to him. It was as though the noise of the ring and craziness of the event had ceased around them and they were the only two people who existed in the whole world.

West Virginia . . . Seth . . .

Her heart raced and she covered it with her hand, shaking her head as her fingers gripped the comforter.

No. No, it wasn't him. Stop this!

"This is madness, Griselda Schroeder," she whispered, using the name she hadn't uttered since it was officially changed to Zelda Shroder by the Child and Family Services Agency in D.C. to protect her identity following her abduction.

Sitting cross-legged on the bed, she reviewed the facts, as she knew them to be:

> 1.   Holden Croft left West Virginia with Caleb Foster ten years ago, and despite ten years of Internet searches and a private investigator funded by her secret stash, no trace of Holden had ever been found. Even if he had managed to survive life with the Man, why would he willingly take the name Seth? And why would he ever return to West Virginia?
>
> 2.   Holden would be twenty-three, and Seth looked to be thirty.
>
> 3.   Holden had been short and stocky. Yes, he was only thirteen when they'd lost each other, but Seth, the fighter, was a huge, tall guy.

She tugged her lip into her mouth, scooting back on the bed to lean against the headboard and think. Something was bothering her because something about Seth being Holden actually felt right.

Holden was a fighter. Always had been.

She thought back to the first time she'd ever seen him—holding his own with Billy. Time and again, he'd challenged the Man, telling him that his name wasn't Seth and hers wasn't Ruth. Time and again, when the Man lifted his hand to Griselda, Holden would push her out of the way and take the beating. The morning the Man found her on Holden's side of the cellar, the beating she got was so bad Holden had jumped on the Man's back, trying to choke him with his small arms to drag him off Griselda. His reward had been several bruised ribs and a bloody back when the beating was over.

It isn't Holden, she insisted, running her hand over her hair to feel where the strands were stuck together with dried blood. But something in her heart was already unfurling—hope, hope, desperate hope.

"He wouldn't come back here. He's only twenty-three. He would *never, ever* go by Seth," she whispered. "Just because you *want* him to be Holden doesn't make it so."

Tears burned her eyes, and she swiped them away. It had been a huge mistake to allow Jonah to coerce her into coming on this trip. It was completely messing with her head, which throbbed painfully. As soon as Jonah got out of the shower, she'd insist that they pack up and head home.

She pulled her duffel bag off the bureau and threw it on the bed, pulling out a pair of jeans, a white T-shirt, and a gray sweatshirt that said "Georgetown" in navy-blue block letters. Despite the streaks of blood in her hair, she wasn't interested in showering. All she wanted to do was get the hell out of West Virginia as soon as possible and go home.

Jonah came out of the bathroom, standing in the doorway with a towel wrapped around his waist, and ran his hands through his wet hair.

"Jonah," she said, standing by the edge of the bed and looking up at him from where she'd been digging through her bag for clean underwear, "I want to go. I want to get out of here."

"Baby, we still got the cabin until four."

"No. Now. My head's killing me. I want to go home."

"Me and Shawn are going fishing."

"Jonah, I never ask you for anything."

He searched her face, then shrugged. "I'll talk to Shawn about it. Maybe we can leave a little early." He pushed a Q-tip around his ear with a grimace. "Damn, but that fucker screamed right in my ear before he collapsed last night, and it's still making my head ring."

Her face whipped up from the duffel bag, staring at him. Every cell in her body was suddenly on high alert.

"Jonah," she said breathlessly, her fingers and toes going cold, like she knew, like she knew exactly what the answer would be before she even asked the question. "What did he yell?"

Jonah grimaced, wrinkling his nose as he kept poking the Q-tip in his ear. "Uh . . . sounded like . . . um, Jesus, I don't know. Grizz. Yeah. Guh-guh-guh-Griiiiiiiiizzzz. Like that. Fucking loud." He shrugged, turning back into the bathroom.

Her whole body had gone stock-still when he said the name. Frozen, fixed with shock and disbelief and . . . belief. The bathroom door closed with a click and she gasped, "Holden," covering her mouth with her hand. She wanted to go to him, wanted to run out of the bedroom, out of the cottage, down the steps of the porch and onto the road. Run and run and run until she found him, until she stood in front of him, looking into his unfathomable gray eyes.

Her body felt flushed and weak as her knees buckled, and she collapsed onto the bed, curling up as though protecting herself from blows. Her heavy, throbbing head ached and spun as tears rushed down her cheeks, and she quickly surrendered to darkness.

CHAPTER 8

Seth

He heard her soft crying before he opened his eyes and reached his hand out, feeling her hair beside him on the bed.

"D-d-don't cry, Gris," he murmured, stroking her hair. "Don't cry."

"Seth? Honey? Oh my God. Are you awake?"

"G-G-Gris?" he mumbled again, even though he knew it wasn't her voice. It made him feel frightened that it wasn't her. Who was *here,* and where was *she?*

"Honey, it's Gemma."

"N-n-no," he sobbed, blinking his eyes shallowly. They were too swollen to open all the way. "Wh-wh-where's Gris?"

"Gris? Who's . . . ? I don't—honey, you took a bad shot to the back of the head." She raised her voice, telling someone to get a doctor before turning back to him and speaking slowly. "And you . . . you were . . . stabbed a few times. Seth, what do you remember?"

"*Wh-wh-where's G-G-Gris?*" he screamed.

Darkness.

***

"Wh-wh-where's G-G-Gris?" he screamed, shooting bolt upright in the motel bed. Melon-colored light filtered through

cheap polyester curtains, casting the small room in an orange
glow. Sweat dripped into his eyes, and he used his free hand to
wipe his forehead.

"Shut the fuck up!" yelled Caleb from the bed beside him,
rolling back over and snoring a few seconds later.

Seth pulled on the handcuff that bound one wrist to the bed
frame. He'd gotten used to sleeping with one arm over his head.
Even though he swore he wouldn't run, Caleb wordlessly
chained him to the bed every night before heading out to the
local bar. After the first night, Seth had learned not to drink
anything before bed.

One night, when Caleb left for the evening, he actually
forgot to chain Seth up, and it hadn't really occurred to him to
run. There was no one to call, nowhere to go. Theoretically, he
could use the motel pay phone, call information, and ask for
child protective services. He could tell them that he'd been
kidnapped almost four years ago, and yeah, they'd probably
come and get him and arrest Caleb, but then what? They'd
remand him back into the D.C. foster care system. Back into a
"family" where there was a good chance that the "parents"
abused and neglected the kids. It would be a matter of time until
something unspeakable happened to him with some other
unexpected and unknown monster.

At least Caleb was a known entity.

And over the past year, Caleb's temper, rantings, and
ramblings had subsided substantially, almost as though
murdering Gris had been a miracle cure for Caleb's particular
brand of crazy. Caleb finally seemed to have some measure of
peace in his life, like he had achieved the goal of a life's work in
killing her.

If Seth mentioned Gris, he still got a hard and immediate
wallop across the face, but the bad beatings had not restarted
since leaving West Virginia, and Caleb's references to Ruth
were less and less frequent. And the idea that they were actually

brothers was a very real and constant delusion for Caleb, who seemed to believe that they were four years apart in age, though Seth guessed the gap was closer to forty. Caleb would ruffle his hair affectionately now and then and call him "little brother" almost all the time. What was strange was that there was a genuine tenderness in these gestures, almost as if Seth truly was Caleb's beloved little brother, and sometimes, shamefully, Seth allowed himself to believe it.

Mostly, Seth told himself he didn't care if Caleb wanted to pretend they were brothers. The reprieve from daily beatings was such a relief, Seth never argued. When Caleb said, "My little brother will have the grilled cheese, and I will have the . . .," Seth said nothing. He kept his face blank, like it was the most normal thing in the world that they should be brothers with a four-decade age difference. And there were even times, when strangers or waitresses gave them funny looks in diners, when Seth felt defensive, almost protective of Caleb, which confused him terribly.

When Caleb returned back to the truck or motel room after drinking in the evenings, he'd lie down to sleep, mumbling in circles about how he'd finally cut the cancer out of their family, how he'd destroyed the evil and saved Seth from everlasting damnation. And during these times, Seth would clench his eyes shut and ball up his fists as a thick and sharp hatred of Caleb overwhelmed him, boiling and raging in his adolescent body until he shook from it. He would imagine killing Caleb or jerking the wheel out of his hand when he was driving on the highway and killing them both. He would imagine finding a hammer and burying it in Caleb's head as he slept. There was a sick but solid pleasure in imagining all the ways he could avenge Griselda's death. But he was only fourteen years old, and he wasn't a murderer. Dreams of vengeance did not translate into action, only into a constant, simmering, burning frustration.

Caleb kept saying they were headed to the sea, but as far as Seth could tell, they didn't travel in a straight line and they never stayed anywhere for more than a day or two. They mostly slept in the truck, but occasionally in motels. Caleb kept his money in a metal box and the key always on his person. Where he'd gotten the money, Seth didn't know, but it was enough to live on because neither of them worked, but they ate twice a day like clockwork and Caleb drank every night.

The part of Seth's heart that hid the memories of Griselda hated Caleb with a fierce passion, but it was also true that after a year of living with Caleb, Seth had made a resigned peace with his life. With Griselda gone, there was nothing to fight for, nothing to live for. He was dragged around from town to town without rhyme or reason, but he had food to eat and a dry place to sleep, and when Caleb wasn't drunk and ranting, he was the quietest companion you could ever imagine.

Seth had known a better life, and he'd known a worse life. He knew the terror of the unknown and balanced it against the comfort of the known.

For lack of another option, he could stand this life until he was old enough and strong enough to free himself from it.

The only thing he couldn't *stand was that every night, in his dreams, Gris returned to him. Her blue eyes swam with tears, her little fists clenched tightly by her sides, her horrified face contorted in agony, pleading for his life, as an ocean of rushing water separated them.*

***

"Mr. West?"

A bright light was shining directly into his eyes, first one, then the other, and he winced because it was making his head ache.

His first thought was, *Get that fucking light out of my face.*

His second thought, which knocked the first one off the block, was, *Where is Griselda?*

"Yeah," he rasped, his throat scratchy and raw. He managed to get one eye mostly open. "Wh-where am I?"

"Hospital, son. You don't remember coming here?"

"No, sir. Water?"

"Of course. Nurse! Water, please." The man put his hands on his hips, standing back to take a look at Seth's face. "You were injured pretty badly last night. Four stab wounds. Luckily none hit a major organ, but all needed stitches, and we gave you a pint of blood. You'd lost quite a lot. Concussion, of course. Your nose was broken, so I reset it. Fracture on your cheek should heal up in a few weeks. Sewed up a few cuts on your face too. Your ribs'll be painful for a little while, but they weren't broken."

The nurse returned with a cup of water, and Seth took it gratefully, holding it to his lips with trembling fingers.

"There was a woman here."

The doctor nodded. "Your girlfriend. Gemma Hendricks."

"No one else?"

"Quint and Clinton Davis brought you in last night and came by to check on you this morning."

Seth nodded, then flinched. "This morning? What time is it now?"

"I'm sure you're disoriented. You were brought in around ten last night. Ms. Hendricks arrived early this morning with the Davises and stayed for about an hour until they cleared out to go to work."

"Wh-what time is it now?"

The doctor looked at his watch. "After two."

"N-no one else has come?"

The doctor shook his head slowly. "No, son. Are you expecting someone?"

"N-no."

He turned his aching head away, closing his burning eyes. Had he actually seen her? Or had it just been his mind playing tricks on him, his battered head wanting to believe she was still alive? She'd looked so real, but this sort of delusion had haunted Seth before.

"We'd like you to stay for another night, Mr. West, just to rule out—"

"I'll go home today," he said resolutely, opening his eyes to look at the doctor. He could barely afford the treatment he'd already received, let alone more time in the hospital.

"I wouldn't advise that. Your stitches could—"

"I'll be fine."

The doctor huffed. "I'm not comfortable discharging you."

"I'm not comfortable staying."

"I really can't—"

"Then I'll discharge myself."

The doctor shook his head in disapproval. "At least let me get some fresh gauze and antibiotics together for you. You'll have to change the dressings once, maybe twice, a day. I can instruct Miss Hendr—"

"Instruct *me*."

"Mr. West, there are people who care about you, willing to help. I think—"

"Instruct *me*."

"Fine. Give me an hour to put together a sheet of instructions and some supplies."

"Thanks, doc."

The doctor gave Seth a troubled look before patting his shoulder and turning to leave the room. Seth watched him go, then turned his face to the windows that looked out over the hospital lawn.

He desperately tried to pull his memories of last night from his throbbing, fuzzy head.

Taping his hands . . . "To Make You Feel My Love". . . Clinton's warning . . . meeting Eli in the ring . . . the fight . . .

He flinched.

. . . seeing Griselda.

He closed his eyes, fixing on the memory of her face. Blue eyes, golden hair, chin scar. It was her—it *had* to be her. Every night since the day she'd been murdered in the Shenandoah, Seth had dreamed of her. Every night since he was fifteen years old, he'd fallen asleep staring at her face. He knew her face like the back of his hand. Better. He knew it better than anything else in the world, and there was no way he could mistake it. Either the girl from last night was her, or he was ready for a straitjacket, because he was going as crazy as Caleb.

"G-God, Gris," he whispered as tears burned his eyes. "How are you alive?"

How was it possible? Had she managed to escape that day? Had Caleb shot her, but she somehow survived? Had she been buried alive, but escaped after they'd driven away? But the blood on Caleb's shirt. The grave. Caleb said he'd killed her. Could he have been lying? Seth needed answers, and he needed them now.

More memories of last night teased him, and he flinched because the harder he tried to remember, the more his head throbbed. She had been arguing with someone last night. Who? He blinked. The college boy in the polo shirt. Seth's fingers clenched into fists, and he tightened his jaw. Who the fuck was that guy? And why was he upsetting her? He winced, searching his memory. The college boys were standing with Quint, and she was yelling at one of them. Quint. He needed to get to Quint. Now.

He looked around the room wildly for a telephone, but there was none. His jeans were draped across a chair on the other side of the room. It took more strength than he had for Seth to swing his legs over the bed, but his wrist yanked him back, still attached to an IV. He pulled it out, grimacing at the sharp pinch.

Resting on the side of the bed, his chest, right under his

pecs, burned like crazy, and he looked down to see a white bandage stained with brown blood and freshly seeping red. Wincing, he stood up carefully, his head swimming as he shuffled toward the chair, steadying himself by holding on to the foot of the hospital bed. He lurched once and landed in the chair, trying to catch his breath. After a moment, he reached for his jeans and pulled them on, moving slowly, finally standing to yank them to his waist. Three more wounds on his left hip and lower back throbbed, so he didn't zip or button the pants.

His face was slick with sweat as he made his way to the hallway, resting in the doorway for a minute before he took slow, careful, barefoot steps to the nearby nurse's desk.

"Mr. West, what are you doing out of bed? I must insist—"

"I need a phone."

"You *need* to get back in bed."

His voice was scratchy but firm. "*The phone. N-now.*"

Her mouth dropped open, but she picked up the phone sitting in front of her and raised it to the counter where he was leaning. He nodded in thanks and picked up the receiver, dialing Clinton's cell phone.

"Clinton here."

"It's Seth. Pick me up."

"Dang, Seth. They letting you out already?"

"Where's your pop at?"

"What time's it? Almost three? His shift's just ending. Probably heading for Rosie's 'bout now to grab a cold one."

"Come pick me up. I gotta talk to him."

"Yeah, yeah, sure. Let me just tell Chick I gotta go. Be there soon."

A bolt of pain shot through his chest as Seth lowered his arm, and he dropped the receiver with a trembling hand. The nurse rushed around the desk, carefully putting her arms under his shoulders and guiding him back to his room.

CHAPTER 9

The insistent knocking on the door woke Griselda from a deep sleep, and she sat up slowly, getting her bearings. The shock of Jonah's news must have knocked her out. Though she didn't remember falling asleep, she was lying in the center of the bed in the fetal position. She caught a look at the clock: twenty-five past three.

Standing up, she listened to the sound of more knocking, then walked through the open door of the bedroom. A note sat on the dining table:

You were sleeping. We went fishing. Back by four. –J

She took a deep breath and made her way to the door.

Pushing the curtain aside, she looked through the window to see Quint standing outside on the porch. As he raised a hand in hello, she let go of the curtain. He was probably here to collect on the bets Jonah and Shawn made last night.

He knows Holden. He'll know where I can find Holden.

She sucked her bottom lip into her mouth, worrying it between her teeth. With Jonah, Shawn, and Tina gone, she was all alone in the cottage, and she knew nothing about this guy, except that he'd had a creepy interest in her last night. Was he a sicko? Would he hurt her? But the question of her safety was quickly eclipsed by the fact that Griselda knew how much pain she could tolerate, and whatever Quint meted out was worth the possibility of finding Holden.

Still, she could be cautious.

She pushed the curtain aside.

"What do you want?" she asked through the glass.

"Need to talk to you."

Her eyes widened. "To *me*?"

"To you, Griselda."

Her name. Her full name that she hadn't been called since that terrible day on the Shenandoah. She gasped softly, unlocking the door.

"How'd you find me?"

"Your boyfriend. Told me last night where y'all were staying."

She nodded once, barely able to breathe, waiting for him to continue.

"You want me to come in, or you want to come out here and talk to me?" he asked, stepping back as the door swung open.

"Come in," she whispered, though neither of them moved. "How do you know my name?"

Say it, she thought, desperately. *God, please just say his name to me so I know for sure that it's him.*

"Seth," he said simply.

Tears coursed down her cheeks as she nodded at him. It was true. Oh God, it was true. It was Holden in the ring last night. Holden, who went by Seth now. Holden, who had returned to West Virginia. Holden, who was huge and looked thirty. Holden, who fought other men for sport.

"Holden," she whispered.

"Come again?"

Through glassy eyes, she looked up at Quint. "Where is he?"

"I can take you to him."

Griselda nodded, walking through the doorway and following Quint to his truck without a second thought, without even closing the door or walking back inside for her purse.

They rode in silence for several minutes before Quint spoke. "Figured out how I knew you."

"Oh?"

"You reminded me of someone, but I couldn't figure out who. I realized it last night when we were carrying him into the clinic. He has a tattoo of your face. On his arm."

"Oh."

"Yeah. And under it, it says 'H+G.' Told me today that the *G* was for Griselda."

Tears brightened and burned her eyes, and she nodded, turning her head to look out the window.

"Only one time Clinton gave him shit for that tattoo. He came to a few hours later, with one less tooth."

Her lips wobbled, tilting up a little.

"He's a fierce fighter, Seth. Has been for the four or five years we've known him. He doesn't say much, but I always wondered what happened to him to make him that way."

Griselda swallowed, her lips tightening again.

"He works with my boy, Clinton, at the glass factory."

She didn't answer. She didn't trust her voice.

"Yeah. You're a quiet little thing. I get it. I'd quit yammering, but hell, I just get nervous. Seth shouldn't'a discharged hisself from the hospital like that. And you're here, and he's got your face on his arm, and I just . . . heck, I don't know what's going on."

Several more minutes passed in silence before she gathered the courage to speak. Her voice was soft and a little broken when she did. "I haven't seen him in a real long time."

"How long?" asked Quint.

She swallowed past the lump in her throat, shaking her head. She couldn't say anything else. She leaned her head against the window, and her eyes fluttered shut as she remembered the last time she saw him.

***

"R-r-r-r-uuuuuun!"

Griselda's face crumpled as she watched the butt of the Man's rifle slam into Holden's head. Holden's voice cut off immediately, and he slumped to his side, knocked unconscious. Cutter barked from the riverbank, howling and pacing.

"Goddamn it!" she screamed, lurching forward, then catching herself just in time before slipping. "Goddamn you! No!"

She looked at the rushing water between her and Holden. They were separated by seven or eight large stones, in deep, rushing water, but even if she got to him, then what? She couldn't fight the Man. She couldn't drag Holden along with her. There was only one question she needed to answer: should she go back with the Man, or should she try to make her escape and send help for Holden?

"I said to shut up, dummy," mumbled the Man, letting go of Holden's shirt. His head hit the rock with a clunk, and he lay there limp and motionless.

"Holden," she sobbed, staring at his lifeless body. She lifted watery eyes to the Man, speaking through clenched teeth. "You're going to hell."

"You first, Ruth," he spat, raising the rifle.

Her eyes widened as she stared back at him. She hopped two rocks farther away before turning back to face him. Her eyes dropped desperately to Holden's body before cutting to the Man's narrowed eyes, which glared through the shotgun sight.

"Why? Why did you do this to us?" she sobbed. "We never did anything to you!"

"Ya led him down the devil's pathway, sissy, with yer spring tits an' tight ass. Ya damned him to the fiery pits by churnin' up his lust. Yer my sister, but I'd kill ya soon as look at

ya, Ruth."

"I'm not your sister! I'm not Ruth!"

"True enough. Yer no sister of mine no more. Yer a lyin' temptress bitch'n'heat. An evil whore of Babylon sent to destroy my brother with yer wicked ways."

"Holden's not your brother! He's not Seth!"

The Man's face reddened with fury, and he cocked the gun, taking aim.

Griselda turned her back to him, stepping gingerly onto another rock as the gun sounded and a bullet whizzed past her head.

"Noooo!" she screamed, slipping, then righting herself. "No! Stop!"

"Yer pure evil, Ruth. Ya need to be put down like a rabid dog."

Concentrating on her steps, she moved more quickly.

Don't look back, no matter what. Our feet are small. Stone to stone. I jump, you jump.

Tears burned her eyes, and her body was rigid with fear as she tried desperately to keep her balance. She heard him cock the gun again.

"Stop it! Sto-o-o-p," she sobbed, choking on her words. She chanced a helpless look back at Holden, who still lay motionless on the large rock. "Oh, Holden. Holden, I'm so sorry . . ."

Another gunshot and the bullet splashed a foot in front of her.

She screamed, "No! Stop!" before taking another step forward.

Move, Griselda. Keep moving. Don't look back. Get to the woods. Find help.

She pushed herself to keep moving. Stone to stone, her feet slipping, her aching muscles compensating for balance. Wondering if a bullet would suddenly tear through her with every step she took made it hard for her to keep her balance, but somehow she managed to move forward. Finally she could see the pebbles under the water, and she jumped into the knee-deep river, wading as fast as she could toward the rocky shore.

Finally on dry land again, she turned around.

They were gone.

***

"This is it," said Quint, and Griselda realized that the truck had stopped.

They'd parked on a traditional, all-American, if somewhat run-down, Main Street, in front of a two-story brick building. The lower level had a lackluster coffee shop, whose glass door, in peeling paint, announced "RITA'S" and "W rld's est Co fee." She raised her eyes to the second level and saw two windows facing the street. Apartments.

"You want that I come up with you?" asked Quint.

"No," she said, staring up at the windows. In the right window, two hands were pressed flush against the glass, though she couldn't make out the body attached to them. It was him. She knew it. She felt it.

Quint fumbled with his breast pocket, finally handing her a key. "This'll get you in."

She reached for it with trembling fingers.

"I should warn you. Seth's in bad shape. He was stabbed a few times last night, nose broke, ribs bruised. Concussion. Cheek fracture. Ain't no way he shoulda left the hospital, but all he could talk about was finding you. Said he'd beat me like Eli if I didn't come for you and bring you to him."

"I'll take care of him." Griselda shifted slightly to look into Quint's gentle blue eyes. "Won't be the first time."

Quint's lips tightened in sympathy, but he only nodded. "Tell him I'll come by tomorrow with food and such."

"Thank you," she said, reaching for the door.

"Griselda," said Quint.

She turned to face him.

"I don't know who you are, but he . . . well, he feels something fierce for you."

She wiped her eyes and nodded, shutting the door behind her.

The key opened the door at street level, and she looked up the dingy stairs, taking a deep breath. For ten years, Griselda had searched for Holden, saving her money for detectives, maybe even hoping to set up a life with him once she found him. And now here she was, closer to him than she'd been in half a lifetime, about to look into the gray eyes that she'd dreamed of all that time, and suddenly she felt terrified.

What do you say to the person you loved so deeply as a child? The person you imperiled when you stepped into a madman's truck? The person you betrayed when you turned your back and left him behind? How do you make amends for the lost years and broken promises? My God, what do you say?

A door opened upstairs, and she heard the soft shuffling of bare feet on a linoleum floor. She took a deep breath, and when she looked up, there he was: Seth from last night. *Holden*, standing at the top of the stairs, staring down at her. He wore unbuttoned jeans, his torso bare but for three or four tattoos, and bandages that covered a good section of his chest under his heart and over his hip.

"G-G-Gris?" he asked softly, his voice breathless and broken, but in it she heard Holden's, and her ear, so lonely for him for so long, inclined to him.

Tears filled her eyes, and she nodded as they spilled over the rims of her eyes, trailing down her cheeks. She started crying in earnest, but her lips tilted up as her feet started up the steps, one after the other, faster and faster until she made it to the top, standing across from him, staring into his battered gray eyes.

"Oh my God," she whispered.

His face was beat-up and bruised, but as wet as hers, and

he sniffled as he held out his hand to her. She looked down at it—the fresh cuts stole her attention first, but then she noticed the familiar tan freckles splashed across his white skin like constellations, and she gasped, lifting her head with a beaming smile as she started sobbing.

"Oh my God . . . Oh my God . . . Oh my God . . ."

She reached for his hand, tentatively at first, but the moment they touched, his fingers curled around hers with strength and purpose, pulling her to him.

"He said you were d-dead," he murmured.

"No," she whispered. "No, I made it across."

"My G-God, Gris, you're alive."

His eyes trailed across her face, up to the crown of her head, following her amber hair to her shoulders, back to her eyes, which he searched carefully, sweeping down her cheekbones to her lips, to the scar on her chin, where he fixed his gaze for a long moment before looking up again.

"C-can I—?" His eyes glistened as he held out his free arm, as though he wanted to hug her but needed permission to touch her. She stepped into him, letting him wrap her gently against his body as she lay her cheek on his bare shoulder.

With her flush against him, his left hand shifted, fingers entwining with hers, and he leaned forward, resting his cheek against her head.

"You're alive." He said it again so quietly it was like a thought that stole some breath to be heard.

"Yes," she sobbed, closing her eyes and wrapping her left arm around him until her palm lay flush and curved against the back of his neck.

"He said, uh, he said he shot you."

"He tried, but he missed."

Holden shuddered, holding her tighter. "The g-g-grave—"

"Cutter."

"No. He said C-Cutter ran off."

"He lied. It was Cutter in the grave, not me." Griselda looked up at him, shaking her head. "The police found him buried in the front yard. After you left."

His face contorted. "C-Caleb s-s-said that w-w-was y-y-y—"

"Breathe," she said without thinking.

He did. He took a deep gulp of air, his chest pushing into hers. She felt him sway a little, which reminded her how badly he was injured.

Worried because they were so close to the top of the stairs, she stepped away from him and noticed that his face was not only wet because he was crying, but because he was dripping with sweat. Beads started in his hair, running down the sides of his face. She looked down at his chest and realized that what had looked like brownish blood from a distance was actually pinkish red and spreading. He was bleeding and probably needed his bandages changed.

She searched his eyes, which were still wild and disbelieving. His shock at seeing her was masking the pain, but he needed to lie down before he lost his strength, and she needed to re-dress his wounds.

She lifted her chin toward the apartment behind him.

"Can we go inside, Holden?"

He gasped, drawing away from her, searching her eyes for a long moment.

"Seth," he whispered firmly, then took her hand and pulled her through the open apartment door.

CHAPTER 10

She's alive. She's alive. Gris is alive.

It was an endless litany in his head and a celebration in his heart as he guided her into his home.

"Holden, I think—"

He turned to face her after closing the door behind them. "I don't go by Holden anymore."

She flinched. "It's your name."

"N-not anymore. I go by Seth."

She dropped his eyes, looking down at the floor. "I don't understand."

"I haven't been Holden in a long time."

"But you're not Seth."

"Yes, I am." He sighed, wondering where to even begin. "Gris," he started, but before he could gather his thoughts, she interrupted him.

"If you're Seth, does that make me Ruth?" she asked, her voice soft but bitter as she cut her eyes to his.

"*N-nothing* makes you R-Ruth," he said harshly, clenching his jaw and staring at her for a long moment before shuffling past her into the small living room. He lowered himself onto the tattered sofa, the pain from the movement making him gasp.

"Lie down all the way," she said, putting her hand under his arm to help ease him down. "Where are the clean bandages?

This one under your heart looks seepy. I'll change it."

"Are you a nurse?"

"No."

Lying flat on the couch, he looked up at her, still in a state of semi-shock that after so long she was suddenly here. In his apartment. With him. Near him. Touching him. He had so many questions: Where had she been all these years? Had she ever tried to find him? Was she okay? Did she still dream of him as he dreamed of her?

"G-Gris. J-just talk to me."

She met his eyes briefly before looking back down at his wound. "After I bandage you up, okay?"

"You're still stubborn."

Her eyes flashed to him, and her whole face softened before it crumpled, tears tumbling from her eyes. She gestured to the back hallway off the living room.

"Bathroom back there?" she asked through sobs.

"Yeah," he said, watching her go, hating it that she had to leave his line of sight even for the two minutes it would take for her to collect the supplies.

When she came back a few minutes later, her face was dry, though her eyes were still glassy and puffy from crying. She knelt down beside him on the floor, reaching for the bandage near his heart. He reached up gently, closing his fingers around her wrist, then sliding them up to clasp the back of her hand to the palm of his.

"Leave it for a minute."

He twisted his neck until his cheek rested on the coarse, nubby material of the old couch, staring at her face.

"I never thought I'd see you again."

She clenched her eyes shut, wincing as fresh tears fell down her cheeks in rivulets.

"I hoped," she gasped, and her sweet breath touched his cheek like a blessing. He let go of her hand, reaching to place his palm on her cheek, swiping away the tears with his thumb. She leaned into him, opening her shattered eyes. "God, how I hoped."

"Wh-where have you been, Gris? What happened after—"

"Please let me change the bandages, Hol—"

"Seth."

She grimaced instantly, drawing back from his hand and letting it drop back to the couch. She stood up and looked down at the bandage.

"I need to clean it with some warm water."

Without meeting his eyes, she turned and crossed the room and into the kitchen. He listened as she ran the water to warm, rummaging around for a bowl. The pain was ratcheting up now that his adrenaline had stopped pumping, and the area below his heart where he'd sustained the deepest cut burned and throbbed like a fever. Finally she returned, placing the warm water on the floor beside the couch. Without warning, she reached for a corner of the bandage and ripped it off.

"Jesus!" he cried, his eyes shooting open wide from the pain.

"I can't call you Seth. It's not who you are."

He made a groaning sound, followed by a short exhale of stored breath. When he jerked his chin up to look at her, he found her less sad and more angry for the first time since their reunion.

"Yeah, it is," he bit out. "You saw me last night. It's *exactly* who I am."

"No," she said firmly, then more softly, "No, Holden."

She shook her head, dipping a paper towel in the warm water and gently dabbing at the incision over and over, mumbling under her breath. It was an action so familiar his heart contracted, compressing his lungs, which struggled to draw a full breath.

"*. . . Seth . . . . .name of a danged crazy perso—*"

"Stop mumbling, Gris."

Her eyes darted up to meet his. "Zelda."

"Huh?"

"My name is Zelda. I don't go by Griselda anymore," she said tartly, "and I sure as heck don't go by Gris."

Though he tried to catch her eyes, she kept them down as she made this speech, concentrating on his wound. She folded another paper towel and pressed it gently against his chest until the skin was clean and dry. With sharp ripping sounds, she tore open two bandages, arranging them carefully over the clean incision before tearing off strips of white surgical tape to secure them.

"Z-Zelda?" He tried it out, and it felt so devastating and wrong and foreign to his mouth that tears burned at the backs of his eyes.

"Yeah?"

"No. I c-can't c-call you that."

"Too bad." She reached down for the basin and stood up, giving him a hard look, her beautiful lips in a taut, angry line. As she stared at him, her face softened, and she reached into the supply basket for an amber vial of pills. "You're in bad pain."

"I've known worse."

And because she knew this was true, her eyes flooded with tears, and the muscles in her throat visibly tensed, as though swallowing an ocean of terrible memories. He watched her, feeling every emotion that crossed her face, remembering that when she flinched, she blinked quickly first, and when she was trying not to cry, she clenched her teeth and tried to swallow the sadness away. He saw it all. He felt it all. He remembered it all.

Still holding the container of painkillers, she twisted the top off with her teeth and leaned down to let one white pill spill onto the couch beside his face.

"I'll get you water."

She headed back to the kitchen, where she placed the

basket on the counter, and he heard the water running in the sink again.

"You know what?" she called to him, stepping out of the kitchen and standing across the room with her hands on her hips.

"What?"

She stalked back to the sofa, dropping to her knees beside him and offering him a glass of water.

"I ain't calling you Seth."

Her use of the word *ain't* was so unexpectedly familiar, it pinged in his brain like a ball peen hammer as he gulped the water. When he lay back down, she reached for his arm. Her hands were soft and warm and a little damp as she turned his forearm over to look at the underside.

His heart beat like crazy as her eyes found her face in the swirls of ink, and she gasped, staring for a long moment before suddenly bending forward to press her lips against his skin, against the letters "H+G" tattooed there. The pain of his injuries and the shock of seeing her again? In terms of intensity, it all paled in comparison to the sensation of her lips touching his skin, and it was several seconds before he realized he was holding his breath. As he forced himself to exhale and drag in a shredded gasp, she raised her head to find his eyes. Bending his arm at the elbow, she showed the tattoo to him.

"You didn't get 'S+R' tattooed on your arm, Holden—"

"Gris . . ."

"It says 'H+G.' 'Holden plus Griselda.' So, I don't give a good goddamn *fuck* who you are to Quint or Clinton, or, or, or to *the Man* or anyone else—"

"G-Gris!"

"—because you are *Holden* to me. I lost too much, and I held on too long for someone named *Holden*, so you either get used to me saying that name again or—"

"G-G-Griselda!"

"What?" she yelled.

"Okay."

"Okay what?" she asked, holding her breath.

"You win."

"What do I win?"

"F-fucking call me Holden if you have to! Jesus!"

Her face, which was frowning, softened immediately, her lush lips tilting up as a rogue tear trailed down her cheek.

"Holden," she whispered, on a let-go breath, reaching forward to brush his hair off his forehead and press her lips to his skin.

His eyes fluttered closed at this reward, and his aching heart eased, knowing the first real shred of peace since the last moment he'd seen her.

Gris. My Gris. She's here. She's alive.

Her lips parted as she drew back, and she took a deep, shuddering breath before leaning back and sinking down on her haunches. She found his far hand and wove her fingers through his, then lay her arm gently across his chest, resting just under his neck, careful to avoid his injuries. He knew she was crying when she lowered her head beside his on the sofa. The crown of her soft golden hair nuzzled his cheek as he readjusted his fingers so that his palm was flush with hers.

"Now what?" he murmured near her ear, trying not to close his eyes. The pills were kicking in, and the pain was finally subsiding, but he fought against the lull of exhaustion that threatened to pull him under. They needed to talk. He needed to find out where she'd been, how she'd survived, who she'd become. He needed to be sure she'd still be here when he woke up.

Her voice was tender but felt far away. "Now we rest for a little while, and then we'll talk."

"Gris—"

"Don't worry, Holden. I'm not going anywhere. I promise I'll stay."

"Okay," he sighed, tightening his grip on her hand before closing his weary eyes and yielding to sleep.

***

"I better go back," said Gris, burrowing her forehead into his neck, her breath soft on his skin.

"N-n-not yet," he whispered, holding on tighter to her body. "Stay."

He'd noticed her breasts more and more lately, since they'd both turned thirteen. They weren't big like an adult's, but they weren't small like a child's anymore either. They were obvious under her worn-out yellow dress and more pointy when it was chilly. He tried not to look at them, especially during the day, when the Man would beat him for even peeking at Gris, but he liked the way they felt—all warm and soft—pushed up against his chest at night or in the early morning, like now.

"Okay," she sighed. "I'll stay for a few more minutes."

"G-Gris," he whispered. "W-what'll it be like?"

"When we're grown-ups?"

"Yeah."

She leaned back a little, looking into his eyes, the dawn sunlight filtering in through the crack in the cellar doors making her hair more blonde than red.

"Well," she said, her eyes lighting across his face before settling on his eyes again, "someday someone will find us here. We'll be rescued, and they'll take us back to D.C. And because we had so much trauma, they'll put us in the same foster home again. And I'll still come to you every night just like now."

"Mm-hm," he encouraged her.

"And we'll go to school and study real hard. Soon enough, we'll be eighteen. And then you'll buy me a ring at the mall and ask me to marry you."

"Yep."

"And it won't be a fancy wedding because we got no family, but maybe Marisol will come."

"B-b-but not Billy."

"Nope. He ain't invited," she agreed. "And one day we'll have babies."

"And we'll never, ever leave them. W-w-we'll be the best p-parents ever, Gris."

"Yep. The very best. And we'll buy a little house, not in the city, and we'll work real hard to make it nice. We could have a garden, 'cause we know how to do that."

"I don't ever w-want to g-garden again."

"Why not? Ain't the vegetables' fault that the Man makes us grow 'em."

"I hate everything about b-b-being here. 'Cept you."

She touched her forehead to his. "Holden, I—"

Suddenly the lock clicked at the top of the stairs, and her eyes flew open. She rolled soundlessly to the floor, and Holden watched in horror as she crawled as fast as she could to the panel while the Man's heavy boots made their way down the stairs.

They'd discussed this before, and Holden know that Gris had a terrible decision to make. If there wasn't enough time to get back to her room, she would huddle against the door and act like he'd forgotten to lock her in last night. She vowed to never risk letting him know about their panel, or they'd lose each other for good.

Holden's heart sank as she made her decision, moving past the panel to huddle against the door to her room and pretend that she'd slept there.

The Man finally stepped onto the dirt floor, and Holden clenched his eyes shut, desperately hoping that the Man would believe that he was asleep and that Gris had slept several feet away from him beside her door.

"Wickedness!" bellowed the Man, the two tin oatmeal bowls crashing to the floor and scuttling across the room.

Holden's eyes burned with fear, but he opened them to see

the Man reach down and grab Griselda's braid, yanking her head up. "Wicked, evil gal sleepin' in here with Seth!"

"No, sir," she sobbed. "No. You f-forgot to lock me in l-last night. I slept by the door, sir. Didn't even look his way. Not once."

Still holding her hair, the Man drew his hand back, and his palm cracked across her face, making her head whip to the side. She grunted, a throaty sound that ended in a higher-pitched whimper. As he drew his hand back again, Holden threw back the blanket of his bed and jumped up.

"D-d-don't hit her again!"

The Man's hand stilled, and Holden's eyes shot to Griselda's. The expression on her face, which was bright red on the side that had just taken the smack, begged him not to get involved.

"Ya tellin' me what to do, half-wit?" asked the Man, turning to Holden and loosening his grip on Griselda's hair.

"I'm t-t-telling you d-d-don't hit her again!"

The Man's eyes blazed with fury as he released Griselda's hair, pushing her head roughly against the panel wall as he stalked toward Holden. His hands fell to his belt buckle. He unbuckled it and pulled it off with one yank, the whipping noise making bile rise in Holden's throat.

"Ya want her beatin', little brother?"

"Y-y-yes, s-s-sir," said Holden, staring at Griselda, who mouthed the word "no," shaking her head.

He'd asked her to stay. She'd tried to go back to her room, and he'd asked her to stay because he wanted to feel her body next to his. No matter what the Man said, Holden couldn't bring himself to believe that touching Gris, that loving her, was evil. But it was his fault she'd been caught.

Yes, he wanted her beating.

He pulled off his T-shirt and threw it on the bed, facing away from Griselda as the terrible blows started landing.

CHAPTER 11

It took Holden a while to fall asleep. He fretted for a bit, mumbling incoherent words with full-body flinching and an almost painful grip on her hand.

After a good twenty minutes, Griselda finally heard his breathing shift to a deep, even rhythm. His hand, still tightly bound with hers, finally relaxed. He was sleeping peacefully.

You still have nightmares, she thought. *Just like me.*

She sighed, wondering what episode of his life had just tormented him before he found peace. Her heart hurt to imagine there had been more misery in his life than that which they had endured in the cellar together. But chances were, there had been. Chances were, his life had been a living hell.

She was comfortable enough where she was, kneeling on the floor beside him with her head touching his. It was a position she remembered well from their childhood nights in Caleb Foster's cellar, and she thought ruefully that Holden's smelly, nubby couch wasn't much of an improvement from the rank mattress that had been his cellar bed.

It was very quiet in his apartment. She could hear the occasional car horn or muted voice from the sidewalk below, but it was unexpectedly peaceful. The late afternoon sun softened the drab room with a golden light as Griselda looked around at Holden's home.

The walls were probably once white but were now badly scuffed and slightly discolored. The cigarette smoke she smelled was old and stale, so she assumed the previous renter had smoked and Holden just hadn't bothered repainting. The carpet, like the sofa, was brown and nubby, and showed several cigarette burns throughout.

In addition to the sofa where they rested, there was a dingy, scratched-up coffee table, a mustard-gold velour easy chair that had seen better days, and below the windows she'd glimpsed from Quint's car, a TV on a wooden crate with a gaming console attached. The small, simple kitchen was beyond the front door, and to the right was a small kitchen table with two chairs. On the table, which had a neat stack of mail and a couple of books, there was also a vase that held a single daisy.

Oh, she thought, unexpected jealousy slicing through her like a blade. *Of course.*

She hadn't actually given it any thought until that moment. But of course a twenty-three-year-old man as built and fierce as Holden would have a girlfriend. It's not like Griselda had a right to expect or assume that he'd lived his life as a monk since that day on the Shenandoah. It's not like she had lived like a nun either, she sniffed, thinking briefly of Jonah.

What irritated her, and made no sense at all, was how much it hurt. And not just that he had a girlfriend, but that he had a whole life that didn't include her. He lived in West Virginia, he worked in a glass factory, he had friends she'd never heard of, he fought other men for sport and profit. She didn't know him. She didn't know him at all anymore. *That* part of him was—as much as she hated to admit it—someone named Seth.

And yet.

He wore her face and their initials on his arm, dyed into his flesh so she would be a permanent and constant part of him. Though he'd obviously learned how to control his stammer, it still got away from him when he felt overwhelmed or emotional.

Forbidden names like Ruth and Cutter still caught on his tongue, and he still breathed deep the instant she told him to. As she'd bandaged him, his eyes still searched hers for truth and comfort, just as they had so long ago, when he was only Holden.

***

". . . hope wasn't lost, however! The dark knight arrived on his jet-black steed—"

"Steed?"

"Horse," she said impatiently, losing the rhythm of the story every time he interrupted. She was annoyed with Holden today. He'd taken her beating yesterday morning, and he shouldn't have. The Man had already gotten her once in the face, and he generally didn't hit her more than four or five times. When Holden got involved, it made the made the man so much madder that he got fifteen or twenty lashes on the back. Holden didn't seem to understand—if she lost him, her life was over. He had to stop talking back.

"—and he battled the fearsome witch with his sword, which was steel, forged in the fiery canyons of—"

"What's 'f-forged'?"

"Made. Crafted."

"Oh, right. G-go on."

". . . in the fiery canyons of Hades. He chopped off her head with one flaming blow, and it rolled across the room to land at the feet of the princess."

"Eyes open?"

"Eyes are always open when someone's dead," she said, shivering as she remembered all the times she was sure Joellyn was dead, staring straight ahead and barely breathing.

"G-gross," he said. "Then w-what?"

"Then nothing," she said, flipping over on the cot so her back was to him. "You interrupted me so much, I can't barely keep my place."

"D-d-does the kn-knight save the princess?" asked Holden

from behind her.

"Of course. It wouldn't be a fairy tale if she was locked in the witch's hut forever."

"Well, then, c-c-can you just finish it?" he begged her, placing his hand tentatively against her back. "Just so I c-can see it in my head? I p-promise I won't interrupt no more."

Griselda pursed her lips, looking straight ahead at the darkness of the cellar. Though she couldn't see it, she knew there was a tool bench across from the cot where they were lying. It had hammers and saws, and sometimes she had a terrible idea: that when the Man came downstairs with their breakfast or dinner, she would slam one of those hammers into his head. Except, if she didn't kill him, he'd kill them.

She flipped over onto her back, folding her hands on her chest and staring at the ceiling. Holden shifted slightly, and she could feel his eyes on her, needing the comfort that her silly stories provided. And she needed him too. Without him, she'd have no one to care for, no one to love, no one with whom to endure the long, dark, lonesome hours.

"Fine." She drew in a deep breath, and her chest expanded just enough for her side to brush into his, which made her tummy flutter. "Holden?"

"Yeah?"

"Don't talk back to him." She felt the hot tears gather in her eyes. Pain hurt. Fear hurt. But she could bear pain and fear. The thought of losing Holden was unbearable. "Please. Just . . . let me take it sometimes."

Holden took a breath, then swallowed. "I hate him. I hate it when he yells those things at you. C-c-can't stand it w-w-when he beats you."

"I don't care if he yells at me. I don't even care if he beats me. I can't stand it when you make him mad and he starts in on you but worse. It scares me, Holden."

Holden was silent for a long time before asking, "He ever

t-t-touch you funny, Gris?"

She swallowed down the lump in her throat. "No. You?"

He shook his head. "Nope."

"I don't want to talk about that," she said quickly, a shiver breaking out across her body.

Though the Man didn't seem to have a special interest in either her or Holden like that—like Mrs. Fillman had seemed to have in Billy—that he might develop such an interest was the stuff of Griselda's worst and darkest nightmares.

"We have to escape, Holden," she murmured. "We have to try and escape."

"F-f-finish the story."

"I can't."

"You c-can," he said. "Just b-breathe."

She took a deep breath, trying to remember where she'd been in the story, trying to let go of the terrifying thoughts of Holden leaving her and the Man wanting her.

"Okay," she said. "Let's see . . . Well, the witch's head landed at the feet of the princess, but she didn't scream because she didn't notice it. She was staring at the knight, dressed in black, standing just inside the door of the cottage. He sheathed his sword and crossed to the fair maiden, dropping to his knees as he broke the chains that bound her. Then he carried her from the witch's lair. Though they hadn't seen each other for one hundred and one years, they were as much in love as ever. The knight kissed the princess in the sunshine, and they lived happily ever after."

"The end," whispered Holden, as he always did.

"The end," said Griselda, her heart still heavy and frightened as she burrowed her forehead into the sweetness of his neck. She couldn't fall asleep, but she closed her eyes, the words "We have to escape" playing in an endless loop in her head.

***

When Griselda opened her eyes, it was dusk in the small apartment, and she knew immediately where she was. What she didn't know was who was sitting a couple feet away from her in the mustard easy chair, staring her down with narrowed eyes.

"Ain't this cozy," the woman observed.

Griselda blinked, starting, trying to pull her hand away from Holden, but it was still held securely at the base of his throat, and she didn't want to wake him by wrenching it away.

The woman narrowed her eyes. "Are you G?"

"G?" asked Griselda, reviewing the situation with a still-sleepy head. She was in Holden's apartment. She'd tended to his wounds and fallen asleep. So who was this woman sitting a few feet away from her, shooting her daggers?

She glanced at the vase on the kitchen table.

Aha.

The daisy.

"G. For 'Gris,'" the woman said, spitting out her name like it was a bad word. She shook her head, her ponytail swinging from side to side and releasing a strong smell of fast food grease. "He calls out yer name in his sleep."

"Oh." Griselda dropped her eyes for a moment, hating it that this woman knew what Holden said in his sleep.

"I know yer her. I recognize you from the ink, so don't deny it. 'Sides, he never holds on to me like that."

"Yes. I'm Gris."

"Of course you are."

"And you're . . .?"

"His *girlfriend*. Gemma."

His girlfriend. Griselda had already known, but it pinched something inside to hear it confirmed.

"Another G," Griselda said softly.

"Yeah, but not the one on his arm." Gemma crossed her own arms over her chest. "So who are you to Seth?"

"Someone from a long time ago," said Griselda.

"Like a sister?" Gemma asked, tentatively.

"Foster sister."

Griselda glanced at their tightly bound hands before looking back up at Gemma, her silence giving Gemma the rest of an answer she didn't like.

"You stayin'?" demanded Gemma. "Now that yer here?"

Griselda shrugged. She had no idea how to answer that question, but for the second time since she'd arrived at Holden's apartment, she thought of Jonah. She briefly, and without much emotion, wondered if he'd left for Maryland, or if he was still here, wondering where she was, worried about her. Without her purse or her phone, there was no way to know. She'd simply . . . disappeared.

"Hey!" said Gemma, snapping her fingers twice in Griselda's direction to get her attention. "I asked you a question."

Griselda didn't particularly like being snapped at. Her voice was low and unfriendly when she replied, "I don't know."

"I been with him six months."

Griselda stared at her, unmoving, uncaring.

"I spent all the morning with him at the hospital until I had to go to work. I went straight back there after work. 'He's left,' they told me. 'Checked himself out,' they told me. I come here, let myself in, and here you are. Holding his hand. Asleep." She took a deep breath and narrowed her eyes. "I should slap yer face off yer neck."

"I wouldn't," Griselda said tightly.

Gemma flinched, taken aback by the sand in her rival's tone. "Ain't nothin' gonna happen tonight anyway. He couldn't get it up if he wanted to."

Griselda stared at her, grateful for the cloak of semidarkness that concealed her blush. She was no innocent, but the last time she'd seen Holden, he was thirteen. Her mind hadn't progressed to a point yet where it could process that he could—that *they* could—that their bodies could . . .

Gemma stood up, brushing her hands on the front of her tight jeans. "Tell Seth to call me when he wakes up. We got things to discuss."

Without moving more than necessary, Griselda nodded curtly, watching Gemma head out the door, which clunked shut loudly. Holden gasped, his eyes flying open.

"Where's Gris?"

"Here. I'm here. Shh. Shh, now," she murmured, adjusting their fingers so he'd know she was real.

"I'm dreaming," he panted, blinking his half-asleep eyes at her.

She shook her head and spoke tenderly. "No, Holden. It's me. I'm here."

"It's you," he gasped, his eyes widening before fluttering closed again. "Gris. Don't go 'way."

"I won't," she promised as he fell back into a deep sleep.

This time he hadn't tightened his hand on hers, so after watching him sleep for a few quiet minutes, she slipped her fingers from his without waking him. She pulled a tired-looking, thin blanket off the back of the couch and covered him, relieved when he didn't stir.

Standing up and crossing the room, she locked the apartment door and fastened the dead bolt and chain.

"No more visitors tonight," she muttered, feeling unsettled by Gemma's sudden appearance, threats, and departure. Though it had been many years since Griselda fought physically with another woman, she was in good shape—likely, she'd still hold her own. No, what bothered her was that, even after a lifetime in the foster care system, she didn't like the vulnerable feeling that came from being woken up by a stranger, and after years living on her own or with Jonah, she was unaccustomed to it.

Her stomach growled, and Griselda realized that she hadn't eaten since Rosie's last night. She opened the refrigerator to find milk, three cans of beer, half a package of hot dogs, half a bag of buns, an apple, ketchup, mustard, and an onion. She opened the cabinets and didn't fare much better: a can of coffee, half a bottle of cooking oil, two half-empty boxes of cereal, and a few cans of soup.

A sudden sharp memory of her early childhood assaulted Griselda and made her grimace. Until the age of six, she had lived in an apartment with her meth-addicted mother, Joellyn, in Anacostia, the worst neighborhood in Southeast D.C. They'd rarely had enough food unless Griselda's grandmother made the trip from Baltimore to check on them and bring groceries, and when she did, it was always the same: hot dogs, apples, milk, and cereal. She said that you could live on those four things for breakfast, lunch, and dinner if you had to, and she was right. Griselda often had.

Griselda paused, staring at the cabinet and wondering if she'd shared that story with Holden at some point or another. Perhaps she had. And perhaps it had been advice he'd inadvertently taken. How strange to know that her grandmother's wisdom was still in use so obscurely, so many years later. Her grandmother had died a few days before Griselda's sixth birthday, and Griselda spent that birthday being dragged by her mother to her grandmother's poorly attended funeral, after which they returned home and her mother dosed herself hard enough to stay in an almost dead stupor for days.

Not long after that, Joellyn started a kitchen fire, and Griselda was taken away from her mother. With nowhere else to go, she was assigned to her first foster family. She saw her mother only twice after that, and when she was returned to the foster care system after her escape from Caleb Foster, she was informed that her mother had died of an overdose while Griselda was in West Virginia.

Shrugging off the bad memories and plucking a can of chicken noodle soup out of the cabinet, she opened the lower cupboards and found a solitary saucepan, which she placed on the stovetop.

Her hands shook a little as she emptied the contents of the can into the pan, and after the soup was on the stove, she took a seat at the small table, staring at Holden's sleeping form.

Now what? he had asked her before falling asleep, and the question reverberated in her head as she stared at him. *Now what?*

For ten years she'd been searching for Holden, and now she'd suddenly found him. He wasn't dead, but he was drastically changed, and she recognized that leaving now might be easier in some ways. She could walk out of his apartment as he slept and move on with her life, knowing he was safe and alive. Maybe, as a way of making amends, she'd send him some money so he could move to a nicer place. He could go back to his life with Gemma, and she could go back to hers with Jonah.

And yet, her longing to know him again tightened its grip on her heart and demanded she stay. Finding him, but not taking the time to know him, seemed like a waste of the miracle she'd been granted. Just being near him again felt strangely hopeful— like a chance to be whole again after long years of being broken. No matter who he'd become, she wanted to know him. She *needed* to know him. She needed to know what had happened to him, how he had survived, if he was okay. Some part of her—a very potent and tenacious part of her—had never let go of Holden through ten dark and lonely years. Might be that someday she'd walk away from him. But not today. Not tonight.

Noticing his phone on the table beside her elbow, she picked it up, dialing Jonah's number.

"Who's this?"

"Jonah, it's me."

He exhaled in a rush. "What the *hell*, Zelda? What happened? Where the fuck are you?"

"Doesn't matter."

"Doesn't matter? We've been waiting here for you for more'n three hours. Shawn was saying how you had a head injury and maybe you'd wandered off. Drowned or something. Your purse is here. What the fuck is going on? Where are you? We'll come get you."

She took a deep breath and exhaled slowly. "No. I'm not going back with you."

"Wha-What does that mean?"

She looked at Holden sleeping peacefully across the room, then got up to take the boiling soup off the stove.

"It means what I said. I'm not going home. Not right now."

"What the fuck, Zelda? You been crazy ever since we got here."

She was silent, wedging the phone between her shoulder and ear as she rummaged for a bowl and poured the steaming soup into it.

"What about your stuff? Your purse and your phone?" he asked.

"Take it all home for me, I guess," she said, opening the drawer beside the sink to find two sets of silverware and no more. She took a spoon and closed the drawer. "I don't really care."

"You don't care. And then what?"

"Live your life."

"Live my life. The rent? The bills?" he snapped. "Your job?"

"You figure out the bills for now," she said, shuffling to the table, careful not to let the hot soup slop over the side of the bowl and burn her hands. "I'll handle my job."

The reality was that there was not much she cared about in this world. Her apartment and its contents? Nope. Her purse and phone? Replaceable. She cared about Maya, to whom she hoped to explain everything someday, and the McClellans, who might or might not fire her from her job. She would miss little

Prudence very much if she was fired, but even Prudence wasn't enough to keep her from Holden. So, as much as it would hurt, she'd accept that consequence.

There was only one person in the world for whom Griselda truly cared. One person. And unbelievably, after a decade apart, he was sleeping a few feet from her right now.

Jonah cursed under his breath. "You know what? You are—you are one bat-shit, crazy-ass bit—"

"I'll see you when I see you," she said, pressing the red End button on Holden's phone before holding down the power button to turn it off entirely.

If Jonah called back—and she was sure he would—she didn't want to risk waking up Holden. If his voicemail greeting gave the name Seth, Jonah might come looking for her here, but then, Jonah's only connection to Seth was Quint. And somehow she didn't see Quint giving up Holden's home address to her jackass of a boyfriend.

Which meant—for now, at least—she was free.

CHAPTER 12

It was nighttime when Holden woke up, but the apartment maintained a dim glow of ambient light from the Main Street lamps beneath his window, even in the middle of the night. He'd never purposely live in a place where the nights offered a pure, black darkness. Not willingly, anyway.

"Gris?" he ground out, trying not to move.

"I'm here," she said, and his eyes focused on her standing up at his kitchen table and walking across the room in bare feet.

She was beautiful.

She was so fucking beautiful it made his eyes burn.

She'd taken her sweatshirt off. All she had on was a pair of jeans and a white scoop-neck T-shirt. Her hair was back in a ponytail, and he didn't know if she wore makeup or if she was just naturally stunning, but he'd be willing to bet on the latter. She'd been a tall, skinny girl, but she must have stopped growing at some point, because she was definitely shorter than his six feet by several inches, but still trim. And now the slight adolescent curves that had so intrigued him a decade ago were filled out and womanly—the swell of her breasts, the gentle curve of her hips—and even with four stab wounds, three bruised ribs, two black eyes, a broken nose, a fractured cheek, and a concussion, Holden's body reacted, his dick stiffening, even though he had no business thinking about Griselda in that way.

She squatted down beside the couch, her face a few inches from his, and he could smell the fresh, clean scent—like soap or laundry detergent—that clung to her skin, and he knew that when he closed his eyes to die, that was the last memory he would reach for: the sweet smell of Griselda on the night he found out she was still alive.

"How you feeling?" she asked, her voice low and gentle as she offered him a glass of water.

He struggled to sit up a little. "Good. Yeah, um, better."

She held the glass to his lips, and he took several deep gulps before lying back down with a soft groan.

"Holden . . .," she said, giving him a look.

"Everything fucking hurts," he admitted, wincing. When he looked at her face, though, it was impossible not to grin. "Except my heart." He paused, spellbound by the sight of her so close. "But even my heart hurts a little."

His eyes dropped to her lips, and he watched as they tilted up a little. "Why's that?"

"Because I missed all of this. I missed ten years of . . . You . . . are so beautiful."

"Aw, look who got smooth." She laughed softly, placing the glass on the floor, and he knew that if the room had been brighter, he would have seen a pink blush color her cheeks.

"I hate to say it," she continued, still grinning at him. "But you don't look so good."

"Yeah, well. Didn't know you were coming. No time to pretty up."

"How often do you do it?"

"It?"

"Fight like that."

He heard the censure in her tone and looked away from her, up at the ceiling, shrugging his shoulders defensively. "From time to time."

"I'd think you would have had enough of being beaten up," she said, picking up the glass.

"I don't do it to get beaten. I do it to win," he muttered.

She sighed, heading back to the kitchen with the empty glass, and Holden watched her: the gentle sway of her hips, the silent touch of her little feet across the carpet. The last time he'd seen those feet, they'd been cut up and bleeding, the Shenandoah rinsing them clean.

"You want something to eat?" she asked.

"I don't have much."

"You have all the basics," she said. "My grandma used to say—"

"—hot dogs, apples, milk, cereal. Breakfast, lunch, and dinner."

She leaned her elbows on the kitchen counter. "I wondered if you'd remembered that."

"I remembered," he said softly. *I remember everything. I've lived on memories of you for ten years.*

"So what'll it be?"

He shifted on the couch, the spike of pain in his chest wound making him wince. "I think I have some soup too? Up in the cabinet?"

"Yep," she said without checking. "Tomato or chicken noodle?"

"I don't care which. You don't mind heating it up?"

"Nope," she said, pulling his saucepan from the drying rack. Since Holden never left anything in the sink, and she was familiar with the small stock of food in his cabinets, he assumed she'd made herself some soup too.

"How long was I out?"

She opened the cabinet next to the stove and took out a can of soup, pulling on the metal tab to open it. "Um, a few hours. Three or four?"

"You ate?"

"I did. I hope you don't mind."

"What's mine is yours, Gris."

She stared at him for a moment, then turned her back to him, pouring the soup into the pan. He was hungry, but he wished she'd leave it for now.

"Come talk to me while it's cooking."

She gave it one last stir, then turned to face him, crossing the room to stand behind the easy chair across from him, which still felt way too far away.

She pulled her bottom lip into her mouth, looking at him like she was trying to decide something. Finally she said, "While you were asleep, your, uh . . . your girlfriend, Gemma, stopped by."

"Oh yeah?" *Fuck.*

"Mm-hm. She was, uh, upset to find me here. Said you should call her so that you two could discu—"

"G-Gris, listen—"

"Holden," she said, her eyes sad, "I don't want to disrupt your life."

Well, I want you to. My life was shit until a few hours ago. My heart only started beating again when I saw you walking up the stairs toward me.

Risking the pain of sitting up, but wanting to face her, he braced himself on his elbow, carefully lowering his feet to the floor, then leaned on the back of the couch trying to keep his chest and stomach as flat as possible.

She quickly stepped around the chair and sat down next to him on the couch. If he'd have known that trying to sit up would make her rush to his side, he would have tried it as soon as his eyes had opened.

"You okay? Move slow," she said, putting her hand on his arm.

He panted lightly from the pain, turning his head to the side to look at her and covering her hand with his. She sat a few inches away, on her knees, her body facing him, that clean scent so fine and so welcome it was almost making him light-headed.

"You smell good," he said, staring into her blue eyes.

She flinched, her eyes darting to his neck for a moment before sliding back up to his face. She lingered on his lips—only for a split second—but he noticed, and it made his breath catch as his skin flushed with heat, chased by shivers.

This girl. This girl. God, what she does to me with just a look. The thought made his head race, only stopping when it acknowledged that she already had someone in her life who got to do more than look—he got to touch her, be with her, give her pleasure. Holden's lips tightened.

"W-who were you with last night?"

She pulled her bottom lip into her mouth again, holding it between her teeth as she stared back at him. This was something he didn't remember her doing when they were kids, but it was one hundred fucking percent distracting, and he prayed she wouldn't drop her eyes to his lap, where his dick twitched and swelled.

"Um. Jonah."

"And who is Jonah? College boy? B-boyfriend?"

"We live together," she said, holding his eyes but pulling her hand away.

Well, if he needed something to deflate things, finding out she lived with fucking Jonah was the perfect pin.

"Married?"

"No," she said quickly.

"Engaged?" He flicked his eyes to her bare fingers.

"No," she said, shaking her head for emphasis. "It's not like that. We just live together. He didn't go to college. And frankly . . . I don't know if he's my boyfriend anymore."

He lifted his eyes back up to hers, peripherally noting the way her breasts moved up and down with her short, shallow breaths, and desperately trying not to drop his eyes to stare at them. "Why not?"

She searched his eyes, scanning them carefully, as if looking for answers to unasked questions. Her lips parted, but the soup suddenly boiled over, hissing and spitting, and she jumped up to take care of it without answering his question.

***

Griselda's heart galloped as she padded across the crappy brown carpet back to the kitchen, relieved for a break from the intensity of their conversation. With her back to Holden, she took a deep breath, finally filling her lungs, and flicked her tongue over her dry lips. When he stared at her like that, she could barely think.

She turned off the burner and took the clean, dry bowl she'd used from the drying rack beside the sink. Lifting the soup from the stove with a solitary pot holder, she filled the bowl and placed the pot in the sink to clean later.

She could feel his eyes on her from the moment she left the couch. Turning back to him, she asked, "Do you want to eat over there or at the table?"

"Here, if that's okay. I have a little table," said Holden, pointing to a folding table leaning against the wall by the TV.

She set up the table in front of him, then went back for the soup, swearing she could *feel* the heat thrown off by his steady gaze. It was discomfiting, making her feel nervous and excited, too self-aware and too aware of *him*.

After she placed the bowl and spoon before him, she made the safer—and yes, spineless—choice to sit in the easy chair instead of beside him again. As he'd slept, covered with the blanket, she hadn't studied him closely, but now, seated across from him, she allowed herself to explore him with her eyes as he leaned forward to take a spoonful of soup.

His burnished blond hair was still thick and unruly and too long in the front, where two rogue curls dipped over his forehead as he leaned forward to blow on the soup. His chest was firm and sculpted with muscle, and though his abdomen was hidden by the collapsible table, she checked out the tattoos on his upper chest as he placed his lips on the rim of the spoon. An angel had been inked just below his neck, and her unfurled wings spread across the length of his body, from shoulder to shoulder. The light was too dim for Griselda to make out the details, but she knew in her gut that the angel was somehow connected to her, and her heart clenched with the certainty that grief had been its designer.

She slid her eyes from his right shoulder to his upper right bicep, which bulged slightly with defined muscle tone, and found four black roses. Under the first two she read "Cory and Will," a red banner under their names with the date "11.14.99." His parents. He'd only told her the story once, but she'd never forget it.

Holden had spent the night at his grandmother's house so that his parents could have a date night for their tenth anniversary. When his grandmother drove him home the next day, the smell of gas in the small apartment was unmistakable, and his parents were dead in their bed from carbon monoxide poisoning. One of them had turned on the stove to make dinner and gotten distracted—dinner was never made, and by morning they were gone.

The third of the four black roses read "Gran," with a red banner noting the date "2.4.01." His grandmother, and guardian, who'd died of a heart attack only fourteen months after his parents' deaths, leaving Holden utterly alone in the world.

And finally, under his grandmother's rose, a final black rose dripping with two drops of bright red blood that read "Gris," and the date "6.12.04."

Her breath caught as she jerked her eyes to his face, only to find him watching her with such steady, unspeakable sorrow, such unfathomable tenderness, it made her face crumple. Her neck bent forward, her chin resting on her chest as two huge tears plopped into her lap.

"G-Gris," he whispered, his voice soft and broken. "I thought you were dead."

"I know," she sobbed, reaching up to smear her tears with her fingers, but unable to stop them from falling.

"Stop crying, Gris. P-please stop crying, or I'm going to have to get up and walk over there to hold you, and damn it, as much as I'd like to do that, it would hurt like hell to move, so please . . ."

She sniffled loudly, taking a deep, ragged breath before looking up at him. "I'll stop. I'm okay."

"Okay," he said, nodding as he drew his spoon back through the soup, watching her with haunted eyes. He sipped the cooling soup, then swallowed. "I'll change it."

"The rose?"

"*Your* rose," he said. "I'll have it colored red and cover up the date."

"You don't have to do that," she said.

"The angel is you too, Gris," he said, placing his hand over the angel's face, over his heart. Then he twisted his right arm to show her the tattoo of her face and their initials. "And you already saw these."

Her eyes still welled, so she blinked quickly a few times and took another deep breath. She jerked her chin toward another tattoo that peeked out from the inside of his left arm. "What's that one?"

He raised an eyebrow, purposely turning the arm inward as he took another sip of soup. "N-nothing."

Intrigued, Griselda leaned forward. "Holden? What is it?"

"Ten years is a long time to be stupid," he said, staring at his soup bowl.

"You don't want to tell me?"

"Not really."

"Will you anyway?"

He put the spoon in the bowl, looking up at her with a

conflicted expression, then turned his arm outward, showing it to her. It looked like a bunch of haphazard tally marks to her—four lines crossed through, another four crossed through. He stared at her face as he twisted his arm, and she counted over eight bunches, then nine, then ten, seeing countless others before raising her eyes to his.

"What does it mean?"

"It means I was lonely," he whispered, his face defensive and challenging as he stared back at her.

Her lips dropped open, and she sat back in her chair, holding his eyes, her stomach lurching as she realized how many women he'd been with, how many times he'd been touched and held and loved . . . by someone other than her. It knocked the wind from her lungs, and an uncomfortable lump rose up in her throat.

"Oh."

He didn't say anything, just stared back at her, unapologetic, unsmiling, uncertain.

"I see," she said, her voice breathy as she finally exhaled.

Telling herself she had no right to judge what he'd done to cope with the misery that had been his life, she still couldn't help how much it hurt. She wished it didn't, but it did. God, it hurt so much.

"How many?" Her eyes flicked to the tattoos. "Total?"

"I stopped counting."

"Why count at all?"

"It felt . . ." He shrugged. "C-comforting."

He didn't blink, and his face didn't shift expression. He didn't explain further. He just stared back at her, letting his truth sink in.

Finally she broke eye contact with him, looking out the window as she took a deep breath, her tongue darting out to wet her lips nervously.

Griselda had lost her virginity in her third post-Holden

foster home, at the age of seventeen, and slept with four other boys in quick succession. She'd been looking for a connection, for a safe haven, for belonging, but she never found it. She found only disappointment and an aching, intense loneliness for what she wanted and couldn't have. Just short of getting a bad reputation, she graduated from high school, and once she started working for the McClellans, Griselda cleaned up her act, emulating Sabrina McClellan, concentrating on work and swearing off of men.

Until Jonah.

Jonah had bulldozed his way into her apartment, into her bed, into her life, and to her everlasting shame, she'd allowed him to stay.

"Why isn't he your boyfriend anymore?" Holden asked, as though he could read her mind.

"Jonah?"

"Yeah."

"Because I called him on your phone while you were sleeping and told him I wasn't going home with him. I told him to leave without me. I said I was staying here for a little while." She swallowed past that big lump in her throat, wondering if she'd been foolish to make such a rash decision for her life. Would Holden mind that she wanted to stay? Could she bear it if he asked her to go?

Holden didn't say anything, and she bit her bottom lip again. It was getting raw from so much biting, but she couldn't seem to help it. Releasing it self-consciously, she reached up and ran her finger over the irritated skin, before adding, "He didn't like it."

Holden's eyes were wide and searching, resting on her lips, then skating back up to her eyes, his breathing ragged and audible. The spoon fell from his fingers, clattering to the bowl and splashing a bit of red soup onto the cheap folding table.

"You're staying?"

"Just till I know you're okay," she said softly, feeling embarrassed, because he had tally marks and a girlfriend. They barely knew each other as adults, and he certainly hadn't invited her to stay.

"You're staying," he said again, his voice less tentative but still giving away little.

Her cheeks heated up as she looked away from him, bracing her hands on her knees to stand up and get moving. "I don't have to. Listen, if you don't want me to stay, I can—"

"G-Gris," he said sharply, a fierce edge to his voice.

She cut her eyes to his.

"I want you to stay." He paused, as though trying to figure out what else to say. "I want you to stay." His eyes glistened as he stared at her, and he blinked several times. His voice broke as he repeated one more time, "I w-want you to s-stay."

CHAPTER 13

Once Holden had finished his soup, Griselda rinsed the pot, dish, and two spoons, placing them in the drying rack, and helped Holden to his feet so he could use the bathroom. After pissing, he paused in front of the mirror to check out his face and winced at what he saw.

Both eyes were discolored and badly swollen, and his cheek was a blackish color and very tender when he grazed it with his fingertips. His nose had a white bandage over the bridge, with tape between his eyebrows and on either side of his nostrils. He pulled the tape off gingerly, cursing softly from the pain and swallowing at the deep purple color. His lips had somehow managed not to get split, but there were several other ugly contusions on his face, mostly scabbing over now, but not pretty.

You look like a fucking animal. It's a wonder she doesn't run away.

His eyes drifted to the bandage under his heart and then to the larger bandage on his hip that covered three stab wounds. Peeling that one away, he took a peek. Neat black stitches had closed the three incisions. He counted four on one, five on another, and seven on the longest. Covering them back up, he flinched as he smoothed the tape over his skin and shifted his eyes to his chest. How Eli had managed to stab him in the chest wasn't entirely clear, but Holden had been so distracted by seeing Gris, Eli must have reached around from behind and Holden never saw it coming. The doctor said it was just a few millimeters from his heart. He'd been lucky.

Lucky didn't even scratch the surface.

He was alive. And Griselda was alive. He knew better than that doctor. He knew that there was no luck left in the entire world tonight, because all of it—every last fucking drop—belonged to him.

Opening the bathroom door, he stepped out slowly, looking left into his bedroom. Some stupid, horny part of him half hoped that Gris would be lying on the bed, waiting for him with a playful grin, but his room was neat, quiet, and empty.

He leaned his head against the doorway, trying to get a fix on reality before rejoining her in the living room.

As a rule, Holden didn't connect with women emotionally. Physically? No problem. But he hadn't met a woman since Gris who could get through to him emotionally. No matter how many women he'd bedded, the end result was always the same: the face that always flashed through his mind as his body climaxed was Griselda's. It didn't matter whom he was with. It didn't matter that Griselda was dead, or that her face was still teenaged in his fantasies, which, he knew, was a big leap beyond creepy. An argument could be made that he'd searched for years for someone to replace Griselda in his mind, but his memories of her were too potent to displace. For a decade, she'd been his deepest, most impulsive, most unavoidably instinctive sexual trigger. For as long as he could remember, she was the beating heart of his sexual life. Whether he liked it or not, it had always been that way.

Why? Because as an adolescent with raging hormones trapped in a terrifying life, Griselda had not only been Holden's only source of solace and tenderness, but she'd been his first taste of feverish, passionate desire. He'd watched her body blossom into curves day by day, and felt those growing curves press into his body at night when he held her. She'd been the first girl to touch his heart and his body with tenderness. She'd been his family, his best friend, his confidante, and companion. He'd loved her fiercely and unconditionally, and her brutal loss had only served to idealize her in his mind and his heart. She was everything he wanted, everything he'd lost, something he could never have.

Now suddenly, after ten years, the girl of his dreams had been delivered to him, and it didn't matter that they'd been reunited for only a handful of hours. His body had roared to life in ways he'd never experienced as an adult man: his heartbeat erratic, his blood pumping wildly, his skin primed for her touch, his lips starving for a taste of her. In every possible physical way, he wanted her. Badly. Urgently. He wanted the tactile satisfaction of touching her, the warmth of her body beside his, the sound as she drew breath, and the feel of it when she exhaled against his throat. He wanted to reassure himself that she was actually alive and not just a beautiful and cruel delusion. And no matter who she had become, he never, ever wanted to let her go.

Besides his very real and visceral physical desire for her, he also wanted to *know* her again. He wanted to be as intimately familiar with her heart and mind as he'd been ten years ago, when he could read every nuance of her tone, every expression that crossed her face. They'd been so close, so in tune with each other, words had been almost unnecessary. For a decade, he'd grieved the loss of that kind of closeness. He desperately missed it. And now that she was here with him, he wanted it back.

Taking a deep breath, Holden turned back down the short hallway, toward the living room, and tried to calm his body down. Despite his longing to instantly reconnect with her in every possible way, emotionally and physically, he needed to slow down and try to relax. He didn't want to scare her, for God's sake, and, he reminded himself, this wasn't just any girl to be taken or had.

This was Griselda, risen from the dead.

Taking a few slow, halting steps, he walked back into the living room, where he found her sitting on the edge of the couch, head bent forward, talking on his cell phone. Though his instinct was to sit beside her, he purposely stood across from her, giving her space, trying to read her face.

". . . I am so sorry, Mrs. McClellan, but I don't have much family, and I need to stay here for a little while and take care of him. Yes, ma'am. Mm-hm. My foster brother." She paused, looking up at Holden. "Yes. It's been a long time."

Holden raised his eyebrows to ask her if everything was okay. She shrugged, before looking back down at her lap, but her body was tense.

"I know that. I'd never leave you in the lurch, and I would have given you more notice, but his injuries—it was a bad, uh, accident."

Holden lowered himself into the easy chair across from her, wincing when his ribs ached from the movement.

She exhaled, and her shoulders finally unbunched. "Oh. Okay. Thank you. That's really . . . nice of you." She used the back of her hand to swipe at her eyes, even though her voice remained level and even. "I appreciate that. Mm-hm. He's going to be okay. Yeah. Please give her a kiss for me. Tell her I promise more stories when I come back. Okay. Yes, I will. Bye."

She pressed the End button, looking up at Holden. His first guess was that she looked bewildered, but he wasn't sure, and he hated it that he couldn't read her better.

"I used your phone," she said. "I hope that's okay."

"What's mine is yours, Gris," he said again.

She gave him an uncertain grin, but it faded quickly, and she glanced down at the phone again, furrowing her eyebrows. "My, uh—Jonah called a few times while it was off. And it looks like he left some messages. I don't want them. Just delete them, okay? I would've deleted them for you, but I didn't have your voice mail pass code."

"Sure," he said, taking the phone from her extended hand. It was warm from being pressed against her ear, and he curled his fingers around it. "Was that your boss?"

"Yeah. She didn't fire me," said Gris, laughing in surprise. "She said she'd find a replacement for one month and hold my job."

"A month." It hurt to smile, but Holden couldn't hold it back, because having thirty days with her felt like a miracle. Still, he didn't want to push her. "You staying here for a month, Griselda?"

"I—I don't . . . I mean, I *can*, but I don't . . ." She looked down, her cheeks turning pink.

"Stay," he said simply, the words falling from his lips, as they had a hundred times before in Caleb Foster's cellar. He caught her eyes as they blinked at him uncertainly.

Stay, he thought, wishing he was sitting beside her so he could tuck a stray lock of reddish-blonde hair behind her warm ear. *Stay forever. Don't ever leave me again.*

"I'll stay for a while," she said, standing up and taking two folded towels off the arm of the couch. She spread them out across the cushions, smoothing them with her hands and treating him to an awesome view of her backside, which served to distract him from what she was doing for an extra moment.

"What's with the towels?" he finally asked.

She turned slightly to look at him, "Making up a bed for myself."

"No, Gris," he said, leaning forward a little and groaning softly when pain radiated from the trio of cuts on his hip. "I'll sleep here. You sleep in my bed."

There was an irony to his words, not lost on him, since she'd *been* in his bed many, many times, but had never once been able to *sleep* in it. She shook her head, glancing up at him before taking the thin blanket he'd been using before and laying it over the towels.

"You're injured," she said. "You need your bed."

"It's big," he said softly, the words tumbling from his mouth before he had a chance to approve them. "Sh-share it with me."

Her head whipped up, and she pulled her lip between her teeth—*damn it*—her blue eyes searching and cautious. "I don't think so."

"Why not? Wouldn't be the first time."

She tilted her head to the side, pursing her lips and crossing her arms over her chest defensively. "That's an awful lot of tallies on your arm."

"I'm not looking to add another tonight."

"I just don't—"

"G-Gris," he said, in pain and beyond exhausted. He didn't want to fight with her. He wanted the sweetness of her body next to his. He wanted the luxury of falling asleep beside her without the sound of boots coming down the basement stairs. He wanted to talk about everything that had happened to both of them, but not tonight. Tonight he just wanted to know that she was breathing beside him as he fell asleep. "Sleep. *Just* sleep. Beside me. Next to me. Please."

He hated the uncertain look on her face, the way she looked at him like she was trying to find him. It made him feel lost.

"I'm too weak to do anything else," he said lightly, offering her a small grin.

Her lips tilted up a touch in answer. "Promise?"

He stood slowly, holding his hand out to her. His heart thundered as she reached for it, pressing her palm against his and letting him curl his fingers around her hand. "Promise."

***

Following Holden into his bedroom, Griselda tried to ignore whatever misgivings she had about how quickly things were moving between them. After a decade, they'd seen each other last night, found each other this afternoon, and here she was, planning to sleep beside him in his bed tonight.

And yet where else would she sleep? The pull to be with him, to touch him, to reassure herself that he was safe and strong, was powerful. She had crossed the finish line of an exhausting journey, and all she wanted was a safe and warm place to close her weary eyes and rest her bewildered heart. Could there be any better place than beside Holden, whom she'd loved so fiercely, lost so brutally, and missed so terribly these long ten years?

He had changed a lot, yes, but he was still Holden, who'd loved her and fought for her. He was still the gray-eyed, sweet-smelling boy who'd made life bearable when it should have killed her. He was still the keeper of her memories, the only sanctioned guardian of her heart. The need to share his space, to feel the heat of his body resting beside hers, was as visceral for her as it appeared to be for him. She didn't want to let him out of her sight. Now that she'd found him, even altered, she didn't want to spend a moment away from him. Whatever uncertainty lay ahead of them, tonight she wanted the solace of his heart beating next to hers.

"Will you crack the window?" he asked, lowering himself to the bed and exhaling like everything hurt.

She dropped his hand and crossed the small room, unlocking the window and pushing it open halfway. It looked out at the brick exterior of another two-story building and didn't offer much of a breeze, but the sounds of a small American town—the occasional whoosh of a car, people strolling in the evening, a dog barking in the distance, the voices of people coming and going from the café below—it all served to make the room feel less isolated. And she understood the appeal. She chose the hum of humanity as her preferred lullaby too.

Turning around, she found Holden lying on top of his comforter, his head on one of two pillows, his arms flat by his sides. His eyes were closed, and in the dim light provided by one bedside lamp and whatever glow made its way through the window, he was beautiful.

A little over six feet tall, his long torso rippled with partially inked muscle that tapered down to a V, disappearing into his unbuttoned jeans. He was lean and hard-bodied, but his chest was covered with scars, and Griselda knew that if he turned over there would be even more. She flinched as the sound of the Man unfastening his belt buckle echoed in her head. How many times had Holden's back been torn open?

Cast out his wickedness and sin, oh Lord, and make him clean again!

More times than she could count on two hands. She shivered, crossing her arms over her chest, and forcing Caleb Foster's voice from her mind.

Tilting her head to the side, she skimmed her gaze down his denim legs to his bare feet, and a sad smile spread across her face to see that his—like hers—still had silvery white scars across the top where the sharp brown corn husks had sliced through their feet that disastrous day. Identical scars that would always remind them that she had escaped and he was left behind.

How could he forgive her for leaving him? How could his eyes gaze at her with tenderness when she had gotten in the truck first but he had been the one left behind at the river?

Don't ever hate me again. Promise.

I p-p-promise, Gris.

She clenched her jaw, her eyes brimming with tears.

"You gonna stand there all night staring at me?"

"Maybe," she murmured.

There was no rule book for how you were supposed to behave when you found the foster brother with whom you were kidnapped thirteen years ago, with whom you lived in filth and terror for three years, whom you'd lost but had loved and longed for every day since. There was so much to learn about each other. So much they knew about each other on one level, but so much they didn't on another.

"I think I'm in shock," she whispered. "I can't believe I'm here with you. I don't know how to do this. You're you and I'm me, but we're so different. What happens next? How do we even—?"

His eyes opened, and he took a deep breath, then sighed. Raising his hand, he held it out to her. "Come lay down."

She closed the distance between the window and the bed, sitting down on the edge. His fingertips touched her back, and she twisted her neck to look at him.

"I want to know you again," he said, his gray eyes soft. "I want to know what happened that day on the river, how you got away, where you went, and everything that happened next until you showed up at that fight last night."

"I want the same," she said, a tear falling over the rim of her eyes and sliding down her cheek.

His voice was tired, heavy. "I want to know if you've had a good life. I want to know why you decided to stay here tonight and not go home. I want you to . . ."

"What?"

"I w-want you to tell me a story."

Two more tears slipped down her cheeks as she turned away from him, smiling to herself, and reaching forward to pull the chain on the bedside lamp. Then she lay her head down on the pillow beside his, swinging her legs up on the bed and straightening them. Her arm lay flush against his, and in an instant she was back in that hot, smelly station wagon, Holden on one side, Marisol on the other. And then time skipped forward, and she was lying on that disgusting cot in the Man's cellar, Holden's scrappy body beaten and tired and frightened beside her. And then time skipped again, catching up with itself, and she was here, now, in his apartment, and they were all grown up, finally reunited, arms touching again.

His skin was hot, partly because it was June but partly because his body was fighting to heal. But feeling him beside her was so familiar, her eyes fluttered closed in relief, and she released a long, low breath through her lips, letting the rest of her body finally relax beside him.

"Gris?" he said after a while, turning his head on the pillow to face her.

She twisted her neck to mirror him, opening her eyes. "Yeah?"

"I'm so tired."

"Me too."

"Let's sleep."

"Okay."

"You're alive."

"I am."

"You finally found me."

"I did."

"You're lying next to me right now."

"Yes."

"And this isn't a dream."

"No."

"And you'll be here when I wake up?"

"I promise."

"Okay," he said, closing his eyes. "Will you tell me a story while I fall asleep? I always w-wished you could do that when we, uh—when w-we w-were . . ." His voice drifted off, and she felt him breathe deeply, just as she used to tell him to. She realized that he did it to control his stammer, and something about that made her so happy and so sad, she held her own breath, concentrating hard so she didn't sob. "It was so d-dark at night once you left me."

"I'll do it now, Holden," she said, her voice breaking a little.

The back of his hand was flush against the back of hers, but he twisted it, pressing his palm to hers, entwining his fingers through hers, like he'd done a thousand times before. And her fingers remembered. And her heart remembered. And both felt like they'd finally come home.

"Once upon a time," she began, "there was a princess named . . ."

"Griselda," he mumbled, almost asleep, eyes still closed.

A tear slipped out of the corner of her eye, sliding slowly into her hair.

"No," she said, smiling at him as more tears silently joined the first. "Moonlight. Princess Moonlight."

CHAPTER 14

"I got an idea, Holden." Griselda cast a quick glance to the porch, where the Man dozed in the shade before she squatted back down in the garden, turning the earth over and over with a small trowel. "It's been dry lately. Real dry."

Holden's eyes darted to the porch before he squatted down beside her, the chain around his ankle making a soft clinking sound. She noticed that his left eye wasn't swollen anymore, but it was still a little discolored, light blue, lavender, and yellow making an ugly circle of tie-dye on his otherwise tanned, freckled skin.

"And?"

"And that means the river will be lower. We'll be able to see the rocks."

"W-w-what r-r-river?"

"The Shenandoah, Holden. I keep thinking about the drive that day. I don't think it's more than a few miles away."

Holden flinched, quickly focusing his attention on the sack of seeds to his right, and Griselda cursed her bald delivery. Mentioning the Shenandoah always upset Holden. But they had to escape. She couldn't explain it, but lately she felt like the Man was giving up on their redemption. He was quieter, but his face was colder and meaner. She was frightened about what he'd do if he decided that they were beyond saving. They had to figure out a way to leave.

She knew Holden's memory had gone straight to the day of their kidnapping because his stammer was worse than ever when he responded. "Th-th-three miles? F-f-five miles? You don't even know for sure. And th-th-that's a lot on foot, Gris. B-b-barefoot."

They'd outgrown their old shoes long ago and hadn't been given new ones. On the flip side, however, their feet had toughened up over the past two years.

"Holden, breathe." She searched his eyes. "We have to go. I think this is our chance."

"W-w-when?"

"Day after tomorrow. Sunday morning. It's the only time he's gone for a full hour."

"He'll c-c-come after us."

"We'll have a forty-five-minute head start."

"W-w-won't be enough."

"It'll have to be. We have to do this, Holden. Remember what you asked me? About him touching me funny?"

Holden's head snapped up, and his eyes drilled a hole in hers. "H-h-has h-h-h-he—"

"No. No, not that." She shook her head. "No. But his rants are getting shorter. The beatings are getting worse. I'm afraid . . . I'm afraid that he's going to—"

"K-k-kill us," finished Holden.

Griselda nodded.

"W-w-what if the w-water's t-t-t-t-t—" He took a deep breath through his nose and held it before exhaling loudly. "—t-too high, Gris? I c-c-can't swim."

Holden almost never cried, no matter how bad things got, so Griselda's heart lurched when his eyes watered and a tear escaped from the corner of his eye, rolling down the side of his dusty face and plopping on the dirt between them. She reached up quickly and caught the next one, curling her fingers around it.

"It won't be too high. It's dry. Hasn't rained in eight days. He'll come down with our breakfast as usual. Then he'll go to church. As soon as we can't hear his truck anymore, we'll go too."

"W-w-what about the, uh, l-lock?"

"Well, this morning while you were still asleep, I poked at it a little. The wood on the cellar doors is soft from all the snow we got this winter. I think, once he's gone, we can use a hammer or some other tool and force a hole through it. We just got to be ready and move fast."

She knew her plan wasn't rock solid. It was a long way to the river. Several miles, at least, and that was if she remembered the direction correctly. But if they could get there, and get across it, Cutter would lose their scent. They'd cross over to the woods on the other side and keep running. Keep running until they were far away, until they were safe, until—

"Okay." Holden's breath was ragged, but when Griselda looked up, his face was stoic and his tears were gone.

She gave him a small smile, determined not to let him see how frightened she was. *"We can do this. I promised I would find a way to save us. It's my fault. It's my—"*

"N-n-no, Gris. It's not your fault." He shook his head, his gray eyes searching hers desperately. *"G-G-Gris, whatever happens, I w-w-want you to know—I l-l-lov—"*

"Ruth and Seth!"

Holden's eyes widened, and he scrambled away from her, his ankle chain clanking loudly as he stood up quickly and reached down for the seed sack, which spilled open. He squatted down again, furiously trying to push the seeds back into the burlap.

"What've I told ya 'bout idle hands, ya heathen filth?"

The Man's boots thudded down the porch steps toward them. Griselda's heart was in her throat as she turned away *from Holden, digging small holes as quickly as she could, her hands trembling as she tried to keep the row straight and even.*

"Ya don't fool me, Ruth. I saw ya head to head with yer own kin, ya filthy gal. Plannin' bold an' lewd acts!"

Oh God, please. Please. Please not today. Please leave us alone.

"Temptin' my brother into a life of wickedness beyond redemption. Whisperin' yer whorish secrets in his ears."

Griselda kept her head down, tears burning her eyes as urine slipped through her threadbare pink bathing suit, trickling down her thigh.

As best she could tell, he was standing right behind her. Then she heard the sound of his belt buckle being unclasped, and she dropped the trowel, hunching over until her forehead pressed into the dirt, and covering her head with her shaking hands.

"W-w-wasn't her f-f-fault."

The Man's boots, so close to her crouching, shaking body, pivoted in the dirt.

"Come agin?"

"W-w-wasn't her f-f-fault, sir. Sh-she needed some seeds, and I d-d-dropped 'em. Sh-she was only helpin' me c-c-collect 'em."

Griselda held her breath. It was so silent, she couldn't imagine what was going on between them, but she still braced for the landing of the belt on her back. She protected her head, curled as tightly as possible, the dirt pressed against her face.

"She's a-blindin' ya with her evil ways, Seth." The Man's voice was thoughtful, almost gentle with sorrow. "I see it happenin' all over agin. Yer almost lost to me."

It felt like an eternity before she heard the Man turn and walk away from them, his footsteps slow and halting. She stayed curled in a ball until she heard the truck engine turn over, and then she finally unfurled her body, her crotch soaked, her muscles complaining.

She looked up at Holden, who held the sack of seeds, staring at the driveway where a puff of dust followed the hasty departure of the Man's truck.

"We gotta go soon, Gris," he said without stammering. "We gotta go soon."

***

In his sleep, Holden had pulled her against his body. He woke up holding her in his arms, his heart pressed to her back, his lips a breath away from the warm skin of her neck. For the first time in longer than he could remember, he hadn't woken up in the middle of the night, sweating and cold, the word *Rrrruuuuuun* reverberating in his ears like the echo of a gunshot. He'd fallen asleep with his hand braided through hers, listening to a story about Princess Moonlight, who was jealous of Lady Starlight and smitten with the Sun King . . . and he'd woken up with Griselda in his arms.

His knees were bent, spooning hers, and his erection strained uncomfortably against the confining denim of his jeans, but he ignored it because any discomfort was worth the heaven of holding her. Though his face didn't hurt quite as bad as yesterday, his stab wounds were still tender, throbbing steadily. He tried to remain completely still. If he moved, she might move. She might move away.

Though he'd lived with Gris for three long years, and held her against his body more than once, he'd never had the luxury of sleeping beside her, or waking up next to her, and he savored this precious first—the warmth, the peace, the contact. And he hated that a month made it finite.

"Morning," she said, her voice low and gravelly, her chest pushing against his arm as she took a deep breath.

"You're still here."

"Promised I would be."

"What time is it?" he asked, closing his eyes and snuggling

into the warmth of her neck.

"I don't know."

"Is this okay?" he whispered.

She turned in his arms, pillowing her head on her elbow, and pushing her strawberry-blonde hair over her shoulder. His arm was still draped over her hip, and he tightened it, pulling her closer. He felt it again—that thick, deep, heavy feeling in his gut that he'd felt yesterday, when she stood at the bottom of the stairs looking up at him—that feeling that life would end if he had to go another day without looking at her. It made his twenty-three-year-old heart beat fiercely with desire and longing. It took his breath away.

"It's better than okay," she said, the breath from her words kissing his lips.

Her eyes were bright and blue, and he looked away out of habit because blue eyes had broken his heart for ten years. It would take a little while to get used to seeing them staring back at him. He stared at her lips instead, pink and pillowed, and ached to kiss her, but common sense overruled him. *Don't push her*, it warned him. Until he knew where they stood with each other, he needed to give her the space and freedom to let him know what she wanted.

"Where you been, Gris?"

"The Shenandoah. Then Charles Town. Then D.C. Now mostly Maryland."

"Mostly?"

"I work in Georgetown."

"What do you do?"

"I'm a nanny." Her lips tilted up as she said this. "For a little girl named Prudence. Her daddy's a congressman."

"Friends in high places."

"'Friends' would be a stretch."

"But they're good to you? The McClellans?"

Her body stiffened. "How do you—?"

"You were talking to her on the phone last night and said her name. Mrs. McClellan, right?"

She took a deep breath, letting it go, and he felt her body relax. "Right."

"Gris? You think if there's any way I knew where you were that I wouldn't have come to you? Nothing could have stopped me." His voice broke, and he swallowed the lump in his throat. "But up until Saturday night, I thought you were dead." He paused, blinking his eyes and working to control his voice. "I never looked for you. I'm so sorry about that. I'm so d-damn sorry I b-believed him."

"You have nothing to be sorry for," she whispered, her voice tender in their fragile little early morning cocoon.

"I should have known he was lying."

"You were a kid. You must have been scared out of your mind."

Ruth's dead, little brother, an' you can thank me for puttin' an end to her evil ways. She ain't never comin' back to torment you with her wickedness.

Holden flinched at the memory.

"I dream about him," whispered Gris, her eyes tired and frightened. "Almost every night."

"Last night?"

She nodded. "We were in the garden. Talking about leaving . . . escaping."

Holden remembered the conversation like it was yesterday. "*I* used to dream about *you*. At the river. Almost every night."

"Used to?"

"Maybe I still will, but last night I didn't. I guess, uh, I g-guess seeing you alive, somehow . . . I don't know. I just slept."

She leaned forward to press her forehead to his. "I wish I could stop seeing him in my head, hearing the sound of that belt buckle . . . Leviticus . . ."

"Stop. D-don't." It was impossible to pull her closer since

her body was flush to his, but he tried. "He's d-dead, Gris. Caleb's dead. C-Can't hurt us ever again."

"What?" She sucked in a swift and urgent breath, then released it, her body trembling against his. "He's—he's dead? When?"

Holden slid his hand up her hip, over her waist to her arm, finally landing on her face to cup her cheek, his thumb swiping gently over the damp softness. "A while back. He was hit by a car in Oregon. He's gone, Gris."

She shimmied down a little, bending her head into his neck, her shoulders shuddering as she dragged in a ragged breath. Silent sobs racked her body, and it killed him for two reasons: one, because only kids who needed to learn how to hide their tears cry that way; and two, because Caleb had been dead for six years, and she hadn't had the peace of knowing he was gone.

"I looked for death records," she said. "On the Internet. At the library. I searched for 'Caleb Foster' over and over again, but there was never anything . . ."

Holden leaned back, threading his fingers gently through her hair. "He d-didn't go by Foster. He went by West. Caleb West."

"Oh," she said, nodding, tears still coursing down her face. "Caleb West." She breathed through her nose, a jagged, jerking sound mixed with sobs. "I can't stop crying. I don't even know *why* I'm crying. I hated him. I'm not sorry."

"You're relieved," whispered Holden, stroking her amber hair.

"Yeah, I . . . I am." She took another deep, shaky, gasping breath. "How do you know? That he's dead?"

His throat suddenly ached from the lump lodged there. He tried to swallow it down, but it wouldn't budge.

"How . . .," she said. "You would've been . . . seventeen." She drew back, her watery eyes searching his face, brows furrowing, confusion hijacking her expression. "Wait. Why—

Holden, were you still . . . with him?"

He let his hand fall from her hair as he rolled over onto his back, staring up at the ceiling. The movement made his hip hurt. His chest too. Thank God his face didn't hurt as much today. He placed his palm over his heart and felt his lungs inhale and exhale as he closed his eyes.

"Holden?" she said.

"Hmm?"

She shifted a little, and when he opened his eyes, she was leaning up on her elbow, her expression grave. "What were you—I mean, you were still with him? At seventeen?"

He turned to look at her, clenching his jaw, his fingers curling into the skin of his chest.

"Yeah," he muttered, his voice breathless in his own ears.

"You stayed with him?" she asked, her eyes and voice stunned.

"Yeah."

"Oh." She blinked at him, her lips slightly parted, then dropped onto her back, but he quickly realized that no part of her body was touching his anymore. After several long moments of silence, she said softly, "I'm glad he's dead."

And Holden, who'd been holding his breath, replied, "M-me too."

***

Griselda didn't know why it shocked her so much to learn that Holden had stayed with Caleb Foster for four years after her escape, but it did. It shocked her. It upset her. It damn near leveled her. Because surely there would have been many, many opportunities for a seventeen-year-old to escape, and yet he hadn't. He had remained with their captor and tormentor until Caleb Foster died. It was almost unfathomable. And she wasn't sure she even wanted to know why. She wasn't sure she'd be able to understand if he'd stayed of his free will, and if he was somehow coerced into staying, she didn't know how she'd bear hearing the story. For years she'd wanted to know what had happened to Holden, but in her head, he'd most likely been killed, or, having escaped from Caleb Foster at some point, he'd re-created himself, like the heroes in the fairy tales she spun.

Turns out he *had* re-created himself. But not because he'd escaped and started a new life. No. After living with the Man for four additional years, he'd *chosen* to become someone named Seth West.

It suddenly struck Griselda how little she knew about the adult version of Holden. Her fingers felt cold, and her stomach jumped as she slid to the edge of the bed, swinging her legs over the side. Had she somehow expected Holden to be an older version of the exact person he'd been at thirteen? She tugged her lip between her teeth, thinking. Yes, she had. But he wasn't. He was someone else entirely, and it made the situation feel complex, confusing, disappointing, and perilous.

Did she believe he would hurt her? No. Though she knew he was capable of great violence, and she had no guarantee he wouldn't turn it on her, in her gut, she knew she could trust him not to hurt her.

But she'd deeply loved the person Holden had been so long ago. The question that made her want to weep was, If she got to know him now, would she *still* love him? Because she wanted to. She desperately wanted to love Holden.

"G-Gris," he said softly.

"Breathe," she murmured without thinking.

He did. He took a deep breath, groaning slightly as he let it go.

"I n-need to start at the beginning. It's the only way you'll understand."

Her whole body felt heavy and too tired for the journey ahead.

"W-will you look at me? F-finding out you're alive is like

a m-miracle to me, and—"

She didn't turn around. "I just don't know if—"

A loud knock on the door cut off her thoughts, and she stood up, glancing down at Holden, still lying on his back.

"Should I get that?"

"Who's there?" he hollered, anger and frustration thick in his voice, loud enough that Griselda jumped.

"Seth?" The voice, traveling through the living room, down the hall, and into Holden's bedroom was faint, but Griselda's eyes hit the floor the second she heard the name Seth, and that unpleasant, nervous feeling in her stomach multiplied.

"Yeah?" he yelled.

"It's Quint! Brought you some food."

Holden groaned as he braced his palms on the comforter and sat up slowly, swinging his legs to let his bare feet fall to the floor.

"I'll go," said Griselda. "Take your time."

Relieved to be walking away from Holden for a few minutes, she headed for the living room and unchained the door. Quint stood in the hallway, holding a brown sack in each arm.

"Morning, Griselda," he said politely.

"Morning."

He looked into her eyes, then swept his glance away, catching sight of something—or someone—over her shoulder. "Seth. How you doing?"

"Better'n yesterday, worse'n tomorrow," he said gruffly. "Come on in, Quint."

CHAPTER 15

Being around Griselda this morning was like crossing a minefield.

Holden knew she was shocked that he'd stayed with Caleb for as long as he had. Hell, it wasn't like he didn't have mixed feelings about it too. But she needed to give him a chance to explain how it was—how it was to be thirteen years old and utterly alone in the world. No parents, no grandparents, no Gris.

It hadn't mattered where he went or with whom. He didn't care. His life had felt so bleak, so totally devoid of any possible goodness or happiness, he didn't even give a shit that he was called Seth and more or less forced to pose as Caleb's kid brother. He didn't care that he slept with an arm chained over his head until he was almost fifteen. He didn't care that he'd been called dummy by the other freshmen because he was sixteen when he enrolled in high school but had only a fourth-grade education. He didn't care that Caleb would go off on benders for days on end. He didn't care that he'd had no one and nothing to love since he was thirteen.

He didn't care, because everyone he'd loved had died or been killed.

Carbon monoxide.

Heart attack.

Gunshot.

They were gone. They were all gone.

Caring about someone hurt. Caring about someone led to heartbreak. And since Holden didn't care about Caleb, he was the perfect companion. The ones he'd loved were gone, and Holden was breathing, and life was worth nothing and about nothing. Life was just going through a series of motions until he joined those he'd lost. And all that those motions required was food, water, sleep, and air. So he'd stayed with Caleb, yes, because Caleb gave him food and water. Caleb didn't molest him while he slept. He barely spoke to Holden, and when he did, what he said didn't matter anyway.

Caleb had also murdered Griselda.

And Holden hated him with a black and desperate passion, even as Caleb kept him alive.

"You want that I put these away, Seth?" asked Quint, walking into the apartment and hefting the bags onto the kitchen counter.

"I'll do it," said Griselda. She looked up, catching Holden's eyes, and he tried to soften his expression for her, but she looked away too quickly to appreciate his efforts.

"Uh . . . can I, uh . . . can I talk to you a minute?" asked Quint in a low whisper, gesturing to the hallway.

"Yeah." Holden glanced at Griselda, who was unloading the groceries. "Thanks, Gris."

"Uh-huh," she muttered with her back to him.

"I'll b-be back in a minute."

"Mm-hm."

He gave her back a last, longing look before turning toward the door, his hip and chest starting to ache again from all the sudden movement, his face throbbing like hell. He followed Quint to the hallway and pulled his apartment door shut, looking up at the man who'd been like a surrogate father to him since he'd arrived in Charles Town five years ago.

"I, uh . . .," Quint took the grubby John Deere cap off his

head and rubbed his straggly gray hair, looking up at Holden, then away. "I . . ."

"Spit it out, Quint."

Quint looked up again, leveling his eyes with Holden's. "I know who you are."

Holden kept his face blank. "Oh yeah? Who am I?"

Awkwardly scrubbing the back of his neck, Quint grimaced. "You're that kid went missin'. You and her."

Holden took a step back and lifted a foot to the wall behind him. "W-what makes you think that?"

Quint shrugged. "Don't forget a name like Griselda. Not when she's kidnapped less'n ten miles from here. The *H* on your arm . . . that's for Holden, right?"

He stared back at Quint, saying nothing.

"I remember because of the *H* and *G*. They said you two was like a modern-day Hansel and Gretel. Holden and Griselda."

Holden licked his lips, then folded them between his teeth, making his mouth a thin, terse line.

"Can't imagine what you . . ." Quint stopped, his bluish-gray eyes distressed. "Can't imagine what you two went through. I'm, uh . . . I'm awful sorry for it."

Clearing his throat first, Holden took a deep breath and let his leg fall back to the floor. "N-not much for reminiscing about it."

"You ain't seen her since then? Since she . . . got away?"

As much as he liked Quint, his business with Griselda bordered on sacred, and he wasn't going to stand here with him gossiping about it like a couple of old ladies.

His eyes went flat, and he turned away. "I appreciate the groceries, but . . ."

"Dang, Seth, you're always so short-tempered. Now, wait a second. I don't want to get in your business."

"Then . . ."

"Chick won a couple hundred last night. He saw the

damage to your face, and the whole town knows about the—the damn *knife* Eli pulled. Told Clinton to tell you to take a couple of weeks off at half pay. You don't need to go back to work for a little bit."

Honestly, Holden hadn't once turned his mind to his job. If Griselda was planning to stay for a month, he'd stay with her, and if that meant losing his job, so be it.

"Need a month," said Holden.

"He didn't offer a danged month."

"Still need it."

Quint shook his head. "I'll tell him."

"Okay then." He gave Quint a look as if to ask, "We all done here?" then turned to open his door.

"Seth, that asshole boyfriend o' hers musta called me ten times last night."

Holden stiffened, then turned back to Quint, his eyes narrowing. "He still here?"

Quint shrugged. "Don't know. My bet, he's too much a pussy to come lookin' for me, and definitely too much of a pussy to come lookin' for you. But you can't fight, neither, Seth. Not like you are. You're weak right now."

This was news. He didn't realize he'd *need* to fight Jonah, but come to think of it, Gris had been a little cagey about her boyfriend, turning off his phone, asking him to delete messages. Did this guy hurt her? Give her a hard time? Goddamn, if anyone touched a hair on that woman's head, Holden would kill him.

"Seth. Back it up."

"He f-fuckin' comes near her—"

"He won't." Quint reached into his hip pocket and pulled out a set of two keys on a simple keychain. "You know how to get to my cabin, right? Up by Berkeley Springs."

Holden eyed the keys and nodded.

Quint shrugged again. "So? Head outta town for a few

weeks. Spend some time with your . . . with her. Get better."

Feeling grateful and overwhelmed, he reached for the keys. "Thanks, Quint. I don't know how to—"

"Clinton would likely be dead if not for you," said Quint, putting a hand on Holden's shoulder. "You straightened him out. And you and that gal, what you been through . . . well, I'm glad to do it, son."

Holden nodded at Quint, thankful but wondering, after this morning, if Gris was going to be interested in heading to a remote hunting cabin with him. It appealed to Holden—to have a quiet, safe place to get to know her again. No asshole boyfriends. No Gemma. Limited cell service. They could just take their time talking and walking, sleeping and eating. Learning about each other, remembering what they loved, letting go of what hurt them. If he could get her to go.

Quint squeezed his shoulder, then released it.

"Might add that Gemma's plenty pissed at you. Was at the Poke and Duck last night spouting off about yer, uh, about yer visitor."

Holden took a deep breath. He knew it wasn't fair to leave town without speaking to Gemma, but he also knew it was highly unlikely that she'd be able to hear anything he had to say. Quint read his face like a book.

"She won't find out where you are from me," he said, chuckling to himself as he headed back down the stairs. "Take care, now, Seth."

"Holden," he called after his friend.

Quint stopped and turned around, nodding. "Holden."

***

Putting away the groceries was just an excuse to stay busy and stay away from Holden. Last night, after his breathing had changed to a deep and even rhythm, she had stared at his face for hours, searching for the boy in the battered face of the grown man, and crying softly when she found him. In the star points of his eyelashes, in the freckles that were almost hidden by the discoloration from his broken nose, in the small brown mole over the left side of his lips. She stared at his face until her eyes were so heavy she couldn't keep them open anymore, and then she flipped over, pressing her back to his front, and sighing with contentment when he reached for her and pulled her close in his sleep.

She could see it in the softness of his eyes and hear it in the tenderness of his voice: she still meant a great deal to him. And part of her was relieved to know it. But part of her was afraid. Because Griselda was sorely out of practice with loving anyone.

Aside from Maya, about whom Griselda cared deeply, and Prudence, whom she loved in the easy way that adults are able to love children, she hadn't allowed anyone remotely near her heart. She had no other friends. She liked and respected Sabrina McClellan but kept their relationship professional. And Jonah? She despised him.

And now here she was with Holden, and love was back on the table, except she didn't know how to find it, how to allow it, how to nurture it, how to hold on to it. It frightened her because everyone she'd ever loved—her mother, her grandma, Holden— had left her alone in the end. And Holden wasn't who he used to be. He had changed. And that frightened her too.

It made her wonder again if the best play, the safest play, was to just go home. She could slip downstairs, call Jonah collect, and he'd come get her. He'd rough her up a little, but then he'd get turned on, and he'd treat her sweet for a while. She'd go back to work tomorrow morning with a long-sleeved shirt on, and Maya would be sassy, asking questions about Zelda's weekend in West Virginia. Her empty, meaningless life would just keep moving forward.

Or she could take a risk.

She could take a risk and stay, find out who Holden had become, settle their past, figure out their future.

Her hands, which had been flattening and folding the empty grocery sacks on the counter, stilled.

Their . . . *future*.

She blinked several times, trying not to panic, but panic was already setting in. Griselda didn't think about her future, didn't trust it, didn't plan for it. She didn't read the college brochures Mrs. McClellan had given her; she didn't think in terms of marriage or children. The future was a luxury for people who had goals and support and love. Griselda lived. She ate, she drank, she breathed, she worked, she slept. She didn't plan for the future.

And yet the word had entered her brain so effortlessly, as if something in her head—or her heart—had given way, had somehow given her permission to entertain that word, to think about it, to consider it for the first time in her adult life.

"Gris?"

She jumped, startled by the sound of his voice. She didn't even realize Holden had walked back into the apartment.

"Yeah?" she said, putting her palm over her racing heart.

His perfect lips quirked up. "I didn't mean to scare you."

"I'm not scared of you," she answered, and felt her own lips tilt up in response to his as she realized that she was telling the truth. Love? Change? The future? Those things scared her. But Holden? No. She could never be truly scared of Holden, no matter what choices he'd made after their life in the cellar. Even in the handful of hours they'd spent together, there was enough about him that she recognized, that she remembered, that she *knew*. Once upon a time, he had held her heart in the palm of his hands, shielded her body with his over and over again, soothed her battered soul when there was no other comfort. And those same arms that had protected her as a child had held her as she slept last night. She'd woken up with them wrapped around her this morning. No matter what, she knew in every cell of her being that she wasn't scared of Holden Croft.

"Well, that's good," he said, that little smile still lingering on his lips, making her heart race and sing.

"Everything okay with Quint?"

"Yeah. It's fine. He, uh, he gave me this." Holden opened his fist to show her a set of keys.

"Keys?"

"To his cabin. It's out of town an hour or so." His tongue darted out to lick his lips, and something deep inside Griselda coiled with heat. "Said we could use it for a few weeks. Get away from here."

"Just you and me?"

"Gris," he said, "I know I look, uh, different. R-rough. And I know you're bothered that I go by Seth and stayed with Caleb. But I want the chance to know you, and I need the chance for you to know me. And, w-well, if you d-don't like me, I w-won't try to keep you by me. I'll let you go."

Oh God, Holden, never *let me go.*

"But I'd like to introduce myself to you." He stood up a little straighter. "I'd like that ch-chance."

He swallowed, still staring at her, and she found herself lost in his eyes. They were still swollen and scabbed, but they were gray and soft too.

"I know I look broken, but—"

"Holden," she said, blinking furiously because this was so damn hard and she was about to cry again. "Are you whole or broken?"

He blinked back at her, his jaw tightening as he clenched it, his nostrils flaring. He was trying not to cry just as hard as she was.

"I'm b-broken," he finally whispered. "But I think I could be whole again."

She didn't bother swiping at the tear that rolled down her cheek. Nodding at him, she held out her trembling hand. "Let's find out."

CHAPTER 16

Gris had prepared him a plate of fried apples and a bowl of cereal, insisting that he sit down at the kitchen table and let her gather a few things together for them. He told her where to find a duffel bag, and every time she poked her head back into the living room, she had a question about where to find something else. He had to hand it to her—she was thorough, packing up towels, sheets, and toilet paper, just in case. When he said as much, she paused, her pretty face quirking up in a grin.

"I think it's the nanny in me," she confessed, her cheeks rosy.

"You babying me?" he asked, taking another mouthful of fruit and thinking that fried apples had never, ever tasted so sweet.

She rolled her eyes and shook her head, turning back into the hallway and rustling around in his bathroom cabinets. It occurred to him that she'd probably find the 48-pack of Trojans he'd picked up the last time he was at Walmart. And though he should kick himself for thinking it, he couldn't help hoping that she'd slip a few in his bag, just in case.

He wasn't totally sure what had changed between his confession that he'd stayed with Caleb and her willingness to join him at Quint's cabin, but he wasn't foolish enough to ask her. He was about to have her all to himself for a few weeks, and that's all that mattered.

"I'm changing your bandages before we go," she shouted from the back hall, and he chuckled softly to himself, popping the last apple in his mouth and starting on the cereal. Damn, but she was just as bossy as ever, and he loved it because it felt so familiar it almost made him want to weep. Instead he shoveled a spoonful of cereal into his mouth and chewed slowly, savoring the sounds of Griselda moving around in his space.

Twenty minutes later, the dishes were washed, his bandages were changed, his bag was packed, and he was locking the apartment door behind them. Griselda had his duffel bag thrown over her shoulder, and the two brown sacks, repacked with groceries and other supplies, filled her arms.

As she descended the stairs in front of him, he admired how strong and self-sufficient she was, putting away the groceries, making his breakfast, packing his bags, making his bed, and straightening up the apartment before tending to his wounds and repacking their supplies. She was cheerfully and effortlessly efficient without complaining or asking for thanks, which made her unlike every other woman he'd ever known.

He wondered if that part of her had been inadvertently nurtured during their years with Caleb, when their survival had depended on strength and hard work. From March to November, they'd work in the garden every day, from seven in the morning until five in the evening. From November to February, they'd work in the barn, canning the fruits and vegetables they'd carefully cultivated in the warmer months. Once or twice a week, Caleb would load a few boxes in the back of his truck, and when he returned drunk a few hours later, the boxes were empty and ready for more.

Holden couldn't speak for Griselda, especially after all these years, but for him the work had been a blessing. For the most part, when they were silently working, Caleb left them in peace, and when Holden thought back on those days, if he could eliminate fear from the equation, he recalled a whole and quiet communion with Griselda, every hour, every minute, of every day. Their days blended together in a monotony of work, but at least they had each other, and for him, that not only made it bearable—in some ways, it had even made those days precious.

"You okay with the stairs?" she asked, glancing back at him.

His deep thoughts scattered, and he nodded. Though his hip, chest, and face still hurt a lot, it wasn't as bad as yesterday, and the Advil he'd taken while she changed his bandages was beginning to take the edge off. As long as he moved slowly and carefully, it wasn't unbearable.

"Where's your car?" she asked, holding open the door at the bottom of the stairs.

Tilting his head to the left he said, "Around the corner. The piece-of-shit Ford pickup."

As he came up behind her, she headed through the door and turned onto the sidewalk. But suddenly her efficient pace stilled, and she stopped abruptly at the mouth of the alley. One of the grocery bags in her arms started to slip, but she tightened her grip on it at the last minute. Her head whipped back to look at him, her eyes wide and panicked, and her lips parted in dismay.

He flinched, reading her face a second too late.

Fuck.

She'd been in that truck once before.

***

The second Griselda looked around the corner, she recognized the truck because of the faded bumper sticker on the back that read "Rosie's Barn Bar." It was Caleb Foster's truck. The one he'd used to abduct them.

Unconsciously, for most of her life, she'd looked for that bumper sticker on the back of every red truck she'd ever driven behind, on every road, every highway, everywhere she'd ever traveled. And now here it was. Sitting in an alleyway parking lot in West Virginia, like it had been there all along.

"That's his . . . his . . ."

"It's n-not his anymore," said Holden from behind her. "It's mine."

"You *kept* his truck? You *wanted* his . . ." Her words drifted off, and she searched his face, dizzy from breathing way too fast. With increasingly sweaty palms, the groceries started to slip again.

He pulled the bags from her arms, wincing from the effort, and set them down on the pavement, before placing his palms gently on her cheeks. His gray eyes were gentle and compassionate as they stared back at her.

"L-listen to me, Gris. It's not his anymore. It's mine. And I kept it because I was, uh, seventeen and I had nothing and he took good care of it. It got me from Oregon back here. And yes, maybe if I'm honest, I k-kept it because I had nothing left of you but memories . . . and one of those memories was you sitting next to me in this truck. So, yeah. I k-kept it. But it's *not* his. It's mine."

She locked her eyes on his as he spoke, searching them for a lifeline, and her heart stopped racing as she found it in his words.

He'd kept it because of *her*.

He'd kept this truck because once upon a time, for twenty minutes, on the worst day of their lives, she'd sat in this truck holding a puppy on her lap after he'd begged her not to get in, then followed her anyway.

It was so heartbreaking her breath caught, and she let her cheek fall onto his shoulder, her face turned into his neck. His arms came around her, strong and solid, holding her against his chest, and she let herself relax against him, closing her eyes. He hadn't been able to shower this morning, but he'd cleaned himself up in the bathroom after breakfast, and he smelled like fried apples, soap, and sweat. The heat of his throat warmed her lips, and without thinking, she leaned forward and pressed a kiss to his skin.

He gasped, holding his breath, motionless except for his fingers, which slowly curled into fists on the back of her T-shirt.

Molten, melting heat spread out from her belly, making deep and hidden muscles clench with longing as her nipples pebbled, straining against his chest. She felt him harden through his jeans, pushing insistently into her thigh. She drew back, then pressed her lips against his throbbing pulse once again.

A soft, strangled groan released from the depths of his throat, the vibration faint but thrilling against the sensitive skin of her lips. His breath finally released in a pant, falling hot against her ear and making shivers run down her back.

"Holden," she whispered, her breathing quick and shallow.

"Gris," he murmured, the low sound making her toes curl in her sandals.

"We should, um . . . we should . . ." Her lips were so close to his throat, they grazed his skin like butterfly kisses both times she said the word *we*.

"Huh," he groaned softly, making no move to release her, though his fingers uncoiled, flattening against her lower back.

She swallowed, a fog of intense, aching desire making her warm and light-headed. On a purely physical level, her mind skated swiftly to what it would be like to *be* with Holden, and her heart thundered against his as she imagined her nakedness pressed against his, his lips kissing hers, his hands exploring the peaks and valleys of her body, the hardness between his thighs pumping into her.

He was far more experienced than she, but if the tenderness in his eyes was any indication, he'd be careful of her, anxious to please her. Her sex flooded hot and wet at the thought, dampening her panties as she closed her eyes to concentrate on the hard angles of his body pressed against hers, wondering what they would feel like without clothes between them.

Bothered and way beyond hot, her mind finally interceded, thrusting common sense on her consciousness like a bucket of ice water to the face.

The *last* thing she and Holden needed was to complicate this reunion with sex.

Besides, taunted her cruel mind, *he has a girlfriend . . . and a shitload of tally marks.*

She pulled away from him, straightening her head and opening her eyes. "I guess we should get going."

He cleared his throat, his gray eyes almost black as they searched her face with brutal intensity, finally resting boldly on her lips. "Yeah."

"Sorry about that," she said, feeling her cheeks color, and wishing she didn't like it so much that he couldn't stop looking at her lips. "You kept the truck because of me, and that's . . . I don't know. It's sad and it's nice and it's . . . confusing."

"You're confused?" he asked, still holding on to her tightly, adjusting his stance slightly so that his erection strained against her sex, not her thigh. "About what?"

Her eyelids fluttered a little, and she forced herself not to roll her hips into him. "I think . . . I mean, I think my feelings are a little, uh, all over the place. I'm glad to see you . . . I'm relieved you're okay . . . I'm . . ."

"You're what?" he asked, finally sliding his eyes from her lips to her eyes.

"I'm . . .," she started breathily, then pulled her bottom lip between her teeth.

"Stop doing that," he growled softly, his eyes never leaving hers.

She released her lip.

"Breathe," he said.

She took a deep breath.

He dropped his arms and took a step back, though he still

drilled her eyes with his. "You're right. We should get going."

He turned away from her and walked to the driver's side of the truck, opening the door, and stepping carefully inside.

***

Fuck.

Fuck, fuck, fuck. Damn.

He flashed a look in the rearview mirror and saw her pick up the two grocery sacks and place them carefully in one of the two crates bungee-corded in the bed of the truck. She hefted the duffel into the other crate, then turned around, her back to the truck, her hands on her hips. She needed a moment. He understood completely.

Glancing at the tally marks on his arm, he knew that there was no mark inked into his skin—not one—that could come close to the moment he'd just shared with Griselda. And my God, they hadn't even kissed. Her lips had barely touched his throat for more than a few seconds. If they ever . . . God, if they ever . . .

He grimaced, adjusting his pants and trying to relax. Looking in the rearview mirror again, he wondered if she was doing the same. He had felt her nipples, stiffened into points, pressed against his chest as she kissed his neck a second time. She'd been every bit as turned-on as he was.

Fuck.

He wanted her so badly—every inch of his body pulsed impatiently for her touch—and yet . . . and yet . . .

In some ways Holden had grown up too fast, but in others his growth had been stunted. He knew this about himself. He acknowledged it. For the most part, he had endured life, not lived it. He had a shitty factory job and a crappy apartment, and he slept with the light on half the time and woke up screaming the other half. His bank account was meager, and he had very few friends. He fought other men for sport because the rage in him was ceaseless. He used women for pleasure and was a rotten boyfriend to Gemma, because hell, he wasn't sure he knew how to love someone anymore—how to put someone else's interests before his.

But despite every bad thing he knew about himself, he also knew this: Griselda made him want to live again. Griselda made him want to be a better man.

There was so much rocky terrain between them, a new emotion every minute, a fragile trust that he couldn't bear to risk. For the first time in his life, there was a woman inside the body, and her feelings—her heart—were more important than his dick getting attention. If he fucked this up with her, he might never get another chance. The stakes were too high.

Besides, he didn't even know if he deserved her. And before she could belong to him, he needed to know he was worthy of her. Whoever was with Gris, himself included, needed to earn her first.

Reminding himself that he needed to give her the space and time to decide what she wanted had calmed him down a little by the time she finally opened the passenger door and swung her body into the cab of the truck.

She gave him a shy smile as she buckled her seat belt, her cheeks still flushed, her eyes still a little dilated.

"I'm sorry," she said.

"Don't need to be."

"I shouldn't have done that."

"It's okay, Gris."

Her blush deepened. "Well, I, uh, I promise to keep my lips to myself from now on."

There were about twenty places he'd rather have her lips than kept to herself, and they were all throbbing for her attention right now. But he didn't argue. Holden hid his wince by turning the key in the ignition and letting the old truck roar to life, then placed his arm over the seat to back up.

Griselda rolled down the window.

Ten minutes later, Charles Town disappeared in Holden's rearview mirror, and the countryside of West Virginia beckoned them to keep moving forward.

CHAPTER 17

It didn't take long for Griselda to fall asleep beside him, and Holden couldn't help sneaking glances at her as he drove through the lush green fields dotted with vibrant trees that flanked either side of Route 9 West.

He had to admit it was strange to be back in this truck with her for the second time in his life, and he couldn't help thinking about the first time. His lips tightened as he remembered Caleb's first words to them—the first time Holden realized he was trapped with a madman: *Ruth? Ya ever make me wait like that agin, I'll strip the skin off'n yer back.*

Holden had known that something wasn't right with Caleb Foster the first time he laid eyes on him. His elementary school had done a program about stranger danger in third grade, and his mother had always warned him about taking rides with people he didn't know. But the thing about having your life upheaved and being placed in foster care? Everyone was a stranger, and you were forced to accept them into your life. You were told that they were your foster "mother" and foster "father," even if you hadn't laid eyes on them before your placement, even if they drank too much and forgot to give you dinner. You were instructed to live in their house, sleep in the bed they provided, and follow their unfamiliar rules. You were, more or less, *encouraged* to place your naive trust in total and complete strangers.

So Holden understood why Gris had gone willingly with Caleb after the tragic miscommunication between them, and the thing is? Somewhere inside, he knew what was going to happen if he got in that truck, but he couldn't bear to watch her go off with Caleb alone. He was already invested in her.

The first time he ever saw Griselda, on his first night at the Fillmans' house, she'd been standing in the hallway outside the room he shared with Billy. She had a toothbrush in her hand, so he guessed she was headed to the bathroom, but she'd paused in his bedroom doorway, watching Billy taunt him with his dead father's Orioles cap, punch him, and call him a retard for stammering. Her blue eyes flashed with fury, small hands fisting by her sides, and Holden knew—*he knew*—that she would be important to him. Her indignation had also given him the courage to fight back because he didn't want her to think he was some little wimp who let older kids push him around.

As Mrs. Fillman lit into him about punching Billy, he ignored her, shifting his eyes to Griselda instead. Leveled by her soft, steady, compassionate gaze, suddenly everything that had just happened with Mrs. Fillman and Billy didn't matter. In a world full of heartache, turmoil, and strangers, she somehow felt familiar. She felt like grace in a graceless world. All he could see was her kind face, her pretty hair in neat braids, her kinship, her solidarity. For the first time since losing his grandmother, he felt a genuine connection to someone, and to let Griselda know that his heart recognized hers, he had winked at her.

Shifting his eyes back to the road, Holden grinned, remembering her tall, scrawny body and huge eyes that used to take in everything around her. How desperately he'd wanted to belong to her, to mean something to her, to protect her— whatever it took to be in her life. A little indignation with a side of compassion and he'd been a goner from the start.

He would have sold his soul to be close to her.

His grin faded.

In a way, that's exactly what he'd done.

But would he trade it? If he could go back to that day on the side of the road, knowing what he knew now, would he choose differently? Would he choose to stay rooted to the pavement as she drove away with Caleb Foster?

The answer was swift and final: no.

He wouldn't have changed his decision.

He would have followed her. No matter what, he would have followed her.

Go to the ends of the earth for you . . . to make you feel my love.

***

As they pulled into the driveway, Holden looked at the dilapidated farmhouse in front of them. During the twenty-minute drive, the Man had been mostly quiet, only muttering a few times, and Holden couldn't quite make out what he was saying. Something about "wickedness" and "evil ways," and once he'd looked at Gris venomously, narrowing his eyes and spitting out "the path to hell" before turning his wild eyes back to the road.

Gris still held the puppy on her lap, but she wasn't smiling anymore. She looked at Holden despairingly, her eyes telegraphing her terror and acknowledging the grave mistake she'd made by getting into the truck. Desperate that she not be too frightened, he mustered the courage to wink at her once, then looked out the window like he was enjoying the view so she wouldn't see the stark horror invading his eyes too.

"We're home. Git out."

The Man grabbed the puppy off Griselda's lap, making it cry from his rough handling, and Griselda's eyes cut to Holden's as the Man slammed his door shut, leaving them alone.

"It'll b-b-be okay," he whispered.

"How?" she whimpered.

"We'll d-d-do what he s-s-says and r-r-run away later when he's asleep."

Suddenly the door beside Holden was jerked open.

"Ya got to be stronger, little brother," said the Man, darting a lethal glance at Griselda before settling his watery eyes on Holden. "Can't succumb to her temptress ways this go-round."

"Y-y-yes, s-s-sir," said Holden, stepping down to the dusty ground, utterly confused by the Man's words but anxious to appear agreeable.

"Beg the Lord for salvation from yer wickedness," he added, looking back at Griselda. "An' maybe He'll forgive ya."

"Yes, sir," she mumbled, tears thick in her voice, as she stepped down to the driveway beside Holden.

Don't cry, Gris. Please don't cry.

"Ye'll live in darkness till yer evil ways is purged! Till yer worthy o' the light."

Holden stared up at him, watching as the summer sky turned gray with storm clouds.

"Ye'll work yer fingers so the devil knows there ain't no playground for his pleasure."

Griselda's hand touched Holden's, and he folded his fingers over hers as the Man stared up at the sky.

"Can't be no cleft in yer remorse! Ya hear?"

The puppy in his arms was whimpering, but the Man didn't seem to notice how tightly he was gripping the small animal.

"For the wages o' sin is death!"

The sound of water hitting the ground made Holden look down to see a puddle between Griselda's dusty sneakers where she'd peed. At the same time, fat raindrops started falling, as though the Man's angry ranting had the power to hide the sun.

Suddenly the Man looked down at them, his eyes widening at the sight of their clasped hands. The fury on his face was immediate and terrifying. Throwing the puppy to the ground, he *ripped their arms away from each other, hurting them, staring up at heaven and wailing, "Cast out the wicked!"*

His fingers squeezed their skin painfully as he dragged them behind him, around the back of the house. Letting go of Holden's arm for a moment as he opened the storm cellar doors, Holden looked wildly at the woods that surrounded the property on all sides, wondering if he should try to run. But one look at Griselda, who had tears streaming down her face, closed the door on freedom. He didn't run. A second later Caleb Foster grabbed his arm again and dragged them down into the darkness of their first night in hell.

***

"How long was I out?" Griselda asked him, waking with a start to find the truck was stopped.

"Not long," said Holden, flicking a quick glance at her, then looking back out the windshield. He took a deep, shaky breath, then sighed, shaking his head a little like he was shaking something away. "Thirty minutes or so."

She scrubbed at her face with her hands, then stretched her arms before crossing them over her chest. They were parked in front of a Target. "Where are we?"

"Martinsburg. I thought . . . well, you're welcome to use my toothbrush, but you're so skinny, I don't think my jeans will fit you."

Her lips tilted up. "Aw! You'd loan me your jeans?"

"What's mine is yours," he said.

"You keep saying that."

"I keep meaning it," he said, without looking at her.

"I have no money," she said. Since she was careful with her money and had been self-sufficient for several years now, it was an uncomfortable admission.

She felt his eyes on her. "What's mine is—"

"I get it," she said, looking up and rolling her eyes at him, "but I'm paying you back someday."

He shook his head, grinning at her. "Still stubborn as hell."

"I'm no freeloader, Mr. Croft."

"Okay, Miss Griselda. Fine. If you insist, you may pay me back for a couple pairs of jeans and a few shirts."

"Miss Griselda, huh?"

"Well, I ain't calling you Z-Zelda," he said, parroting her words from yesterday.

She opened her door and stepped out of the truck, stretching again. She felt a familiarity coming back to their relationship and she loved it. Not that she'd ever had a home she loved, but if she had, she imagined this is what it would feel like to come home.

He walked around the hood of the car, holding his hand out to her, and she took it, letting him weave his fingers through hers as they walked through the parking lot.

"However, as long as we're talking about Zelda," he said tartly, and her heart skipped a beat as his fingers squeezed hers gently, "why don't you tell me something about her that I, uh, don't know?"

"I thought you hated that name," she said.

"Maybe I'll like it more once I know her better."

Griselda was both relieved and sorry when he dropped her hand and handed her a red plastic shopping basket. Relieved because their physical connection—their raw chemistry—was fierce and relentless, and sorry because a rash, impulsive side of her wanted to encourage it, explore it, test it, and savor it.

She sighed, her body and mind at war as she stepped into the air-conditioned store.

"So?" he asked.

"Right. Zelda." *Um . . . Zelda wants to jump your body like a monkey and hang on for dear life while you—* "She loves kids."

Holden was silent, so she looked up to find him grinning at her with such a sweet expression, her tummy flipped over.

"Not surprised," he said. "I always thought you'd be an amazing mom."

His words from long ago—*We'll be the b-best p-parents ever, Gris*—floated through her mind, making her feel warm. Her free arm brushed into his, and she didn't move away so it happened again, each time sending delightful little shivers up her arm.

"What else?"

"I love my job."

"Tell me about it," he said, his fingers brushing against hers like a tease.

"I work Monday through Friday, eight to six. The house is in Georgetown, and it's so beautiful, Holden—it's like something you'd see in a movie. She has little soaps in the bathroom in the shape of birds, and they smell like . . . well, like clean fresh air and roses. Everything's perfect. Everything's lovely. Sabrina—she's my boss—goes out most days, and it's just me and Pru. I make her lunch, take her to the park, do her laundry. Sometimes I—"

"Pretend it's your house, and she's yours."

Griselda grinned, nodding at his perception. "That's harmless, right?"

"You always did love spinning fantasies, Gris."

"She's such a happy little girl, it's not just a fantasy, Holden. There are really children who grow up in safe, happy places, and I love that. I love seeing what it looks like for a little girl to have such a beautiful childhood." She didn't say this with self-pity, but she worried it sounded that way. "Not that I . . . I mean, mine could've been worse, I suppose. You get what you get—"

"—and you don't get upset," finished Holden, surprising her by remembering Mrs. Fillman's favorite catchphrase. As though reading her mind, he added, "D-didn't much like Miz Fillman."

Griselda turned into the women's clothing section, scanning a clearance shelf for size-four shorts. She didn't look at Holden when she asked, "What do you think was going on between her and Billy?"

Finding three pairs of denim cutoffs, she pulled them off the shelf and into her basket and looked up at Holden. His expression had darkened, and his jaw was tight. His eyes searched Griselda's before answering. "Sh-she was molesting him."

Griselda flinched. She'd suspected, of course, but it was dreadful to hear it confirmed. "How do you know for sure?"

"I pretended to be asleep while it was happening."

She winced, reaching out to touch his arm, and he stepped closer to her.

"God, Holden."

Her hand skated down his arm, clasping his hand.

"Only happened once while I was there," he said. "B-but I was only there for three nights."

His fingers entwined around hers, and she stepped back, pulling him with her between two racks of T-shirts that afforded them a little more privacy. "I'm sorry."

"D-don't be sorry for me. Be sorry for B-Billy. Cost a lot to be the favorite."

"He was mean. Billy. He was so mean," said Griselda, flashing back to Mrs. Fillman's adoring glances at Billy in the rearview mirror of the station wagon, and feeling sick.

"The worst of it, Gris? I was glad. I was so fucking g-grateful it was him and not me. How fucked-up is that?"

"No," she said, squeezing his hand and stepping closer to him. "No, that's not fair. You were a little kid. You didn't wish anything bad on Billy. You just wanted to be left alone."

Holden dropped her eyes, looking down at the floor.

"All those years together, and you never told me," she said softly.

"I kn-knew you were scared about Caleb," he said. "You know, doing that to us. I didn't want to give you more reason to be, uh, worried."

He had protected her from it. Just as he'd protected her with his body time and again, taking whippings meant for her. Overwhelmed with gratitude, she let the basket fall from her fingers and wrapped her arms around his neck, pulling him against her. His arms came around her easily, strong and warm, clasping her lightly to his chest as he buried his face in her hair. She could feel his heart hammering against hers, and whether it was a result of terrible memories or the rush from holding each other, she couldn't be sure. But an embrace whose original motive had been comfort quickly shifted for Griselda as her body leaned into his, alert and aroused in the space of an instant.

Her breathing shallow, she locked her fingers on the hot skin of his neck, the ends of his silky dark-blond hair curling over her hands. She arched her back a little, pressing her body closer to his as she rested her cheek on his shoulder, her warm breath fanning his neck.

"Nobody ever took care of me like you," she whispered close to his ear.

***

Holden trembled, her words sending tendrils of pleasure from his brain, spreading warmth throughout his body. His heart throbbed against her chest, and he clenched his eyes shut, fighting against the waves of paralyzing emotion and reckless desire.

It scared him to feel so much after so long of feeling nothing. It scared him to want her so badly when he had no idea if she would be receptive to an advance. He longed to love her. He longed to kiss her. But neither were safe choices, because, poorly timed, either could lead to her loss.

He tried to take a deep breath, but it sounded shaky and ragged in his ears. Her hair smelled like sunshine and soap, and her sweet curves felt like heaven. She'd arched her back before whispering, her breasts pushing against his chest, and his hypersensitive, over-aroused body was just about at its breaking point.

Opening his eyes, he pulled away from her, knowing that his skin was flushed and his eyes probably close to black. His arms dropped to his sides, and his chest heaved up and down.

"I'm, uh, I'm going to go get some bandages and such," he panted. "M-meet you at the checkout?"

She flinched almost imperceptibly, her tongue darting out to wet her lips as her wide blue eyes searched his face. He read her expression perfectly: she was confused by his abrupt withdrawal and shaken up by what was happening between them. His skin was hot and ready for her touch, but the tally marks on his arm itched like a reminder, and he dropped her eyes, stepping away.

"I'll see you in a bit."

"Yeah. Sure," she said, sounding bewildered.

He looked up to catch her pulling that bottom lip into her mouth like an unintentional dare. Before he changed his mind, hauled her up against him like a caveman and had his way with her right smack in the middle of Target, he pivoted and walked quickly away.

The reality was that Holden hadn't had to use much self-control where women were concerned. If he liked the way a woman looked and she liked the way he looked, he fucked her. Hard, fast, slow, easy. In a men's room. Against a wall. In a strange apartment. In the back of his truck. His technique varied based on his mood, but his patience didn't. He didn't have much. He didn't need much. He was hard-bodied and good-looking, and more than anything, he simply didn't give a shit about any of them, which was apparently the biggest turn-on of all.

Keeping Gris at arm's length was a test of will for Holden. It was forcing him to develop a skill set he didn't have: the patience to wait for a woman he actually cared about. Hell, for a woman he practically worshipped.

He threw one look back toward women's clothing, glad to see that she wasn't staring after him looking hurt, and detoured through office supplies to get to the pharmacy. Suddenly something caught his attention: the words *Writer's Journal* in black and white on a red background. Plucking the notebook off the shelf, he flipped through it, looking at the blank, crisp pages and wondering if she ever wrote down her fairy tales. Tucking it under his arm, he browsed through the pens, finding a couple that looked nicer and fancier than the others and were a little more expensive. Holding the notebook and pens, he turned back toward first aid supplies, his chest and hip aching for the first time in an hour. Walking around the store was likely overdoing it.

Just as he made it to the Band-Aid aisle, his phone buzzed in his back pocket. With his free hand, he pulled it out, looking at the screen and grimacing. His phone must have just gotten a strong signal, and it was a series of texts from Gemma coming in one after the other, and they were not happy.

FUCKING COCKSUCKER!

You left town without even telling me, Seth?

With your fucking foster sister?

You better call me right the fuck now and explain what the hell is going on.

We NEED to talk.

I am not playing.

Holden sighed, looking down at the phone again before turning it off and shoving it back into his pocket.

He didn't want to care, but being around Griselda was already changing him, and he had to admit he felt a little bad. It had been cowardly to leave Charles Town without talking to Gemma. He should have stopped by the DQ to break things off clean and let her know that things were over between them.

Honestly Holden had no idea why he'd let Gemma hang around so long. He didn't love her. He didn't even really like her all that much. She'd been Clinton's high school girlfriend for a year or two, but things hadn't worked out for them, and she'd moved away after high school. When she moved back home a few months ago, around Christmas, she'd set her sights on Holden. At first, Holden kept his distance out of respect for his friend, but Clinton swore that they were ancient history and he didn't care if Holden spent time with her. Plus, she'd been relentless. And smart. She'd figured out quick that if she cleaned up and shut up during sex, she was ten times more likely to come.

But Holden and Gemma were not a match—they had almost nothing in common. They both liked getting drunk on a Friday night and sleeping in late on Saturday morning. They had friends in common, like Clinton and some of his other high school buddies, and they both lived the same marginal, shit-job, uninspired life. But Gemma didn't know that deep inside Holden preferred sketching and reading to tractors and fights. She didn't know that he was content with quiet and didn't require loud country music at all times to fill up the silence. She didn't know that he despised the incessant chatter of reality shows. And she didn't know that he couldn't give two shits about her hair, nails, or clothing. Frankly he really just didn't give much of a shit about her at all. If she called him—right this minute—and told him she'd taken up with someone new? All Holden would feel is relief.

And the minute he broke things off, she would see all this in his eyes, be hurt, make a scene. She'd show up at the Poke and Duck for the next few months telling anyone who would listen what a selfish cocksucker Seth West turned out to be. And, well? What man walked into that shit show willingly? Was he a coward when it came to the wrath of Gemma Hendricks? Absolutely. He'd just as soon avoid her.

Unless Gris wanted him.

Unless Gris wanted him all to herself.

And then he'd say what he needed to say to Gemma, and to hell with what she said or thought for the rest of his life. If Gris belonged to him, the rest of the world could go to the devil and he wouldn't even notice.

Picking up some Advil, bandages, tape, antiseptic ointment, and small scissors, he balanced everything on the writer's notebook and headed to the checkout area, looking for Griselda.

Didn't take long to spot her.

It was as if his heart, his body, his very soul, was so finely tuned to her, if she was within a hundred-mile radius, he'd know. He'd just know, and everything in him would gravitate to the smallest particle of her.

She gave him a cautious smile, which made him feel a little bad, and he reminded himself that even if he never got to touch her, kiss her, or make love to her, just being around Griselda was better than any of that with any other woman. And it was true. Holy shit, he thought, his grin answering hers, it was fucking true.

"I think I got everything," she said, swinging her basket, and his glance darted down, widening when he realized there was a rainbow of colorful bras on top of the T-shirts and shorts. Hot-pink satin, black lace, aqua blue, and white. White with a little pink bow in the center and—*fuck*—matching panties.

He clenched his jaw, looking up to smile politely at her as his dick swelled in his jeans.

"What'd you get?" she asked, stepping forward in line, unaware of the chemical reaction taking over his body.

Holden glanced down at the medical supplies hiding the notebook. Suddenly he felt a little embarrassed about the gift, like a twelve-year-old with a crush on a pretty girl. And that made him instantly remember that once upon a time, he *had* been a twelve-year-old with a crush on a pretty girl. *This* girl.

"Nothing much. Few things."

"Mysterious," she said, her eyes twinkling. "Remember, I'm paying you back."

No, you're not, he thought, but anxious not to be at odds with her, he just nodded

She offered him her basket. "You mind if I use the bathroom real quick?"

"Go ahead."

He took the basket in his hand, and she smiled before walking over to a store employee to ask where the bathroom was. Her hips swayed gently as she changed direction, heading toward the little in-store café. He watched until he couldn't see her anymore, his mouth dry and his pulse beating in his throat. He hated like hell to let her out of his sight.

"Sir? Sir, are you ready?" asked the red-smocked kid working the register.

Glancing up, Holden realized it was his turn and placed his things on the belt, then turned his attention to her basket. He removed her new underthings, trying not to be weird about handling them, but unable to suppress the images of them pressed against her sacred, hidden places. The aqua against her nipples, the little pink bow sitting under her belly button, the white cotton kissing her—

"Cash or credit?"

"Huh? Oh. Cash."

"Eighty-six fifty."

Holden took his wallet out of his back pocket, peeling out five twenties and handing them over as the cashier finished bagging their things.

"Your wife's real pretty," said the kid, holding out Holden's change and gesturing with his chin to Griselda, who was making her way back to him.

"My . . .?" Holden asked, looking from Griselda back to

the cashier in confusion.

"Your wife. She's hot. Nice going."

Holden chuckled softly, a surprised sound, holding out his hand as the kid poured the bills and change into his palm.

Your wife.

Your wife.

Your wife.

The words ricocheted in Holden's head, and he stared, dumbfounded and grinning, at the cashier as Griselda slipped beside him, nudging him with her hip.

"We all good here?" she chirped, smiling at the beaming kid and taking the two plastic bags he offered her.

Holden turned to look at her, his heart spilling and tripping over itself. "Yeah. We're great."

CHAPTER 18

"How long until we get there?" Griselda asked as she buckled herself back into the red truck.

"Forty minutes, give or take," he said, wincing as he sat down.

"You're in pain."

"I'll take another Advil. I can rest once we get there."

"Want me to drive?" she asked, fishing the Advil out of the Target bag and opening it.

He shook his head, taking the two brown pills from her palm and swallowing them without water. "Naw. I'll be okay."

"Okay."

He glanced at his seat belt, then back at the windshield, clenching his jaw and reaching forward to turn the key in the ignition.

"You're not buckled," she said, and it occurred to her that twisting his torso to grab the belt would likely hurt his side.

"I'm fine," he said.

"No, you're not. Let me help you," she said, unbuckling her own seat belt and sliding across the seat until her hip was flush with his. As she looked down at their jean-clad thighs side by side, she heard his almost-soundless gasp, and it made her heart speed into a double-time beat. Her eyes slid up his chest to his face, which was set stone hard, staring straight ahead, his posture stiff and muscles rigid. His fingers were curled tightly around the steering wheel, the whites of his scabby knuckles stark and straining, like he was bracing for something.

Or some*one*.

My God, she wondered. *Do I do this to him?*

"Holden," she whispered.

He didn't turn to her. He swallowed deliberately, his nostrils flaring a little.

With her outside hand, she reached across his chest, turning into him, her breasts brushing his shirt, her ear close to his lips as she leaned around his body. She was close enough to hear a ragged breath drawn and held as she leaned over him. Close enough to catch the flutter of his eyelids out of the corner of her eye as her left nipple grazed his chest and hardened.

She pulled the belt over him, leaning back to buckle it. The echo of the loud click faded, but she stayed frozen in place. The entire space felt charged—electric and hot—like their T-shirts were the only thing preventing incineration, and if their skin happened to touch, they'd both go up in flames.

"Gris," he said his voice low, his face tense. "If you don't move over . . ."

"Oh," she murmured, breathless with longing.

He finally bent his neck and looked down at her, his dark and stormy eyes close, so close, slamming directly into hers.

"Please," he begged her.

Her tongue darted out to wet her dry lips, and his eyes dropped to her mouth. He closed his eyes, swallowing tightly.

"P-please, Gris," he whispered. "I'm so fucking weak."

The desperation in his tone moved her to action, and she quickly scooted back over to her seat, reaching for her belt and buckling it quickly, staring straight ahead as he started the truck and backed out of the parking lot without another word.

With the silence between them tense and brooding, Griselda rolled down her window to distract herself and rested her elbow on the windowsill as they left Martinsburg behind.

That morning, when she kissed his neck, she'd felt his erection straining against his jeans, but he'd made no move to kiss her, even though she was making a move on him. Embarrassed that she'd been so forward, she promised not to kiss him again, and he'd graciously laughed it off. But she couldn't seem to stop reaching for him—while they were in Target, she'd wrapped her arms around him again, arching into him. She could tell that she physically affected him, but again, he hadn't taken advantage of the situation. In fact, he'd pushed her away and left her alone to shop. And now, yet again, she could tell that his body responded to her closeness, but again he pushed her away, practically begging her to stop touching him.

Though she felt strongly that he cared for her and wanted to spend some time with her, she could see that he was holding himself back, almost painfully, from touching her. They'd slept next to each other, sure, but that was probably more a celebration of their reunion—a throwback to when they'd been kids together. He certainly hadn't made a move on her, and heck, she'd been in his bed. He could have.

She sighed, thinking about the daisy on the kitchen table, and Gemma's face flashed through her head. *He calls out your name in his sleep . . . His* girlfriend *. . . I been with him six months.*

That must be it, she thought. *He's attracted to me, like he's probably attracted to nine women in ten, but he's* committed *to his girlfriend.*

Then why is he going to a remote cabin to spend several weeks alone with you? her hopeful heart demanded.

Because you're childhood friends who endured a painful experience together, reasoned her head. *Because he needs closure just as much as you do.*

Friendship.

Closure.

Desperately she thought back on the past two days, but despite their attraction to each other, he hadn't said or done anything to indicate that he would cross the line from a cherished friendship to . . . something more. He wanted to know what had happened to her, he wanted her to know what had happened to him, he wanted to know if she'd lived a happy life. But, no matter how much she wanted to add subtext to his words, in reality there probably wasn't any.

He held her hand easily . . . as he always had.

He lay beside her easily . . . as he always had.

But, while she was foolishly hoping, deep in her heart, that he could see her and love her as a woman, the reality was that he was only seeing her and loving her as his resurrected foster sister, his dear childhood friend.

She clenched her eyes shut, wincing in embarrassment and disappointment.

Despite Gemma, he is *attracted to you,* said the devil on her left shoulder. *You could push things. Over eighty tally marks says he'll eventually fold.*

But he won't belong to you, protested the angel on her right. *Besides, if you care about him, you won't do that to him. He has a girlfriend. He's obviously trying to stay committed to her. If you truly care for him, you'll support him. You'll do everything you can to help him be good.*

She glanced at his beautiful face, looking past the black-and blue, to find the boy she'd loved in the man sitting beside her. Maybe he couldn't be *her* man, but he wanted to be her friend, and if that's all he could offer, then that's all she would take.

***

Holden turned down the access road, looking for the reflective lights that would indicate Quint's hidden driveway. Relieved that the uncomfortable drive on the bumpy, unpaved dirt road was brief, he pulled in front of a log cabin set in the middle of a vast and quiet clearing bursting with wildflowers, and cut the engine.

The cabin itself was small, made of light wood logs and trimmed with green shutters. It had a covered porch, where two rocking chairs rocked idly in the midday breeze on either side of the green-painted front door.

Holden had been here a couple of times before, joining Quint and Clinton for hunting weekends, and he knew that inside there was a common room with a small kitchen, dining table, woodstove, futon, and two chairs. In the back of the cabin was a tiny bedroom with a full-size bed and a no-frills, utilitarian bathroom. A rustic ladder led from the common room to a loft, where there were two twin mattresses for extra company. Though the whole space was probably only 800 square feet, Quint occasionally rented it out for up to six guests, but Holden wasn't sure how six people could move around in the snug space.

There were no electrical wires—the stove and fridge ran on propane, and a generator hardwired to the small dwelling provided enough power for a microwave, a few lights and a couple of outlets. It wasn't a fancy spot, but Quint and Clinton kept it in good shape. Wondering what Griselda thought of it, he turned to look at her for the first time since she'd buckled his seat belt.

She was staring at the cabin through the windshield. "It's like a doll's house . . . or an enchanted cottage. I almost expected it to be made of candy."

He couldn't help grinning, because of course Griselda would romanticize an old hunting cabin into something charming and whimsical like an enchanted doll's house.

Looking back through the windshield, he saw it through her eyes: small and charming, like something out of a fairy tale.

"I guess," he said.

"I like it," she said softly. She unbuckled her seat belt but stayed put.

Since she'd leaned over him to buckle his seat belt, and he'd warned her that he was on the brink of kissing her, she'd kept her distance. The way she'd scooted back across that seat like her ass was on fire told him something too: he was right about her not wanting to jump into anything with him, and he was right about practicing patience and self-control so he wouldn't scare her away.

Still, a thread of hope wouldn't be denied entirely. She had kissed his neck this morning, hadn't she? Yes. And she had wrapped her arms around his neck in Target, pushing her body against his. She was attracted to him—of that he was certain. But she'd also told him that she was confused. And he didn't want to add to her confusion. He wanted her to be comfortable with him. Time and patience, he reminded himself, reaching down to unbuckle his belt too.

He turned to her. "Well, I guess we should . . ."

"Yep. I'll get the bags and groceries. Why don't you just go rest a bit?"

"I can help—"

"Nope. I insist. Go rest. Get a nap. I'll wake you up for hot dogs in an hour," she said, offering him a little smile.

"You sure? I feel a little bad leaving you to do everything."

"Do I look like I mind?" she teased.

You look beautiful. You look amazing. You look like the girl of my dreams.

"Nope," he said. "You look as strong as that little girl who somehow made it across the Shenandoah."

She flinched, sucking a deep breath into the back of her throat. Her eyes widened, stricken, and her lips parted with a gasp. "Holden—"

He realized his mistake immediately. They hadn't talked about her escape yet, and he saw the immensity of her guilt change her face as he mentioned it so offhandedly. "I don't mean that in any bad way, Gris. That's just the last way I remember you."

Her lip trembled. "I should have . . . I should have stayed. I should have turned back," she said, her eyes welling with tears. "I'm sorry. Holden, I'm so damn sorry. I shouldn't have run."

"N-no," he said, reaching for her shoulders and making her face him with a small jerk. "D-don't you *ever* say that to me. Not ever again. You got away. Do you have any idea how grateful I am that you escaped? I am going to thank God every day for the rest of my life that you got away and lived and found me again." Tears streamed down her face, and he felt his own eyes burning in communion with hers as his fingers curled into her shoulders. "I told you to run, and you ran. You ran, and I'm g-glad, Gris. I'm happy you made it. I'm n-n-not s-s-sorry and I'm n-n-not—"

"Breathe," she said, tilting her head to the side until her cheek rested against the back of his left hand. She closed her eyes, letting go of the breath she'd been holding.

Holden watched her, savoring the touch of her soft cheek pressed against his skin. It took every last reserve of his strength not to run his hands down her arms and pull her against his chest. But he didn't. He'd wait for her. He'd wait forever if that's what it took for her to invite his touch, to want it.

Finally she opened her eyes, taking a deep breath and smiling at him. A relieved and happy laugh made her shoulders shake a little as she stared back at him like something magical had just happened, and Holden would swear that, from now until the end of his life, he'd never see anything more beautiful than Griselda smiling back at him in that moment.

"Thank you," she whispered, her tears still streaming. "Thank you so much, Holden. Thank you."

"For what?"

"For forgiving me."

He shook his head. "There's nothing to forgive."

"There is," she whispered, turning her face just a little to press her lips to the back of his hand.

"Gris," he ground out, the sound painful and pleading.

She looked up, nodding at him, as though remembering herself, then righted her head as he quickly slipped his hands from her shoulders.

Taking a deep, ragged breath, she used her palms to wipe her face and turned to him. "Doll's house?"

"Yeah," he said, fishing the keys out of his jeans and handing them to her. "You go on in."

She nodded, letting herself out of the truck. And Holden watched her go, begging God and every angel in heaven for more than just a month with her.

***

Holden was lying down in the back bedroom, so Griselda took her time placing their clothes on an empty shelf in the linen closet between the bedroom and bathroom, and unpacking the groceries. Quint had purchased a few luxuries for them—in addition to milk, mac and cheese, and a loaf of bread, he'd included a dozen eggs, some fresh berries, a package of chicken legs, and a box of frozen hamburgers. Rifling through the kitchen cabinets, Griselda also found some basics, like flour, sugar, cooking oil, and spices. She grinned, thinking that she could dip the chicken legs in beaten egg, then dredge them in flour, and fry them up. It wouldn't be the fanciest feast, but it had to be better than hot dogs, and if memory served, Holden loved fried chicken.

Pulling the canister of flour down on the counter, she rummaged through a cabinet beside the propane stove for a frying pan. Finding one, she placed it victoriously on the stove. She felt like singing, like dancing, like living. Like *living*.

Looking out the window over the sink, at the meadow of sweet wildflowers, she paused, breathing deeply and acknowledging the brutal and massive weight that Holden had just willingly and lovingly lifted from her shoulders. For most of her life, she'd felt guilty about two terrible things that she'd done: getting into Caleb Foster's truck, and running across the Shenandoah River without Holden. And now, in the space of minutes, he'd relieved some of her burden.

Leaving the frying pan, flour, and chicken for a moment, she crossed the small living room and headed out the front door and into the field. She couldn't remember the last time she'd felt so lighthearted that she could take pleasure in something trivial or beautiful, so tears fell from her eyes as she leaned down to pull bluets, buttercups, black-eyed Susans, and white aster into a wild and colorful bouquet. Bringing the warm blooms to her nose, she breathed deeply, then looked around at the field of flowers, the trees in the distance, and the bright sun shining down on her slick, upturned face.

"Thank you," she whispered, watching the drifting clouds break up the clear blue of the summer sky with thick puffs of cheerful white.

Turning back to the house with her bouquet, she wished there was a way to love Holden how he wanted to be loved, instead of the way she did. But the truth she was forced to acknowledge was that she had never seen Holden as a brother, and he'd always been more than a friend. She loved him in a way that was necessary, not luxurious. She loved him like the tide loves the sand—trapped together, one lost without the other, pushed and pulled, but never ripped apart. She loved him in a deep and singular way, almost as though God had crafted one heart in heaven, then split it between Holden's body and hers, fating her to a never-ending longing to be with him, or a fractional life without him.

She sat down in one of the rocking chairs on the small porch, propping her feet up on the railing and wondering if he felt this way about her, or about Gemma, or about anyone at all. And was he capable of loving someone like this? He'd stayed with a monster like Caleb Foster until he was seventeen, then he'd returned to West Virginia, the site of their abduction and captivity. At some point, he'd started working a job he didn't appear to care very much about, lived in an apartment that was one step above a hovel, and beat up other men for money. And the tally marks on his arm. She winced, thinking about them, about the stark and vicious loneliness that would make him keep looking so desperately for someone to assuage it.

Swallowing over the lump in her throat, she closed her eyes and let the warm afternoon breeze fan her cheeks and the scent of wildflowers soothe her aching heart. He'd given her the most incredible gift today in easing her terrible regret. Desperate to return that kindness, she vowed—again—not to get between Holden and Gemma. If Gemma filled the hole inside Holden, Griselda was grateful for her and would do nothing to jeopardize or endanger his happiness.

***

Waking up to the smell of fried chicken and the sound of singing, Holden kept his eyes tightly closed, convinced that he was still dreaming, because he had no one to make him fried chicken, and the singing voice sounded strangely like Griselda's.

"I'm living in a kind of daydream . . . I'm happy as a queen."

Someone was singing "The Very Thought of You," an old song that Griselda's grandmother had loved more than any other song.

"And foolish, though it may seem . . . To me? That's everything."

Sometimes, when Caleb Foster had left for Rosie's and they lay side by side in the darkness, she would sing it to him, and he still remembered every word.

"The mere idea of you . . ."

"The longing here for you," whispered Holden, blinking his eyes to open them, and looking around the tiny bedroom in

225

confusion before the events of the last two days came rushing back to him.

He was in Quint's cabin.

Griselda must be making fried chicken.

And Griselda was singing.

"You'll never know how slow the moments go 'til I'm near to you . . ."

Staring up at the ceiling, his eyes watering with tears, he smiled. This was the stuff of dreams: his amber-haired, blue-eyed girl coming back from the dead and banishing every shred of devastating loneliness from his life with her warmth and stories and off-key voice singing poetry while she fried chicken in the tiny kitchen of a remote hunting cabin. Too fantastic to be true. Too heartbreaking to be real.

Sitting up carefully, he was relieved to find that his nap had chased away a good bit of the aching in his hip and chest, and even his face wasn't throbbing very much anymore. His heart was a different story.

Now that they were here together, all alone, out in the middle of nowhere, it was going to be harder than ever to keep himself from advancing on her. Glancing down at his hand resting on his thigh, he felt the impression of her lips pressed against his skin and groaned softly. The next time she did something like that, he was just going to come out and say it: "Unless you want my hands on your body, you need to stop doing that." Then she could skitter away, but at least she'd have been duly warned about his intentions.

"I see your face in every flower, your eyes in stars above. . ."

This girl. Everything about this girl made him want, made him long, made him yearn to *change* his life, *start* his life, finally *live* his life after a decade of going through the motions. He wanted to get a better job to take care of her. He wanted to stop fighting because she disapproved of it. He wanted enough money to have every tally mark lasered from his arm. He wanted some sort of guarantee that she'd never, ever leave him again. And he wanted all of it now. Yesterday. Ten years ago, and every day since.

Standing up slowly, he let his body settle into an upright position before taking his time crossing the hall to the bathroom and then heading out into the common room.

She stood at the stove with her back to him, her feet bare, her hair in a ponytail, the mouthwatering smell of fried chicken filling the entire cabin with goodness. Holden leaned against the wall, crossing his arms over his chest, a grin taking over his face as he watched her.

"It's just the thought of you—the very thought of you, my love," she sang, using a fork to transfer a golden leg to a paper towel–covered plate.

As she reached forward to turn off the stove, some of the leftover grease in the frying pan spat up at her and burned her wrist.

"Ow!" she yelped. "Damn it!"

With a sudden rush of adrenaline, Holden crossed the kitchen in two strides. He turned on the faucet and grabbed her arm to thrust her wrist under the cold stream. He held it there, wincing at the red blotch developing on her white skin. When he lifted his eyes to hers, she was staring at him with a surprised, curious expression.

"It's just a little burn."

He shrugged, still holding her arm, staring down at the burn.

"You were asleep," she said.

"You were singing."

"Too loud?"

"No."

"You remember that song?"

"I remember."

He slid his palm down her arm to cradle her wrist from below.

"The stove's still on," she said.

Without dropping her hand, he took a step closer to her, reached around her waist with his free hand, and flicked the burner off.

"I made fried chicken," she said softly, her cheeks flushed.

"I can smell it."

"You like fried chicken. I mean . . . you must have mentioned it to me a hundred times when we were—"

"It's still my favorite."

They were both silent for a few seconds, and Holden knew he should drop her hand and step away from her, but he couldn't. She'd hurt herself doing something kind for him, and it just about shredded his heart.

Just another moment, he told himself. *A few more seconds touching her and then I'll move away.*

"Sorry about the singing," she whispered, unmoving, her breath kissing his throat.

He jerked his neck to face her, his thumb curling into her palm, his eyes searching hers for mercy.

"I loved it," he murmured.

She stepped forward, closing the distance between them, her lips parting, her breasts grazing his chest through his T-shirt as she stared up at him.

"Holden, I . . ."

Every breath she took seemed to draw him closer to her, as if she was breathing him, not air. He leaned forward, into her, his free hand reaching for hers.

"G-Gris . . ."

Her eyes, dark blue and churning, flicked to his lips, lingered there, then slid back up his face and seized his.

His self-control snapped.

After all, he was only human.

CHAPTER 19

Tilting his head, his lips landed flush on hers as his fingers slipped between hers, folding, binding their hands together. She pulled her hand out of the water, wrapping her arm around his neck, and sinking her wet fingers into his hair. His free arm encircled her waist, crushing her against his chest as his tongue traced the seam of their lips. She opened for him, touching her tongue to his and swallowing his groan as he squeezed her fingers, pushing her against the counter with his body.

Releasing her hand, he lifted her onto the countertop beside the sink, reaching back quickly to turn off the water. She parted her knees so he could step between them, and his hands landed on her hips, his fingers kneading her skin through the denim of her jeans. Wrapping her other hand around his neck, she locked her fingers together while sliding her tongue against the velvet heat of his.

He dragged her roughly to the edge of the counter, fitting the softness of her pelvis flush against the hardness of his. She raised her legs and locked her ankles behind his back, whimpering softly as he sucked on her tongue.

His hard chest pushed into hers, every deep and gasping breath crushing her breasts as her fingers broke free from each other and tangled frantically in his hair, trying to push him closer, closer, as close as possible. His fingers slipped beneath her T-shirt, skating up her back to unfasten her bra, as his tongue stroked hers into a frenzy.

Spreading her fingers in the silk of his hair, she leaned her head to the side, guiding his mouth to her jaw, letting her neck bend back as he kissed a path from her lips to her throat. His palm curved around her ribs, the pad of his thumb stroking the pillow of her breast, finding her nipple and massaging it into a tight, aching point. His other hand followed, cupping her breast and rolling her other nipple between his thumb and forefinger.

"Holden," she moaned, arching her back to slam her hips into his and whimpering when his fingers increased their pressure on her overaroused skin. He pushed her shirt and bra up over her breasts, baring them, and Griselda raised her arms so that he could lift them over her head.

Panting with want, her hands dropped to the hem of his T-shirt, shoving it up over the ridges of muscle until he grabbed the shirt at the back of his neck and whipped it over his head, throwing it to the floor.

For just a moment, half naked with each other for the first time ever, they were still, his bare chest a shadow away from hers, grazing her sensitive, straining nipples with every breath. With his hands at his sides, he held his breath and stared into her eyes, searching them, waiting for something.

And then she knew—somehow she knew. He was waiting for her. For permission.

"Yes," she gasped, her palms landing flush on his cheeks as she jerked his face to hers, their teeth clashing together as his tongue tangled with hers, the heat of his chest slamming into the heat of hers.

His hands were suddenly under her bottom, and he lifted her effortlessly into his arms, kissing her deeply, madly, blindly, like the world would end if he stopped, and she wound her hands in his hair, the past and the present colliding into a moment she'd dreamed of since she was a child. Keeping her legs locked firmly around his waist, he carried her from the kitchen into the back bedroom and lowered her onto the bed, following her down, covering her body with his.

Her hands slid down his body, tracing the angles of his collarbone, the deep groove of his spine, the tight band of muscle at his waist that flexed under her touch. She felt the texture of a hundred scars crisscrossing his flesh, evidence of Caleb Foster's fury and Holden's willingness to protect her time after time. Tears blurred her vision as she slipped her hand into the waistband of his unbuttoned jeans and under the elastic of his underwear, her palm landing on the hard, hot skin of his ass. Her fingers flexed on the taut skin, and he gasped, stealing the air from her lungs and making him laugh softly.

"Gris," he said, leaning back from her, his elbows on either side of her head, his hands gently cupping her cheeks. His face was a mixture of emotions: tenderness, surprise, arousal . . . and concern. His smile faded as his brows knitted in worry. "Are you sure about this? Oh G-God, Gris, I w-want . . . I want you so much, but I don't want to hurt you."

She knew the truth of his words because, in all her life, the only person who'd never hurt her, never let her down, was Holden. And yet, time and again, she had hurt him. And here she was, lying beneath him, tempting him to cheat on his girlfriend when he'd been trying so hard to be good.

She pulled her hand out of his pants, holding it suspended awkwardly in the air for a moment before letting it land tentatively on his back. The tears in her eyes trickled down her cheeks as she turned her face to the side, away from his trusting, searching eyes.

"G-Gris? What is it? Gris?"

His fingers brushed her damp cheeks tenderly, and she pulled her bottom lip between her teeth, clenching her eyes shut.

"I don't want to hurt *you*," she said.

"Are you afraid you will?"

She turned back to him, opening her eyes. "I want you too, Holden. I want you so much. It feels like I've wanted you forever."

His lips quirked up a little, and his worried eyes softened. "Then . . ."

"But you have a life. You have a girlfriend you love."

He looked confused for a moment, then narrowed his eyes. "Gemma?"

She swallowed, nodding miserably. "Gemma."

He stared down at her chin before capturing her eyes again. "You think I love her?"

She wet her lips, willing herself to stop crying, because she didn't want to make this more difficult for him. "You've been with her for six months. She sleeps in your bed. She has a key to your apartment. You're . . . together. I don't want to ruin that for you. I've already done so much to hurt you. I couldn't bear it if . . ."

Holden's eyes closed slowly, and he dropped his hands from her face, rolling off her chest to lie beside her. He released a loud, low, barely controlled sigh.

She couldn't hold back the tears anymore, because she was so desperately emotional about him, and this rejection—even though she'd suggested and encouraged it—was more painful than she'd anticipated. They streamed down her cheeks as she stared up at the rough wood ceiling, feeling miserable.

Then, when she least expected it, she felt his fingers touch hers, reach for hers, effortlessly weaving between hers, his palm adjusting and readjusting until it was flush with hers, joined between them.

"Griselda," he said, "I don't love Gemma. I don't even like her that much."

Her relief was so visceral, the dam of warmth pooled in her belly broke forth, flooding her insides with heavenly release. She sighed, taking a slow, deep breath, and letting her bunched muscles relax.

"You don't love her," she breathed, exhaling with a small sound of pleasure.

"No."

"But you've been together for months."

"We've been *fucking* for months. That's all."

"Ah," she sighed, her relief changing from a warm and soothing feeling of deliverance to a gathering, like a seed of anticipation that grew rapidly, making her heart speed up and her sex ache, throbbing to be filled by his.

"I don't . . .," he paused, his body rigid beside her. "G-Gris, I'm not sure I know how to love someone. Sometimes I feel like that part of me is . . . b-broken."

"It's not," she said with certainty, rolling onto her side and resting her cheek on her arm to stare at his face in profile. Her need to touch him, to continue where they'd left off a moment before, made shivers of want break out across her skin, changing her breathing, further quickening her galloping heart.

"How do you know?" he asked, hope breaking his voice.

"Because I know. Because I know *you*. Because I know your heart. Because that part of you might be hidden, but it isn't gone."

It was his turn to flinch, before scrubbing his hand over his forehead. "What about you? You're with someone too. Jonah. You're living with him."

"I don't like him either," she said without thinking, licking her lips as she focused solely on Holden.

"We're both with people we don't even like," said Holden, reading her mind. "Do you have any idea how fucked-up that is?"

Yes. But we can change that. Starting right now.

"I'm not with Jonah anymore," she said, her voice soft and even. "And I'll never be with Jonah again."

"Why not?" asked Holden, his voice low and his eyes

fierce as he rolled onto his side to face her.

"Because for the rest of my life," she said, dropping his eyes to gather her courage before lifting her chin and spearing him with her gaze, "I only want to be with you."

***

Her words knocked the wind out of Holden's lungs, and he inhaled sharply, staring at her in shock, and realizing that she was right: he *was* still capable of loving someone. Some deep and hidden part of him recognized this was true because the feeling that welled up inside him was so much bigger than love, so much wider and stronger, and filled with so much grateful, intense wonder, there wasn't another word to describe it.

Kissing her for the first time a few minutes ago, touching her breasts and sliding his hands along the warm softness of her skin, had felt glorious, but it had also felt like stealing something. He'd been aroused beyond belief, but he'd felt guilty too—like he was taking something that she hadn't offered. And now, here she was, the girl of his dreams, telling him that she belonged to him. Telling him that what he was taking was already his. Telling him that she wanted only him. Forever.

"Oh God, Gris. M-me too," he said. "I'll break up with Gemma as soon as we go back to Charles Town. It's over. It was over the second you walked back into my life."

"I'm ruined for anyone but you, Holden. I always have been."

He thought of the marks on his back and the marks on his arm, the countless nights spent looking for an antidote to Griselda's iron hold on his heart, even from the grave. "M-me too. I'm ruined for anyone but you."

"So we'll try this?" she asked, her eyes searching his with a heartbreaking, hopeful uncertainty that made him desperate to reassure her, to let her know how deeply and irrevocably he would love her for the rest of his life if she would only give him the chance—the honor—of being with her. "Being together?"

"We've always been together," he whispered reverently, reaching for her, his fingers landing on the bare skin of her waist and pulling her close. She was soft, so soft and warm, and his heart thundered in anticipation of finally having her. "Even when we were apart, we were still together. Even when I thought you were gone, you still lived inside my heart."

"I never gave up hoping that I'd find you," she said, flattening her hand over that heart, which beat wildly for her. "There were times . . ." She winced, swallowing painfully. "There were times it was the only thing keeping me alive."

Her admission crushed him because he was no stranger to that desperation, and he exhaled the breath he was holding, leaning forward to rest his forehead against hers, nuzzling her nose with his as his lips brushed hers tenderly.

"Is this real?" he whispered, his eyes glassy and burning. "Is this finally real?"

"This is real," she said, reaching for his cheek to pull him closer and kiss him more deeply.

She rolled onto her back, and he followed her, pressing her into the mattress and swallowing her moan as he moved their locked palms over her head. Plunging his tongue into her mouth, he stroked hers with increasing urgency, and she arched her body against his, her breasts flattening under his chest muscles as he surged against her, pushing his erection into the softness between her thighs. His free hand skimmed down her side to cover her breast, and she gasped. Sliding down her body to take the rigid point between his lips, he swirled his tongue around her nipple before sucking it into his mouth.

"Holden," she moaned, burying her hand roughly in his hair, her fingers pulling the strands, curling into his scalp to keep him in place.

Grazing her sensitive skin with his teeth, she cried out, and he released her hand, covering her slick breast with his palm as his mouth drifted over the valley of warm skin to find its twin.

As he teased it with his tongue, Gris whimpered again, her little noises of pleasure making him hotter and harder, his dick throbbing with the need to bury itself inside her.

"Are you wet, Gris?" he growled, blowing on her nipple and watching as goose bumps rose on her pink, flushed skin. "Are you wet for me?"

She whimpered as he slid his hand over the soft skin of her belly, opening the button of her fly with a quick flick of his fingers and smoothing his flat palm under the elastic of her panties. His fingers skimmed over her trimmed, curly hair, unable to keep himself from anticipating the way she would tease and tickle him as he moved in and out of her body. Clenching his jaw, he slid his middle finger between the slickened folds of her clit, finding the erect nub of hot flesh and loving the way her hips rose off the bed to meet his touch.

"Jesus," he murmured, his thumb pressing her bundle of nerves like a button as he slipped two fingers inside her slippery sex. She was soaked and ready for him, and they'd only just gotten started.

He didn't want to go fast with her—he wanted to savor every moment—but the way she writhed under him, and the way his dick pulsed with every movement, made him rethink his plan. She needed him and he needed her. Romance could wait. Right now, he just needed to be inside her.

"Gris, I want you," he said, stroking her intimately and looking up to watch the play of pleasure and emotion on her beautiful face. She was so fucking perfect, the muscles in his stomach clenched and his chest hurt, *hurt*, with how much he felt for her.

With his fingers still lodged inside her, she leaned up, reaching for his jeans and pushing them down to his hips. His dick—long, thick, and hard as a rock—caught on his boxers, and he slipped his fingers out of her to reach down and release himself from his clothing.

She gasped, either from the loss of his fingers pleasuring her, or because he was finally naked before her. His raised his eyes to hers, watching her lips drop open as she stared down at him.

"Holden. Oh my God . . ."

He was big. He knew this not because he'd seen a lot of naked men with whom to compare himself, but because her reaction was fairly commonplace for him. The follow-up ranged from delight to fear, but the initial reaction was always one of mouth-dropping surprise.

He watched her face as she stared at him, trying to read her reaction, his heart throbbing with hope, then swelling with relief as she looked up at him with dark blue eyes. She licked her lips and demanded, "Get my jeans off. Now."

She lay back, and he reached for her fly, yanking it down. Slipping his fingers into the waistband of her jeans and panties, he pulled both down her legs with a jerk, throwing them to the floor.

Settling back over her body, naked together for the first time in their lives, he lined up his heart over hers, his hands sliding down the sheets to find and bind their fingers together. He looked deeply into her eyes, and she parted her legs so he could settle between them.

"I was tested six months ago," he said, hating that he had to mention it, but anxious for her to know that he was careful.

"Gemma?" asked Gris.

"We use condoms. But I . . ." He paused, feeling a little like a selfish prick without knowing her birth control situation. "I don't want to use one with you. We *c-can* . . . but, I just—"

"I don't want to either. I have an IUD," she said, raising her knees and locking her ankles on the back of his ass. "I want to feel you."

"Are you sure, Gris? I fucking w-want you right now more than I've ever wanted anything in my life. But unless you're sure

. . ."

"I don't know what will happen after this," she said, her dark eyes full of tenderness and uncertainty. "What happens after this?"

"I'll make you come. I'll hold you while you sleep. I'll change for you. I'll live for you. I'll never let you go," he promised, capturing her top lip between his and kissing her.

Her eyes glistened with tears when he drew back, and she squeezed his hands. "Promise me?"

"I p-promise, Gris."

"Breathe," she said, arching her pelvis into him to let him know she was ready.

He braced himself over her, positioning himself at the slick, pulsing opening of her sex, then paused, holding her eyes. "Gris, ask me if I'm whole or broken."

She gasped as he pushed slowly, inch by inch, into the heaven of her hot, wet sex. She panted softly, "Holden, are you . . . whole . . . or broken?"

He clenched his eyes shut, his arms shaking as he tried to control himself. The sensation of her sucking him forward was fucking unbelievable, but he moved as slowly as he could, savoring every moment of their joining, of the moment he became one with Griselda in every possible way. And finally the tip of his erection could move no farther. He was fully lodged inside her. He was one with the only woman he'd ever loved, could ever love, would ever love.

His dick pulsing, his heart throbbing, he opened his eyes and found her dark blue ones staring back at him with such trust and tenderness, he flinched and almost wept.

"I'm whole," he whispered. "*You* make me whole."

Tears filled her eyes, spilling out of the corners and into her hair as she palmed his cheeks, frantically pulling his face down to hers. He pulled out to the entrance of her sex, then plunged forward again, moving slowly and gently, anxious not to hurt her, reveling in the tender nerve endings of their bodies, stroking and kissing as his lips devoured hers.

Her palms smoothed over his rough back, and he felt her fingers curl into his skin, her fingernails making him flinch as he pulled back slowly then pushed carefully into her again with a groan of pleasure, a sheen of sweat breaking out across his brow.

"It's okay," she panted, releasing his lips and bending her neck so her head strained back into the pillow. Her dark eyes owned him. "I won't break. I want you, Holden. I need you. Take me home."

He bent his head, his damp forehead landing on her shoulder as he moved faster, the friction from his movements and the hot fucking noises from the back of her throat making him swell inside her. Her legs locked around his waist, and her arched body took him deeper and tighter with every thrust. He felt the swirling beneath his abs, the way every muscle bunched and tightened, the way his dick started vibrating inside her, and then she screamed his name, the walls of her sex pulsating around him like fucking heaven.

Staring at her beloved face, contorted in ecstasy, he felt it—the marriage of past and present, the walk on a country road, fairy tales told on a crowded cot, her eyes in the sunshine, her parted lips, stubborn heart, gentle soul. He paused at the precipice for only a moment before stepping forward into forever, letting go, opening his heart and releasing his body as her name passed his lips and he surrendered to the inevitability that was his deep and eternal love for Griselda.

CHAPTER 20

"Do you know what 'Griselda' means?" he asked her, stroking the hair from her forehead, as they lay tangled together.

"No," she said, smoothing her hand over his chest and breathing deeply. The small room smelled like sex, and she wanted to memorize the smell of her body belonging to his.

"It has two meanings. One is 'dark battle' and the other is 'gray fighting maid.'"

Kissing the warm skin between his pecs, she rested her lips on the tiny foot of the angel inked there.

"You're both," he continued, his fingers making leisurely runs from her temple to the ends of her hair, then back again. "You won the dark battle because you're a fighter."

Griselda took a deep breath and thought about his words. "I don't feel like much of a fighter."

"Why not? You're the strongest woman I ever met, Gris. Ever."

She rested her arms on his chest, her cheek on her forearm, gazing up at him. "My life . . . it doesn't look so good."

"Hey," he said, his eyebrows knitting together as he slipped his hands under her arms and dragged her up his body. "D-don't say that."

She gave him a small smile. "I admit, it's improved quite a lot in the last few days, but . . ."

"But what?"

She tilted her head to the side, her smile fading. "I was in a shitty relationship with a pretty awful person. I have no ambition, no future, no education, no prospects. I have one real friend, and she doesn't even know . . ."

"...what happened to us?"

Griselda shook her head. "People know what they read. 'A girl escaped her abductor after being held captive for three years. The boy she was with is still missing.' After I escaped, they took me back to D.C., but other than giving them the approximate location of Caleb Foster's farm, I didn't tell them much about our time there. They sent me to a therapist, but I just . . . I didn't want to talk about it. I didn't want to relive it all. And then when they came and told me you were gone without a trace? I never opened my mouth about it again. To anyone."

"Why not? Might have been good for you to talk about it."

"I left you, Holden. I left you there. I left you with a monster, and I ran away."

"I told you to run. I'm glad you ran, Gris." Holden paused for a moment. "He shot at you, didn't he?"

Griselda's eyes welled as she remembered. "I told him he was going to hell. He said, 'You first, Ruth.' I was screaming at him that you weren't Seth and I wasn't Ruth, but he raised that gun and fired . . . and I ran."

"You didn't run when I told you to run?"

She shook her head. "No. Not right away."

"J-Jesus, Gris! He c-could have—"

"I've thought about it a million times, Holden. I don't know for sure, but I don't think he wanted to kill me. He shouldn't have missed the shots he took, but he did. I just think he had this crazy notion that he could save you from me, and needed me out of the way."

Holden took a deep breath and sighed. "I figured it all out, you know."

"Seth and Ruth?"

He nodded. "Yeah. I put it all together. He talked about it a lot, but it wasn't as crazy as when we were at his place. Not as much Leviticus," he said, laughing softly and bitterly. "More just . . . his memories. All mixed up, though, thinking I was really Seth."

"They *were* his brother and sister, right?"

"Yeah," said Holden. "Several years younger than him. Twins. When we left, he brought this old box of pictures with him. I looked through them a lot, piecing it all together.

"The pictures were square with muted colors, and old. They were stamped with dates from the seventies. An older brother standing beside two younger siblings, you know, like headed to church on Easter or something. The three of them in a backyard. On the porch of that house. Caleb was the oldest and tallest, and then Seth and Ruth would stand beside him, always holding hands.

"I noticed something, Gris. In every picture with the three of them, there was a small gap of space between the twins and Caleb, like a boundary. And in every picture, Seth stood in the middle beside Caleb, never Ruth. There were several pictures of Caleb and Seth together, and in those pictures, Caleb looked like a totally different person . . . like, resting his elbow on his little brother's head, or his arm around Seth's scrawny neck, smiling down at his little brother with, like, pride and love. And you know, Seth looked happy too. Not joyful, and maybe a little wary, but okay.

"But, Gris, in the pictures of Seth and Ruth? Seth *glowed* with happiness, his eyes soft with secrets, or with adoration or something, when he stood beside Ruth. Their hands were always bound together, and nine times out of ten, Seth smiled at Ruth while Ruth smiled for the camera. She was real cute. Like you. Full of life and hope with big wide eyes. He was . . . crazy about her."

Holden paused as Griselda wrapped her head around this information. "Do you think they . . ."

"Yeah," Holden breathed. "I think they were in love with each other. I'm sure of it."

Griselda winced as she digested this. A brother and sister in love with each other? It was unnatural. Wrong. How had it happened? Or was that a mystery that would never be solved for her and Holden?

"C-Caleb caught them."

"What?" she gasped, her mouth dropping open as her eyes cut back to his.

Holden nodded. "He caught them having sex. I don't know how old they were . . . teenagers, I guess. Fifteen, maybe sixteen. They were a churchy family, very devout, strict parents. From what I could gather, I'm pretty sure he kept it a secret for Seth. And I think it destroyed something inside Caleb. Seeing them together. Knowing about it."

"And he killed them."

"I don't know." Holden shrugged. "The box with the pictures had an old clipping about it. That barn we did the canning in? That was rebuilt after the original barn burned down. They found a bracelet of Ruth's in the ashes. 'They were burned in the fiery pits of hell.'"

Griselda shivered as Holden's eyes held a faraway look for several more seconds before coming back to earth and focusing on her.

"Holden . . . you sounded just like him."

"He said it all the time," said Holden dismissively.

"He killed them," she said. "I know he did." She rested her cheek on his chest, just below his neck, and wrapped her arms around his chest. "We were next."

"Maybe. Probably. Which is why I'm so glad you ran, Gris." He leaned down, pressing his lips to her head. "I'm so fucking g-grateful you got away."

Griselda took a deep, shaky breath as she closed her eyes. "He killed them. He killed his own brother and sister, and he would've killed us too."

***

As she settled back down on his chest, Holden resumed stroking her hair, and soon her breathing was deep and even, and he knew she was asleep.

The warmth of her skin pressed against his made him want her again, but he didn't want to wake her up. She needed sleep and he needed to let her sleep because he intended to have her over and over again until he was so far under her skin that she wouldn't be able to leave him at the end of a month. That was his plan anyway.

Making love to her had rocked his world, shifting it on its axis, and making his life without her wither away like an untended garden. She was his light and water—his sustenance and hope, and he wanted to forget the years that came after the Shenandoah and before yesterday. He ached from so much lost time when he could have been with her. Glancing at his arm, he winced, imagining the tally marks magically floating off his skin and dispersing into the wind like dust, until only one remained— the only one that would ever matter.

He hated that he'd shared that experience with so many before her, and yet, in a strange and twisted way, he'd always shared it with her. Because she was whom he wanted, dreamed of, longed for. He'd always dreamed of her at the moment he fell apart. And now the dream had come true. It was her hot sweetness surrounding him, her lips moving under his, her soft breasts crushed under his chest. She was real, and she was his.

She moaned in her sleep, and his hand, which had stilled, moved quickly to her crown, smoothing her amber hair lovingly, and she snuggled closer to him, knees bent against his hip and breath fanning his chest.

He loved her.

God in heaven, how he loved her.

It wasn't that he didn't know how to love anymore, as he'd feared. It was that he didn't *have* anyone to love until Gris reappeared in his life. And now that she had, his only wish was to never be parted from her.

Sighing deeply, he thought about their conversation, zeroing in her words—*He killed them, I know he did*—and hating it that his mind felt so conflicted about her conclusion. It confused Holden that he couldn't immediately jump on that bandwagon. Caleb deserved accusations and hate—his behavior to them had proven him capable of atrocity—and yet Holden wasn't actually sure that Caleb had killed his siblings, or if their accidental death had pitched him into a madness wherein he believed they'd gotten their just desserts for engaging in incest. Had he engineered the fire? Or had the twins been sleeping in the barn and died accidentally when a lamp got kicked over? Had Caleb murdered them willfully? Or had he been plagued with guilt for keeping the secret that killed them? Holden wasn't sure. He never had been.

He'd thought about saying as much to Griselda, but she would never understand that his feelings about Caleb were less cut-and-dried than hers. He hated Caleb, of course, but he also felt a deeply unwanted protectiveness toward Caleb that he was ashamed of—that made him feel perverted and twisted and weak. Further, he felt a sympathy for Caleb that he couldn't completely abandon either. It was deep-seated, maddening but constant. He felt guilty that he didn't hate Caleb as much as he should. He felt sick with himself that he felt compassion for someone who was very likely a murderer and definitely a kidnapper. He felt disgusted that any part of him should feel protective of the man who claimed to have killed Griselda.

But Caleb had also kept him alive.

And once they left West Virginia—once Caleb perceived that Holden had been "saved" —he hadn't been cruel to Holden anymore.

Caleb was a monster, yes, but he was a principled monster in his own way, which made it difficult for Holden to hate him with Gris's blind fury. He wished he could because eventually she'd sense the conflict in him. She was already upset by his admission that he'd stayed with Caleb until his death. That wasn't even the worst of it, because she'd probably decided that he was somehow coerced. He hadn't been. He'd stayed because he had nowhere else to go, and because his life with Caleb hadn't been as bad as it could have been.

Holden dropped a hand to his heart. He'd have to figure out a way to help her understand because if he couldn't, surely he would lose her.

Breathing deeply, he closed his eyes, concentrating on the warmth of the beloved woman draped over his chest, and praying that when the time came, he'd be able to make her understand.

***

"Seth, you gonna call me?"

He finished zipping his jeans and looked up at her, trying to remember her name. Fuck. His dick was still slick, and he had no fucking clue what her name was.

"Uh, sure."

She pulled up her panties and straightened her dress, crawling to the edge of the pickup and holding out her arms like she wanted him to help her down. He turned away from her, and after a minute, she got down on her own.

"Junior prom is next week. You taking someone?" she asked.

Fuck no.

"I'll, uh, t-take you home," he answered, ignoring her question.

She'd smiled at him over the Cheetos when he stopped in at the Super-7 Gas 'n' Sip for a pack of Camels twenty minutes ago. All it had taken was a lift of his eyebrows in invitation, and she'd joined him in his truck, where they snacked on Cheetos and she told him her life story before he boned her senseless in the back.

"Maybe I don't wanna go home yet," she whined. "Where you from anyway?"

He got into the driver's seat, opening the pack of cigarettes and shaking one out. Holding it between his lips, it took him two shitty convenience store matches to light it, and he sat back, giving her a couple of minutes to decide whether or not she wanted a ride.

He'd taken the truck from the parking lot of Grady's, Caleb's watering hole of choice, and he intended to have it back there by eleven, when Caleb generally started for home. Maybe tonight Caleb'd kill himself on the bridge as he made his way back to the double-wide they shared at a mobile home park just out of town.

Whatever-her-name-was decided she wanted the ride, and as she opened the passenger door, Seth looked away, taking a long drag on his cigarette. No matter how many girls spent time in this truck with him, only one had ever mattered: the first girl who ever sat next to him in the front seat. Blue eyes flashed in front of his face, and Seth winced, burying them.

"You gotta pick up your brother later at Grady's?" When he didn't answer, she decided to get mean. "My daddy says he's real strange."

Holden turned over the ignition.

Fuck her.

And fuck Caleb.

"You don't say much," she sighed as they pulled out of the lot behind the Super-7. "Go left up here. But you fuck real nice."

Seth drove in silence for several minutes, hoping she'd shut up for the rest of the ride. He felt dirty and disgusted, and the hole inside of him was bigger than ever.

"'N-n-nother l-left?" he asked, stopping at a stop sign and waiting for her to tell him how to get to her house.

"You wanna fuck me again sometime?" she asked, running a finger down his arm.

Honestly? He couldn't care less. It would be her or someone else, and whoever it was, she wouldn't matter.

He shrugged.

"Left," she said, a pissed-off tone creeping into her voice. "You know, I'm just trying to be friendly. You show up here outta nowhere in the middle of junior year acting real quiet and a little retarded, and living with a brother who looks like your grandpa. You might try being a little nicer. Just sayin'." She huffed softly when he didn't reply, crossing her arms over her chest. "Up there. Second house on the right."

Seth pulled up in front of a crappy little house, with three cars out front and a Christmas reindeer on the scrubby front lawn, even though it was May. His mother had always taken their decorations down by New Year's, he recalled, clenching his jaw, and pushing the image of her pretty freckled face from his mind.

The girl turned to him, her eyes narrow. "You know what? I take it back. You don't fuck nice. You fuck too hard, and your dick's too big. Freak."

Then she flounced out of the truck and slammed the door.

And Seth, who didn't have much more than a big dick going for him, peeled out of her driveway, hating her, hating Caleb, hating himself, hating this disgusting fucking joke of a life.

He laid on the gas, going faster, though the little roads were small and curvy in this neighborhood. He blew past a stop sign and onto a main road, pressing harder on the gas and watching the speedometer move to 75 . . . 80 . . . 85 . . . He'd never driven so fast in his life, and a smile curved the edges of his mouth. Woods whooshed past him on both sides, and he rolled down the window to let the wet, cold Oregon air into the cab, taking a drag of his cigarette before tossing it out the window.

The speedometer needle kept moving . . . 90 . . . 95 . . . 100 . . . Out of the corner of his eye, he saw massive trees. Trees that had been there for a thousand years. Trees that would wreck a truck on impact if it was going a hundred miles an hour, and kill whatever sorry thing was breathing inside it.

He channeled every bit of strength in his sixteen-year-old body and pushed so hard on the gas pedal that his foot ached. The needle rose to 110. He took his hands off the wheel and closed his eyes, a dreamy, ethereal feeling coming over him. He was going to go home. In a minute, he'd be with her again. With her, and his mother, and his father, and his grandmother. He'd be with all of them again. He could see her face as clear as day, feel her fingers woven through his, hear her voice in his ears . . .

Holden, are you whole or broken?

Stone to stone. I jump, you jump.

Keep your fingers over the letters.

The loud blare of a semi horn roused him from his daze. His eyes shot open, and he blinked at the oncoming headlights, slamming on the brake. The truck bucked and shuddered as it slowed down, skidding on the damp road, out of control until the last second, when Holden jerked the wheel and managed to get out of the way of the oncoming sixteen-wheeler. He was drenched with sweat and crying like a baby as he pulled over on the side of the road.

After an hour of useless sobbing, he returned the truck to Grady's and stepped into the tattoo parlor next door.

And that night, for the first time in years, he fell asleep with his fingers over the letters once again.

***

His eyes opened slowly, and then he gasped, because, *oh my*

God, his dick was surrounded by heat and wet, and, holy shit, nothing had ever felt so good.

Looking down, he saw Griselda's hair spread over his abdomen, golden and gleaming in the afternoon sun streaming through the window. Her lips held him tightly as her tongue worked his tip, and he clenched his eyes shut, thrusting his head back on the pillow.

"Gris," he groaned.

Her mouth stilled, and when he looked down, she'd moved her hair to the side and was grinning up at him, his fat dick still in her mouth.

"Relax," she said, before sucking purposefully as her hand held his shaft in place.

He tried to. He truly did. Because normally a blow job from a beautiful woman was something he'd just lie back and enjoy, but as good as it felt, what he really wanted was to be inside her again.

"Wait," he panted. "Wait . . . can we . . .?"

She slid her mouth off of him, her face a little confused as she caught his eyes. She ran the back of her hand over her glistening lips. "You don't want me to?"

"I do," he said quickly. "Definitely. But I miss you. I want to feel you. I want to hold you."

She'd been kneeling between his legs, but now she scooted up, straddling him with her knees on either side of his hips. Her full breasts swung lightly with the movement, and he stared at them, his mouth watering to taste them again.

"You want me . . . here?" she teased, still holding his rock hard dick by the base, her hand moving ever so slightly, pumping him, driving him crazy.

"I want to be inside you," he told her, keeping his eyes open, though they threatened to roll back in his head.

She leaned up on her haunches, positioning his erection beneath her, then sank down, impaling herself fully with a combination sigh and moan that rose from the back of her throat.

"I'll do anything for you," he pledged, blinking his eyes as he reached for her hips.

Griselda leaned forward and kissed him, her breasts flattening against his chest as she slipped her tongue into his mouth. He clutched her against him, lifting his hips to pump into her as their tongues tangled, tasting each other, swallowing each other's sighs. When she leaned back, Holden reached forward to palm her breasts, watching her eyes flutter closed as he pinched her nipples, driving up into her faster and faster, loving the way her breath hitched and panted, coming out faster and more jagged.

Feeling the pressure build deep in his pelvis, he jackknifed suddenly, wrapping his arms around her as she locked her ankles around his waist. Leaning down, he took her nipple in his mouth and sucked hard enough that she screamed his name, her sex flooding and convulsing around him, pulling him higher, sucking him deeper. He bellowed her name into the sweet, damp skin of her neck, holding her tightly as he climaxed, pulsing in waves, emptying himself.

"Gris . . . Gris . . . Gris . . .," he murmured, kissing her neck as her limp body sagged against him. "I didn't know it would be like this."

"I did," she said, leaning into him, her wrists crossed at the back of his neck.

He rested his forehead against her chest, his arms like iron bands around her body. "I love you," he said, the words passing through his lips like a blessing, like a benediction.

"I know," she whispered in a breaking voice. "I love you too."

He clenched his eyes shut, overwhelmed by the simple sweetness of her words, the truth in them, the comfort of them, the rightness of them in his ears, the eternal yes of them.

Shifting them carefully back down on the bed without

breaking their connection, he stayed deeply embedded in her as he stroked her hair from her face.

"I've always loved you, Gris."

"Me too," she said, softly but certainly, a little smile touching her eyes. "Always."

"You won't leave me?" he asked.

"Never."

"We'll stay together," he said.

"We will."

"And get married."

She nodded.

"And have babies."

A tear snaked down her cheek as she nodded again.

"You want babies?" she asked, giggling and crying at the same time.

"I want yours. I want our kids to be safe. I don't want anybody to ever hurt them. I'll keep an eagle eye on them, Gris. I'll make sure they have somewhere to go if anything ever happens to us. I'll love them just as much as I love you. I'll take care of them. I p-promise."

"I believe you," she said. "Holden?"

"Hmmm?" he asked, a contentedness and security he'd never known making him warm and drowsy.

"I'm hungry."

"Pretty sure my woman made some fried chicken earlier," he said, kissing her lips tenderly.

"Yes, she did."

She pulled away from him, and he missed her warmth immediately as she rolled to the edge of the bed, sitting with her back to him.

He felt her uncertainty suddenly and wanted to reassure her. "We'll be okay, Gris. We're together again, like we always should have been. W-we'll be okay now."

Looking at him over her shoulder, she smiled sadly. "I

hope so, Holden."

Then she stood up, grabbed her jeans off the floor, and left the room.

CHAPTER 21

Griselda plated the food, and they ate at the kitchen table—a feast of cold chicken and apple slices washed down with ice-cold well water—and all the while they traded shy, happy, knowing glances, staring at each other, then looking away, shaking their heads with low, bemused laughter, both quietly delighted and just a little overwhelmed by what had just happened between them, by the words they'd spoken and the promises they'd made.

Holden wore nothing but unbuttoned jeans, and she stared at his chest—his strong, beautiful, sculpted chest that memorialized her loss—as much as she liked, biting her lip when he caught her, then giggling when he threatened to take her on the kitchen floor if she didn't stop.

His eyes were soft with love, but alive with wonder, and every moment she spent with him, he looked more and more like the boy she'd known so well and loved so much. She could have happily watched him forever. Heck, she thought as she rinsed the dishes, that was the plan, wasn't it?

As she stood at the sink tidying up, Holden went outside to the truck. When he came back a few minutes later, Griselda placed the clean plates in the drying rack by the sink and turned to look at his sweet smile, and noticed both hands were hidden behind his back.

"What you got behind your back, Holden Croft?" she asked, her eyes teasing.

His cheeks reddened a little as he showed her a notebook and three pens, holding them out to her.

Her eyes flicked questioningly from the items in his hand back to his face.

"It's a gift. Maybe a d-dumb gift, but I thought . . . well, I thought you could write out some of your stories while we're here."

The lump in her throat was so immediate and huge, she dropped his eyes, trying to swallow over it, but it made her own eyes burn with tears. He'd gotten her a gift.

With shaking hands, she reached for the notebook and pens, staring down at them as one fat tear rolled down to the tip of her nose and splashed onto the notebook cover.

"Gris?" he said, reaching out to tilt her chin up. "You okay?"

"I love them," she whispered, clutching them to her chest and trying to get herself under control. "No one's . . . I mean, I haven't gotten a gift in . . ."

He flinched, leaning forward to kiss her tenderly before drawing her into his arms, the notebook and pens trapped between their hearts.

She felt foolish for crying. It was such a kind, thoughtful gesture, and she was ruining it with self-pity. But aside from the homemade birthday card that Prudence had made for her this year, and the extra fifty dollars in her paycheck at Christmas and on her birthday, Griselda didn't receive gifts. Not now. Not ever. Not from her mother, not from her grandmother, not from any of her foster parents, not from Maya, and certainly not from Jonah. Not counting the extra money from the McClellans, she hadn't received a gift since . . . well, since Holden had handed her a bouquet of buttercups on her thirteenth birthday, almost ten years ago.

"Get used to it, Gris," he said against her hair, still holding her tightly. "I'm going to get you presents whenever I want to. W-whenever I feel like it. I'm going to give you so many presents, you'll barely remember what it felt like to have none."

She could feel him clench his jaw against her temple, a sign that her tears were making him emotional too.

"My daddy used to give my mama gifts all the time," he continued. "He'd come home from work with a flower or a candy bar. Sometimes he'd go into a department store and collect free perfume samples. They didn't have much, but they took care of each other. And that's how I'm going to be. I'm going to take care of you."

With every bit of her heart, Griselda wanted to believe him, wanted to trust that after a lifetime of fear and loneliness and abandonment, it was possible to finally be happy. But just like before, when he'd said, "We'll be okay now," something inside her was skeptical. Part of her doubted she deserved happiness. Another part insisted that as much as she wanted it, something bad would happen, because something bad always did. Unlike Holden, Griselda had never had a good example of a loving relationship. All she'd ever known was turbulence, and as much as she wanted something safe and solid with Holden, she wasn't entirely sure how to get there.

"So what do you think?" he asked her, leaning back to look into her eyes and swiping the last tears from her cheeks. "Want to write down a few stories?"

"You remind me of Mrs. McClellan," she said, sniffling through a deep breath, then grinning at him.

"How so? She as handsome as me?"

"Full of yourself."

"The most beautiful girl in the world was in my bed all afternoon. I get to be cocky."

She rolled her eyes at him, gesturing to the porch with her chin and reaching for his hand. "Want to sit outside a while?"

He let her lead him outside. He scooted his rocking chair next to hers, and they both leaned back, letting the low sun warm their faces as they rested their bare feet side by side on the rough-hewn railing.

Griselda closed her eyes, breathing in the scent of wildflowers and fresh air. "Mrs. McClellan wants me to go to college."

"College?" he asked in surprise. "College. Wow. That would be something, Gris."

"I can't afford it."

"We'll figure it out," he said softly, and she marveled at his words, unable to stop the terrifying burst of hope in her heart that sang, *I'm not alone. I'm not alone anymore.*

"I have a little money," she said, realizing that her Holden fund was now available to be spent. "Not enough for college . . . but almost thirteen thousand saved."

He was silent for so long, she opened her eyes and turned to him. He stared at her in awe.

"You're rich," he said.

"It was all for you. To find you. I was saving up for this private investigator in New York. Supposed to be the best."

"For me?" he asked. His fingers reached for hers and squeezed. "You d-didn't give up."

"Never."

"Well, I think you should go to college, Gris."

She shrugged, looking down at the notebook. "I don't know. Some colleges have writing programs, you know? For people who like writing stories. And Mrs. McClellan talked a little bit about scholarships. I don't know, though. I don't know anyone who ever went to college except for her."

"You shared your stories with her?" Holden asked.

"I make them up for Pru. I guess she overheard."

Holden grinned, squeezing her hand again. "I love that."

"So does Pru."

Drawing her hand away from his, she opened the new notebook on her lap and uncapped one of the pens. She opened the cover, and wrote neatly in the middle of the first page:

FAIRY TALES

by Griselda Schroeder

She stared at her name, wondering what it would feel like to really see her stories in a book, in print, to know they were read to children before bed, ensuring sweet dreams. One of her foster mothers, Kendra, had told her she was good with kids, and Mrs. McClellan thought she had talent. Of course, Holden, who'd always loved her stories, would encourage her. Maya would get on board too. But was it actually possible to change your whole life like that? To make your dreams come true?

Her stomach clenched, and she closed the notebook, looking out at the flowers. It was simply too much good at once. She didn't trust it. She wished she could, but she didn't. Girls like Griselda didn't get new beginnings and happy endings—it was safer to anticipate disaster than embrace happiness. And yet . . .

She turned slightly to look at Holden, whose head was back against the chair, eyes closed. The bruises around his cheek and eyes had improved a lot since yesterday. The discoloration over the lid was already gone, and though the reddish black below his eyes was still visible, it was turning yellow now. His cheek was still swollen, but like his eyes, the discoloration was already improving. His lips—lips that had touched hers so lovingly all afternoon—were pillowed and perfect, and his nose and cheeks were dotted with freckles. Just over the left side of his lip, closest to her, there was a larger, darker freckle, and suddenly she longed to kiss it, to own that tiny part of him just in case she ever lost the rest.

"Holden?" she asked softly, still staring at his face. "Why'd you stay so long with Caleb Foster?"

***

He was grateful that his eyes were closed so she couldn't read them as his stomach dropped. He'd known this question was coming, of course, but he dreaded having to answer it. He could barely get his own head around the conflicted feelings he had for Caleb. He didn't know how to explain them to Gris.

He took a deep breath, turning to her and opening his eyes slowly. Her face, so beautiful in the golden sun, made his lungs freeze with fear and longing, and he held his breath before letting it out with a hiss.

"I'll try to explain," he said. "W-will you try to understand?"

She nodded slowly, her body shifting in her rocking chair to face him. His eyes dropped briefly to her breasts then skated up to her lips, praying that those parts of her wouldn't be forever off-limits to him after this conversation.

"K-kiss me first?" he asked, a feeling of panic almost choking him.

"Tell me first," she answered, sitting back, staring away from him, out at the meadow.

So he did. He told her about waking up on Caleb's front porch, a fresh grave in the front yard, blood on Caleb's shirt.

"He told me you were d-dead. He changed our names. I was c-crying for you, so he knocked me out again," he said, his hand instinctively touching his temple. "When I woke up, it was n-nighttime and I was sitting in his t-truck. I don't know where we were. Somewhere in western West Virginia, I guess. Maybe K-Kentucky. The first few w-weeks . . . I don't r-remember them all that w-well.

"D-during the day, we'd drive. S-sometimes we'd s-sleep in the truck. S-sometimes he'd get a motel room. When we s-slept in the truck, he handcuffed me to the s-steering wheel. When we s-slept in a motel, he handc-cuffed me to the bed. Said I needed to be ch-chained up until R-Ruth had loosed her power over me."

"Holden," she said softly, and he turned to her, watching tears run down her face.

"He drank a lot. M-most nights. Wherever we were. He'd ch-chain me up first so I couldn't run." He looked at Griselda, feeling stunned by the force of the memories, that dead feeling he'd lived with for so long coming back to him as he relived those days. "N-not that I would've run."

"Why not?" she asked, her face contorting with confusion as she smoothed her tears into her hair.

He wanted to touch her, wanted to hold her, but he didn't dare reach for her. It was hard to keep talking, but he did his best to explain.

"B-because inside . . . I was d-dead." He swallowed. "You were g-gone. My f-folks and gran were long g-gone. Didn't m-matter what he d-did to me. I didn't c-care."

"What . . . What *did* he do to you?" she asked in a terrified whisper.

"He fed me," said Holden, looking out at the wildflowers. "He gave me a place to s-sleep." He swallowed the lump in his throat. "He never t-touched me wrong."

"But he still beat you?"

Holden shook his head, clenching his jaw. "Only w-when I mentioned you."

She was silent as she absorbed this. "He just . . . stopped?"

"Yeah," said Holden, nodding. "He said he'd c-cut the c-cancer out of our lives, and I was s-saved."

"Because I was dead."

Holden finally turned to her and whispered, "Yeah."

Her forehead creased as her eyebrows furrowed together in confusion. "Did you . . . God, Holden, did you . . . *like* him?"

"Sh-short answer? I hated him."

"Long answer?" she asked.

"It's c-c-complicated," he said, his heart racing faster as he tried to figure out how the fuck to explain his actual feelings.

"I need to hear it," she said, her voice low and thick, her tears still falling. "I want to understand."

Holden swallowed painfully, clenching his jaw before nodding. "In his m-mind . . . he thought I was Seth. He truly b-believed it. And he truly b-believed that killing Ruth would save Seth." He winced as he looked at her. "I know it sounds c-crazy, but in his own way, he was p-protecting me . . . uh, Seth.

"When we went to diners, he'd order his food, then turn to me and ask, 'What'll it b-be, little b-brother?' all p-pleased and p-proud that I was w-with him. And the waitresses would look back and f-forth between us, at the age difference, and s-sometimes s-snicker, and I'd f-feel . . ." He felt the old anger surge up. ". . . *mad*. B-because he was just t-trying to . . . you know . . ."

She'd dropped her glance to her lap halfway through his remembrance, but now she looked at him, her face white and destroyed. "He wasn't," she paused, taking a deep breath, "your *brother*. He *abducted* us. He *tortured* us."

"You th-think I don't know that? I was th-there, Gris." He shifted in his chair suddenly, showing her the crisscrosses of mangled scar tissue on his back. "You th-think I d-don't remember? I remember!"

He turned back to find her red-faced and furious.

"Do you? 'Ye'll live in darkness till yer evil ways is purged! Till yer worthy o' the light.' Remember that? 'Can't be no cleft in yer remorse! For the wages o' sin is death!' Death! *My* death!" she ranted, tears streaming down her face.

"I kn-know the f-fucking words as well as you!"

"Then how? How could you feel . . . *affection* for him?"

"It w-wasn't f-f-fucking affection!"

"What was it then? When those waitresses snickered? What was it? What was it when you thought of him shooting me in the back?"

"Hate!" Holden screamed. "F-f-fucking hate!"

Birds that had been sunning on the roof took flight, their wings beating against the warm summer air, seeking sanctuary.

"Well. You sure as hell didn't hate him enough to leave."

"I was th-thirteen years old, ch-chained to a bed or steering wheel every n-night of my f-fucking life for two years. Even if I c-could get away, where the f-fuck was I going to go?"

"Back to D.C.?" she suggested angrily.

"B-back into the system so someone like M-Miz F-Fillman could m-m-molest me in my sleep?"

"Not all foster parents are molesters," said Griselda, her voice losing some of its conviction.

"Enough are," answered Holden. "Or d-drunks. Or they b-beat on you. Or they f-forget to f-feed you."

"Fine. The system isn't paradise. But it had to be better than staying with a child abductor! An abuser! A crazy fucking madman!"

"I was *d-d-dead* inside. Everyone—*everyone*—I had ever loved was d-dead," he said, his voice breaking and eyes burning. "He didn't b-beat me. He f-fed me. I had a warm place to sleep. By fifteen, we were settled in Oregon, and I enrolled in high school."

"As Seth West," she said.

Holden nodded.

"You took his name."

"After t-two years with him? What the f-fuck did it matter?"

"It mattered because your name was Holden. Maybe I could have found you if you'd still been Holden."

"You couldn't have f-f-found me, Gris, because you were f-f-fucking *d-d-dead*!" he yelled. He took a deep breath as she stared back at him, their gazes in a deadlock.

She stood up, dropping the notebook on the chair, her face disgusted and sad and furious. "I'm going for a walk. Don't follow me."

"D-don't f-fucking leave. Gris, talk to me!"

"I can't," she said, putting her leg over the railing and following it with her other, and his heart clenched because he suspected it was so she wouldn't have to risk touching him as she passed by his chair.

"Please," he said softly to her retreating form, but she never turned around.

***

Griselda walked purposefully through the meadow, refusing to look back at him despite his quiet plea, which threatened to break her fucking heart in half.

Not only had he stayed with the Man, but he'd developed some sort of—what? Holden refused to call it affection, but it sure as hell felt like that!—*softness* for Caleb Foster. Almost as though some part of Holden had believed himself Seth West and had accepted Caleb Foster's protection, and even, when snarky waitresses giggled at them, returned it.

This was the man who had abducted them, tortured and terrified them, whom Holden believed had killed Griselda, murdered her in cold blood and buried her. She'd been dead only two years, and Holden was living it up with Caleb, eating his food, sleeping in a space he provided, going to high school like the holy hell of West Virginia had never even fucking happened.

That's not fair, her heart whispered gently, interrupting her inner tirade.

She stepped out of the meadow and into the woods, the not-too-far-away sound of a stream drawing her to the left.

He'd been kidnapped too—*because of you!* her heart reminded her—and he'd endured more than his fair share of beatings. He'd been brave, but she knew he'd been as terrified as she. He'd tried to escape and failed while she had succeeded. He'd essentially been abducted again, this time alone, with no one for comfort, and his dearest friend dead. He said he'd felt dead inside, and Griselda believed it, her tears falling faster as she imagined his thin wrist shackled to the truck wheel, to motel beds, freedom close but never possible. He'd reminded her that he was only thirteen, still a child, and he'd lost everything and everyone that mattered to him. And yes, he could have escaped and gone back to the system, as she suggested, but he was right. She flinched, remembering Mrs. Fillman's hand on Billy's thigh at the park. Holden, with his blond hair and all-American freckled face, would have been easy prey.

Caleb Foster fed him, offered him a warm place to sleep, didn't beat him, and eventually let him attend high school like a normal kid.

She couldn't imagine it had been a good life, but she knew, as he did, that it could have been worse.

The sound of trickling water was louder now, and she came on the stream she'd been seeking—not too wide across, maybe fifteen feet, and not too deep either, but clear and clean, with some big rocks for sitting by the shore. She sat down on one, took off her sandals, and stuck her feet in the water.

I'll make you come. I'll hold you while you sleep. I'll change for you. I'll live for you. I'll never let you go.

Did she believe him?

I'm whole. You make me whole.

After these revelations about Caleb Foster, could she trust him?

I've always loved you, Gris.

She sobbed, and her body came alive as she thought of the reverent way he'd touched her, looked at her, made love to her.

You won't leave me? he'd asked. And she'd answered, *Never.*

And she meant it.

She'd held on too long, hoping to find him again, and finding him was too miraculous, too right, too good to give up, because he'd succumbed to some fucked-up version of Stockholm syndrome. She could allow him to have some gratitude to Caleb Foster for keeping him alive.

And then it occurred her.

Despite everything Caleb Foster had done to them, she had to admit, she felt some gratitude too.

She was grateful that Caleb hadn't shot and killed Holden that day. She was grateful that he'd taken care of Holden so Holden *didn't* run, ending up in some fucked-up foster family that could have broken his spirit. She was even grateful that Caleb had taken such good care of his truck so Holden could return to West Virginia.

She'd long held the belief that Caleb was an irredeemable monster, and he was, but she also couldn't deny that things could have been worse for Holden. He could have been killed. He could have been further abused. He could have been starved or trafficked or any number of other unthinkable horrors. Instead, as Holden pointed out, he'd been fed, he'd had a place to sleep, he hadn't been beaten anymore, he hadn't been molested. He'd survived.

Her lip twitched in objection because she despised Caleb and didn't want to humanize him, but once the window to that train of thought had been opened, she couldn't close it. The Holden who had made love to her today was, in some part, a product of the care he'd received from Caleb during their years apart, and for that she could be grateful.

"Still pissed?"

Startled, she looked up to find Holden standing behind her.

"I told you not to follow me," she said, turning back to the river.

"Not good at listening to directions, I guess."

"Obviously," she said, slipping her sandals back on and standing up to face him. He'd thrown on a long-sleeved flannel shirt and buttoned two buttons, but his feet were still bare and his jeans were still undone.

He looked at the river, eyes narrowed. "What if you came

across someone out here? Some perverted hunter who wanted to hurt you?"

She gave him a sidelong glance. "You might be feeling better, but you still have two bruised ribs. You're not in any shape to be my protector. You're weak."

"Like hell," he said, his eyes flaring.

She huffed. She didn't want to be mean to him, but it would take a little time to understand what had happened to him and how it had made him into the man he was now.

"I hate it that you stayed with him," she said.

"I know. Sometimes I do too."

"But I can also understand. What Miz Fillman was doing to Billy . . . I'm glad that didn't happen to you."

"I didn't like him, Gris," he said gently, reaching for her. He put his arm around her waist, pulling her against his chest, and she didn't resist him. "I was a broken kid. And yes, he was evil, but to my mind he was the least of possible evils." He sighed against her hair, holding her tighter. "So I stayed."

"I don't want to judge you for it."

"Then don't," he said. They stood silently for a while before he spoke again. "I'm not weak. I want to take care of you, Gris."

"I can take care of myself," she said softly, unwilling to surrender completely.

"I'm strong," he whispered near her ear. "Let me do it instead."

She let her muscles relax against the warmth of his chest, cherishing the solid comfort of him, memorizing the feel of him holding her so tenderly. Placing her cheek on his shoulder, she looked out at the river.

"It's an awful lot to digest, Holden. So much has changed all at once."

"So take your time," he said, one hand rubbing her back. "We've finally got time, Gris, and I ain't g-going anywhere."

CHAPTER 22

Minutes turned into hours, hours into days, into the end of their second week together, which found its own fragile identity, its own tentative rhythm.

During the day, Griselda sat in the rocking chair on the little porch, filling her notebook with stories that she read to Holden in the evening. Many nights, he'd make a fire in the fireplace, and they'd sit side by side on the futon as she read, his arm around her shoulders, his lips kissing the top of her head whenever he felt like it.

They hiked in the woods daily, swapping stories about their lives in the time they'd been apart, and occasionally sharing a happy memory from when they were together: the times they'd seen wildlife on Caleb Foster's property; their birthdays, which they'd celebrated quietly together in the dark cellar; and the couple of times Caleb had tripped over their chains and knocked himself out for a few hours.

They held hands. They kissed. They held each other and laughed. They held each other and cried.

They visited the little stream many times, soaking their feet in the cool water, picnicking on the rocks and skinny-dipping. More than once, Griselda stole Holden's clothes and ran back to the cabin through the woods, jumping into bed, breathless and sweaty, giggling and naked when he caught up to her there.

His injuries healed quickly, and by the beginning of the second week, his face looked almost normal but for some small spots of yellow, and while his ribs would needed a couple of more weeks to mend, they didn't ache anymore. The doctor had advised Holden that his stitches would dissolve in about six days, and sure enough, they had. He wasn't a hundred percent yet, but he was certainly on his way. He hadn't started working out again—Griselda had forbidden it—but he'd found an ax in the cabin, and he was aching to get outside and chop some wood, use his muscles, feel strong and whole again.

Especially because he'd finally listened to the messages left on his phone by her fucking asshole of an ex-boyfriend. He'd been checking his messages, deleting texts from Gemma without reading them and writing back to Clinton, who asked how he was doing. He remembered Griselda's request that he not listen to Jonah's messages before deleting them, but his curiosity got the better of him and he listened anyway.

Part of him wished he hadn't.

Jonah's hateful voice, calling Gris a bitch, a cunt, and fucking garbage, made Holden's fist curl with rage as he listened in disbelief, tamping down the murderous instinct to get in his truck, drive to Maryland, find this dickhead, and beat him until his mouth and fingers didn't fucking work anymore. He wondered in what other ways Jonah's aggression had manifested itself toward Griselda. Had he hit her? Had he beaten her? If Holden ever found out that Jonah had laid a hand on her in anger, he'd better start looking over his shoulder because Holden would be coming for him.

After he'd listened to the messages, he sent a text to Jonah's number: *She's done with you. You ever go near her again and I will end you, you cocksucking fuck. Seth*

Since then, Jonah had written back a steady stream of expletive-laden messages to Holden, a couple per day, mostly at night, calling Griselda and Seth every filthy name in the book. Holden didn't read them anymore, but suffice it to say that his foot was good and ready to find a home in Jonah's ass should they ever have the bad luck to meet in person.

It wasn't lost on Holden how fucked-up their sex lives had been—him, sleeping with anyone who opened her legs in an effort to exorcise Griselda from his life, and her, shacking up with a total asshole who appeared to have no respect for her, and zero concept of the amazing woman he'd been lucky enough to have in his arms.

It bothered Holden tremendously that Griselda would invite such a person into her life—and yes, into her bed— because he felt she deserved so much better. Better than Jonah, for sure. Even better than himself, lowly factory worker and fight club headliner that he was. It angered Holden that he didn't have more to offer her, but the more time he spent with her, the more he wanted to remedy that. He wanted to be everything to her: her best friend, her confidant, her support, her partner, her lover.

Her lover.

From the moment she'd walked back into his life, Holden had wanted her, as though sleeping together, joining their bodies in the most intimate possible way, would somehow bind them together. And in some ways, it had worked. Learning how she liked to be touched, moving inside her, watching her face as she climaxed—because of the depth of his feelings for her, it was like nothing he'd ever experienced before. And when she slept naked, curled up next to him, her head heavy on his chest, her hair soft and golden on his skin, Holden felt a peace he'd never known.

And yet he sensed her reluctance to commit to what was happening between them and what it could mean to both of their lives. When he tried to talk about what would happen at the end of their month together, she suggested they enjoy the time they had. When he mentioned college, she smiled, but she didn't engage in the conversation. When he asked about her life in Maryland and D.C., she glossed over the McClellans and her friend Maya, invariably changing the focus of the conversation back to him, like her real life was an off-limits topic.

He knew that they'd been reunited for only a couple of weeks, but he was anxious—and yes, perhaps unreasonably so—to know that she bought into the idea of a future together. And it frustrated him that, though her feelings for him seemed genuine, she didn't appear to trust that when he said he loved her, he meant forever.

He had two more weeks to convince her that this wasn't just a pause in their mediocre lives before they returned to reality. Holden truly believed that this month, reunited, spending time together, learning about each other, loving each other, was just the beginning of the rest of their lives. He'd do whatever it took to convince her of it too.

"You awake already?" she asked him, her voice still fuzzy from sleep.

"Sunshine woke me up," he answered, stroking her hair.

"Mmm. That's nice."

"What should we do today?'

"Mmm," she murmured, still half asleep. "More of this."

He chuckled, a low, satisfied rumble. She wiggled a little against him, and his dick sprang to life, growing and pulsing with every beat of his heart.

"Maybe go into town?" she asked, rubbing her breasts against his chest.

"Sure. If you want."

"I want," she purred, dropping her lips to his chest and sucking his nipple into her mouth.

"Ah," he gasped, his erection pressing urgently against her hip. "Gris, unless you want me inside you, you better stop."

She paused, looking up at him, her blue eyes sleepy but

tender. "Of course I want you inside me. I'd let you live there if I could. So you'd never be farther from me than . . . me."

It was a rare allusion to the future, so he took it and filed it away, feeling hopeful. Flipping her to her back, he settled his weight on his elbows and looked down at her. "How'd we find each other?"

"You were fighting in a field. I showed up."

"It was a one-in-a-million chance."

Her eyes drank in his face, resting on his eyes, then his cheek. "I hate it that you fight."

"I'll stop."

"But the money?"

The several hundred dollars he'd made at that fight had been financing their little retreat, and they both knew it. "I'll figure out something else."

She nodded, offering him a weak smile before looking at his lips despondently. He read her expression easily: uncertainty, insecurity, doubt.

"I will, Gris. For you, for us. I'll figure it out."

"I know you will," she said, but he could tell she wasn't convinced.

"You'll have to trust me."

"Not my strong suit," she said, arching her back a little so her breasts pressed into his chest, distracting him, which he knew was her intention.

"Work on it," he suggested, circling his hips, then drawing back to position his dick where she wanted it.

"Okay," she said, licking her lips, her eyes dilating to black with anticipation.

He slid into her slowly, staring deeply into her eyes, watching as they flinched, narrowed, fluttered, then closed, her head pressing back into the pillow as her lips parted with a gasp, chased by a sigh. He felt it too—all of it—the slick heat that meant she was ready, the subtle ripples in the walls of her sex that massaged him, the wonder of their bodies joining, the comfort of being as close as possible, the excitement of having her to himself for however long she welcomed him.

"I love you," he said through panted breaths, wishing she would open her eyes. "As long as we're together, we can figure it out. I . . . I'd do anything for you."

She wet her lips, pushing her head back into the pillow as he pulled out as far as possible before sinking into her again.

Whimpering, her fingers skimmed up the uneven scar tissue on his back, burying in his hair, and she leaned up, pressing her lips to his. Holden quickened his pace, his tongue plunging into her mouth as his sex merged relentlessly into hers.

His muscles started bunching just as the moans in the back of her throat got louder, and he demanded, "Tell me, Gris. Say it."

"I . . .," she panted, gasping and whimpering as her inner walls clamped down on his dick, sucking him forward with their pulsating contractions. "Oh God, I love you!"

Her words made his eyes burn, and he thrust deep inside one last time, yelling her name as he surrendered to heaven.

***

"You really want to go into town?" he asked her a few minutes later.

Griselda scooted to the edge of the bed and swung her feet over the side. "Mm-hm. We need a little food, and believe it or not, I need another notebook."

Writing down her stories over the past two weeks had become almost as addictive as Holden, giving her a purpose she'd never enjoyed so much before. In addition to the various characters she'd created for Holden and Prudence—Princess Sunshine and Princess Moonlight, Prince Twilight, Princess Stormcloud, Lady Starlight and the Sun King—she created a fairy tale world where these characters lived with sun, moon, and star fairies, and where the evil Glacier Queen and her minions of Freezites and Hailions threatened to steal every bright, warm, and beautiful thing from the Kingdom of the Sun.

Every day, as she stared out at the wildflowers, with Holden flipping through one of Quint's many birding books in the rocking chair beside her, she escaped to a world where her characters struggled to live and love, to survive and thrive together.

She loved it.

I love this cabin and these wildflowers.

I love every minute in Holden's arms and every second writing down my stories.

These are the best and happiest days of my entire life, and I will be grateful as long as I can have them.

But an underlying melancholy wouldn't leave her alone. She'd been unloved by her mother and never close enough to her grandmother for any real affection. She'd unwittingly orchestrated Holden's abduction and abandoned him to Caleb Foster as she escaped across the Shenandoah. Sooner or later, he'd rethink everything. Someday soon, the sex wouldn't be new anymore. They'd be all caught up on each other's lives. The surprise and wonder of their reunion would wear off, and when it did, he'd decide that he didn't love her anymore, that she wasn't worthy of his love. Even though she knew it was coming, it would break her in half when he walked away, so she tried not to let go of her entire heart. She tried to protect a small part so that she was able to bear it when he finally turned his back on her.

This can't last. This can't last. This kind of happiness can't be yours. Don't get too comfortable.

"Filled the whole notebook, huh? Well, I'm not surprised at all. The Glacier Queen sure makes things tough on the Sun King." Holden grinned at her. "So you want to shower first? Then we'll head into town?"

She nodded, slipping off the bed and stretching her naked

body in a thick, bright stream of morning sunshine.

"Keep that up, you won't get to the shower for another hour," he said, and though his voice was light, when she looked at his dark eyes, she knew he wasn't entirely kidding.

Winking at him, she headed for the tiny shower. She looked back just for a moment to see him take his phone off the bedside table and narrow his eyes at the screen.

And that was something else.

As much as he said he'd break things off with Gemma when they returned to Charles Town, she knew that he was still reading her texts. She saw Holden's eyes cloud over with anger and frustration as he typed into his phone when he thought she wasn't looking. It made her edgy. It made her wonder.

Sometimes she thought about Holden's tally marks—he'd been with so many women—and although he reassured her that she was the love of his life, she had to admit the marks bothered her. She mostly believed that he loved her right now, and certainly not one of the women represented on his arm, including Gemma, knew Holden in the same way she did, but it was a hell of a lot of tally marks.

She flushed the toilet and reached into the tiny RV-size shower to turn on the hot water, letting it warm up. She didn't believe that she was a conquest or a tally mark to Holden, but she cringed inside when he talked about the future or alluded to them staying together beyond the time they spent at this cabin. And she feared that his feelings for Gemma weren't quite as cut-and-dried as he let on. He'd been with her for six months. That had to mean *something*, right? Griselda appreciated that he *said* he'd break things off with Gemma, but until he did, she had to prepare herself for him possibly going back to her, didn't she? She'd be stupid and naive not to.

Winding her hair into a bun, she stepped into the shower, lathering her body with soap, the space between her legs tender from so much lovemaking.

She'd never had sex like the sex she had with Holden. It was the kind of sex written about in the trashy novels she and Maya used to sneak off Kendra's bedside table: tender, rough, hard, soft, fast, slow . . . heaven. All of her lived, and some of her died, in his arms, her heart swelling with the sort of love she'd barely thought possible, her soul withering with the thought that these days were finite.

But she had to face the possibility that living in a doll's house and writing fairy tales was just a beautiful fantasy, a vacation from the real life that would start up again the moment they headed home. Their lives wouldn't disappear just because they'd found each other. Gemma and Jonah, jobs and bosses, Clinton and Maya—they were all still there, waiting.

And Griselda simply didn't know how to reconcile the two lives.

Here, in the woods, clinging to each other every moment, they were Holden and Griselda, who had a unique history and deep emotional attachment. But out there? In the real world? They were Zelda and Seth. Jesus, the rest of the world didn't even know their real names. They lived two very different lives, where fairy tales and college and gray-eyed, sweet-smelling babies felt impossible.

"Gris? You almost done?"

"Almost," she said, turning around to rinse the soap off her body. "One more second."

One more second.

One more minute.

One more hour.

One more week . . . with you.

She took a deep breath and pushed her worries out of her mind for now. She refused to ruin the time they still had by letting her mind even consider the future. Might be they'd go their separate ways when it was time to leave the cabin. Probably, even. But for now, Gris belonged to Holden, and

Holden belonged to her, and if she had to, she'd live on these days for the rest of her life.

CHAPTER 23

Holden took her hand as they headed into the Food Lion in Berkeley Springs.

She'd been quiet after her shower, like something was bothering her, but she told him she was fine when he asked. Though he didn't believe her, he decided not to press it. He knew enough about women to know that when someone was "fine," she probably wasn't, but she wasn't going to tell you what was *not* "fine" until she was good and ready. So be it.

As they walked through the sliding doors, his phone buzzed in his back pocket. Once. Twice. Damn it, he'd meant to leave it at the cabin. Fucking Jonah was on a rampage today.

Griselda dropped his hand and looked up at him with wide, unamused eyes.

"Shouldn't you answer that? Might be important," she said all sassy, reaching for a shopping basket and charging into the store without him.

Fine. Hmm.

He caught up with her in the produce section. "Something wrong?"

"Your phone's been fascinating you all morning," she said, gazing at the bananas like she'd never seen one before in her life.

"We can't afford bananas," he said gently.

She picked one up and held it between her ear and mouth like a phone receiver. "Hello? Oh, Gemma! What an unexpected surprise. Your boyfriend? Of course. He's right here." She handed him the banana with a sour look, then turned on her heel and started toward the apples.

Holden stood frozen, staring at the bananas. Holy shit. She was jealous? Griselda Schroeder was jealous. He forced himself not to smile as he followed her to the bins of apples.

"How about *green* apples?" he suggested. "Like the color of your skin."

"And sour," she retorted, "like your girlfriend's disposition."

"Well, now," he drawled, "since my girlfriend's yelling at me in the middle of the danged Food Lion, I guess that's about right."

Her face didn't soften as she whipped around to face him, one hand on her hip, mad as hell.

"Why does she keep texting you?"

"You're assuming a lot."

"Oh . . .," she said, crossing her arms over her perfect breasts and raising her eyebrows in challenge. "It's *not* Gemma who keeps texting you?"

"Among others," he admitted, unable to lie to her, but not especially anxious to tell her he'd been trading several days' worth of insults with Jonah.

Her eyes flared open, dropping to the tallies on his arm, then back to his eyes. "Well, don't let me keep you from the . . . *others*!"

"F-fuck," he muttered as she sped away from him, realizing how she'd misinterpreted his words. He'd meant Jonah and Clinton, not other *women*, for Chrissakes. He had his hands full enough with her.

He followed in her wake, giving her a few minutes to shop solo and hoping she'd calm down. When she got to the frozen food aisle, he sidled up to her and nudged her with his hip. She didn't turn around.

"I didn't mean other *women*," he said to her back.

She huffed, opening the freezer door between them and leaning inside.

"Gris, I'm not talking to any other women, but I can't help it if Gemma texts me."

"You could've broken up with her."

He grimaced. Yeah, he could have. "Well, I didn't. We hadn't even spent twenty-four hours together yet. W-we hadn't even . . ."

She drew back, slamming the freezer door, and gestured at him with a package of frozen green beans.

"What? We hadn't even what?"

"W-well, hell, I didn't know how things were going to go with us. I was prepared to be friends if that's what you wanted."

"In which case you'd be glad you held on to Gemma? As a backup? For your . . . *needs*?"

"No. Hell." He stared at her, shaking his head slowly. "I can't win today. You getting your period or something?"

If he'd thought her eyes were furious before, they quickly changed to glacial. "Because the only excuse for my being pissed about your girlfriend sniffing around would be hormones?"

"Gemma's *not* my girlfriend." Holden swallowed. "G-Gris—"

"Uh-uh. You'd best tell *her* that, not me! You freely admit that Gemma keeps texting you, and you've been texting all damn morning, and you're *sleeping* with me. So pardon me if I don't like it. Why don't you go wait in the truck and leave me alone?"

She threw the green beans in her basket and started walking down the aisle again, and Holden stalked away in the other direction.

Twenty minutes later, she joined him in the truck. As soon as she sat down, he turned to her. "Your facts are wrong. I'm not texting her back. I've been deleting her messages!"

She buckled her seat belt with a loud click. "So . . . who?"

"Who *w-what*?" he spat, pissed that they were even having this stupid quarrel about nothing, as he backed out of the parking space.

"Who do you keep texting?"

"It doesn't matter."

She rolled her eyes and crossed her arms. "Eighty-somethin' tally marks says it does."

"They don't *mean* anything, Gris!"

"They do to me!" she yelled.

"F-fucking Jonah! Jonah, okay?"

She froze, her whole body going still.

"What?" she said, like he'd knocked the wind out of her with a sucker punch. "Wh—? Jonah? How? Why?"

"I listened to his f-fucking messages. I know I said I w-wouldn't. But I was curious. He's got a f-filthy f-fucking mouth, Gris."

He glanced at her, and she was staring at him, slack-jawed and wide-eyed.

"So I texted him if he ever came near you again, I'd d-do something about it."

Out of the corner of his eye, he saw her shoulders relax and her body deflate. "You been trading texts with . . . Jonah?"

Holden glanced at her, then dropped her eyes. He stared out the windshield at a red light and nodded. He was surprised to feel the soft, warm touch of her hand on his cheek.

"Look at me," she said.

He did.

He did, and this time all the air was sucked out of his lungs because this girl did things to his heart and his body with her eyes, with just a look.

"You ever going to stop protecting me?"

"No."

"Shoot. Jonah." Her lips quirked up a little, and she laughed so softly it was almost like a sigh. "I guess you're trading insults."

"He's an asshole, Gris."

She nodded but didn't seem to want to talk about Jonah. "I'm sorry I gave you a hard time."

"I'm sorry I made you think I was texting Gemma . . . or any other girl."

"I'm sorry I yelled at you."

"I'm sorry I listened to the messages when you asked me not to."

"I'm sorry I didn't trust you," she whispered.

The car behind them beeped, and Holden turned back to look at the road as she dropped her hand from his face. "We'll be back at the cabin in two minutes, Gris, and I have some things to say. You're going to listen, you hear?"

"Okay," she said, folding her hands in her lap.

He pulled onto the dirt road that led to the cabin, and a moment later he cut the engine, parking in the gravel by the porch.

"Come on."

"Where we going?"

"Come on," he said again.

He got out of the truck and walked around to her side, holding out his hand to help her down. She took it, and he pulled her into his arms.

"You listening to me?" he asked, his lips close to her ear.

"Mm-hm," she murmured, leaning into him.

"I need you to listen g-good, now."

"I am. I promise."

"You don't want me to fight? I won't fight. You want me to break up with Gemma? She's gone. You want me to quit my shit job, give up my apartment in Charles Town, and move to Maryland? Done. You want to go to college? I'll make it happen.

"I've been half d-dead for ten years, Gris, but then you walked back into my life, and I came alive again. You make me want to live. You make me want to be a better man.

"I love you, and when I say that, I mean that you're my reason for breathing, for eating, for drinking, for sleeping, for *living*. I will *never* hurt you. I will *never* leave you. I will *always* protect you. There is no one more important to me than you, and as long as I live, there never *w-will* be."

Her shoulders were shaking when he finished. She wrapped her arms around his neck, pulling his face close and pressing her lips to his, her salty tears mixing with the taste of him. This was a different kiss than the others they'd shared—it was sad, yes, but it wasn't tentative. In its own glorious way, it felt like a kiss of surrender, of Griselda finally believing that he belonged to her and only her, and that she could start to trust her feelings for him, and their commitment to each other.

She rested her cheek on his shoulder. Her face turned into his neck, her lips close to his skin.

It took him a second to realize that she was saying something very low.

"What, angel?"

"I got into the truck first," she sobbed so pitifully it was almost like a child's terrified whisper. "I got you abducted, and then three years later, I left you there while I escaped."

"No, baby—"

"I deserve every bad and dirty thing I get. I ruined your life. I did that to you, Holden, and someday when the shock of me being alive wears off, you're going to look at me and hate me for it."

He held her closer, tighter, until he could feel her heart thrumming against his, the short sobs of breath fanning his neck as she wept. As clear as day, he heard his own words from long ago in his head, *I w-won't ever hate you again. I p-promise, G-Gris.*

"I can't hate you. I already promised."

She sobbed harder, taking a ragged breath that made him clench his jaw, scrambling for a way to make her see that whatever bad had happened as a result of getting into Caleb Foster's truck so long ago, it didn't matter. The good in Griselda, in them together, outweighed the bad one million to one.

"Gris, listen," he said, leaning back to look at her. She kept her eyes down, tears of shame and sorrow streaming down her face. "You gotta hear my w-words."

"I just . . . I'm so sorry, Holden . . ."

"Listen to me, because this is the truth, Gris." He tilted her chin up with his finger, capturing her eyes and making sure she was focused on him. "You saved my life."

"No—"

"You saved my life," he said firmly. "Four times now, you've saved me."

"That doesn't even make sense."

"It does."

She shook her head in defeat, so he continued.

"You saved my life at the Fillmans because, for the first time since my g-gran died, I felt connected to someone. To you. And pressing my arm against yours in that stupid station wagon made me feel . . ." He shook his head, searching for the right words. "Alive."

"That's not—"

He cut her off. "I wouldn't have survived the cellar without you."

"You wouldn't have *been* in the cellar without me."

"Woulda coulda shoulda," he shrugged. "Doesn't matter. What matters is that I *was* in the cellar, and you were there with me, and having you there k-kept me alive."

"Holden, you're twisting—"

"No, I'm not. I'm telling you *my* truth, the truth of my life as I see it. Third time? When you ran, we both survived. Gris, think back. Think back to that day in the garden right before we escaped. We were sure he was getting ready to k-kill us. And if you hadn't run, if you'd come back with us, he probably would've, because he could see what we meant to each other and he hated us for it. Instead, you ran . . . you got away, and he believed I was saved. If you hadn't run, good chance we'd have both been dead a long time ago. You ran, and it saved b-both our lives. Certainly saved mine."

She was still shaking her head, so he cupped her wet cheeks, smiling into her face tenderly as his own eyes welled with emotion. "Stop shakin' your head, Griselda Schroeder, because this is my truth, and I am sharing it with you, and you need to respect that."

She looked up at him with wide, glassy eyes.

"Four times. The Fillmans'. The cellar. The river. And you saved my life again on Saturday night, when you showed up at that fight. You saved it when you walked into my apartment building on Sunday afternoon. You saved it when you agreed to stay with me for a month . . . because my life was a dead thing, Gris, and you made me want to live again. You came back from the dead and brought me back from the dead w-with you.

"And it fucking k-kills me that you ever thought you deserved some dickhead like Jonah in your life because you deserve the best, Gris. And that's exactly what I want to be for you: the best. Exactly what you got coming to you."

"Holden," she sobbed, leaning forward to kiss him.

He held her face in his hands, leaning away so her lips wouldn't touch his. As much as he wanted to get her naked and sink into the sweetness of her body, he needed to see it in her eyes first—that she believed him, that she would allow herself to love him and consider a future with him.

"No, sweet girl. N-not yet." He smiled at her tear-streaked face, letting his thumbs swipe away some of the wetness. "First I need to know you heard me."

She searched his eyes, her bright blue ones circled with pink from her tears, huge and glistening.

"You mean it?"

"Every word."

She licked her lips, clenched her jaw, and sniffled, taking a deep, shaky breath that made her breasts push into his chest. "You think I saved you?"

"I know it. You're my savior. My angel."

Her eyes were searing as she stared at him, as though seeking a glimpse of his soul to verify that his words were true. The almost imperceptible nod of her head was his first indication that she'd found it.

"I'm your angel?"

"I got the wings on my skin to prove it."

"You going to marry me, Holden Croft?"

"As soon as you say yes."

"You going to help me go to college?"

"I'm going to insist."

"You going to be the father of my babies?"

"Yes, ma'am," he said, the idea making him so hard, so fast, he felt dizzy with desire for her. "Hell, yes."

"Then I think we should get in some practice," she said, finally smiling at him with her whole face, sassy and confident, finally—*finally*—believing what Holden had known from the first time he'd laid eyes on her: they belonged to each other, and they always would, until the end of time.

***

Griselda stepped away from him and took his hand, leading him into the cabin, walking purposefully through the small common room to the tiny back bedroom, which was bright and sunny.

Standing just inside the room, she didn't know if it was the heat of Holden's body behind her or the warmth of the mid-morning sun that made her skin feel so hot. Her heart throbbed with anticipation and longing. Her eyes closed slowly as she felt Holden's hands land on her shoulders. Pushing away the hair on the back of her neck, he dropped his lips to her skin, nuzzling and sucking gently as one of his hands looped around her waist, resting warm and flat on her abdomen, just beneath her breasts.

She leaned back, into him, tilting her neck to the side to give him better access to her throat, to the pulse there that rocked and throbbed. He pulled her closer, his erection bumping her backside as his hand drifted lower, over her belly, into her shorts, under her panties, his longest finger landing effortlessly on her aching clit. She let her head fall back on his shoulder as the pad of his finger rubbed and circled, pulling breathy whimpers and urgent moans from the back of her throat as she thrust shamelessly against his digit. Two of his fingers dipped lower, slipping into her drenched sex and making her gasp with the sudden feeling of fullness as his thumb continued pressing and rubbing her clit. His other hand let go of her hair, smoothing over her shoulder and down her chest, into her bra, cupping her breast and freeing it to gently pinch her nipple into a tight, aching point.

"Holden," she gasped, every part of her body electric, on fire, aware of his every movement, inside, outside, rubbing, stroking, pinching.

"What, angel? Tell me," he murmured, his lips like a feather touch under her ear.

"I want . . .," she said, her breathing quicker and more ragged as her body, his plaything, gathered, bunching together in anticipation of imminent release.

"What do you want?" he asked, taking the soft lobe of her ear between his teeth and biting.

She fell apart standing up, supported by his arms, her sex

convulsing in ripples and waves, her head a dead weight on his shoulder as her knees buckled. Suddenly she was swept up in his arms, and he was placing her in the center of the bed, unbuttoning her shorts and slipping them down her legs. He raised her arms over her head and a moment later her bra and shirt joined her shorts on the floor and she was completely bare, bathed in the warm sun, staring up at the love of her life, who quickly shed his jeans and threw his T-shirt on the ground.

He reached for her legs, spreading them slowly before kneeling on the bed between them, the mattress depressing a little from the solid mass of his body joining hers. Reaching forward, he ran his fingers from her clit to her opening, letting the slick of her recent orgasm coat his skin. Holding her eyes, he touched himself, circling the tip of his shaft until it was shiny with her essence, and fuck, but it was the most erotic thing Griselda had ever seen in her entire life.

"What do you want?" he asked again.

"I want you," she panted, her body clenching with arousal, desperate to feel him moving inside her.

"Who do you love?"

"I love you."

"Who do you choose?"

"You," she said, letting go of the tightness inside that had made her so cautious of looking beyond tomorrow.

"Forever, Gris," he said, placing his hands on her hips and pulling her toward him, lifting her pelvis a few inches off the bed and resting her backside on his knees as he guided her sex to his.

"Forever, Holden."

Pulling her forward with one swift yank, he buried himself to the hilt. She gasped with surprise, but her eyes held his with a tenderness, an intensity, that humbled him because he could read them so clearly, and he knew that she had finally surrendered everything to him. She wasn't holding back anymore. Her heart, her life, her future—it all belonged to him.

"I want you," he said, pushing her hips away, then pulling them back again until they were perfectly joined.

"I love you," he said, sliding her back and forth on his hard, swollen, pulsing dick.

"I choose you," he said, placing his hands under her back and raising her up into a sitting position on his knees, keeping himself lodged deep inside her body.

Her breasts were crushed against his chest, and he thrust up slowly, taking his time, watching her eyes roll back in her head before he leaned forward to capture her lips with his. His tongue swirled around hers, and he felt her ankles lock around his back, her legs flexing tighter and tighter around his waist as the walls of her sex clenched around his penis, which moved faster with each thrust.

"Wait for me," he breathed, feeling the gathering, the heat, the swirling in his belly, the stars behind his eyes that told him his climax was building, was almost ready to burst.

"I can't, Holden . . . I . . ."

His hands skated up the damp skin of her back, cradling her skull from behind, forcing her to look at him.

"I jump, you jump," he said, the words falling off his tongue easily, even though they'd originally been hers. He searched her dark, heavy-lidded eyes. "Wait for me, Gris."

"Come with me, Holden," she gasped, her inner muscles so tight their bodies were truly one.

"I am," he rasped "Now!"

Wrapping his arms around her body and thrusting one last time, they came apart together, clasping and crying out each other's names as their bodies moved to a primal rhythm of love and surrender and pleasure.

"Forever, angel," he whispered against her shoulder, gently laying her back down on the bed, then pulling out of her and rolling behind her. He drew her into his arms, profoundly grateful, deeply in love. He was whole, happy, alive, back in captivity, his heart and soul owned by hers. Then, now, and . . .

"Forever," she answered, curling her body against his and falling asleep in his arms.

CHAPTER 24

"Holden?"

"Yeah?"

"You ever think about dying?"

Only all the time.

They'd been with the Man for six months now, and the beatings never stopped for more than a day or two before they did something wrong that made him start up again. On the list of forbidden behavior?

1. *Looking at each other.*
2. *Talking to each other about anything other than the work at hand.*
3. *Whispering to each other.*
4. *Touching each other, even by accident.*
5. *Referring to each other as Holden or Griselda.*
6. *Back talk.*
7. *Crying, talking, or moving when he was reading from the Bible.*
8. *Crying at all.*
9. *Addressing him as anything other than "sir."*

No doubt there would be more, but this list was hard

enough to keep from doing. Not looking at each other was the worst of it, though, thought Holden, forcing himself not to look up.

Gris was stirring the huge vat of corncobs, then transferring them to a massive barrel full of ice and snow from outside.

It was up to Holden to take the cooled ears and cut the kernels off the cob with a corn stripper so he could pack the corn in the canning jars. When he had enough, he'd add a pinch of salt and pack the kernels, leaving an inch of room on top.

When he had six jars, the Man would take them to the pressure canner on the other side of the barn. That's where he was now. That's how come Gris had risked talking.

"N-n-no," he said, looking up uneasily to see if the Man was walking back toward them, loosening his belt buckle to whip their backs. "And you shouldn't either."

"Can't help it," she said, picking up the tongs and transferring the blanched ears one by one.

She'd already burned herself twice this morning, and he couldn't bear it if it happened again. "C-c-concentrate on what you're d-doing."

Holden measured a teaspoon of salt into the next jar. He reached for a handful of kernels and emptied them into the jar. One after another, packing them in, not too smooshed, or the Man would throw the jar at the barn wall and tell Holden to do it again. His eyes flicked nervously at the wall where October's applesauce had crusted on the weathered wood like cement. His temple throbbed from the memory.

Gris walked back to the boiling cauldron, her ankle chain jingling. Like Christmas bells, Holden thought for a moment, thinking they must be close to Christmas now. Not that Holden had anyone missing him this Christmas. His gran had passed last year. He chanced a quick glance at Gris, thinking if he had to spend Christmas with anyone, he was glad it was her, no matter where they were.

"Ch-Ch-Christmas is coming. D-d-don't think about d-dying. Think about Ch-Christmas," he muttered without looking up.

"Christmas," she murmured wistfully. "Ain't never had a Christmas like you see on TV."

Holden looked up, but the Man was still at the canner, out of sight.

"It's magical. Someday, when I'm a d-d-dad, m-my kids are going to have the b-best Ch-Christmas ever. You too, Gris."

"You'll be a good daddy, Holden. The best."

The best, he thought, reaching for another handful of kernels. No matter what, I'll be the best.

"Yes, I will, G-Gris. I guarantee you th-that."

***

At first Holden thought the knocking was an extension of the dream he was having about canning in Caleb's barn during that first cold winter. He shivered and pulled Griselda closer as his mind tried to reconcile the dream from reality. Canning = dream. Hunting cabin = real. Gris worried about dying = dream. Gris in my arms = real.

The knocking continued.

Knocking = real.

He blinked, squinting his eyes, and realized that it was barely morning. Dawn, at best, maybe four or five o'clock. And yes, someone was knocking on the cabin door. He bolted upright, every cell on high alert as he grabbed his jeans off the floor and pulled them on, buttoning and zipping before taking his T-shirt off the floor and jerking it over his head. What if fucking Jonah had somehow figured out where they were?

Satisfied that Griselda was sleeping peacefully and determined to keep her safe, he closed the door quietly and trekked barefoot through the common room. Whoever it was, he'd better not be bringing trouble, because Holden was ready.

He cracked his knuckles, standing beside the front door.

"Who's there?" he growled, his voice low and menacing.

"Seth? That you?"

His shoulders relaxed. It was Clinton.

Holden unlocked the door and threw it open.

"Almost gave me a heart attack."

"Sorry," said Clinton, offering Holden a cup of hot Dunkin' Donuts coffee as he stood on the porch. "I know it's early."

"Early? It's still *nighttime*."

"Nah," said Clinton, taking a step back. "It's almost five. I gotta be at work at seven, so I thought I'd catch you early and then drive back down."

"What's up?" asked Holden. "Your dad okay?"

"Dad's fine. Your, uh, your friend up?"

Holden shook his head, opening the spout on his coffee cup. "She's asleep."

"Come on out here and sit with me a spell?" Clinton settled into the rocker that Gris always sat in while she wrote her stories.

"Uh, sure." Holden pulled the door shut behind him, wondering what was so important that Clinton would leave Charles Town at four o'clock in the morning to visit him. "Someone bothering you?"

"Nothing like that."

Holden sat down, propping his feet on the railing. It was cool, the early-morning air misty over the wildflowers. For a second he considered waking up Gris because it looked like something out of her stories.

He turned to Clinton. "So?"

Clinton took a long swig of coffee, then leaned forward with his forearms resting on his thighs. "You need to come back, Seth."

Holden bristled at being called Seth but didn't correct his

friend. "Your dad rent out the cabin?"

Clinton shook his head, grimacing, then sipped his coffee again. "I don't know how to . . . aw, hell, Seth. Gemma's pregnant."

His lungs deflated. His hand pressed against his racing heart as he stared at Clinton's somber face. "Wh-what?"

"She's been trying to get a hold of you. Says you keep blowing her off, not answering her texts. She's sick all the time. Finally broke down and told me why."

"It's a lie," said Holden, feeling dizzy. He blinked his eyes, trying to clear his head. "W-we used protection."

"She mentioned that. Said that a few nights, after drinking too much, though, maybe you two weren't all that safe. Maybe the protection was . . . faulty."

"It's n-not mine."

Clinton clenched his jaw, his eyes flashing. "She's not perfect, but she's not a whore. And she's not a liar. Gemma wouldn't say this unless it was so."

Holden's feet dropped from the railing, and he placed the coffee on the floor by his chair, raking his hands through his hair. Gemma was pregnant? With his child? He closed his eyes, listening to his heart beat in his head.

"H-how f-far . . .?"

"How far along is she?" Clinton shrugged. "She says twelve weeks. Just went to the doc a few days ago because of all the throwing up. Thought she had a nasty stomach bug. Turns out she's knocked up. With your baby."

His baby. His child. He couldn't help the way his chest tightened with something painful and awesome at the thought. He was going to be a father.

Then he winced.

But not of Griselda's baby. Of Gemma's.

"Jesus," rasped Holden, glancing at the cabin door, then back at Clinton.

"You gotta come home and take care of her, man."

"The fuck I do."

"It's your kid," ground out Clinton, his coffee cup frozen in midair on the way to his mouth.

"And I will take care of it. It's mine and I want it and I will be there for it—I mean, him . . . or her." He paused. "But Gemma is a g-grown-ass woman, and—"

"Fuck you, Seth." Clinton put his coffee cup on the ground and stood up, bracing his hands on the railing. "She's the mother of your fucking kid. She needs you. You need to come home. She was at the Poke and Duck last night—"

"W-wait, what?" Holden jumped to his feet, staring at Clinton. "She was at the Poke and Duck, d-drinking with my k-kid in her—"

"*Your* kid?" Clinton scoffed, facing Holden. "I just told you that you got to come home and take care of her, and you practically told me to go fuck myself."

"She better not be p-poisoning *my b-baby* with—"

"She was drinking ginger ale. I know 'cause I was buying 'em for her. Jesus, Seth. Give her a little credit."

Holden backed up a little, crossing his arms over his chest and leaning against the railing. His baby. His child. His kid. A father. *I'm going to be a father, Gris. I'm going to be the best daddy in the world.*

"They're a package deal right now," said Clinton. "Her and the baby. And they both need you."

"Sounds like you're filling in just fine. Listening to her woes and buying her sodas."

Clinton gave him a sidelong glance. "She ain't my girlfriend."

The word *anymore* hung heavy between them, and despite the fact that Clinton had outwardly approved of Holden and Gemma's relationship, Holden had to wonder if that was entirely true.

"Ain't mine either . . . once I get back. I want to be with Gris. I'm breaking things off with Gemma, Clinton."

Clinton's head whipped around to face Holden, his face reddening. "The *fuck* you are!"

"It's *my* life, Clinton."

"You know, you're a cold bastard, Seth. I appreciate that you helped me get on the straight and narrow. Got me off the drugs. Helped me get a decent job that I like. But you've got an ice cube for a heart." He shook his head, pursing his lips, his eyes angry and narrow. "She's the *mother* of your *child*. And she needs you. I don't know what you got going on with, uh, Gris. But you need to come and deal with Gemma fair and square. And let me tell you something else: It's Friday morning. You don't come home by tomorrow night? I'll tell her where you are. And she can come on up here and deal with you herself. I owe her that. Fuck, *you* owe her that."

Holden stared at his friend, who shook his head with disgust, then pushed past him and trudged to his truck.

"And you better get your fucking priorities straight, man! It's your *kid!* A fucking kid, goddamnit!"

A moment later, Clinton's truck was screeching out of the driveway, throwing up dust and gravel as he sped away, giving Holden the finger.

***

Griselda felt the bed depress a little as he joined her and pulled her against his chest, his breath warm on her neck. It was early. Earlier than they usually woke up. She could tell because the room wasn't awash in bright sun. It was dim and grayish-blue. And that wasn't the only thing that felt off: Holden's hot, velvet-steel erection wasn't pressing against her bare backside, firing up her body with longing and anticipation. In fact, she could feel the rough denim of his jeans pressed against her bare skin. He was already dressed.

She turned around in his arms, surprised to see him wide

awake, his face a mask of worry. He stared at her with such sorrow—such terrible, terrifying sorrow—her breath caught and her heart started to race.

"Holden?"

"G-Gris," he said softly, wincing as his eyes searched her face with such grief it hurt to look at him.

"What happened? What's wrong?"

"G-Gris," he said again, a whispered sob. He dropped her eyes, staring down at the sheets between them.

"You're scaring me," she said, her fingers tingling as panic sluiced through her body. "Tell me what's going on."

"Clinton came to see me."

"This morning? Is someone . . .? His father?"

Holden shook his head, swallowing. "No. Gemma."

"God, is . . .? Holden, is she okay? Did something happen to her?"

His eyes, so deeply regretful, seized hers. "She's p-pregnant."

Pregnant.

Pregnant.

She heard the word in her head, staring at Holden's lips as it reverberated around the room. His girlfriend was pregnant. Gemma was pregnant with Holden's baby.

"Oh," she gasped, her vision blurring as tears filled her eyes. Another woman was pregnant with Holden's baby. Gemma would be the mother of Holden Croft's baby, not Griselda Schroeder.

It's a strange thing to feel your heart break. Cartoons would have you believe it's like breaking a cracker. It snaps in half, with red crumbs falling to the ground, leaving two jagged halves sitting side by side. All you'd have to do is shove them together and they'd look like one again.

That's not the way a real heart breaks. It's not clean. It doesn't snap in half. When a heart breaks, it somehow stays whole. It keeps beating. It keeps pumping. Only the person who owns it knows that it's been shattered.

She placed a palm on his T-shirt and pushed away from him, sitting up, covering her breasts with the sheet and dropping her eyes. Suddenly she was Eve in the Garden of Eden with her naked body, broken heart, and empty, aching womb.

"G-Gris," he said gently, not reaching for her. "This doesn't change things."

She clenched her eyes shut to stanch the tears because she knew good and well that was a lie. In a minute, he'd tell her that he owed it to Gemma to go back to her, and while the cabin had been fun, it was time to say good-bye.

"W-we can still be together. I can be with you *and* be a father to my child. I don't want to be with Gemma. This doesn't change things."

She looked up. She leveled him with her gaze.

"This changes *everything*."

He shook his head. "It doesn't. I still want you. I still love you. I still choose you."

She used a corner of the sheet to wipe the tears away. "She's having your baby, Holden."

"Yes. But I'm in love with *you*."

She looked away from him, trying to get her head around his words. Was what he was saying possible? Could they still be together? He'd change his mind, wouldn't he? Wouldn't he want to try to build a family with Gemma?

"She's the mother of your child. Don't you want—"

"I'll do right by her," he said. He reached for Gris's hand, but she yanked it away. "But I *love* you. I want to be with you."

"There's a baby to think about now."

"And I'll take care of him or her . . . and you'll be the most amazing stepmother."

Stepmother. God.

"There's a place for you in all of this, Gris. I want my son or daughter to know you as well as he or she knows me and Gemma. From the day that baby's born, I want him or her to know you and love you. I mean, one day this baby will be a sister or brother to *our* kids," he said. "All I've done for an hour is think. And this is what I know: there's room for all of us. How can a baby have too much love?"

Her lashes were soaked with tears as she scooted back toward him. He'd not only thought of her, he'd planned for her part in his life and his baby's life. Her heart was so swollen with love for him she didn't know how much bigger it could possibly get.

Last night, when he'd told her that she'd saved his life four times, her walls had finally tumbled down and she'd allowed herself to glimpse a future with him. And as much as she didn't anticipate it including a baby by another mother, the fact that he didn't miss a beat when considering her place humbled her and proved his love more than anything else could have.

"I love you," she said. "I'll do anything I can to help."

"I'm sorry it's not yours," he said, reaching out to palm her cheek.

"It's okay. Our time will come." She twisted her head and kissed his hand. "You're gonna be a dad, Holden."

"The best daddy there ever was," he said, his eyes dancing with happy tears.

CHAPTER 25

As much as Holden had tried to convince her that everything could be worked out to accommodate everyone, the drive back to Charles Town was quiet and a little somber. Their month together had been cut in half, and Clinton's news, while happy in one breath, was unsettling in another. So much needed to be hashed out. So many hurdles needed to be overcome.

Griselda, whose faith in Holden and her as a couple was still fragile, felt herself pulling away from him. She had given him her heart, her body, and her soul, and part of her wished she hadn't. Part of her wanted to protect herself now, and the only way she knew how to do that was run . . . except he wasn't telling her to go this time. He was counting on her to stay.

As far as Gemma knew, she and "Seth" were still together—he hadn't broken up with her. Holden insisted that his first point of business with the mother of his child would be to break up with her, but as much as Griselda didn't like her rival, she didn't like this plan either. She hated the idea of upsetting a pregnant woman, and as much as Holden insisted that his relationship with Gemma had been casual, Griselda couldn't imagine her taking the news of a breakup with equanimity.

But Holden was dead set on the idea that honesty was best at this point, and he was determined that they could rationally figure things out. He wasn't giving up his child, and he wasn't giving up Griselda. The problem? From Griselda's limited knowledge of pregnant women, they *weren't* rational, and a rejected girlfriend/pregnant woman? The least rational woman of all. Holden had no idea what he was walking into.

Griselda did. And her heart ached for the future they'd imagined. A future that felt further away and less likely with every mile closer to Charles Town.

"Holden," she said, "I want you for myself. You know that, right?"

"Yeah."

"But I just think . . . I think breaking up with Gemma first thing is going to, well, upset her. I think it's going to be hard for her to . . . you know, be reasonable."

"I'm not going to act like you and me aren't together, Gris. She deserves the truth. And I promised you I'd break it off as soon as we returned to Charles Town."

"Yeah, she does, and yeah, you did. But maybe you could, you know, give it to her in stages."

"Stages."

"Yeah. Like, first, make sure she's feeling okay. Ask about her health. About the baby. Give it a day or two. Then maybe talk about growing apart or something. I don't know. I just think this is going to go south fast. Why don't you talk to her one-on-one to start? I can wait in the truck."

Holden shook his head. "No. You're coming in with me. We're doing this right from the get-go."

She took in his stony expression, her heart feeling heavy. She wanted to believe that if she'd known about Gemma's condition, she wouldn't have let things get as far with Holden as they had. But it wasn't true. She was helpless around him, pulled to him with a force that felt otherworldly.

Pulling her bottom lip into her mouth, she worried it between her teeth as they zoomed past a sign that read "Welcome to Charles Town." Holden slowed down a little as they rode down Main Street, and Griselda realized this was a pretty little all-American town. Idyllic, even, and perfect for raising a family.

I could have been happy here, she thought wistfully. *But now . . .*

"Check my phone, Gris, would you? Clinton said she might be over at his place this afternoon. Let's find her and get this over with."

Griselda picked Holden's phone up off the seat and swiped the screen to check for new texts. There was only one, from Clinton. *She's here. When you coming?*

She typed back: *On the way.* Then she placed the phone facedown on the seat next to Holden, her hands shaking. "She's over at Clinton's."

"Good," said Holden, his fingers rapping on the steering wheel with nervous energy as they stopped at a red light. "Let's get this over with. Don't worry, okay, Gris? We'll work it out, then we'll go back to my place and talk. You still have two weeks left before you have to go back to work. We can still make the most of them."

She nodded, looking out the window again. It felt like he was completely avoiding the idea of Gemma as the mother of his child—her feelings, her needs, her wants. He was so blinded by Griselda and his longing for her permanence in her life, she worried he was making a big mistake about handling this situation. It made her stomach flip over with foreboding.

He knows her better than you do, part of her reasoned. *Maybe he does know what he's doing. Try to have faith in him.*

"I feel you pulling back from me, Griselda."

"Let's just see what happens," she whispered.

"We're going to figure it out," he said again, like it was his mantra, his blind hope.

She crossed her legs toward the window, watching as they headed out of town into a neighborhood of small one-story houses with neat patches of grass out front.

Holden pulled into a driveway and cut the engine. He turned to her and pried one of her folded hands out of her lap, his eyes tender. "It's going to be okay. She needs to understand that even though I can't be with her, I'll still do my part."

Griselda nodded her head, squeezing his hand before pulling hers away. "I could wait here . . . just until—"

"No," he insisted, his voice taut and low. "You're part of my life. That's how it's going to be. Best she understands that now."

He opened his door, stepped out of the truck, and walked around to her side to help her down. Taking her hand, he laced their fingers together.

"Don't worry," he whispered.

He didn't bother to knock on the front door. She followed him around the one-car garage to a small backyard surrounded by a chain-link fence. She raised her eyes to a slightly elevated deck, finding Quint, Clinton, Gemma, and an older lady, whom she assumed to be Quint's wife, sitting at a redwood picnic table playing cards. Holden pulled Griselda up the stairs, tugging on her hand, and the card players stopped their game to look at them.

"Well, now," said the older lady, smiling at Holden, "look what the cat drug in!"

She stood up, maneuvering over the bench and opening her fleshy arms to Holden, who dropped Griselda's hand to hug her back. "Maudie, this is Griselda."

Maudie leaned back, fixed shrewd eyes on Griselda, and offered her a small smile that landed somewhere between troubled and sympathetic. "Quint told me 'bout ya. Sorry for yer ordeal back-when, honey."

The plump woman wore a cheerful aqua and white striped T-shirt over a pair of too-tight aqua polyester shorts, but she spoke with an accent like Caleb Foster's, and for just a moment

Griselda's blood went cold and she shivered.

"Thanks," Griselda said, sliding her gaze to the table.

Gemma stared daggers at Griselda, her dark eyes narrowed, her palm resting on her mostly flat belly. Next to Gemma sat Clinton, his eyes downcast. And across from him sat Quint, who cocked his head to the side, giving Griselda a can't-win-'em-all shrug and a small, sad smile.

"I 'spect that Seth and Gemma here have some things to discuss," said Maudie, wringing her hands. "Maybe Clinton and, uh, Griselda could come inside for a refreshment."

Griselda's cheeks flared with color as Gemma continued to stare at her with a look of such unbridled hatred she considered fleeing back to the relative safety of Caleb Foster's old truck.

"Griselda stays with me," said Holden firmly, and Clinton, who'd been in the process of standing up, sat back down beside Gemma.

Holden, no doubt sensing Griselda's discomfort, put his arm around her shoulders, and she watched Gemma's eyes burn.

"You feeling okay, Gem?" Holden asked.

Slowly, ever so slowly, Gemma shifted her gaze from Griselda to Holden, fixing her murderous eyes on him instead.

"Yer back."

"I am."

"Well, I ain't talkin' to you with yer whore here," she said.

Holden shook his head, his arm tightening across Griselda's shoulders. "You won't talk to her like that."

"No? 'Cause I think the word *whore* is fittin'. Plain as day you two fucked."

Maudie gasped, covering her mouth and whispering "Lord Jesus" as Quint jumped up and ushered her into the house, leaving the four young people alone.

"Yer a piece of shit who's fuckin' *her* while yer kid's in *my* belly, Seth."

"I had no idea you were pregnant."

"Well, I am."

"And I'll do my part."

"Which is?"

Holden shrugged. "Pay for what needs be. Be a father."

Gemma gasped, like something had hurt or shocked her, and Griselda realized, with some measure of genuine sympathy, that Gemma had been prepared to forgive Holden until that moment. As angry and hurt as she was, if he'd apologized for being with Griselda, Gemma would have allowed him back into her life. In fact, if Griselda was reading her rival's face correctly, it's what Gemma was hoping for. And his words had just sent that hope to hell.

"The fuck you will," Gemma snarled, gathering herself together. "Not with her around."

"What does *th-that* mean?" Holden spat, his body rigid beside Griselda.

"You skip town with this cheap piece of foster care tail, you fuck her for two weeks while I'm pukin' all over the place, and then you come here holdin' her hand? Tellin' me you'll do yer part but also tellin' me we're history?" Gemma's laserlike eyes were narrow, hurt, and mean.

"I don't love you, Gem. I love Griselda. I want to be with her."

Gemma's eyes watered, and she blinked twice before clenching her jaw, her face setting in stony fury. "Is that right?"

Holden nodded.

"Fuck you," growled Gemma.

Holden's voice was gentle, but Griselda could tell it was forced. He was running out of patience with Gemma's anger. "Gem, we can w-work this out. I want to be with Gris, but I'll take care of the hospital expenses. I'll help however you w-want, however you need. I'll be a good father. And Gris'll be a great stepmother."

"Shut. Yer. Mouth!" screamed Gemma, pounding her

hands on the table. "Yer *whore* ain't gonna be raisin' no kid of mine!"

"Gemma, let's just talk," he said, trying to be reasonable. "Let's hash it out. W-we're going to be parents. W-we should—"

"No! You got one decision to make, Seth. *One.* It's me and the baby, or her. You decide. You can have yer fuckin' foster sister whore or yer child. But you don't get to have both, you greedy shit."

"I love her," he said, turning to look at Griselda with desperate eyes.

"Fine," spat Gemma. "Then we got nothin' else to talk about. Get out."

"But I can still be a daddy to my kid. That's *my* k-kid," said Holden, raising his voice and lifting his arm from Griselda's shoulders to point at Gemma's belly.

"Fuck it is. It's *mine.* To do with what *I* want." Her narrow eyes darted back and forth between Griselda and Holden for a moment before she shifted her gaze to Clinton. "You ready?"

"Gem . . ."

"My appointment's in half an hour," she said standing up.

"Gem, let's talk a little more," pleaded Clinton.

"Fuck talkin'. You heard him. He chooses his whore over his kid. I don't want his bastard. You ready to drive me to that clinic or what?"

***

Holden stared at Gemma in horror, his brain refusing to believe what she was saying. She wouldn't do that. My God, she *wouldn't.*

His heart pounded, and his breathing went fast and shallow as he held her eyes and saw no mercy there.

"Gem," he gasped. "W-what're you d-doing?"

"What am I d-d-doin'?" she asked, taunting him. "I don't fuckin' want your kid inside me, Seth. I'ma have it cut out." She turned back to Clinton. "You drivin' me or not?"

"Don't you get out of that f-fucking seat, Clinton," growled Holden, stepping forward and trying to catch his breath. Bile rose to his throat, threatening to choke him. "That's *my* baby. You're not killing *my* k-kid."

"*Yer baby!* Fuck you, Seth," said Gemma, putting her hands on her hips. "It's *my* decision what I do with *my* body. You ain't got no say."

It didn't feel right that he should have no say, and yet he knew it was true: he didn't. She could go to any clinic and walk out fifteen minutes later with his baby left behind in a garbage can. His heart clenched, and he threw up into his mouth at the terrible mental image.

"Gemma," he said, unable to keep the fear out of his voice. "I'm b-begging you not to do this."

"You can beg me all you want," she said. "But I ain't lettin' no whore raise my kid. I'd rather—"

"I'll go!"

Griselda's voice made him start. She stood beside him, her hands clasped in front of her, her chest heaving and her eyes glistening.

"I'll go," she said again, softly, her voice broken. "I'll leave."

"N-no," he said, reaching for her. She stepped away, holding her hands up to fend him off.

"Holden," she said, her eyes so bereft he felt his heart dying just looking at her. "Me leaving is the right choice."

"I won't lose you. I c-can't."

"But you'd lose your baby?" She shook her head as tears ran down her cheeks. "No. I can't let that happen." She shifted her eyes to Gemma, stiffening her spine. "I'll go tomorrow. As soon as I can arrange to be picked up."

"Tonight," said Gemma.

"Tomorrow!" roared Holden, the frustration and fury

distorting his voice almost unrecognizably. "You s-selfish c-cunt!"

"Don't you throw insults at me, Seth West. I still have that appointment . . ."

Holden clenched his jaw, rage making his body so taut he wished he had someone to punch, someone to hurt, someone to hurt *him* so bad that he'd pass out and wake up to find out that all of this was just a terrible nightmare.

"Enough, Gem," said Clinton. He stood and stepped away from the picnic table to head inside. He looked at her over his shoulder before letting the screen door slam behind him. "I'm not drivin' you anywhere."

"Fine," she said, crossing her arms over her full chest and turning to face Holden. "Tomorrow. Works better for me anyways, since I got to pack up my stuff. I'm movin' in with you, Seth. I'm sick of stayin' at my mama's house, and I'm quittin' my job at the DQ. You gotta take care of me now."

"Don't push me, Gem."

She shrugged, giving Griselda one last victorious once-over before following Clinton into the house.

Holden grabbed Griselda's hand, pulling her back down the porch steps and around the garage to his truck. Once seated, he turned to her, his heart thudding in misery, his life suddenly a new version of hell, where the woman he loved was walking away from him.

"You're not going anywhere, Gris. W-we need to talk."

CHAPTER 26

Griselda had known more than her fair share of heartbreak. Unloved and abandoned by her mother, with a father she never knew, she'd been passed around from one foster family to another, barely able to make a connection before she was uprooted again. She'd been abducted, held captive, and beaten. She'd escaped from hell, only to be put back in the system again. As an adult she'd allowed her body to be used without affection and abused without protest. Heartbreak. She was no stranger. She'd known more than most.

But she'd never felt anything like the pain of knowing that she alone stood between Holden and his child. His child's life depended on her walking away, and her decision was quick and final because she loved Holden, and even more, she already loved that baby, just as much as he did.

Better than anyone on earth, she knew his deep and lifelong desire to be a father.

And she knew that he would never forgive her if he ended up choosing her over his baby.

The words "I'll go!" had been ripped from her broken heart with the very knife that clinic doctor would have used on Gemma's belly. A life for a life. Griselda's happiness in exchange for Holden's child. It was a fair trade. Oh, but it hurt to the very depths of her soul.

They rode back to his apartment building in heavy silence, their footsteps echoing up the steps like a death march.

For the two weeks Griselda had been with Holden, her tears had flowed freely—a sign of love, of trust, of faith, of hope—but she had no tears now. Long ago she'd learned how to hold them back to avoid punishment. She'd learned how to eat them, the salt eroding her insides until she ached from the burn. Like now. Like right now.

Holden closed his apartment door behind them and pulled her into his arms. He held her for a long time, and she allowed herself to be held, though her arms hung limp at her sides.

Finally she whispered. "I need to use your phone."

"For what?"

"I need to call Maya and ask her to come get me."

"No!" he exclaimed. "P-please, no," he gasped. "G-Gris . . ."

She felt a cool and inexplicable calm as she pulled away from him.

"Yes," she said gently.

"You're leaving me."

"I am."

"W-we can work it out."

"Not right now, we can't. Not when she could still hurt your baby."

Griselda held out her hand, waiting for the phone.

Holden suddenly dropped to his knees and took her hand in his, his eyes red rimmed and glassy as he looked up at her with desperation and agony. "I'm *b-begging* you not to go."

And all those tears she'd just eaten refused now to be held back and erupted in streams of anguish. "Holden, please. Please don't make this harder for me."

"D-don't go," he pleaded, staring up at her as a tear slid down his cheek. "She'll come around."

"You don't know that." She dropped to her knees in front

of Holden and touched his cheek with her palm. "My being here will just make the situation worse. I think I should go, and you need to work this out with her, and you and I need to . . . to wait."

"I waited ten fucking years for you!" he yelled, dropping his head to her shoulder. "P-please, Gris."

"I can't. I won't come between you and your baby. If she hurts that baby to spite you, you'll hate me, Holden. It'll ruin us. We have a choice right now to do what's right for that baby. I have to go. At least for now."

He leaned up, reaching out to hold her face between his hands. "I'm in love with you. W-with everything I am, I love you. Th-there is no future for me without you. N-no family. N-no love. N-no life. I'll be dead again. I'll be d-dead without your heart b-beating in my chest, G-Gris. D-don't d-do this. G-give her a d-day or t-t-two to c-calm d-down!"

"It's not worth the risk," she sobbed, her voice breaking. "Give me the phone. We'll have a little time left together before I go."

He dropped his hands from her face, pulled his phone out of his back pocket, and threw it on the floor between them. Standing up, he looked down at her with anger and sorrow. "I can't s-s-stand it."

"Then go out for a while," she said. "Go for a walk. Come back when you're ready."

He nodded, turned on his heel, and walked back through the door, letting it slam shut behind him.

With trembling fingers, she picked up the phone and dialed Maya's number.

"M-Maya?" she sobbed as soon as her friend said hello. "It's . . . Zelda."

***

Holden walked down Main Street in the late afternoon sun, past the row of businesses, to the little park beside City Hall. Sitting down on a bench, he hunched his shoulders, letting his neck drop forward in misery.

She was leaving. His Gris, his love, his girl was leaving. By tomorrow she'd be gone, and he'd be alone again.

Only this time he wouldn't be alone with the memory of a dead girl. He'd be alone with the knowledge that the only woman—the only *person*—he'd ever loved was living and breathing two hours away. And he wasn't allowed to be with her.

His thoughts circled in an endless loop, the horror of Gemma's suggestion to terminate the pregnancy balanced against the heartbreak of Griselda offering to leave. The only words in which he found any comfort were these: *I have to go. At least for now.*

For now.

Did she mean that she'd wait for him? That she'd eventually come back? When? When Gemma was past the point of aborting? After the baby came? How long would he have to wait to be with her again? Suddenly the answers to these questions were the only thing that mattered, the only thing that would get him through the anguish of their separation.

He stood up and headed back to his apartment at a clip, anxious to talk to her and come up with a plan. He vaulted up the stairs to the apartment and burst through the door, striding through the living room to the bedroom, where he found Gris separating her meager belongings from his. She was folding them neatly and placing them in one of the two empty grocery bags that Quint had showed up with two weeks ago.

"Hey," she said, looking up at him with red eyes. "You're back."

"Yeah. What did you mean when you said 'at least for now'?"

"What?"

"You said, 'I have to go. At least for now.' W-what did

that mean?"

She sat down on the bed, the white bra with the little bow in her hands. "It means that I don't want to make things worse by being here right now."

"D-does it mean you'll come back?" he whispered.

Her lips parted and she stared up at him, blinking. "Um . . ."

"If you promise to come back, I can bear it," he said, squatting down before her. He took the bra from her hands and placed it on the bed, then took her hands in his. "I won't sleep with her. I won't touch her. I'll sleep on the couch. I'm yours. I'll . . . w-wait for you."

Her lips trembled, and she smiled briefly, then pulled her bottom lip into her mouth for a second. His eyes couldn't help but stare, new memories of their time together—the taste of her, the way her lips felt moving under his, the sounds she made when he kissed her—filling his brain with comfort and longing.

"Me too," she said, with a quiver in her voice. "I'll wait for you. If she ever comes around, I'll tell you where to find me."

"I'll come for you. The second the baby's safe." She nodded, and he unlaced his fingers from hers to wipe a tear from her cheek. "It's so fucking unfair."

"We waited ten years," she whispered, pressing her forehead to his. "We know how to do this."

"We waited ten years," he countered. "It k-kills me that we have to wait any more."

"I'm alive," she said, letting her nose nuzzle his. "I love you," she murmured, closing her eyes. "I'll wait for you." She brushed his lips with hers. "Forever."

"Forever, angel," he said. He placed his hands on her hips and pulled her down onto his lap.

He kissed her fiercely, his hands sliding her tank top and bra over her breasts with urgency. She grappled with his T-shirt, and he yanked it off and threw it on the floor, banding his arms around her and crushing her naked chest to his. He felt the miserable finiteness of their final hours together, and his chest ached from knowing he'd have to watch her leave him tomorrow.

"When is Maya coming?"

"Two or three hours," she said, as his lips kissed and sucked a path from her throat to her ear.

"N-no!" he protested, jerking from her, gazing into her eyes with a look that had to reflect the wild desperation he felt. "It's t-too soon!"

"It's better," she said, settling her palms on his cheeks and pulling him back to her lips. "Gemma said tonight. And a quick good-bye is better."

"I *w-w-wanted* tonight, Gris" he lamented. "I w-wanted forever."

"We have *now*," she said, leaning forward to capture his bottom lip with hers, her tears salty. "And I want to feel you inside me one last time."

His eyes burned as he kissed her, tangling his tongue with hers, trying to memorize the feeling of her small body in his arms. He didn't want to forget the way her softness molded into him, the way she smelled like soap and fresh air, the way her amber hair caught the light and looked like Rumpelstiltskin's gold. His heart, swollen and throbbing with love for her, protested her departure, and he clutched her tighter against himself, his mouth ravishing hers to the point of punishment. Why would she agree to leave him? Why?

"Holden," she gasped. "You're hurting me. Be gentle."

"F-fuck!" he bellowed, releasing her and bowing his head. *"D-don't g-go!"*

With his forehead resting on her shoulder, he clenched his eyes shut, willing any higher power that never gave him one single fucking break in his miserable twenty-three years to intercede, to help, to save him from the stark meaninglessness of life without her.

He received only silence.

He felt her small hands skate up his back, over the lashes, gouges, and scars, until she buried her fingers in his hair, cradling him against her warm, soft body like the mother he'd lost so long ago.

"Holden," she said, her lips near his ear. "Ask me if I'm whole or broken."

He paused for a moment, remembering all the times he'd asked the same of her. In all the time they'd known each other, it was the first time she'd ever asked it of him.

"Griselda," he said, leaning back to stare at her beloved face. "Are you whole or b-broken?"

"I'm whole," she said with a small, certain smile, her fingers gentle against his scalp. "I'm whole because I found you again."

As he inhaled sharply, her face blurred before him until he could barely make out her features. "I'm g-gonna be lost without you."

"No." How she did it, he wasn't sure—though Gris had always been the strongest girl he'd ever known—but she somehow managed to smile. Shaking her head at him, her tears still fell as she reassured him, "No. No, you're gonna be fine. You're gonna to have a baby, Holden. You're gonna be a dad. And you're gonna be great at it."

"I c-can't say good-bye to you."

"Then don't. Just remember the McClellans in Georgetown. You come find me someday if you can. I'll be waiting."

"You'll wait for me?"

"I will."

"Never let me go, Gris."

"I won't."

Reaching for her cheeks, he pulled her face to his, closing

his eyes as his lips found hers. He put his hands under her arms, and he pulled her to her feet, his fingers unbuttoning her shorts as she reached for his and did the same.

Still kissing him, she lay back on his bed, pulling him with her to cover her naked body with his.

They made love slowly, savoring each other, desperate and tender at turns, declaring their love as their bodies climaxed together. And as the afternoon sun fell lower, Griselda lay curled in Holden's arms in a communion of perfect sorrow and perfect understanding. In that moment, they rediscovered the synchronicity they'd known as children, when no words were possible. Only this time, no words were necessary.

When Holden's phone buzzed with the text from Maya saying she was downstairs, he kissed Griselda's head for a long time, his lips lingering on the same crown he'd stroked from his perch on the filthy, striped cot so many years ago.

She rose silently from his bed and dressed with her back to him. When she turned, she stared at him for several unbroken minutes, and he could almost hear her voice in his head from so long ago: *Don't look back, no matter what. Stone to stone. I jump, you jump.*

"Run," he whispered, clenching his eyes shut.

When he opened them again, she was gone.

CHAPTER 27

Griselda would be forever grateful that Maya took one look at her face and said nothing. Standing by the car, she gave Griselda a long hug before taking the pathetic brown paper bag out of her friend's hands and placing it on the backseat.

They rode in silence for a good half hour, with Griselda staring out her open window, feeling so overwhelmed she just let the sound of the wind fill her ears and tried not to think, or feel, or remember. And Maya remained blessedly quiet.

Leaving Holden was the hardest, most painful thing Griselda had ever had to do. In some ways it was worse than leaving him in the Shenandoah because she'd had a taste of what it would be like to live with him, to be in love with him, to be free . . . to be happy. And just when she'd allowed herself to believe in it, it had been ripped away.

Because people like Griselda Schroeder didn't get happy endings, and in the future it would be best for her to remember that.

"Thanks for coming, Maya," she said, turning her weary head to look at her friend. Maya had changed her hair over the past few weeks. It was cut very short, in a pixie style like Halle Berry's, and it complemented Maya's round face and high cheekbones. "You look good."

"Well, you look like shit."

"Thanks."

"When you're ready, you're gonna tell me everything, Zelda," said Maya. Staring at the road, she managed to pull a package of red Twizzlers from the pocket of the car door and hand them to Griselda. "And girl, I mean *everything*."

Griselda tore open the plastic, her eyes welling. "I can't, Maya."

"You have to. If you don't, it's going to eat you whole." Maya grabbed a Twizzler and took a bite. "It was him, right? You finally found him?"

She and Maya hadn't talked about Holden. Ever. After Griselda escaped, she was placed in a foster family and sent to mandatory counseling, which she belligerently attended. Her caseworker and the therapist knew she'd been abducted with a boy, and they knew she'd escaped and the boy had not. But Griselda refused to talk about her ordeal with Caleb Foster. The cellar, the long hours of gardening in the summer and canning in the winter, the cold oatmeal, the hours of Bible reading and accompanying rantings, the beatings. She'd never discussed it with anyone.

By the time she'd been transferred to Maya's house, she was fourteen and a half, and her kidnapping and escape were old news. Not much of the story had followed her except for the broadest strokes. In the very beginning Maya had tried to get Griselda to talk about it, but she'd clammed up tighter than a lock with a lost key, and Maya eventually stopped asking.

"The boy you were kidnapped with, Zel. You found him." Maya took another bite of her licorice. "That's who you've been saving for, right? All these years? And you somehow found him."

Griselda's lips trembled with misery, her eyes burning, though she was sick and tired of crying. "I found him."

Maya nodded, keeping her eyes on the road. "How is he?"

"Changed. The same. Grown up."

"You love him?"

Griselda sniffled, taking a small bite of the candy clutched in her fist. "Yeah."

"And he loves you?"

"Yeah," she whispered, trying to chew, but her teeth stopped working, and her whole body went slack.

He loves me and I love him, but we can't be together.

"So what happened?"

"His girlfriend's pregnant."

"Jesus," sighed Maya. "Give me another."

Griselda took a deep breath and started chewing again, slowly swallowing the mouthful of licorice and handing Maya another braid.

"Tell me about it."

"Finding him?"

Maya shook her head. "No. All of it. From the beginning."

Griselda's hair-trigger reaction was "no." For so long she'd kept her history a secret that she shared only with Holden. Even when they weren't together, it bound them, somehow, that they were the only two people on earth who knew what had happened, who'd lived it, who'd survived it.

"You gotta start talking about it, Z. If you don't? It's eventually gonna kill you."

"Why?"

"Because you can't keep that much sorrow to yourself. I want to bear it with you. I love you like a sister, even though you keep me at arm's length. You know all about my mama, my deadbeat daddy, my murdered sister, and my drug-dealing brothers. You know how hard I fought to get out of there. And all that time I was talking to you about it, you were helping me. Hooking me up with Miz McClellan's babysitting agency, putting in a good word whenever you could. I got a good job now. I'm taking night classes. I'm going to be the first one in my family who gets an associate's degree, and I might even be the first one married legit. And I got here, partially, because you listened. You stood beside me. You helped me. And Zelda, it's my turn to do the same for you. You gotta talk about it, or you'll be stuck back there forever."

Tears rolled down Griselda's weary face as she listened to Maya's words and felt the truth and fragile hope in them. And she found that resonant, comforting, familiar "no" retreating as fast as it had flared. Finding Holden again had opened up something inside her. Knowing he had survived Caleb Foster had freed her of something, and his forgiveness for getting in the truck and leaving him behind had released her from the heavy burden of her guilt. Could she talk about it all? Could she tell Maya everything?

Suddenly her mouth started moving, telling Maya about the first time she ever saw Holden as she stood across his bedroom in the Fillmans' hallway. She told Maya about seeing the Shenandoah for the first time and going to the store in Marisol's place. She explained the mix-up when Caleb *Foster* insisted her *foster* parents had sent him to pick them up. As she talked about the cellar and the ankle chains and the beatings and Leviticus, she realized something important: though she and Holden had shared their feelings about being Caleb Foster's prisoners, it had been a very long time since she'd looked at the story objectively, as a narrative, instead of a memory. And somehow, outlining it as a series of events, instead of a world of hell and heartbreak, took away some of its power over her.

She even felt a detachment to it in some ways, like she was telling one of her fantasy stories. It was her history, yes, but told as a narrative, it wasn't quite as terrifying somehow. What shocked her the most, after keeping it a secret for so long, was how fucking *good* it felt to tell someone. To hear Maya gasp with shock and shake her head with disbelief felt comforting, and the little girl inside Griselda opened her eyes and looked longingly at Maya, loving and needing the compassion, the sympathy, the comfort of someone listening to her story.

Maybe she'd been wrong to roadblock the therapist they'd offered her so long ago. Maybe it was possible to still find one to help her.

"So there he is, fighting this other guy, and you knew it was him? At first sight?"

She shook her head. "No, I had no idea. I mean, I noted that he went by Seth—"

"Which is all sorts of fucked-up, girl."

"—because that name . . . well, it's a hard name for me. But he didn't look like Holden. He looked older and meaner, and his face was unrecognizable."

"Why's he going by Seth?"

"He's not . . . anymore," said Griselda. "And Maya? My real name is Griselda."

Maya did a double take, staring at her friend twice before focusing on the highway again. "Gris—. What?"

Griselda nodded. "They made me change my name when I came back from West Virginia. They were afraid Caleb Foster would try to find me, so they told me I had to change my name. Remember Sandy? That really old social worker with the squeaky shoes and lavender hair? She suggested Zelda. She said it would be easier for me to get used to."

"And Shroder?"

"My birth name was spelled S-C-H-R-O-E-D-E-R."

"God, Zel—Grisel—what the hell do I call you?"

For the first time since she'd gotten into the car, she chuckled softly. "Zelda, dummy."

"I want to hear about what happened after the fight, but I'm wondering . . . whatever happened to the real Seth and Ruth? Do you know?"

Griselda shrugged. "The barn at their family farm caught on fire when they were teenagers. It burned to the ground, and they found items in the ashes that belonged to the twins."

"*Caught* on fire? Or *set* on fire?"

"I don't know, to be honest. I would have said 'set on fire' two weeks ago, but Caleb Foster . . ." She shook her head and sighed. "It's more . . . complicated than that. He ended up treating Holden okay all those years. Like a little brother. Didn't beat him. Didn't molest him. Kept him fed and clothed. In the end, Holden was going to high school like any other kid."

"Any other abducted kid held hostage by a psycho?"

"It all gets mixed up, Maya. You want things to be black-and-white, but they aren't. There are so many shades of gray. I hated Caleb Foster, but I can actually see he wasn't all bad. Is that crazy?"

"Yeah," said Maya.

"He could have killed Holden. Tortured him. Sold him. Molested him. Anything. But he didn't do any of those things. Holden survived, in part, because Caleb Foster ensured it."

"Stop defending him, Z. You're making me want to slap you."

"You don't get it," sighed Griselda.

"I do," said Maya after a couple of minutes. "But it sucks because we shared a bedroom for a couple of years, and I've seen your back, girl. I know what he did to you."

The scars on her back suddenly itched, and Griselda shifted in her seat.

"So tell me the rest. You saw Seth—er, Holden—at the fight, and then what?"

Griselda told Maya about Quint's visit the next afternoon, and leaving her purse and phone at the cabin to go to Holden. She told her about seeing him for the first time, re-dressing his wounds and falling asleep on the floor next to the sofa, her hand tightly bound to his. She told Maya about Gemma appearing out of nowhere, and Quint's kind offer to let them use the hunting cabin for Holden's recovery. When she told Maya how Mrs. McClellan had given her a month off, Maya muttered something about Griselda having the best boss, and when she told Maya about burning her hand and ending up in bed with Holden, Maya sighed.

"Was it . . . good?"

"Yeah," said Griselda, her eyes watering as she remembered his words: *Even when we were apart, we were still together. Even when I thought you were gone, you still lived inside my heart . . . I'm whole. You make me whole.*

"So his equipment . . .?"

"No complaints," said Griselda quickly, her cheeks flooding with heat and probably color.

"What about Jonah?"

"What about him?"

"Where does he fit into all of this?"

"He doesn't," said Griselda. "I'm breaking things off with him when I get home."

Maya glanced at her, concern clear in her brown eyes. "Not going to go over well, Z."

"I can't be with him."

"He's mean, though."

Griselda hadn't given a lot of thought to Jonah since leaving Holden an hour ago. Now her heart started thumping with worry. "Maybe I'll get a restraining order. If he bothers me."

"Maybe you should get a dog," suggested Maya. "Or hey, why don't you come stay with me and Terrence?"

"Invade the lover's nest?" asked Griselda with a knowing side glance. "I don't think so."

"Couch is all yours if you want it."

"Thanks, but I want to go home. And I need to deal with Jonah sooner or later. I'm tougher than I look, Maya."

"If you say so," said Maya unconvinced. "So you run away to a cabin and do the dirty . . . and then what?"

Heaven. "We just . . . knocked around for a couple of

weeks. I wrote down my stories. He read books. We went swimming, sat in the sun, ate, drank, remembered what it was like to be together." She could still smell the fires Holden made in the evening, still feel the heavy comfort of his arm around her shoulders. She swiped away a tear and took a deep breath. "We loved each other."

"Then you found out the girlfriend was pregnant?"

Griselda nodded. "And he insisted he'd reason with her, and it was all going to be okay."

"One big happy family."

Not exactly. "She threatened to get an abortion if he stayed with me."

"Damn, girl! What the fuck?!"

Griselda's heart clenched as she recalled the pleading in Holden's voice when he realized what Gemma was prepared to do.

"He wants kids," she murmured. "He always wanted kids."

Maya was ranting and raving about how some women should be sterilized, but Griselda didn't hear her friend anymore. She zoned out, staring out the window at the light rain that had started to fall as they got closer and closer to Laurel, Maryland.

Would Jonah be home? She braced herself. He'd be furious, and he'd take it out on her. She thought about Maya's offer again, but something inside her rebelled against hiding. It was *her* apartment. *Her* place. Jonah was going to have to get his ass out, and if he wouldn't leave, she'd call the police. Satisfied with her plan, she tuned back into Maya's rant.

"So she made you leave? Zelda?"

Griselda nodded. "Yeah. Me or the baby."

"And he chose the baby."

"No," she said, recalling his words, *I won't lose you. I can't.* "It was *my* choice. I decided to go. He begged me to stay, but I wouldn't risk it. She was crazy, Maya. Ready to go to the clinic and take care of business. I didn't want to be . . . I couldn't bear it if I was . . ."

The events of the last two weeks, and today—and hell, yes, her entire life—overtook her suddenly, and her body was racked with sobs. She bent her head forward and cried loud and long, for herself, for Holden, for that baby whose mother considered killing it. She cried for second chances and lost chances and finding what you want and losing what you love. She cried for the unfairness of it and the frustration of it and the heartbreak of it. For his beautiful words and beautiful body and the way he called her angel and said he'd love her until the end of time. She cried. And she cried. Until finally there were no tears left in her body.

She didn't know how long they'd been sitting in front of her apartment, but the engine was off and Maya sat still and sympathetic beside her in the dark, warm car. "Better?"

"No," said Griselda. "Not yet."

"So it's over?" asked Maya.

"No. Yes." She sobbed, shaking her head, bone weary, spent, and confused. "I don't know. Maybe."

Maya took a deep breath and rubbed Griselda's arm. "It's late. Let's get you inside, and I'll make you a cup of tea and make sure Jonah doesn't bother you. I'll tell him me and Terrence are coming by to check on you later. He won't mess with Ter."

Griselda nodded, giving Maya a small smile. "What would I do without you?"

"We're sisters, Griselda Schroeder," she said, trying out Griselda's full birth name for the first time. "You'll never find out."

Maya took Griselda's spare key off her key chain and handed it to her, and they walked slowly up to the apartment door. The ground-floor apartment windows were dark, and the place had a quiet, unlived-in feeling that unnerved Griselda after more than two weeks away.

Griselda turned the key in the lock, pushing open the door, but it got stuck on something and wouldn't open all the way. Flipping on the light switch to her right, she looked around the back of the door and realized that about two weeks of mail had been piled up under the mail slot. Magazines, catalogs, and bills. Lots of bills, most with the red word "overdue" stamped on the outside.

"He didn't pay one bill," said Griselda, fuming.

"You're surprised?" asked Maya, squatting down to take a handful of mail and bring it to the kitchen counter.

Griselda followed her, finding filthy dishes in the sink covered with crusted food and flies buzzing around. It smelled like decay, and she realized that the garbage hadn't been taken out in weeks. Walking through the living room, she immediately found that her TV, DVD player, and coffee table were gone. A lamp. A chair. Her futon sat dejectedly under the double windows that looked out at the parking area. On one remaining end table was a bottle half full of chaw spit, with a family of flies buzzing around it greedily. Her stomach lurched.

She made it to the bathroom in time to vomit in the toilet that smelled like a latrine. It had been used and left unflushed. She flushed it as she threw up, the smells making her stomach roll over again.

"Fuck me!" exclaimed Maya, peeking in the bathroom and covering her nose with her hand. "Is he a goddamn barn animal?"

Griselda stood up, careful to keep her nostrils closed as she breathed in, and wiped her mouth with the back of her hand. "Pretty close."

She was scared to look in their bedroom, but it was the least trashed room of the small apartment. The bedsheets were crusted with some sort of food or vomit, and it smelled like old socks, but a small TV still sat on her dresser, and a quick check of the closet showed only Jonah's things were missing.

"Maybe he moved out?" asked Maya.

"Sort of looks that way."

"I'll go clean up the kitchen and living room. You got the bathroom, okay?"

"Thanks, Maya."

Maya headed out to the kitchen, muttering about "good-for-nothing jackasses," and Griselda stripped her bed, balling up the dirty sheets and placing them in the bathroom hamper. She opened the bathroom window and took fresh sheets from under the sink back to her room. She made her bed, collected three empty beer bottles—one ringed with red lipstick—and collected the garbage, which had two used condoms among its contents. She greeted this revelation with zero emotion, except for a slight bit of pity for whomever was now saddled with Jonah, and gratitude that it wasn't her.

By the time Griselda finished scrubbing the bathroom sink, toilet, and shower with bleach, Maya had finished the dishes—an amazing feat—scrubbed the kitchen counters, and had the living room in some semblance of order. The fly population diminished every time they opened the front door and took a plastic bag to the Dumpster. And finally, two hours after they'd arrived, her apartment was mostly back to normal.

"He took your TV," said Maya.

"He can have it," said Griselda quietly, remembering that she and Holden had gone two weeks without one and she'd liked the quiet and solitude. "I have the little one."

Maya nodded. "You look exhausted."

"I'm beat."

"Can I make you some tea?"

Griselda shook her head. "I'm going to take a hot shower and go to bed."

"Sounds like a plan," said Maya, opening her arms. "You're so brave, Zelda. So fucking brave. Thank you for sharing the whole story with me."

Tears ran down Griselda's face as she hugged her friend back. "I'm grateful for you, Maya."

"I'm grateful for you." Maya gave Griselda a kiss on the cheek before pulling away. "Lock the windows and chain the door? Just in case?"

"I promise," said Griselda, mustering a small smile.

"I'll see you and Pru at the park tomorrow?"

"Or as soon as I go back to work."

"And you'll call me if you need me?"

"Always."

Maya nodded and let herself out, and Griselda dutifully locked and chained the door shut before stripping off her clothes and taking a hot shower. She belatedly realized she'd left the clothes Holden bought her in Maya's car, but she could get them tomorrow. For now, she just wanted sleep.

She wept in the shower, assaulted by sad and happy memories, her body aching for Holden's arms around her, the touch of his gentle lips all over her body. She missed him with a fierceness that felt new and familiar at once, and though she tried to take comfort in the certainty of his love for her, her loneliness was almost unbearable.

She turned off the water and headed to bed, sliding between the clean sheets without drying off or dressing, and, thinking about Holden's gray eyes and freckles, she cried herself to sleep.

CHAPTER 28

The cellar door creaked open, and a strip of light grew brighter and longer as the sound of steel-toed boots scuffled at the top of the stairs, ready to descend. Cutter whined, but he wasn't allowed downstairs. Six months ago he'd been a sweet puppy sitting on Griselda's lap the day they'd been taken. Today he was as mean as his master, and his teeth were awful sharp.

Without making a sound, Griselda rolled off Holden's bed to the floor, crawled to the paneled wall, pushed aside the loose panel without a peep, and returned to her room. She sat against the wall, holding her knees tightly to her chest, praying Holden would say the words without stuttering this time.

Thank you. Thank you. Thank you. Thank you.

She said the words in her head over and over again, enunciating the th- *and seamlessly sliding to the* you, *as if by concentrating on them, Holden would say them smoothly, without stammering.*

She heard muffled voices, but the sound of a tin bowl clattering across the floor, followed by Holden's sudden cry, told her that her prayers had been in vain. She bent her head to her knees and covered it with her arms, but the blunt sound of palm smacking child still found its way to her ears, embedding itself in her brain.

Stop, *she thought.* Oh God, please make it stop!

She heard the Man yell, "And jus' for that, she don't get none either! Pray for yer souls! Pray all day that He, in His mercy, might remove the wickedness from yer hearts!"

As she lifted her head from her knees, she heard the boots scuffle across the floor, finally making their heavy, deliberate ascent up the stairs, and the blessed music of the lock and bolt clicking.

Griselda counted to ten, then slipped back through the panel. Holden lay on the floor, his nose and lip bleeding, his eyes unfocused as he stared at the ceiling.

"Holden?"

"H-h-hurts."

"I know," she said, scrambling over to him. She sat cross-legged beside him, pulling his head onto her lap. "He gets real mad when you stutter—um, stammer—Holden. You gotta try not to."

Tears rolled down Holden's cheeks as he looked up at Griselda, trying unsuccessfully to blink them away.

"N-n-nobody's c-coming for us, Gris. N-n-nobody c-cares."

She stroked his dirty hair away from his forehead. They were each given a cold basin of water and a bar of soap on Sunday mornings before the Man went to church. It didn't get all the grime off, but by today—Saturday—they both smelled powerfully bad and itched something fierce. But the smell didn't bother Griselda. In fact, she barely noticed it anymore. He was Holden. That meant he smelled sweeter than anyone else in the world because he was her whole world.

"I care," she said. "I care about you, and you care about me. And no matter what, that'll last forever."

"F-forever's a f-fantasy," muttered Holden.

"No, it isn't. Forever is the good stuff," she said, running her fingers through his silky strands of greasy hair, like she'd seen mothers do in movies and on TV. She took the hem of her *grubby yellow dress and dabbed his lip. "And you don't know for sure. Maybe somebody will find us. Someday."*

"W-we don't have anyone to look f-for us, Gris." He crawled out of her lap to his cot and sat down on the filthy mattress. "C-can't be f-found unless someone's looking."

She scooted across the floor to his cot, sitting on the floor beside his legs, leaning her head to the side to rest it on his thigh. She felt safer when they were touching.

"Then I'll keep looking at you," she said, twisting her neck to catch his eyes. "So you won't feel so lost."

He ran his hands through her hair, and she resettled herself on his thigh, letting her eyes drift closed.

I'll keep looking for you.

I'll always be looking for you.

And you'll never feel lost.

Because you'll never be lost.

And we'll be together forever.

Forever, Holden.

Banging. Boots banging. Louder. Closer.

"Wake up, Gris," said Holden, his voice full of panic. He was shaking her shoulders with both hands, and whispering louder than he should. "You gotta wake up!"

"Gris!" he screamed. "Wake up!"

***

Griselda bolted upright, disoriented, the banging from her dream louder, not softer, as her eyes opened. Her heart raced as she realized she was naked, and she stood up on shaky legs, feeling her way to her bureau and pulling out sweat pants and a T-shirt. The banging was real, but it wasn't boots stomping or fists hammering a door. It was banging like a door on a chain being forced open over and over again. He'd unlocked the door but found the door chained closed, and it was only a matter of time until the chain snapped.

Jonah, she thought with dread. *Jonah's here.*

Grappling against the bare surface of her bedside table, she realized that she didn't have a cell phone charging there, as she used to. The only phone she had was a landline on the wall of the kitchen, beside the front door. Looking desperately at the trio of narrow windows in her bedroom, she considered whether or not she could wiggle out of one and decided she probably couldn't. Still, it was worth a try.

She stepped over to the bedroom door, quietly closed it, and turned the lock, then raced to the windows, opening one, and pushing against the screen as the banging sound got faster and more insistent. That chain was not going to last much longer.

"Zelllllda!" he bellowed, slurring her name, menace thick in his voice. "You in there?"

She threw one leg out the window, bending it at the knee, straddling the windowsill. Her leg slipped through the opening to her thigh, but no matter how she shifted her hips, she couldn't get them through. It just wasn't wide enough.

"Open the door, Zelda!"

With one more bang, she heard the door crash open, swinging into the remaining end table beside the sofa, and Griselda pulled herself back out of the window, looking around the room for anything she could use as a weapon. Her eyes zeroed in on a pair of scissors on her desk, and she picked them up, standing on the other side of the bed, her eyes focused on the door.

The doorknob to her room rattled, and she tried to calm her breathing, but this was as crazy as she'd ever known Jonah, and her only hope was that one of her neighbors had heard the ruckus and already called the police.

He banged his shoulder into the door, and it shook but remained shut, and she was cautiously hopeful that it was stronger than she thought, until she heard his running footsteps, and suddenly the door flew open, and Jonah stumbled into the room.

Griselda's entire body braced, her muscles taut and tense. Her only option was to lure him into the room and somehow get past him, into the hallway, through the living room, back out the broken front door. If she didn't, she was trapped.

"So . . . slut," he drawled, his eyes heavy from drinking and dark with fury as he put his hands on his hips. "You're back."

"I don't want any trouble," she said, adjusting and readjusting her sweaty fingers on the scissors she held by her side.

His eyes dropped to them, and he smirked before looking up at her. "And yet you're holding a fucking weapon."

"Please, Jonah," she said, trying to stay calm. "Just go. Just—"

"I'm not going to fucking go, Zelda," he said, taking a step toward her. "This is my fucking home, and you're my fucking girlfriend. The question is . . ." He chuckled humorlessly. "Who exactly have you been fucking?"

"It's not your home. Your name isn't on the lease. This is *my* apartment. You're . . . trespassing," she said, forcing her voice not to waver.

"Trespassing," he repeated, laughing softly for a few seconds and abruptly stopping. The color and expression drained from his face, and his eyes bored into hers. "You fucking cunt."

Her eyes darted to the doorway, but Jonah had placed himself directly in front of it. The only way around him was to leap over the bed, but she'd lose too much time and he'd grab her. Should she scream? Should she just start screaming like a lunatic and hope her neighbors called the police? She listened carefully for the sound of sirens but heard none. Despite the racket he'd made breaking down her front door, it didn't appear that anyone had called the cops.

"Jonah, I was kidnapped when I was a little girl," she said quickly, looking up at him. "I was kidnapped and held captive for three years. And . . . that fighter? Seth? His real name is Holden. He was held captive with me. And . . ."

"Shut the fuck up," said Jonah, narrowing his eyes and shaking his head. He froze when she didn't say anything, and stared at her face. "What the *fuck* are you talking about?"

"It's true. Take out your phone," she said, still trying to breathe normally, though her eyes burned with tears and her heart raced with fear. "I mean it. Take out your phone and type in 'Hansel and Gretel kidnapping West Virginia 2001,' or you could type 'Griselda and Holden abduction Charles Town 2001.' It'll come up. I promise."

He took his phone out of his back pocket, still staring at her with menace. "Don't fucking try anything."

It took him a long time to type because his fingers were big and uncoordinated from the amount he'd had to drink. Finally his thumb slid down the screen, scanning an article, and after a few minutes he looked up at her.

"Fuck." He stared at his phone and Griselda knew the picture he was looking at. It was the same one that had been on "Kidnapped" posters across West Virginia. It was the same one on Holden's arm. "This is you."

"Yeah." She swallowed.

"You were kidnapped."

"With him. I needed to talk to him."

"Your foster brother."

She nodded, and felt a little relieved as Jonah's posture relaxed. Maybe he would leave now.

Jonah glanced back down at his phone and then back up at her, before shoving the phone back in his pocket. "Okay. Fine. So you caught up with your old foster brother. Now you're fucking home. I forgive you. Let's move the fuck on. I'm horny."

"No," she whispered.

His fingers moved to his belt buckle, and her stomach

turned over as he opened the button of his jeans. "Get on your fucking knees and show me how much you missed me."

"No."

"What?" he asked, hands back on his hips, eyes narrowing.

"No. I'm not . . . It's over, Jonah."

"What the fuck does that mean? I didn't say *shit* was over."

"I don't want to be with you anymore."

"Why the fuck not?"

She swallowed, and somehow, some way, her fear receded. It ebbed away, and all that was left was anger. That same white-hot, seething anger that had made her head-butt him in West Virginia.

"*Why the fuck not?*" he demanded.

"Because you beat me and hit me and treat me mean. Because you don't give a shit about who I am or what I want or where I'm going. Because I don't have to put up with your shit anymore, Jonah. I survived three years in a cellar and ten years without Holden. I survived leaving. *Again!* And I *will* survive you, you sick, selfish fuck!"

"You're gonna be sorry you said that," said Jonah, turning the high school ring on his finger so the stone was facing his palm, then, rethinking it, he twisted it back outward again. "Say you're sorry."

"I'm not. Fuck. You."

She raised the scissors and ran at him, screaming as loud as she could. The scissors sunk into the fleshy patch of skin under his collarbone, and when he was stunned and howling, Griselda pushed him out of her way, running out her bedroom door and into the hallway.

R-r-r-r-uuuuuun!

She heard it in her head as clear as day, as loud as if thirteen-year-old Holden was standing beside her.

But this time she didn't escape.

This time the monster caught up with *her.*

Jonah's hand bunched in her hair, snapping her neck back just as she reached the living room. She screamed again as he swept her legs out from under her and she landed on her stomach, the air knocked out of her lungs. Unable to breathe or move, she felt his steel-toed work boot slam into her side once, twice. The third time, she heard the cracking sound of her ribs breaking, and when she tried to take a breath and raise herself to her knees, a sharp, stabbing, unthinkable pain made her instantly freeze.

She moaned deep in her throat, trying to take another breath, stopped by the excruciating pain in her chest.

"You like that, you fucking slut?" bellowed Jonah, his face a mask of rage.

Jonah reached down and grabbed a fistful of her hair, drawing back his fist and slamming it into her face.

Holden's face was inches away, surrounded by a halo of warm light, staring at her from where she lay on her living room carpet. He reached out and ran his fingers through her hair, and his lips touched down on hers like the feathers of an angel's wing.

"Find me," she murmured, though the words were slurred and garbled, like she was talking under water.

I'll keep looking at you. So you won't feel so lost.

She tried to say "I love you," but it hurt too much to breathe. His lips tilted up in a sweet smile.

I love you too. His face was fading, his voice dreamy and far away. *Forever, angel.*

Her hair was yanked again, and her face lifted off the floor. A second later her skull exploded in more pain than she could bear.

Darkness.

CHAPTER 29

Holden was good for nothing.

Since Griselda had left, four days ago, he'd spent almost all his time at work or in his truck, saying little, unable to take pleasure in anything, coming home drunk, as late as possible, and crashing on the couch. Up and out at the crack of dawn, he'd been able to avoid Gemma almost entirely since Sunday afternoon, when she showed up with her car full of stuff. Reminded near constantly of her condition, he'd grudgingly helped her move in, hating every second. She'd taken over his bedroom and bathroom, the strong stink of her cigarettes lingering in the air when he finally stumbled home.

She'd quit her job at the DQ, and he left ten dollars on the kitchen table every morning. Every evening, it was gone. He didn't know what she did with it, but she'd already left one receipt for prenatal vitamins in the same spot to assure him, he assumed, that the money was going to good use and he should keep up the flow.

There were two things Holden was quickly understanding.

The first was that having a baby was expensive. In addition to the $300 a month he planned to give Gemma for her living and prenatal expenses, there was going to be a hefty doctor bill when the baby came, plus all the furniture babies needed. Quint and Maudie were kind enough to offer them Clinton's old crib and changing table, under the condition that they be returned in good condition. Holden didn't mind borrowing old things from good friends, though he could tell that Gemma wasn't happy about hand-me-downs. The couple of times she'd caught him at home, she dropped not-so-subtle hints about him taking on some more fights. But he'd promised Griselda he wouldn't fight anymore, and he worked in a glass factory, not a bank, which left a tight income stream where there used to be wiggle room.

Griselda.

Holden's second realization was that life was barely worth living without her.

Though he agreed with her, in principle at least, that he couldn't risk Gemma terminating the pregnancy, losing Gris had been next to unbearable. He still felt her smooth, warm skin under his fingertips, her small body curved into his. He still heard her belt his name, sweating and gasping, when she came, and whisper his name with aching tenderness when she told him she loved him.

Her loss was everywhere and agonizing. There wasn't a moment that he didn't think of her while awake or dream of her while asleep, tangled dreams of a girl in braids and a beautiful woman. He'd told her, *I'm ruined for anyone but you*, and no truer words had ever been spoken.

As the hours turned into days, the future that had looked so promising a week ago looked bleaker and more empty. If he had to support Gemma and the baby, he'd never make enough to support Gris too. Not the way he wanted to. They'd live in some shithole close to Gemma so he could see his kid, his money going to the baby, unable to help Griselda with college, both of them working like dogs for a mediocre life.

Sometimes his thoughts were so desperate and dark, he wondered if it would be better for Gris to go ahead and find someone else. Though every cell in his body roared and raged in objection to the idea of someone else touching her, loving her, taking care of her, he was a selfish bastard if he didn't let her go.

Twice he'd sat down to write her a letter.

Move on, Gris. Forget me. Go to college and make a life for yourself.

But each time, he had balled up the paper in sorrow and fury and poured himself another shot. He couldn't let her go. Not yet. Oh God, not yet.

He had nothing to live for but his memories of Gris and his unborn child. But despite his longing to be a good father, that baby almost wasn't enough. He was trapped, and life felt hopeless. Foolishly hanging on in the hope that sunshine would break through the darkness—someway, somehow—every day was more lonely and soul crushing than the last.

Waking on the nubby, brown couch, he sat up, rubbed the back of his neck, and blinked his eyes. It smelled like coffee and food, and he narrowed his eyes suspiciously as he noted Gemma in her nightgown standing by the stove. She turned and looked at him, spatula in hand.

"Mornin'," she said, offering him a very small, cautious smile.

"Morning," he rasped, clearing his throat. His head pounded from last night's three-hour date with cheap whiskey, and his stomach growled, reminding him he hadn't had dinner. "What're you doing?"

"Makin' you breakfast."

"Why?"

"Because it's morning," she snapped. She grimaced, then forced her face to soften. "Because I've decided to forgive you for cheatin' on me. It's time for us to move on from that . . . mistake."

He flinched, his body tightening in anger at her use of the word *mistake*. In no universe would Holden classify his time with Griselda as accidental or regrettable. The only thing he truly regretted was letting her go.

"It wasn't a mistake," he muttered.

"Well, whatever it was, it's over now," said Gemma sharply, turning back around to tend to whatever she was cooking.

Like hell, thought Holden, leaning over to pull his cell phone off the end table. *It'll never be over.*

He squinted at the small screen. Three missed calls from an unknown number. Hmm. That was unusual because, besides Clinton and Quint, barely anyone ever called him.

"You trying to get a hold of me last night?" he called to Gemma, wondering if she'd gotten a new number and forgotten to give it to him.

She looked at him over her shoulder. "Nope."

Holden looked back down at his phone, touching the voice mail icon and entering his pass code. He held the phone up to his ear.

"Holden? It's, um, my name is Maya. Maya Harper. Zelda's friend. She called me from this phone number last weekend to pick her up. And, um, oh God, I don't even know how to say this, but Zelda's, she's in the hospital. Jonah, her ex, he beat her real bad. He . . . he punctured her lung and slammed her head against the floor, and, well, they put her in a coma. It's been two days now. And I didn't know if I should call you, but I decided I should. So I don't know. Maybe I was wrong. I'm just . . . I'm so scared. Call me back, maybe, okay?"

Holden was holding his breath, and his body finally rebelled, forcing him to exhale and gasp in another breath. *Fuck! Fuck, no! Shit, shit, shit.* Suddenly he was breathing like he'd just sprinted a mile, and he looked down at the phone. Two more messages. *Oh God. Was she dead? Did she die? Oh, Gris. Oh my God. Please, no!*

He pressed Play for the second message.

"Hi, Holden . . . it's Maya again. I'm worried she'd be pissed if I called you. I'm sitting next to her right now, and . . .

she's still in the coma, but her vitals are good. Her cheeks are pink. They say that's good. Maybe they can wake her up soon or something. I'm visiting her as much as I can, but I've got to go to work too. I'm sorry I keep calling you, but I don't have any family, and Zelda doesn't either, and she's real important to me, so . . . Oh, wait. Doc's coming. I'll call back if there's news."

"Breakfast is ready!" called Gemma.

"Shut up," sneered Holden, pressing Play as fast as he could for the final message.

"Holden, it's Maya. She's gonna be okay." Maya started laughing and crying, and Holden sighed raggedly as she took a moment to catch her breath. "They're . . . Oh, wow. They're waking her up from the coma now, and she's gonna be here for a while longer, but her brain wave function is real good, and they say she'll probably make a full recovery. I mean, her ribs are busted, and she had some intra . . . intracranial bleeding? But I guess she's gonna be okay. So I . . . well, you haven't called me back. I guess I'm sorry for calling you. I thought . . . well, it doesn't matter. Good luck with your, um, your baby. Bye, now."

"I said, 'Breakfast is ready.'"

Holden looked up at Gemma, her image blurred by the relieved tears that crowded his eyes. Gris was going to be okay. Thank God.

"I have to g-go," he said, standing up. He shoved his phone in his pocket and grabbed his keys from the end table.

"Where the hell are you going? I made you some fucking breakfast."

"Th-then you f-f-fucking eat it," he said, striding to the apartment door and walking through it without looking back.

***

"Holden? Holden . . ."

It felt hard to make the words, like her mouth was full of sandpaper and chewing gum, dry and swollen. And her head felt fuzzy, but it was also pounding. Where was she? Was she in

Holden's apartment, or—no, they'd left his apartment and gone to the cabin. Was she at the cabin?

She tried to open her eyes, but they were so heavy, and the sounds around her were so garbled, like being underwater.

"Holden?" she said again, but trying to talk was so exhausting she stopped trying.

Darkness.

***

Holden called Clinton on his way out of town.

"I'm headed to D.C."

"What the fuck, Se—?"

"G-Griselda is in a coma."

"What? Oh Jesus. What happened?"

"Her f-fucking ex-boyfriend beat her up."

"Shit. I'm so sorry, man."

"I ran out of my apartment as soon as I got the message. Gemma's pissed."

"Don't worry about her," said Clinton quickly. "I'll cover for you. Just, uh . . . I'll say Chick had a problem with a delivery and he needed you to take some stuff back to Ohio. You'll be gone a couple of days. Maybe text her, though, okay? So she doesn't go crazy?"

"Yeah. I will. Thanks, Clinton."

"You love this girl."

"Gris? Yeah. She's it for me."

"What's your plan? What about Gemma and the baby?" A protective edge crept into Clinton's voice, and Holden was half tempted to tell his friend to go to hell, or better yet, go to Gemma and convince her that she and Clinton deserved a second chance.

"I don't know. I just . . . I have to see Gris. I have to be sure she's okay."

"Yeah. Call me tomorrow, okay? I don't think I can make this convincing for more than a day or two."

"I owe you, Clinton."

"No, I think we're even now. But we're *even*, Holden. I don't owe you anything else."

With that warning simmering between them, Holden decided it was time to clear the air. "You never got over her, did you? Gemma."

Clinton didn't miss a beat. "I thought I did. Damn, but I wanted to be. Over her. She's pregnant with *your* kid. And that fucking kills me."

"You'd make her happier than me," said Holden.

"She don't want me." He chuckled in that unfunny way that told Holden how much it hurt. "Aren't we all a fucking mess? You want Griselda. Gemma wants you. I want Gemma."

"Yeah. It's a mess."

"I hope Griselda's okay. Call me tomorrow."

"Thanks, Clinton."

Holden hung up the phone and dialed Maya's number as his truck crossed the county line, leaving Charles Town behind.

"Hello?"

"Maya, this is Holden C-Croft."

"Holden. Hi. I'm, um, sorry for all the messages."

"How is she?"

Maya sighed deeply. "Well, she woke up for a little bit, asking for you, but she didn't open her eyes. She's sleeping now. Sometimes it takes a while for the patient to wake up after . . ."

He winced, imagining what she'd been through and cursing the fact that he hadn't been there to protect her. She should have been with him. She should have been safe. He would never, ever fucking forgive himself for letting her go.

"How's her head?"

"Bleeding's stopped. They didn't have to operate, thank God. And the swelling's already going down. But they won't know everything until she wakes up. You know, the extent of the damage. In her brain."

"Got it." He clenched his jaw until it hurt. "And Jonah?"

"Arrested. He's being charged with assault and battery, and possibly attempted murder."

"Good."

Holden had a fleeting thought that Jonah was lucky to be behind bars. If he wasn't, Holden would have tracked him down and killed him with his bare hands. No question.

"She was on a ventilator for her lungs, but she got off that today too. Her ribs will take a while to heal."

"I wish you'd called me sooner."

"I wasn't gonna call you at all, but I got scared." Maya's voice was sheepish and soft when she said again, "She asked for you."

"I'll be there soon."

"Oh, thank God. I didn't know if I should ask . . ."

"When it comes to her? Always ask and I'll always come. Where are you?"

"Laurel Regional Hospital. In Laurel, Maryland. On Van Dusen."

Holden cradled the phone between his shoulder and ear and punched the address into his GPS. "Fifty minutes."

"Great," said Maya. She sighed heavily. "I'm glad. Can you stay a little while?"

"As long as she needs me."

"Okay," she said, relief thick in her voice.

"Thank you, M-Maya," he said, a lump forming in his throat, making his voice sound choked.

"See you soon, Holden," she said, disconnecting the call.

Holden clenched the steering wheel, hating himself for letting Gemma drive Griselda away, and pushing down hard on the gas.

***

"Zelda?"

Someone was calling her name. A man. A man she didn't

know. Why was there a man she didn't know in the cabin?

"Zelda? Can you hear me?"

His voice was distorted, muffled, like he was talking into a pillow.

"Try *Gris*elda," said someone who sounded a lot like Maya.

"Griselda? Can you open your eyes for me?"

I think I can, she thought, but oh God, they were so heavy. She concentrated, trying to take a deep breath, but holy hell, her chest hurt like crazy every time she tried to inflate her lungs. A rusty, whimpering sound echoed in her brain, and she realized it had come from her own throat.

"I think she's coming around," said the male voice again. "Open up those eyes, Griselda."

Using all her strength, she forced her lids to separate, but only one of her eyes would open. She kept it narrowly opened, the light in the room bright and painful.

"Nurse, pull the shades, please."

An older man with gray hair and glasses was staring at her, not too far from her face. Though he looked kind, he wasn't familiar to her, and she still felt panicked. She wasn't at the cabin. Where was Holden? Had the man said "nurse"?

"She's going to be disoriented. Step over here, Ms. Harper, so she can see you."

Suddenly the older man's face was eclipsed by Maya's, and Griselda almost sighed with relief. If Maya was here, she was safe.

"Hey, baby girl."

"MMMaya," she rasped, her throat dry and painful. "You got . . . water?"

"Nurse? Get us some ice chips, please." The older man's face moved beside Maya's, but Griselda stayed focused on her friend.

"Griselda, you're at Laurel Regional Hospital," the man

said. His voice, like Maya's, was distorted, and Griselda had to concentrate hard to make out his words. "You sustained some injuries after an altercation with your boyfriend, a Mr.—"

"Jonah," said Maya. "The night I brought you home."

"Home? No. Cabin."

Home? When did I go home? I should still be at the cabin.

"I drove you home from West Virginia," said Maya, her voice slow and gentle, but still garbled. She turned to the older man, whom Griselda now realized was a doctor. "Does she not remember?"

"Short-term memory loss is common. Was she at a cabin recently?"

"Yes," said Maya. "She spent two weeks at a cabin with her foster brother. I picked her up and drove her home on Sunday."

"So about four days ago. Okay. That's good. It gives us a timeline. It appears she has no memory of the last few days, but that's not at all uncommon." He looked back at Griselda and spoke slowly, "Griselda? It's Wednesday."

No. No, it's not. It's Friday. She tried to take a deep breath and sit up, but the pain in her chest was so sharp she whimpered, leaning back down.

Maya drew closer. "Don't try to move, baby girl. Jonah hurt you, Zelda. He broke a couple of your ribs and punctured your lung. Your head . . ."

"Help, Maya," she sobbed, feeling overwhelmed and as helpless as a baby. "Help. Help me find Holden."

"He's coming, Zelda. I promise he's coming."

She didn't know why she was crying, but her chest hurt and her head hurt and her face hurt. She wasn't at the cabin, she was in the hospital, and Holden wasn't here with her. Apparently she'd been beat up badly by Jonah, but she had no recollection of seeing him, and she couldn't imagine Holden ever letting that happen. She was confused and sad and frightened.

"Her blood pressure's on the rise," said the doctor. "I'm going to give her something to make her sleep."

A moment later their voices faded away, and her eyes closed.

Mercy.

CHAPTER 30

Holden parked his truck in the visitor parking lot, catching a glimpse of himself in the rearview mirror as he cut the engine. He looked like a mess. Same shirt he had on last night, wild hair, red-rimmed eyes, two-day scruff of beard growing in golden-brown. He grimaced, took his keys out of the ignition, and swung his legs out of the truck. Before he saw her, he'd find a men's room and splash some cold water on his face. He ran his hands through his hair, trying to smooth it down. It was the best he could do.

Maya had texted him that Griselda was still in the ICU, though the doctor said they'd be moving her to a regular room soon. She'd woken up once since he talked to Maya, and she'd been so distorted and distressed the doctor had put something in her IV to calm her and make her go back to sleep. Maya said she thought Griselda would be waking up in a few hours and hoped that seeing Holden would help things go more smoothly. Apparently Gris didn't remember leaving the cabin, the confrontation with Gemma, or their horrible, heart-wrenching good-bye. He was grateful for that in some ways.

He strode into the hospital and stopped by the information kiosk to ask for directions. He didn't know what time visiting hours ended and didn't ask. He'd fight anyone who tried to take him away from her. He wasn't leaving until he was sure she was going to be okay.

Stepping onto the elevator, he pressed the button for the second floor, clenching and unclenching his fists as he steeled himself against seeing her injuries.

"Everything okay, son?"

He looked up in surprise. When he entered the elevator, he hadn't noticed anyone else, but a uniformed soldier stood in the corner, looking at Holden with concern and compassion.

"Yes, sir."

"Visiting someone?"

Holden nodded. "Yes sir."

"Hope they're on this side of okay by this time tomorrow."

"Thank you, sir."

The doors opened, and Holden exited the elevator, following the signs for the ICU. When he got to a locked set of metal double doors, he rang the bell but was told by a nurse via intercom that he wasn't on the approved visitor list.

Frustrated, he texted Maya. *They won't let me in.*

Give me a minute. Then, *Sabrina's coming. She'll get you in.*

Holden pushed his phone back into his pocket, assuming that Sabrina was a nurse until the doors opened and a young woman in street clothes stood staring at him.

"Holden?"

This woman was no nurse. She was stunning—superclassy and probably very rich. It only took Holden a moment to realize that Sabrina was Mrs. McClellan. She had to be.

"Mrs. McClellan?"

"Yes. She mentioned me?"

Holden nodded.

"And you're the foster brother?"

"I was. Once."

"And now?"

He shrugged. He didn't know how much Gris would want

him to share with her employer. Hell, he didn't even know if Sabrina knew about what he and Griselda had been through.

Without pushing him for more information, she gave him a grim smile and stepped back so he could precede her through the metal door.

"I warn you, she doesn't look good."

"I've seen it b-before," he whispered, wishing it wasn't true, but it was. He'd seen her face and back cracked open more than he could count, her shoulder dislocated, her wrists and ankles raw and bloody. He was no stranger to Griselda being injured.

"You were in the system with her?" asked Sabrina, walking briskly down one hallway before turning down another.

It smelled like antiseptic and sickness, and Holden's stomach whirled in protest. He hated hospitals. Always had. Especially this one because it held a broken, beaten Griselda.

"Uh, yeah. For a little wh-while."

"And then?"

She had stopped in front of a room, her hand on the doorknob, her eyes looking up at his, inquisitive, sympathetic.

"C-can I see her, please?"

Sabrina nodded. "Yes. Then we'll talk?"

Holden didn't answer as she twisted the knob. He stepped into the dim, quiet room.

"Holden?" whispered Maya.

His eyes adjusted, and he saw a light-skinned black woman approach him from the far side of the room.

"Yeah."

She wrapped her arms around him, catching him off guard, and he stood awkwardly, finally raising one hand to pat her on the back.

"Thanks for coming," she said.

"I need to see her."

Maya released him and stepped aside. "I'll be outside with

Sabrina. Come find me when you're ready, and I'll give you an update, okay?"

Maya brushed past him, slipping silently out the door and leaving Holden and Griselda alone. He made it to her bedside in two steps. He braced himself before opening his eyes.

Gris. Gris. Oh God, oh Jesus.

Her right eye was severely swollen and discolored—black and blue and green—and over it was a gash in her forehead that had been closed with seven butterflies. Her amber hair had crusted blood in it, and her ear was swollen and bruised, with dried blood in the ear cavity and maroon and black bruises underneath.

The hospital sheets were pulled up to her chin, but he drew them down. She was covered in a hospital gown, so he wasn't able to see her chest. IV lines and heart monitor wires peeked out from the light blue fabric. He re-covered her carefully so he didn't disturb anything. Glancing at the monitor over her bed, he noted that her heart rate seemed even and her blood pressure normal.

He sat down in the chair beside her bed. He reached under the sheet for her fingers and held them gently, careful not to disturb the IV port on the back of her hand.

"G-Gris? C-can you hear me? I'm here, angel. I'm here with you. I'm here."

She made a soft sound in the back of her throat, rotating her head a touch so she was facing him in her sleep.

"I love you so m-much," he sobbed softly. "And I'm so f-fucking sorry I wasn't there to p-protect you."

She made that sound again, then sighed, "S'okay."

"I'm gonna stay with you for a while, Gris."

"I jump . . ." she said, her eyes still closed, her lips moving slowly.

"That's right," he said, sniffling. "I jump, you jump."

She was silent for so long, he was sure she'd fallen back to sleep when he suddenly realized she was trying to say something else.

". . . whole or . . . broken?"

He clenched his eyes shut and lowered his forehead to the bed beside her undamaged ear as his tears fell over the bridge of his nose and plopped on the sheet between them. "Whole, angel. I'm w-with you, so I'm wh-whole. G-go back to sleep. I'm here. I'll stay."

She murmured unintelligibly, and a moment later he could tell she was asleep again.

He lifted his head and watched her sleep for a while as his mind tried unsuccessfully to figure out a solution to their separation. He was miserable without her, which made his life in West Virginia completely worthless and almost unbearable. He hated Gemma. He damn near hated his unborn baby, then cringed, taking back the thought because it wasn't true. All he wanted was to be with Gris, and yet he couldn't offer her—or his kid, for that matter—anything good, anything substantial. His life was a train wreck, and he didn't have the first idea of how to get it to a good place—to a place where his love and his child could be safe, could be loved, could be proud of him.

Defeated and despairing, he lay his head back down beside hers, carefully braided his fingers through hers, and eventually fell asleep.

***

"Holden? Holden, wake up."

He blinked, sat up straight, and looked up. Maya and Sabrina stood beside him, and the room was much brighter than before.

"I'm n-not leaving," he said, panicked at the idea of being forced to leave Griselda.

Sabrina cocked her head to the side in confusion, then took a breath, nodding in realization. "Don't worry. Visiting hours don't apply to the ICU. You don't have to leave. You can stay as long as you want to."

"I slept a while."

"So did she," said Maya, with a sad smile. "Best sleep she's had in days. I checked on you two a couple of times, and she wasn't tossing and turning or calling out. Both of you just sleeping like babies. But we thought you might need some lunch." Maya put a hand on his shoulder. "Go on. I'll stay with her. Doc said the meds should wear off in another hour or so."

Holden looked back at Griselda, regretfully pulling his fingers away from hers and standing up to stretch.

"Can I buy you lunch?" asked Sabrina, gesturing to the door.

"I can buy my own," said Holden.

She gave him a polite smile and nodded.

"You need anything, Maya?"

"I already ate, but I wouldn't say no to Twizzlers," she said.

"Coming right up," he said, and he followed Sabrina out the door.

He pulled the hospital room door closed and turned to her. "Thanks for being here."

Sabrina nodded. "Of course. I care very much for Zelda. She's been with us for four years, though I'm ashamed to admit I didn't know her very well before now."

They made their way back through the metal doors where she'd met him, heading for the elevator that would take them to the cafeteria two floors down.

"How long was she with Jonah?" Sabrina said.

She said his name like a dirty word, and Holden liked her for that. He was mistrustful of wealthy people, having grown up in a modest, but happy, home before his fractured adolescence. He didn't have experience with rich folks. They were from a different planet—for all that it mattered, a different universe—that orbited far, far away from his.

But she seemed nice enough, even if she dressed too fancy for a hospital, in flowy pants and a shiny shirt. She wore a gold necklace that was probably real, and her blonde hair was in a smooth, twisty bun on the back of her head. She looked expensive, and that made him nervous, but she was kind to Gris, being here, giving her a job, encouraging her to think about college. Despite her fancy-pants appearance, he needed to give Sabrina a chance.

"Jonah? I don't know. A year. Something like that."

"I noticed the bruises from time to time. I didn't say anything, because I didn't want to embarrass her."

Holden's eyes shot to hers at this confession, but he kept his lips tightly sealed lest he burst forth in a series of curse words that would turn her blonde hair white.

She read his censure with ease, and her cheeks pinkened. "I should have done something."

"Yes. You should have."

"I'm sorry," said Sabrina.

"Gris mighta stayed with him anyway."

"Gris," she said softly.

"Her full name is Griselda."

"Griselda. Zelda. I had no idea," said Sabrina. She took a breath and exhaled heavily. "That's very common in abusive relationships, you know. For a woman to stay with her abuser."

Holden glanced at her, but didn't comment.

"And you were her foster brother?"

The elevator dinged to announce their floor. "Yeah. Before we were, uh, abducted."

Sabrina flinched as Holden held the door for her to leave the elevator. She stood frozen, the color drained from her face. "Ab—"

"Abducted. K-kidnapped." He had no idea what made him suddenly talk about their ordeal. Maybe it was that he sensed Sabrina McClellan really wanted to help Griselda and she needed help, and Holden wasn't in a position to offer much. The least he could do was find someone else who could give her a hand.

Sabrina stared at him in shock until the elevator started buzzing, and then she dropped his eyes and exited quickly. Silent until they reached the cafeteria, she finally turned to him, her eyes stricken. "Kidnapped. My God."

He turned to her, searching her eyes and deciding to trust her with everything. Maya was great, but Holden's guess was that Maya was just squeaking by. Griselda needed someone other than Maya in her court. She needed someone strong, someone who could offer her real support. Perhaps Sabrina could be that person, but not unless she understood the true depth of Griselda's character . . . and need.

"W-we were kidnapped from a country road in West Virginia when we were ten years old and held captive in a man's basement for three years. B-beaten regularly. Forced to work."

"Were you . . .?"

He could see it in her eyes—the terrible question, the worst question.

"No," he said, shaking his head. "W-we weren't molested."

Sabrina took a deep, ragged breath, then nodded, urging him to keep going.

"After a few years, Gris escaped. I didn't. I was told she was d-dead, but she wasn't. She went back into foster care. We . . . found each other two weeks ago. I love her. She loves me. When she came home, her shitbag b-boyfriend b-beat her up." Holden let go of the breath he'd been holding, shrugging in apology for cursing. "I think you're all caught up."

"Dear God," sighed Sabrina, her pink-painted fingernails trembling over her lips.

"She's tough," he said, his lips tilting up a bit in admiration for his strong girl. "She's . . ." He thought of her lying in that bed upstairs, battered and confused, and his heart clenched. He blinked several times, turning away from Sabrina.

They each took a tray, choosing their lunches, Holden careful to remember Maya's candy.

"How can I help?" she asked, once they'd both been seated.

Gauging her sincerity, Holden found her expression open and concerned. A wave of relief washed over him.

"Help her go to college. She wants it. Means a lot to her that you suggested it."

Sabrina nodded emphatically, opening a packet of salad dressing. "Consider it done. Roy and I have connections. We'll help her however we can."

"Thank you," he whispered, wondering what it was like to be so financially secure that someone could mention college and you could wave a magic wand and make a dream come true.

Sabrina swiped at her eyes, but Holden admired her because she was keeping it together and offering to help Gris, despite the shocking news he'd just shared.

"I didn't even know she took it seriously when I suggested it."

"She did," he said, taking a bite of his sandwich. "It would help if she had somewhere to, uh, to go."

"Somewhere to go?"

Holden nodded, swallowing his sandwich over the lump in his throat. "Somewhere else . . . where he w-wouldn't . . . where the memories . . ."

"Oh! Oh, of course!" Sabrina nodded. "Of course she shouldn't go back there where he . . . No. Of course. I hadn't thought about it, but you're right."

"Maybe you could help her find another place."

"Yes. Yes," said Sabrina resolutely, sipping her Diet Coke. "In fact, I have a perfect solution. We have a basement apartment in our townhouse that Roy intends for his mother to move into one day. It's all fixed up and lovely, but for now it's empty. Perhaps she'd stay with us for a little while."

"That'd be good," said Holden, his chest feeling tight with gratitude. She had friends. She had people who'd look after her. He felt relieved.

"Holden? Will you stay? You could . . . move in with her. It might be good for her."

He took another bite of his sandwich, but misery made it taste like paper. He shrugged. "It's not that simple."

"No? No, I guess it isn't. It never is."

"My ex-girlfriend's p-pregnant."

"Ah," said Sabrina, looking down at her salad. "And you're doing the right thing by staying with her?"

"Something like that," he muttered, closing up. He'd talk about Gris as much as he had to in order to ensure her comfort and safety, but his life was not open for conversation.

"Maybe someday . . .?"

Holden looked up at her, closing their conversation with his eyes. "Maybe."

***

"Let's try this again," said the doctor's voice, still distorted, but not quite as bad as before.

Before? Yes, before. He'd spoken with her once before. The doctor. How did she know him?

"Griselda? It's Doctor Leonard. Can you open your eyes for me?"

She tried, but her eyes didn't want to open, and it frightened her almost as much as the garbled, underwater way everyone was speaking.

"Holden?" she whimpered.

"I'm here, angel." His voice was almost clear, low, rumbling right beside her ear. Her heart leaped, and her fingers trembled, grappling under the sheets, seeking his. Suddenly his fingers, strong and familiar, entwined with hers, and she sighed in relief.

She tried harder to open her eyes. One refused to cooperate, but by blinking over and over again, she was finally able to open the other one. It took a minute to focus, but when she did, Holden's face was before her.

"Holden," she said, leaning her neck toward him.

He moved closer, his lips close to her throat, one hand still tangled with hers and the other landing behind her neck gently to still her progress. "I'm here."

"Keep . . . your . . . fingers . . ."

She lost her train of thought, suddenly lost. *What's the rest? What am I trying to say? Why can't I . . .*

"Over the letters."

"Over the . . . letters," she repeated slowly, her panic receding. "Yes."

"Does that mean something?" asked the doctor, who was standing behind Holden, facing Griselda.

"Yeah. From a long time ago."

"I jump . . ." she said, not sure where the words were coming from. They felt jumbled and out of control, like they were floating out of her mouth without permission, from some other version of her life.

"You jump," he said softly, his warm hand stroking the back of her neck.

Yes. I jump, you jump. Yes. That's right.

Holden knows. He understands.

It was a relief.

"Where am I?" she asked, blinking her eyes and looking up at the doctor. And there was Maya beside him. And Mrs. McClellan. Wait. Mrs. McClellan was in West Virginia?

"You're in the hospital, angel," Holden said. "In M-Maryland. You got hurt."

"Yeah," she said, wishing she could take a good, deep breath. "I'm hurting."

"I know," he said, his soothing fingers still rubbing against her skin, the sweet smell of his neck better than any scent on earth.

"I love you," she whispered, closing her eyes.

"I love you too."

"Stay," she said, feeling so very, very tired. "He's not . . . coming back tonight."

"Nope," he said, still holding her loosely. "He's n-never coming back. We're safe."

"Safe," she murmured, surrendering to darkness.

***

Holden waited until she felt limp in his arms, then he settled her gently against the pillow and looked up at the doctor with worry.

"She's skipping around, right?" asked Doctor Leonard. "Skipping around in her memories?"

"Yeah. D-different parts of our childhood. Mixing up the past and present."

"Completely normal," said the doctor, making a note on his clipboard. "Encouraging, even."

Encouraging?

"She d-doesn't know where we are," said Holden, his panic rising. "She d-doesn't remember the last few days."

"She will," said the doctor. "Eventually. Could be later today, could take a while. We won't know until she wakes up again. She needs a little more rest and a little more time."

Time. Something Holden didn't have much of.

"You're good for her," said the doctor, looking up and offering a slight smile before continuing his notes. "You're lessening her frustration by being here. I wouldn't have known what she was talking about."

"I'll stay as long as you need me," he said, looking back at Griselda, who was fast asleep.

"I'm moving her upstairs tomorrow morning. I'm clearing her to leave the ICU."

"Can I stay with her tonight?"

Doctor Leonard looked down at him, over his glasses. "As long as she's still here? Sure. Go ahead. I can ask for a cot."

Holden shook his head. He didn't want to be that far away from her. "No. Thanks. I'm good right here."

CHAPTER 31

It took some convincing, but Maya finally went home at four
o'clock, promising she would return the next day, after work.
Holden had a huge amount of respect and affection for Maya—
she'd essentially stayed with Griselda from Sunday morning
until today, going home only to shower and sleep for a few
hours at a time and using several of her personal days to get out
of work. She was an amazing friend to his girl, and Holden
would be forever indebted to her.

Sabrina McClellan had turned out to be an incredible friend
too. She had left after Doctor Leonard's consultation, to check
on her daughter, Prudence, promising to stop back in the evening
for an hour so Holden could grab some dinner and Griselda
wouldn't be left alone. When he thought of leaving Griselda the
day after tomorrow, he was relieved to think of Sabrina looking
after her, taking her in, encouraging her to go to college. His life
would still be shit, but at least he'd know that Gris was safe and
supported. Maybe it would make leaving her more bearable.

Gazing at her bruised, sleeping face, though, he knew
nothing would make it more bearable. Living without her simply
felt like slowly dying.

He clutched his hands together and bent his head, silently
begging the God of Leviticus to have mercy on him, to help him
be a good father, to help him let Griselda go. And as Holden

prayed, he saw himself—the path of his life—more clearly than he ever had before: a boy who'd been abandoned, then kidnapped, then abandoned again. A teen who'd been seemingly apathetic, while trapped and angry. A man who was fueled by hate and loss.

When Griselda walked back into his life, he found the will to live—to *really* live, to let go of the apathy and anger and make something of himself. And yet, without her, just over the course of four days, all that good energy had disappeared. It was almost as though Griselda was his life force, and without her, life was unlivable.

That was true, he realized, but he didn't like it. He loved Gris, and he wanted her in his life, but he didn't want to be dependent on her. He didn't want to steal that energy from her. It wasn't fair.

In a very real way, it was like his heart had stopped beating that day on the Shenandoah when she "died," and it had been jump-started back to life two weeks ago, when they found each other again. She left for Maryland, and his heart died again without her. But suddenly he didn't want it to keep dying whenever she left the room. He wanted to love her and be with her, but he wanted his heart to be strong enough to beat on its own. He wanted to be strong enough to love her and live for her even when she wasn't standing in front of him. He needed to find that strength.

He wanted to give a shit about his life because that's the only way it was going to get better. He wanted to be strong enough on his own to offer her something good: love, yes, but also true stability, safety, and a real future—not because she fed a visceral part of him that had been badly damaged in his youth, but because he'd figured out how to repair it and offer it to her.

Are you whole or broken?

He wasn't whole. Regardless of what he wanted to believe, he'd never *been* whole, because his completion had always depended on her. But now he knew—he felt it like a fist around his heart, demanding satisfaction—he *wanted* to be whole, all on his own . . . *for* her.

"Holden?"

He turned, in the dim light of the room, to see Sabrina walking in. She was more casual now, in black workout pants and a white T-shirt. She looked younger and more approachable, maybe. Not as fancy. Not as intimidating.

"Hey, Sabrina."

She placed two packages of Twizzlers on a table. "For Maya."

"Nice," he said.

"How's our girl?"

"Sleeping. Doctor checked in before his shift ended. Said she'll sleep odd hours for a few days. He guessed she'll be up for a few hours later tonight."

"Then why don't you get a few hours of sleep while I sit with her? Then you'll be fresh when she wakes up."

He shook his head. "I'm fine."

"Well, you certainly need dinner." She patted his shoulder, urging him to stand up and take a break from his vigil. "I'll be right here next to her until you get back, okay?"

He stood up, giving her room to sit down. "Uh, yeah. Okay."

He was hungry. And he needed to text Clinton and tell him he'd be here for tonight and probably tomorrow night too. As much as he hated it, he'd need to return to Gemma by Saturday, or the devil only knew what she might do.

"Thanks, Sabrina."

She took a book from her leather handbag and shooed him toward the door. "Get some dinner. Or fresh air. Take your time. I'm not going anywhere."

With one last look at his sleeping beauty, he quietly left the room, pulling the door closed behind him.

***

She's being moved from ICU, he typed. *I need to stay tonight and tomorrow night. I'll be back Saturday. Can you cover for me?*

Holden pressed Send, then sat back in the cafeteria chair, hoping Clinton would manage Gemma. He'd just plowed through two burgers, fries, and an apple, and his wallet was looking a little thin. He had some money hidden in his apartment, and he was fairly certain Gemma wouldn't find it, but he'd just spent the last of his fighting money from two weeks ago. He was down to fourteen dollars, and he still needed food tomorrow if he planned to stay another day. Thank God he'd gassed up the truck in Charles Town for the round-trip journey.

Looking around the quiet cafeteria, his gaze landed on the uniformed soldier he'd seen in the elevator that morning. Dressed in a short-sleeved khaki shirt and navy-blue dress pants with a red stripe down the side, he looked proper, but still badass. Maybe because of his shaved head. He handed the cashier some money and waited for his change, then took his tray and started across the cafeteria, looking for the right seat. That's when Holden noticed his limp. It was pronounced and made the soldier move deliberately, as though every step had the potential to hurt. Looking around, his eyes slammed into Holden's, and he nodded in recognition. Changing his original direction, he took a few steps closer and placed his tray on the table next to Holden's.

"Evening," he said, pulling out the chair facing Holden and carefully lowering himself.

"Hey, there," said Holden. He tried not to stare but wondered how the man had injured himself.

"So . . . the person you're visitin'," the soldier said, putting his napkin in his lap. "He on this side of okay yet?"

"*She*," said Holden. "Yeah. They're moving her out of ICU tomorrow."

"Well, oo-rah for that."

Holden nodded, chuckling softly. "Yeah. Okay. Oo-rah for that."

"She your woman? Mom? Sister?"

"She's . . ." Holden looked down, clenching his jaw.

My heart. My life. My everything.

"Aha. I see. *Definitely* your woman."

"Yeah," said Holden. "My woman."

"Well, I'm relieved she's on the mend." The soldier raised his coffee cup in salute, then took a sip. "Damn, but hospital coffee is the worst."

"No argument here."

"But this hospital? It's the worst of the worst."

"You work here?" asked Holden.

"No," said the man. "Well, not really. I'm in Marines recruitment. But I come see the boys here. And at Saint George. And over at Walter Reed. Any of the ones I recruited, I sort of keep an eye on them once they're Stateside again. Especially if . . ."

"I thought you might be in the Army."

"Bite your tongue, son." He squeezed a packet of ketchup on his hot dog. "I was a grunt over in the Gulf. Lost my leg. Now I recruit."

"A grunt?"

"Infantry," he said. He reached his brown paw of a hand across his table and shook Holden's. "Franklin Wainwright Jones, lieutenant, U.S. Marine Corps."

Holden tightened his grip. "Holden Croft."

"You from Maryland, Croft?"

"No, sir. West Virginia, by way of D.C."

Lieutenant Jones took another bite of his hot dog, chewing thoughtfully. "You're in good shape. What do you do, son?"

"I work in a glass factory."

"That's not all, I'm guessing."

"I fight. On the side."

"Fight?"

"Fistfight."

"For cash?"

Holden dropped his glance, feeling ashamed. "Yes sir."

"Helps make ends meet?"

He met Lieutenant Jones's steady, understanding gaze. "Yes, sir."

"Ever thought about enlisting?"

"No, sir. I didn't finish high school."

"Have your GED?"

"Yes, sir."

It had taken Holden endless nights of studying and three passes at the test, but he had eventually earned his GED last year.

"Good enough. First year? You'd make about eighteen thousand. That's your base pay. Then there's hostile pay, fire pay, housing and food allowances. Medical's covered. Tax breaks. Biyearly or yearly wage increase. A career. You'd get special training too."

Enlist? It had never crossed Holden's mind, never even entered his radar. But, he had to admit, something about it appealed to him.

Lieutenant Jones chuckled as he lifted his hot dog. "There I go. You can take me out of the office, but I'm still recruiting."

"Never thought about joining the service."

The older man looked at Holden thoughtfully. "You've got the build. Maybe you should."

"Can I ask you a few questions?"

"Have at it, son."

"How long is boot camp, sir?"

"Recruit training is a twelve-week program."

"And then?"

"Ten days of leave. Then School of Infantry training."

"How long?"

"Sixty days."

"So that's five months right there."

"That is correct, son."

"Then what?"

"MOS. Military Occupational Specialty training. Infantry, communications, field artillery, avionics maintenance. Lots of choices. We figure out where you'd excel, and we put you there. Give you the tools you need. Three to six months is average. Could be a year or more, though, depending on your field." He went into a little more detail about the various specialties, and Holden asked questions, drawn to the lifestyle the lieutenant was describing—the stability, the pay, the pride.

"And then?"

"PDS, son. Permanent Duty Station. Could be anywhere around the world. Could be Stateside."

"So a year of training, and then, uh, PDS?"

"That's right."

"And I'd fight."

"Hell, yes. Almost guaranteed. With the best-trained fighters in the world. Oo-rah!"

Holden took a deep breath, surprised to look up at the clock and realize they'd been chatting for almost an hour and the lieutenant's dinner was long finished.

"What happens next? I mean, how do I—?"

"Slow up, son. You've got someone upstairs who needs your attention today." He shifted in his seat and drew a business card out of his back pocket. He handed it to Holden. "Think it over. Talk to your woman. You're interested? You come find me in Baltimore next week, and we'll talk some more."

Holden looked at the card before slipping it into his back pocket. "I'll do that, sir."

"You're in real good shape, Croft. We could probably fast-track you to basic."

"Meaning?"

"It's June. You pass the entrance exam? I could probably get you to Parris Island by September. That ten days of liberty might even correspond with Thanksgiving, son."

"Lot to think about." Holden's eyes slid to the clock again. "I'm sorry, sir. I have to go."

"I understand."

Holden stood up, offering his hand to the lieutenant. "This has been . . . I mean, thank you, sir. I appreciate your time."

Lieutenant Jones stood up, taking Holden's hand. "I hope to hear from you, Croft."

"Thank you, sir," he said, picking up his tray to clear it, then hustling back upstairs.

***

It wasn't quite as hard to open her eyes this time. One of them still wouldn't open, and it hurt like hell, but the other one had an easier time, and after a few blinks, Griselda focused on Mrs. McClellan's face, reading a book in the chair beside her.

"Mrs. McClellan?" she rasped.

She put down her book and beamed. "Hey, Zelda."

"Is, uh . . .?"

"Holden went to get dinner. He'll be right back."

She tried to take a deep breath, but her mind warned her it would hurt, and it did. She winced, whimpering from the sharp pain. "My chest."

"I'm know, honey." Mrs. McClellan nodded. "Punctured lung."

Punctured lung. Punctured lung. That sounded so familiar. Jonah. And a punctured lung. "Jonah."

"That's right," said Mrs. McClellan, picking up a cup with a straw. "Water? You want some?"

"Yes, please."

Mrs. McClellan helped her sit up, plumping several pillows behind her back. As Griselda sipped the water, she had a sudden, blinding flashback. *You like that, you fucking slut?*

"No!" she yelped, some of the water dribbling down her chin.

"Zelda?"

"He slammed . . . he slammed my face . . . into the . . ." It hurt so much to breathe, she needed air, but she couldn't seem to take a deep breath.

"Yes," said Mrs. McClellan, taking the cup away. She wiped Griselda's mouth and took her hand. "He hurt you. But he's in jail. They're going to put him away for a long time, Zelda. A long, long time. Roy'll see to it. Jonah will *not* bother you again, you hear me?"

"I . . . I . . . Okay," she panted, letting her shoulder relax.

She didn't want to think about Jonah. She never wanted to think about Jonah again. She stared at Mrs. McClellan, but she wanted Holden. She needed Holden. He loved her. He'd take care of—

I'll go!

Suddenly she heard her voice yell the words in her head.

Holden's devastated face.

Her tears.

"Me leaving is the right choice," she said, some of her memories returning, others still foggy.

"What's that, honey?" Mrs. McClellan asked, squeezing Griselda's hand.

"I came home," she said, looking up at her boss, breathless and frightened. "What happened?"

"Maya drove you home. Jonah broke into your apartment and attacked you. Your neighbors heard the noise and called the police. By the time they got there, he had broken your ribs, and you'd passed out from several blows to the head."

"Did he . . .?"

"What?" asked Mrs. McClellan, searching Griselda's face. "Did he what?"

Griselda looked down at her thighs, then back up.

"No!" Mrs. McClellan shook her head emphatically. "No, Zelda. No, honey. He didn't do that. He didn't . . . rape you. The police got there in time. I promise."

"Okay," she murmured, in shock, tears coursing down her face. She wished she could breathe deeper but settled for shallow pants as she wept, repeating, "Okay, okay. I'm okay. Okay."

Mrs. McClellan held her hand, patting it gently as the door to her room opened. Holden moved quickly to her bedside, his gray eyes focused on hers, and Mrs. McClellan stood up to give him room. She slipped out of the room as Holden sat down on the bed beside Griselda. He placed his hands on her shoulders and pulled her gently into his arms.

Her tears streamed endlessly down her face. She'd left Holden and come home. Jonah had broken into her apartment and beaten her. God only knew how long she'd been in the hospital. And Holden . . . Oh, Holden . . .

"You're not . . . supposed . . . to be . . . here," she managed through sobs, clutching him to her, her fingers curled into the fabric of his T-shirt.

"Angel, I *need* to be here."

"But your baby!"

He'd checked his phone in the elevator and found a message from Clinton: *She's buying it for now, but she's pissed you ran out. Won't let her do anything stupid. You gotta understand. She was really mad at you. I don't actually think she would've gone through with it.*

Holden's eyes had narrowed, rage bubbling up as he considered this. By threatening him, Gemma had driven Gris out of his life, into harm's way, into danger. Damn her, but if it was all a ruse for his attention? He'd never forgive Gemma for it. Never.

"It's fine. Clinton's covering for me."

"Oh. Okay. Okay," she said, burying her nose in Holden's neck, wetting his skin with her tears. "Thank . . . thank you for coming."

"Gris, I love you. Hellfire couldn't have k-kept me away."

She sobbed again, then laughed softly, thinking his words came perilously close to Caleb Foster's rants. "Or my wickedness?"

"Or your idle hands."

"Or my heathen ways."

"Or your evil spring tits." He leaned back, and his eyes were glassy, but he managed a small grin. "I fucking love your tits."

She laughed, then sobbed again, unable to stop the next deluge of tears from falling.

And though she knew it couldn't last forever, she savored every moment that he stayed and held her.

And stayed.

And held her.

CHAPTER 32

Griselda was moved to a room on the fourth floor first thing in the morning, and while she still had an IV port in her hand, she was finally allowed to eat solid food for the first time in days. Maya stopped by before work and, opening the licorice Sabrina had thoughtfully left for her, smiled at Griselda from the foot of her bed.

Maya gave Holden her apartment keys and address, and urged him to get away for a little while and go take a shower. He stared at Griselda with hesitation, but she encouraged him to go. After he promised to return in an hour and spend the rest of the day with her, she'd watched him leave, knowing she'd never get used to it. It would never get any easier to watch him walk away.

Maya's eyes tracked his departure before shuttling back to Griselda's face, and then she sat down in Holden's vacated seat.

"Zelda, that man is done and gone for you."

"And I'm done and gone for him," sighed Griselda as she finished off the last of her eggs.

"Any chance you can get him to stick around?"

Undoubtedly she could. She saw his eyes. She knew his heart. If she asked, she had no doubt he would stay. But the life of his unborn child still hung in the balance, so she couldn't. As much as she wanted him, as much as she needed him, she wouldn't ask him to make that choice or sacrifice for her.

"No," she said. "He has somewhere he needs to be more than here."

"He's a good man, Z."

"The best."

"I don't know how you can stand it. To let him go."

"You're gonna make me cry, Maya. Talk about something else." *Something that I can actually have. Something that won't be walking out of my life again in a matter of hours and taking my heart far away.*

"Okay." Maya took her hand and squeezed it. "As it turns out, I do have something to discuss with you."

"Something good, I hope."

"Mm-hm. It is." Maya cocked her head to the side. "You know Sabrina McClellan's been here every day, right?"

"She was here last night. I have to admit, I'm surprised. I've always—I don't know, thought of myself as the help, not a personal friend or anything. Honestly, I feel funny every time you and Holden call her Sabrina. I've been so careful to, you know, be appropriate, be a good employee."

"Well, I think she's amazing, Z. She cares for you a lot. She has your best interests at heart."

"I believe that."

"She asked me to run something by you."

"Oh?"

"Yeah. Thought you might be more open to the idea coming from me."

"What idea?"

"Did you know they have an apartment in their house? The McClellans?"

"You mean the mother-in-law's garden apartment? On the lower level of the townhouse?"

Maya nodded. "That sounds right."

"I've only been down there once or twice, when Prudence wanted to go visit Granny's room. What about it?"

"Well, it seems that the elder Mrs. McClellan has no immediate plans to move in or visit." She squeezed Griselda's hand again. "They want you to consider using it."

"For what?"

"For living, girl."

"You mean, move in? With the McClellans?"

Maya shrugged. "Why not?"

"Well, for one, I *have* an apartment." Griselda chuckled softly in disbelief. "And two, I work for them, Maya. I keep my personal life separate from my professional life. We're not . . . friends."

"First of all, you're not going back to that place—your apartment—after what happened there. Second of all, plenty of nannies live with their families. And third of all, would an employer come to the hospital and sit by your bedside for four straight days? You ask me, that's the action of a friend. A good one."

Griselda considered this. She knew Sabrina McClellan's friends. They were other society women with perfect hair and designer clothing. They drank wine together and talked politics. She and Mrs. McClellan never socialized like that.

And yet they chatted now and then. Sabrina had always taken an interest in Griselda, trying to get her to talk about her experiences in the foster care system and encouraging her to go to college. She raved about the way Griselda tended to Prudence and told her how much storytelling talent she had.

Hmm. Had Griselda misinterpreted the signs? Had Sabrina McClellan been reaching out to Griselda not just as an employer—but in friendship as well?

"You're quiet," said Maya. "Does that mean you're thinking about it?"

"I don't know. I don't know if I'd be comfortable living there. I don't know why she'd suggest it."

"Because she likes you. Because she wants to help you,"

said Maya. She took a deep breath and tsked, sitting back with her arms crossed over her bosom. "Damn, Z. You got people who *want* to help you. You can live there—in a gorgeous apartment—rent free and go to college. You can *get* somewhere in the world. You can *be* something. It's being offered to you on a silver freaking platter. You're so damn suspicious! Why can't you just say yes?"

Griselda stared at Maya, surprised she was getting so upset.

"I'm suspicious because life doesn't just hand you great opportunities on silver platters, Maya. You know that; I know that. Those kinds of things don't happen to people like us."

Maya's eyes flashed, and she looked genuinely angry as she stood up and put her hands on her hips.

"Bullshit. A good thing like that *is* happening to you, and you're too bullheaded to see it, or too scared to just let it happen." She looked down for a moment, as though figuring out what to say, then caught Griselda's eyes, holding on tightly and speaking earnestly. "I've been your friend for almost ten years, Z. Ten years, and I didn't know your real name until five days ago. You never told me about Holden and everything you two went through. You never told me you were looking for him. Listen, I get it—junkie mom, in the system early, kidnapped. You had some bad times. Real bad. Worse'n most. Believe me, I know. I understand. But you're all closed up. And you're stubborn. And suspicious. And you're not doing yourself any favors, girl."

"Maya—"

"I ain't finished," said Maya, brown eyes wide with sass and attitude. "Quit pushing away the people who want to help you, who care about you. I'm here for you. Sabrina's here for you. So I'ma tell you what you're going to do: You're gonna move into that apartment and care for little Miss Pru every day this summer because you love that child and she'll help with the sadness when Holden goes home. And at night you're gonna read through those college brochures Sabrina got you, and use that money you saved to get yourself enrolled. And then when September rolls around and Pru's in kindergarten every day? You're going back to school too. Yes, ma'am. Don't shake your head at me, because that's what you're going to do. You are strong and you are smart, Zelda, but you gotta start letting people in. You gotta trust that they're not all gonna let you down. *I'm* not gonna let you down. *Sabrina*'s not gonna let you down. Just say yes."

Looking up at the friend who'd stood by her despite her secrets, despite her suspicious, stubborn nature, despite her fears, Griselda felt tears flood her eyes and a grin overtake her face. Maybe Maya was right. She could say yes. She could jump at the chance she was being given and hold on tight in the hope that there was something better out there than the life she'd been living.

Maybe it was possible. Maybe, just maybe, she could find the strength and courage to move forward instead of standing still, frozen in time on the banks of the Shenandoah, where her life ended ten years ago.

Her grin faltered, but her tears doubled.

Holden.

What good was any of this without him?

Maya sat back down on the side of the bed, tilting Griselda's face back up with a gentle finger under her chin.

"And I promise you, girl," she said, "you'll figure *that* out eventually too."

"How?" sobbed Griselda.

"Because you and him were meant to be together," said Maya, with a tender, confident smile. "Just not quite yet."

***

As Holden pulled his jeans back on after a shower at Maya's apartment, the card from Lieutenant Jones fell from his back pocket. He picked it up off the floor and sat down on the toilet to look at it.

He'd climbed into bed with Gris last night, sitting against the headboard as she slept with her head against his heart and her body curled around his legs. And while she slept, Holden had taken out his phone and spent some time online looking into the Marine Corps.

Words like *pride*, *leadership*, and *vision* had jumped out at him from the official website, making him feel the sort of hopefulness that his life had only found before with Griselda. He looked at the different units, concentrated in California, North Carolina, and Hawaii, that appeared to be organized by function, which led him to seek out training options. He felt a pull toward the combat-ready units, like artillery and infantry, since they'd been mentioned specifically to him by Lieutenant Jones.

At one point, he stumbled onto a Marine chat room, and he had to keep his laughter soft as he read a thread wherein a new recruit asked about Marine training that wouldn't lead to deployment. The Marines responding had been pretty frank, advising the recruit that if he didn't want to fight, he wasn't Marine material. And Holden felt pride rise up in him as he considered that he'd *want* to fight for his country, for Gris and his baby, for a better life. In fact, it would be a goddamned honor.

I am *Marine material*, said the voice in his head, brimming with hope and pride.

Taking his cell phone off Maya's sink, he dialed the number on Lieutenant Jones's business card.

"U.S. Marine recruitment office. Jones speaking."

"Sir, it's Holden Croft. We met—"

"How's your woman, Croft?"

"Better side of okay, sir."

"Well, oo-rah! What's on your mind?"

"I don't want to wait. I did a lot of reading last night, sir, and I want to be one of the few and the proud. I'd like to come see you tomorrow morning before I head back to West Virginia."

"You sure about this, son?"

"Sure as I can be, sir."

"Oh-nine-hundred tomorrow, Croft. Recruiting Station Baltimore. We'll see what we can do to make a Marine out of a fistfighter."

"Thank you, sir."

"See you tomorrow, Croft."

Holden hung up, slipped the phone into his pocket, and looked at himself in the mirror. For the first time in his life, he didn't see a foster child or an abducted kid or a fucked-up teenager or a pissed-off man. He still saw a fighter, yes, but he saw the potential to be a *good* fighter, an organized fighter, a useful means to a necessary end. Someone who could use his deep well of rage to procure something positive for the world. Holden knew firsthand about fear, pain, and injustice, but he also knew how to stand his ground and push back. And he was going to take those natural skills, those visceral inclinations, and he was going to make something of himself. Someone he could be proud of. Someone Griselda could be proud of. He couldn't wait to tell her.

***

Maya had left for work a little while ago, leaving Griselda to consider the McClellans' offer in peace, without hands-on-hips attitude.

At her core, Griselda was not a very trusting person. She trusted Maya—and Holden—as much as it was possible for her to trust other people, but that was a short list, and one of those people wouldn't be a fixture in her life for the foreseeable future. As Maya had pointed out, Griselda had been cagey even with her best friend about her past, and, if Griselda were honest, her future with Holden. She'd kept herself in a sort of emotional solitary confinement that made it difficult to move forward with her life.

But maybe Maya was right: maybe it was time for Griselda to stop seeing herself as an abandoned child, guilty teenager, or worthless adult. Holden had forgiven her, even telling her that her actions had inadvertently saved his life. Maybe it was time for her to start seeing herself as Holden and Maya saw her—smart and strong. *Smart and strong*. The words felt so good, so right in her head, they almost made her cry, because if she had the will to aspire to any two qualities in her life, it would be those.

If she accepted the McClellans' offer and lived rent free in their apartment for a while, she could still repay them by making herself useful: preparing Pru's lunch every morning and babysitting for free on weekend evenings. She could offer to answer the phones at Nannies on Ninth when she wasn't at class or studying, or mentor new girls looking for a job in child care. And by keeping busy, she wouldn't have as much time to miss Holden.

She winced, and her heart dipped because, while she was planning an exciting and hopeful new life with a gorgeous, rent-free apartment and college, Holden was heading back to West Virginia to work at a glass factory he hated and care for the mother of his child, whom he didn't love. Didn't love . . . *now*, which led her to a terrible thought: What if just being together every day brought them closer? What if he and Gemma looked at that little baby they'd made together and fell in love again? What if Holden decided that he wanted to be a family with Gemma and the baby, and that there wasn't space for Griselda in his life after all? What if he never came looking for her?

Smart and strong.

She wiped away a tear and took as deep a breath as possible, flinching from the pain in her chest and her heart. Because as much as she loved Holden, she still needed to live her life, get an education, be useful, write stories, help others.

No, she'd never fall in love again, because on the day of her last dying, gasping breath, it would be Holden's name on her lips. But she could still have a life. After everything she'd endured, she deserved to have a life.

The thought made her eyes well and her breath catch with surprise.

She *deserved* to have a life.

For so many years, she'd convinced herself that by leading Holden into that truck and leaving him behind on the Shenandoah, she didn't deserve anything good. She deserved every dark, awful thing that befell her. But now, healing through the power of his love and forgiveness, she'd started forgiving herself. And right here, right now, she was giving herself permission to pursue a good life, and Sabrina McClellan was, as Maya had pointed out, offering it to her on a silver freaking platter.

She would always love Holden.

She would always want Holden.

But until she could have him, she was going to live the best-possible version of her life, and one day—*hopefully one day*—they'd find their way back to each other again.

The door to her room squeaked open, and she looked up to see Holden walking in, his dirty-blond hair slick and orderly. His lips—his beautiful lips that had loved her body with such tenderness and passion at the cabin—tilted up into an expectant grin as he drew closer, brandishing a bouquet of flowers from behind his back. They were mostly yellow and lavender like the wildflowers in the meadow where she'd fallen in love with him all over again and for the first time and forever. And as he handed them to her, her eyes flashed to his forearm, where she saw "H+G" etched into his skin and stained in black, right beside the rendering of her face. Her initials. Her face. Her heart beating in his chest. His beating in hers.

She took the flowers from him and smelled them with

pleasure, but her eyes never left his, because after today she didn't know when she would see him again, and aside from the pleasure she felt in his company, there was an aching urgency to remember every stolen second, so she could live on them when they were separated once again.

He seemed to search her face, scanning it slowly, and she felt the heat and tenderness in his gaze as he paused on her eyes, her cheeks, her lips.

"I love you," he said.

"I love you too."

"I have until tomorrow morning at eight."

"That's more time than I thought."

He was so big and stunningly beautiful. She knew how that body loved, how it moved as it loved her, how gentle it could be despite its strength. In ripped jeans and a T-shirt, all hard, strong man with tattoos covering his arms, it was a challenge to see the freckled, blond-haired boy who'd volunteered to walk to the store with her so long ago.

I'll g-g-go t-too.

How far they'd come, together then apart.

How much farther they had to go, apart before together.

"Can you move over?" he asked, coming around to the side of the bed.

She moved very slowly and managed to make a little room for him.

"How're your ribs?"

"They hurt."

He slipped onto the bed beside her, putting his arm around her, and her whole body melted into his.

"What'd the doc say this morning? How much longer will you be here?"

"I can leave the day after tomorrow. The swelling in my head's gone down a lot, but they want two more nights for observation, and they'll do one more MRI before I'm discharged." She looked up at him. "I got worried about the hospital bills. Jonah doesn't have much. I'd need to go after his parents' estate for the bills and I think it's bankrupt. But then I found out the McClellans have taken care of everything."

"They're amazing," said Holden. "I never knew rich people could be so . . . good."

"They invited me to stay in this apartment they have at their house."

He rubbed her arm, and she lowered her head to his chest, lining up her ear over his heart.

"That sounds great, Gris."

"And I've been thinking about going to college this fall."

"You should."

"You think?"

"Hell, yes. Take those writing courses. Show your stories to someone. P-promise me you'll go. No matter what."

She nodded against his T-shirt. "I promise."

She felt his lips touch down on her head, the soft smacking noise of them pursing and kissing her hair, and she closed her eyes, savoring his tenderness, trying to forget how little time they had left together.

"What about you?" she asked. "Back to Gemma? And the baby?"

He sighed. "Funny you ask . . ."

Her eyes opened, and she felt her eyebrows knit together. "Funny? How?"

"I've got some plans too."

"Plans?"

"Uh-huh."

She could hear it in his voice, even in those two little words. The hope. The expectation. She leaned back a little and looked up at his face. "Tell me."

He dropped his lips to hers and kissed her gently, holding her upper lip between his for several seconds of sweetness before releasing it. "Someday I'm gonna do that whenever I want to."

"Promise?"

He nodded solemnly, his gaze never flinching. "I promise, angel."

A rush of relief filled her heart, washing away her previous worries about Gemma.

"Tell me your news, Holden."

"I was useless when you left Charles Town, Gris. D-drinking. Hating Gemma. D-damn near hating my unborn baby. I couldn't see a way out, a way to happiness. And it's not that I deserve happiness, but I don't want him or her to be ashamed of me. I don't want you to be ashamed of me."

"Holden, I could never—"

"Shhh," he said, placing a finger over her lips. "Let me finish."

"Okay."

"*I* don't want to be ashamed of me anymore. I want to *do* something with my life. And that's because of you, Gris." He swallowed, looking at her with so much love it was almost blinding, but she didn't dare look away. "You made me want to live again."

Her lips trembled, and a tear rolled down her cheek, but she didn't interrupt him.

"You're the girl, Gris. You're it for me. I'll do right by my child, but as soon as I can, I'm coming to find you. And when I do, I'll have something to offer you. Something good. A good life. A life I'll be proud of. A life you can be proud of."

She searched his eyes, her heart flipping over with the same hope and expectation she'd heard in his voice. "Tell me."

"I met a Marine recruiter yesterday. He told me all about the Marines, and last night, while you were sleeping, I went on my phone and read everything I could. And Gris? It's what I want. I want to learn how to fight for my country. I want to learn a skill. I want to make a difference. I want to make you proud."

"I *am*," she sobbed, her heart swelling with emotion for this man who'd been through so much but had found the courage and strength to do something positive with his life. "I'm already proud. I couldn't be prouder, Holden."

"I'm enlisting tomorrow, Gris."

She stared up at him. It was a bold and decisive plan—to join the armed forces—but she could see in his face how much it meant to him. Every cell in her body wanted him to know how terribly proud she was, but one loose end that frightened her for him made her whisper, "Gemma . . ."

He placed his palm on her cheek, smiling at her tenderly.

"Gemma didn't want me to be with you. And I won't be. But I don't want to be with her either. I can't make her happy, and she can't make me happy, because there's only one woman in the world who I want, and I'm sorry, but it just isn't Gemma.

"So, while she's pregnant, I'll stay away from you—I'll be in boot camp, then training. I'll have ten days off in November to go see her and the baby, and she'll get regular money from me to take care of her expenses. She can have my apartment all to herself, and I will always do my duty by her and the child. But once that baby's born and I've established my parental rights?" His eyes bored into hers, his expression fierce and unwavering. "I'm coming for you, Griselda Schroeder. You can bet I'll be coming."

Tears streamed down her face as she understood his plan. It wasn't just for her or his child, but for them—for them to bear their separation and to have a real start at a real life together at its end.

"It's true that I'll be leaving you tomorrow morning, angel, but tomorrow isn't an end. I swear to you with everything I am and everything that I'll ever be: tomorrow is just the b-beginning. It's the first day of a journey that ends with us together."

"Together," she sobbed softly, holding his gray eyes with her blue.

"Forever, Griselda. Once you're mine, I'll never let you go."

"I already belong to you."

He dropped his head, and his lips touched down on hers again, gently, then more insistently as his tongue parted the seam of her lips and swept into her mouth. She wanted to turn her body into his, but it hurt too much to move, so she kept her face upturned as he kissed her.

"And I've always been yours," he whispered fiercely against her lips. "From the first day you smiled at me in the Fillmans' upstairs hallway, holding a blue toothbrush and looking worried."

"Will you write to me?" she asked.

He kissed her before sitting up and guiding her head to his heart. "I'd love to, and I will. But it just isn't fair."

"What isn't?"

"You're the writer. Your letters will be ten times better than mine."

"Yours will be wonderful. Tell me what you're doing, what it's like, what you're learning, who you meet. I want to know everything, Holden. I don't want to miss a thing."

"And you do the same," he said, his voice certain and strong, love and hope infusing it with warmth. "Tell me all about Sabrina and Prudence, and keep me updated about Maya's Twizzler habit. Tell me which college you choose, and send me stories, Gris. Promise you'll send me stories I can read before I go to sleep at night. Prince Twilight, Princess Moonlight, Lady Starlight and the Sun King. They're going to end up together, right?"

She shook her head, refusing to give away spoilers. "I'll send them. I promise."

"And when I go to sleep at night," he said, turning over the arm he had draped around her shoulders to reveal their initials, "I'll keep my fingers over the letters. Always. Every night."

Me too, she thought, looking carefully at his tattoo and making a decision to get her own, so that she could go to sleep every night with her fingers over the letters too.

"We're going to make it, Gris," he said.

"I jump, you jump," she answered.

"Only this time," he said, pressing his lips to her hair, "we'll *b-both* make it to the other side."

CHAPTER 33

Moving into the McClellans' apartment proved easier than Griselda had expected. With Maya's help, the McClellans had arranged for all her belongings to be boxed up and delivered while Griselda was still recovering in the hospital. By the time she arrived at the McClellans', all of her things had been moved and lovingly unpacked, so the apartment truly felt like home.

Holden had left her early on Monday morning, heading to Baltimore for his appointment with Lieutenant Jones, and sent her a quick text later that day:

I scored 105 on the ASVAB, which means I can do artillery. Will see doc in Aug and be sworn in. (It's called MEPS.) We should have an acronym too. How about IMYLCILYF?

Knowing that Holden had been worried about the ASVAB test, which measures a potential Marine's aptitude for certain jobs and weighs heavily in placement, she was relieved he did well and had smiled at her phone from her hospital bed.

I'm so proud of you, but you already know that. What is IMYLCILYF?

A moment later her phone had pinged:

I miss you like crazy. I love you forever.

Her eyes teared up, and she typed back quickly.

IMYLCILYF.

She hadn't heard from him since, and that was almost a week ago, but they had agreed not to be in regular communication over the next couple of months, while Holden was living with Gemma and Griselda was settling into her new life at the McClellans'. And it had been her decision, which he lovingly respected.

"Gris," he'd said, nestled together in her hospital bed the night before he left her. "I want to talk about the next few months."

"I don't," she answered, her heart squeezing at the thought of the long separation ahead of them.

"Angel, I won't be able to see you for about five months. We've got to talk about it."

"Stop," she said, her pulse quickening and her eyes clenching shut.

"We've endured worse, and we've survived," he plowed on, tightening his arm around her shoulders. "We're going to be okay."

"I hate it," she said. "I just found you, and now I'm losing you again."

"You're not losing me. I'm yours."

For how long? she wondered. He had two months at home in West Virginia with Gemma. Then swearing in. Then boot camp. So much could happen between then and now.

"Can I ask you to do something for me?"

"Anything," he said.

The thought of him with Gemma was what bothered Griselda the most. She was the mother of his child, and she was living in his apartment. In extremely close quarters. What if Holden decided—after a few weeks—that he wanted to give her another chance? Griselda couldn't begrudge his child the chance to have a loving, intact family, but she wouldn't be able to bear feeling him pull away, an apologetic tone in his writing, his messages coming less and less frequently. It would cycle her into an intense depression when what she needed right now was to get her life back on track with a move, college classes, and a part-time job. She felt an overwhelming need to insulate herself a little, for protection.

She took a deep breath. "Don't write to me until you go to boot camp."

"W-what?"

She swallowed over the lump in her throat. "Go home and be good to Gemma. Make sure she and the baby are healthy. Get ready for the Marines. And when you get there, if I'm still part of your plan, let me know."

"Griselda, you *are* the plan."

"I . . . I know," she said, leaning back to look up into his beloved gray eyes. "But please. Don't write to me while you're with her."

"Damn it, Gris, I have no intention of b-being *w-with* her."

She didn't answer, only stared up at him, begging him with her eyes to understand.

"Fine," he finally relented, his face looking pained. "Fine. On the bus to boot camp, I'll write my first letter."

And if I get that letter, she thought, *I'll know our journey to forever has truly begun.*

Sitting on the plush, beautiful bed in her new bedroom, she picked up her phone and clicked on the week-old text from him, wondering where he was and what he was doing. She wondered if he thought about her as much as she thought about him, and she wished for the day her phone pinged again with the news that he was headed to boot camp and she was still first in his heart.

Placing the pads of her fingers over the words she'd already read a hundred times, she heard his voice in her head:

I miss you like crazy. I love you forever.

Oh, please, God, she thought, leaning back on her bed as she felt phantom fingers worshipping her body and remembered his warm breath fanning the skin of her neck. *Please let it be so.*

***

Holden still hadn't told Gemma about enlisting.

Well, he reasoned, *it was hard to tell someone anything when you barely saw her.*

He spent as little time at the apartment as possible, going to work early and, since returning from Baltimore, eschewing drinking for working out. Visiting the shitty little boxing gym off Norbert Road every night, he refused to get in the ring and fight, but he worked his body relentlessly. Partially he did this because when he went for his MEPS—his physical examination and swearing in—in August, he wanted to be shipped off to boot camp right away, and he knew he needed to be in top-notch physical shape for the Marines to honor that request. And also because the compulsion to reach out to Griselda was so strong and so hard to combat, it was best if he was bone weary by the end of the day, with no moment to think between his head hitting the pillow and his eyes closing in sleep.

It had been four weeks now since he'd kissed her tenderly, over and over again, before leaving her hospital room and heading to Baltimore to meet with Lieutenant Jones. She had tried not to cry as they said good-bye but lost the battle, and he'd come damn close to losing it too.

"I hate it that we can't be together yet," she whispered through tears, her arms around his neck.

"W-we've waited this long," he said in her ear, his voice husky and emotional. Saying good-bye to her would never get easier.

"It feels like we've paid our dues. It feels like we deserve to be together."

"W-we will be. Soon, Gris. W-we're going to get there."

He was gentle with her, careful not to hurt her mending ribs as he held her. He knew it was impossible, but how he wished he could have one last time with her naked, soft and willing beneath his hard, demanding body. He'd never stop wanting her like that. Not now. Not when he had memories that seemed so real he'd get hard and break a sweat in the remembering.

"Last chance, angel. You want to change your mind about writing from now to August?" he murmured against her neck.

The thought of not communicating with her for seven or eight weeks made him sick to his stomach. He understood why she didn't want to hear from him. Would he want to hear from her if she were pregnant with someone else's baby, living in a one-bedroom apartment with him? He understood why it hurt her, but he hated it that anything in his life should injure the woman he loved. His only goal was to make her happy. Forcing himself to focus on the bigger plan that included a happy forever with Griselda, he felt her shake her head.

"No, Holden. I'll miss you like crazy, but I think it's for the best."

The best? The best would be staying in touch over the next two lonely months. Damn it. She couldn't see that?

"Can't you trust me? D-don't you know how much I love you? It doesn't matter if Gemma's sleeping in my bed—I'll be on the couch. I'm not touching anyone until I touch you again."

She searched his eyes, beseeching him to understand before looking away.

"Okay," he said gently, cupping her cheeks and tenderly kissing her lips. "I'll send you a text when I'm headed to boot camp."

"And a letter right after," she added quickly.

"I promise," he said, kissing her more urgently, the early morning sun flooding her hospital room and telling him it was time to go.

How he'd managed to walk away, he wasn't sure. And he'd broken his promise to her that day, texting her from Baltimore, because he figured he wasn't back home with

Gemma yet. But he'd respected her wishes since then.

Holden punched the bag 198, 199, 200 times, then lowered his fists, backing up to a bench, where his water bottle sat waiting.

"How's Gemma doing?" asked Clinton, sidling over to sit beside Holden on the bench. Clinton often joined him at the gym after work, and even though they didn't necessarily work out together, Holden appreciated the company.

He turned to his friend and wiped the sweat off his forehead. "I think you'd know better than me."

"What's that supposed to mean?" asked Clinton, an edge in his voice.

"That you're close to her. You two text each other more than she and I talk."

"Does that bother you?"

"Not at all," said Holden. "You've been in the picture a lot longer than me."

"You going with her to the ultrasound appointment next week?"

"Yeah," said Holden, taking a deep breath.

Gemma had left him a note last night where he generally left her money on the kitchen table. She was having her twenty-week ultrasound first thing Monday morning and had invited him to join her. Holden had read up online, and his heart leaped a little when he discovered that if the baby was in the right position, they could find out if was a boy or a girl. His son or daughter. He couldn't wait to see him or her for the first time.

But the saddest thing about Gemma's invitation was that the only person Holden had wanted to call was Griselda—to talk to her, to share his hopes for a healthy baby, and talk about possible names. Whether she realized it or not, he and Gemma were long past the point of reconciliation. At this point, they were two forced halves of a team, and Holden intended to do his share of the work. He paid her bills while she incubated his child. He respected her demand that Griselda not be a part of his life for now. He stayed out of her way, and, since the morning she'd made him breakfast and he left, she stayed out of his. It wasn't the ideal scenario for bringing a child into the world, but it was strangely bearable, especially since he knew he was leaving soon.

"She's excited to find out if it's a boy or a girl," said Clinton.

"Where're you going with all this?" asked Holden, suddenly feeling a little irritated, like Clinton was trying to guilt him into feeling more for Gemma than he did.

Clinton shrugged. "I don't know. I feel bad about it. I feel bad for the baby because his parents fucking hate each other. I feel bad for Gem because she wants what she can't have. I feel bad about your girl in D.C. because Gem's forcing you two to stay apart. I just . . . feel bad."

"I don't hate Gemma," said Holden quietly, surprised to discover it was true. "I just want someone else."

"But you're living with her. You're the father of her baby. I shouldn't say anything, but I know she still hopes that you two—"

"It's never, ever going to happen," said Holden.

"Maybe you should tell *her* that," said Clinton softly.

"I fucking did. And you were there. And she said she'd k-kill our f-fucking kid."

"She was confused. And hurt. And angry with you."

"Yeah, well. She seemed pretty serious to me."

"Yeah, I guess she did." Clinton sighed. "What a fucking mess."

The next words tumbled from Holden's mouth without a warning and shocked the hell out of him. "I'm leaving, Clinton."

"What?" Clinton turned to Holden with narrowed eyes. "She's pregnant with your kid and you're leaving her? You promised—"

"Calm the fuck down. I promised I wouldn't be with Gris, and I'm not. Having a kid is expensive, Clinton. I'm enlisting."

Clinton's jaw dropped. "What? What the f—? When? You're going into the service? When did *this* happen?"

"I met a Marine when I was down in Maryland at the hospital with Gris. We got to talking, and I just . . . you know, I want to provide for my kid. I want him—or her—to be proud of me. I don't want to work at the fucking glass factory my whole life."

"What's wrong with the glass factory?" asked Clinton.

"Nothing. You've lived here all your life. You'll probably make assistant manager one day. Me? I'm just passing through. Muscle and grunt work. I don't want it forever. I want more."

"So you're enlisting," said Clinton.

"Yeah. Already took the entrance exam. Did okay too. Heading back down to Baltimore in three and a half weeks for my physical, and if all goes well, I'll be shipped off to boot."

"Hell," said Clinton, a fast-growing admiration in his eyes. "You're serious. Enlisting. You're going to be a goddamned Marine, Seth . . . er, Holden."

Because Quint had served in the Army, Holden knew that Clinton had a huge respect for military service, and Holden grinned at the reverent tone in his friend's voice.

"Oo-rah," said Holden softly.

"Damn, Holden. Good for you. That's . . . that's really great. Yeah." He paused. "But what about Gem?"

"I'll be sending my checks to her to help out with the baby. I'll come home after boot and see them. And come on, Clinton, let's just be honest here. I think we both know she won't be alone by then. Not if you play your cards right."

Clinton's cheeks flushed, and he turned away, nodding slowly, looking out at the dilapidated gym, where a few guys were still working out. Finally he whispered, "I love her, Holden."

"I know. Why don't you fucking *do* something about it?"

Clinton's head whipped up, and his eyes met Holden's, searching them, wavering somewhere between hope and caution. "You wouldn't mind?"

"Hell, no."

"It's . . . okay with you?"

"Hell, yeah," said Holden, taking a sip of water. "Make her happy. Fuck knows I can't."

"But your kid?"

"Will always be *my* k-kid," he said tightly. A moment later he relaxed, nudging his friend in the side. "But if *my* kid's going to grow up with some other guy in the picture, I know I'd want him to be you."

Clinton grinned at Holden, then looked back out at the gym. "If she'll have me, I promise I'll love that kid, Holden. I promise you. Won't treat it no different even if me and Gem have more."

Holden nodded, something aching inside him as he realized that his child would likely grow up knowing Clinton better than him. But he'd still be the child's father, and he'd still know that once upon a time he'd broken his own heart to bring that child into the world. He'd changed the entire course of his life. He would never tell his child the threats Gemma had made, but he'd always know that he alone had stood between his child's life and death. Him . . . and Gris. And no one could ever take that away from them.

"When are you telling Gem?" asked Clinton.

"After the ultrasound," said Holden. He took another swig from his water bottle. "She's going to be p-pissed."

"It'll hurt her. But she'll come around."

In the pocket of his gym shorts, Holden's phone buzzed.

"I'm gonna head out," said Clinton. He stood and placed his hand on Holden's shoulder. "Good, uh . . . good talk."

Holden bobbed his chin at Clinton and watched him walk

away before swiping the screen on his phone, his breath catching with a simultaneous burst of love and fear when the alert said he had a new text from Griselda. Was she okay? Was everything okay?

As his heart quickened, he tapped on the messaging icon.

Only there was nothing to read—just a picture she'd sent. On the delicate, white underskin of her wrist, the letters "H+G" had been tattooed.

He stared at the small picture, happiness making him warm, longing making him ache, his breath catching and heart pounding.

A moment later, another text appeared under the picture:

Keep your fingers over the letters.
IMYLCILYF.

***

Griselda knew she wasn't supposed to text him. Hell, she'd been the one who asked him not to contact her, but something inside her had overruled that agreement just this once. She needed him to know that, in spite of the long month since they'd held each other, her love for him was as real as ever. She'd marked her body to prove that her love for him was undying.

Her heart thundered as she stared at the screen. It had been a risk to text him, of course. He might not write back because she'd asked him not to. He might not write back because Gemma was sitting next to him, or because he and Gemma had gotten closer. Glancing at her phone every five seconds, she stood in the upstairs hallway of the McClellans' house while Prudence sang nursery rhymes in the bathtub. Sabrina and Roy were at an embassy event tonight, and Griselda was only too happy to babysit for them.

With sweaty hands she slipped the phone back into her pocket just as it buzzed. She fished it out again so fast she almost dropped it.

I love it.

I love you, angel.
IMYLCILYF.

She sighed, closed her eyes, and leaned against the upstairs hallway wall. She let the marvelous feeling of connecting with her love infuse her body. Her innermost muscles clenched with longing, remembering the feeling of him buried deep inside her, the touch of his lips, his fingers, his body moving against hers. Her breathing became shallow and quick, and her heart throbbed. She missed him every moment of every day. Oh God, how she missed him.

"Zelda?"

Griselda's eyes snapped open, and she peeked into the bathroom at her sudsy charge.

"Your face is all red," Prudence said.

Griselda knew her smile must be blinding because Prudence looked surprised, then returned it, her eyes lighting up in excitement.

"You look like the happiest girl," said Prudence, her toothless, uneven smile making Griselda laugh softly.

I feel like the happiest girl, thought Griselda. *Right here, right now, for one small second, I am the happiest girl.*

He still loves me.

He misses me like crazy.

He loves me forever.

"What do you need, Pru?"

"Can we watch *Tangled* after my bath?"

She chuckled because it had become her and Pru's favorite movie that summer. For Griselda, it had come to mean much more than just a children's cartoon. It was the unlikely pairing of two kindred spirits who fall in love, who change in order to be together, who almost die so the other can live, who finally secure their happily-ever-after. They shouldn't find each other. They shouldn't end up together. It shouldn't all work out, but it does, and Griselda loved it.

"Of course," she said, helping Prudence out of the tub and drying her off with a warm, fluffy towel. "Hurry up and get your jammies on. I'll make us some popcorn."

As she popped two bags of microwave popcorn, Griselda's eyes lingered on the brochure from the University of the District of Columbia that Sabrina had affixed to the refrigerator. Griselda grinned, proud that she would be going there in September. She had filled out her application with Sabrina's help, and just yesterday had been accepted into the College of Arts and Sciences. To celebrate, Maya had taken her out last night for a glass of champagne and to get the "H+G" tattoo on her wrist.

To distract her from the needles, Maya had, well, needled her.

"Girl, for the record, I think this code of silence is crazy."

"I miss him so much, Maya," she said, wincing as the little needles punctured her skin. "But I don't want to influence him one way or another. If he wants to be with me, I'll get that letter in a few weeks. If not, I'll just have to move on with my life."

"And you'll be okay with that?"

"If he wanted to give his baby a family with a mother and father?" She took a deep breath, her heart hurting. "I won't say it wouldn't hurt. It would. Badly. But if that's what he wants, that's what I want for him."

"I'd fight for him."

"Come on, Maya. What would you have given to have your mama and daddy happy together? I can't take that away from someone else."

"You mean the baby."

"Yeah," she said, unable to keep the sadness she felt out of her voice. "If Holden and Gemma want to give their baby a family? I won't stand in their way."

"And you were also the one who insisted on leaving so Gemma wouldn't abort it." Maya shook her head. "You're too good, Griselda Schroeder."

"No," she argued. "I'm not so good. But I know how it feels not to have a family. I wouldn't wish that on any kid."

"So part of you hopes he stays with Gemma?"

"No!" she said. "No. I can't lie. I hope he writes to me. I hope he chooses me. You see? I'm not such a good person, Maya."

"Yeah, you are. Most girls? They wouldn't give a shit about some other woman's baby. And they wouldn't give him the space to figure out what he wants."

The needle stung like hell, and her skin felt so hot, like sunburn. And this was just a small, quarter-size tattoo. Griselda winced, thinking about the huge tattoo on Holden's chest, the angel wings that spanned his whole body. How had he borne the pain? The answer came quickly: Because it had been nothing next to the pain of losing her.

"I just want to be sure he doesn't ever regret being with me." She sighed. "It was really emotional seeing each other again, and we sort of jumped into a . . ." She blushed. "An intense relationship. I think we need a little time to be sure it's what we want."

"You need *time*?" asked Maya, raising her eyebrows.

"Maybe a little," Griselda confessed. "I hate being away from him, but I think that's good. It tells me this is real. It tells me it isn't all about impulse and sex. It's . . ." She shrugged. "It's real. It's what I want."

Maya looked impressed. "Look at you, being all wise and shit. My little girl's growing up."

"It hurts to be apart," said Griselda, laughing softly at her friend, "but it's not all bad."

"Oh, no? Most days it looks like it sucks."

"Give me some credit! I got rid of Jonah. I'm enrolled in college. I'm taking help from people," she said, giving Maya a pointed look. "You're right. I'm . . . I'm growing, I guess. But all of that happened because of Holden. He was the . . . spark."

"That started a fire," teased Maya, thrusting her hips suggestively. The tattoo artist stopped what he was doing and stared at her. "I'm taken," she said, giving him a look. "So while you're doing all this growing, what about Holden?"

"He's growing too. He's going into the Marines. He's not going to keep fighting other men in a field or working somewhere he hates. He's got a plan, a purpose. Direction. You should have seen his face when he told me about it. And you know what? All of that happened because of me. You see, right? We're good for each other."

"I see," said Maya.

The tattoo artist slathered his work in Vaseline and told Griselda to stay seated for a few more minutes while he wrote up her bill and found a sheet of instructions for tattoo care.

"When will you see him again?" Maya asked.

"If everything goes according to plan? November."

"Thanksgiving," said Maya, grinning back at her friend. *Thanksgiving.*

Her longing and anticipation for her future—for *their* future—made her heart race as she waited for the tattoo artist to return with her bill. She'd have so much to be thankful for this year. If he chose her. If he chose them.

Prudence bounded down the stairs just as Griselda poured the popcorn into two bowls. She then filled two sippy cups of lemonade since Sabrina didn't allow Prudence to have an open cup in the media room.

As the movie started, Prudence snuggled against Griselda on the couch, and Griselda dropped her eyes to the tattoo on her wrist, thinking,

Keep your fingers over the letters, Holden.
I will too.

***

It was a girl. He was having a daughter.

What an awesome sight to see her there on the screen, the

outline of her body and the bubbles that rose from her mouth as she bobbed around inside Gemma. He'd seen her skull, her spine, her legs and feet, heard her little heart thumping, galloping like a race horse. She was a living miracle, and she was his.

He and Gemma hadn't said much to each other in the way to the clinic, or in the waiting room, but as the technician turned up the sound on the monitor, Gemma grabbed his hand, and he squeezed it, grinning down at her. Whatever differences they had, this little baby belonged to both of them, and Holden already loved her.

In the truck on the way home, Gemma looked at the pictures they'd been given, and turned to Holden with a smile.

"I've been thinking of names," she said. "What do you think of Karisma?"

Not much, thought Holden, saying nothing.

"Or Destiny? Or Jasmine?"

Holden swallowed, fighting the urge to tell her that he didn't like any one of those names.

Gemma sighed loudly, obviously annoyed with him. "Clinton likes Hannah."

"'Hannah's good," said Holden.

"Yeah?" asked Gemma, placing her hands over her belly. "What do you think, l'il one? You like Hannah? You want to be named by yer Uncle Clinton?"

"*Uncle* Clinton?"

"It's what he calls himself. I don't have no sisters and brothers, and neither do you, so we may's well take family where we can find it."

"Hannah what?"

"Hannah West?" asked Gemma.

"My real last name's C-Croft."

Gemma shrugged. "Okay. Hannah Croft."

Hannah Croft. Hannah Croft. The name was so magical, so

amazing, he almost felt like laughing.

Gris, I'm having a baby girl, and her name is Hannah. Hannah Croft.

"So, uh, maybe we could try a little harder? For Hannah?" asked Gemma, reaching over to place her hand on Holden's thigh. "We could be a real family, Seth—um, *Holden*. We could get a place, raise her together . . . maybe even get mar—"

"Stop," said Holden, pulling into the parking lot of the city park with a screech and gently taking her hand off his thigh. He faced her, keeping his voice gentle. "No, Gem."

"Why not?" she demanded. "I made you happy once. At least a little happy. You let me stick around!"

"You deserve better than someone who lets you stick around. You deserve to be loved."

"Then love me!" she said with tears in her eyes. "I'm sorry I did that terrible thing, saying I was gonna have an abortion. I never woulda done it. I was so mad at you. I was hurt, and I wanted to hurt you. Whenever you were drunk, you'd talk about havin' kids one day, and I just thought . . . I thought . . ."

Wait. What? It all came together in a rush, as Holden held his breath, staring back at her in shock.

"You did this on p-purpose," he said, his voice low and bewildered in his ears. "W-we didn't *forget* to use a condom . . ."

Her cheeks flared with color, and she shrugged slowly, in defeat. "I wanted you to love me. I thought . . ." Her words trailed off, her expression miserable. "Before I put it on you, I poked holes in it so it'd break."

Holden nodded, surprised that he didn't feel angry with her. He just felt sorry—terribly, awfully sorry for her that she was so lonely for someone to love and to love her back that she'd tried to trap him.

"I'm leaving, Gemma," he said gently.

The tears in her eyes slipped down her cheeks. "I'm sorry!

I'm so sorry! You don't have to leave! *I'll* leave. I'll go back to my mama's house, and I'll—"

"Gem," he said, reaching for her hand. "It's okay." He held her hand, looking down at the black-and-white picture of his daughter. "I'm not leaving because of what you just told me. I'm enlisting. It's been in the works since June."

She gasped, sucking in a ragged breath of surprise. "The military?"

"Marine Corps."

"Oh," she sighed, sniffling. "Yer leaving?"

"Yeah," he said. "In a couple of weeks. But I'll send home a steady paycheck for you and Hannah. I can offer her great benefits. Health care. Education. She'll never want for anything, Gem. I'll be sure of it. You either. I'll take care of both of you."

She sniffled again, tilting her head to the side. "The Marines. That's . . . well, that's good, Holden. That's something. Good for you. Hannah'll proud of her daddy for serving." Suddenly Gemma's lips lifted into a smile, and she gasped lightly. "She kicked!" She laughed, looking up at Holden. "You want to feel her?"

He glanced down at her belly, nodding. She guided his hand to her rounded, swollen stomach, flattening it over the yellow T-shirt she wore.

"Just wait," she whispered.

A moment later, his tiny daughter kicked her foot into his hand. He looked up at Gemma in amazement. "Oh, Gem! Oh, wow! She's really in there!"

Gemma smiled back at him, wiping a tear away with the back of her hand and nodding. "I'm sorry, Holden. I'm sorry I did this to you."

Hannah kicked again, and Holden looked up at her mother's teary face. "I'm not."

"Someday . . . you think we could at least be friends?" asked Gemma.

Holden smiled at her and nodded, removing his hand and starting the truck again. "Friends. Yeah. I think so."

***

"Sure you won't come with us?" asked Sabrina, sitting on Pru's bed and watching as Griselda packed her daughter's suitcase for the McClellans' annual August vacation on Cape Cod.

"Thanks, Sabrina, but not this year. School starts in a week. I think I better go over that syllabus again, buy the books, supplies . . . you know."

"College girl," said Sabrina, grinning. "I'm proud of you, Zelda. So proud."

Griselda's cheeks flushed as she glanced at her boss before heading to Prudence's closet to find her favorite flip-flops. "I couldn't have done it without you."

"Have you been writing stories this summer?"

She had been. Inspired by *Tangled*, she'd stayed busy, writing her own fairytales a little bit every night, and filling up four composition notebooks on her shelf.

"I have. I promised . . ."

"Holden?" asked Sabrina.

Griselda nodded, tucking the flip-flops into the suitcase pocket.

"How is he?"

Griselda shrugged. "Good, I guess."

"You guess?"

Griselda tugged her bottom lip into her mouth. "We decided not to talk until he headed to boot camp."

Sabrina raised her eyebrows. "That must be hard."

"It is," said Griselda.

And now was the worst of it. Every minute, every hour, of every day, she hoped for a message from him—something, anything to let her know that he was on his way to boot camp and she was still first in his heart. It had been weeks since she'd texted him with the picture of her tattoo. Weeks without a word.

Was he still hers? Did he still miss her like crazy and love her forever?

"When does boot camp start?"

"Any day now, I suppose."

"Aha. You know, I could have Roy find out if he's—"

"No," said Griselda, looking up to seize Sabrina's eyes. "You're so good to me. But no. If he enlists and wants to let me know, he'll be in touch."

"You have a lot of strength."

Smart and strong. Strong and smart. She was doing her best to be both, to live both.

"How's Maya? She hasn't been by lately."

"She's good. She's an awfully good friend to me."

"She is," said Sabrina. "I like her very much."

Griselda grabbed Pru's favorite bunny, Nermal, off her bed and put him in the center of the suitcase before zipping it closed. "I think that's everything."

Sabrina sighed. "Car should be here any minute. Guess I'll go get my purse."

Griselda picked up the suitcase and started down the stairs just as the doorbell rang, no doubt the car service driver, ready to take the McClellans to the airport.

"I'll get it!" she called to Sabrina.

Setting Pru's suitcase next to the other bags in the front foyer, she opened the front door. But it wasn't the limo driver. She gasped, hurtling herself into Holden Croft's muscular arms.

CHAPTER 34

When she opened the door, every thought, every word, even breath, failed him. She was so beautiful—so utterly beloved—all Holden could do was stare at her until she gasped, and then he opened his arms so that she could fall into them.

"Holden, Holden, Holden," she laughed and cried, her arms winding around his neck and her sweet mouth so close to his throat he could feel her panted breaths, and his body hardened, wanting her.

He lowered his forehead to the crown of her head, closing his eyes and breathing in the fresh, clean scent of her hair, of her skin—of her, his heart, his love, Griselda. Beside himself with emotion, he stood there holding her, unable to move or speak, frozen on the McClellans' front steps with his woman back in his arms after two long months apart.

"Why are you here?" she murmured into his neck. "Is everything okay?"

He finally tried his voice and found it husky. "I'm headed to Baltimore, Gris. C-couldn't stop myself from coming to see you, but I have to be there by one."

She leaned back, her expression tangled between pride and sorrow. "Today's the day?"

He nodded, tightening his grip around her. "I ship out to boot camp today."

She took a deep, ragged breath and scanned his face, her eyes finally resting on his lips. "We have a few hours."

He bent his head, kissing her and stealing her breath away. She was soft and pliant, melting into his body as his tongue swept into her mouth. Her fingers threaded into his hair, her fingernails grazing his scalp as he groaned into her mouth. She tasted like tea and honey, heat and home, and every part of her fit into every part of him, like a puzzle piece, like the missing half of his soul.

"I missed you. I missed you almost as bad as before," he said. "All I want—"

"Ahem."

Holden's head jerked up to see Sabrina's surprised face concealing a grin.

"Maybe take it inside, you two? You're giving our neighbors quite the show."

He felt Griselda's chest shudder as she giggled, and Holden pulled her closer. "Hey, Sabrina."

"Good to see you again, Holden." She cocked her head to the side. "Heading to boot camp?"

"Yes, ma'am."

Sabrina's attention was captured by something behind Holden, and he turned to see a limo pull up. The driver followed Sabrina into the house to collect their luggage, and Griselda peeked her red face out from her cocoon against his neck.

"The McClellans are headed to the airport."

"Is that right?" he asked, unable to keep a huge smile from breaking out across his face. "Which means we'll be alone?"

She nodded, matching his smile, and leaned up to press her lips against his.

"Who's Zelda kissing?" asked a small person's voice from below.

Holden drew away from Gris and squatted down to look Prudence in the eye.

"I bet you're Prudence."

She smiled up at him, her twin blonde braids shiny in the morning sun. "I bet you're the Sun King."

"Oh, you think so?"

The little girl nodded solemnly. "Yes. Your hair's got some gold like mine, and you're bigger than my daddy."

"Hmm. If I'm the Sun King, who does that make Zelda?" he asked, hooking a thumb up at Griselda, who stood beside him on the landing, beaming down at them.

"Lady Starlight, of course." She lowered her voice and leaned closer to Holden. "'Cause she's in love with you."

Holden whispered. "Are you sure? 'Cause I'm definitely in love with *her*."

"Can I tell her?"

"Better not," said Holden. "Wouldn't want it to go to her head."

Prudence looked up at Griselda, then gave Holden a gap-toothed grin. "I think she already knows."

Holden chuckled, then stood up and put his arm around Gris. "Well, she's terrific."

"I know she is," said Griselda with pride in her voice.

Just for a moment—a second, really—he wondered about Hannah. Would she be blonde-haired and gray-eyed like him? Or dark-haired and blue-eyed like Gemma? And would Gemma put her hair in braids? And would she think her daddy was the Sun King based on her stepmama's stories?

"You must be Holden," said a well-dressed man in his thirties holding a suitcase in one hand and offering his other to Holden. "Roy McClellan."

"Yes, sir. Good to meet you, sir," said Holden, shaking his hand.

"Bree tells me you're enlisting?"

"Yes, sir. If all goes as planned, I'll be headed to Parris Island tonight."

"Well, oo-rah, Marine. Good luck to you."

"Thank you, sir."

Roy nodded at Griselda and pushed Prudence toward the car. "Time to go, peanut."

"Bye, Sun King," she said, and he winked at her.

Griselda leaned down to give her charge a big hug. "You be good for your daddy and mama?"

"I will, Zelda. I'll miss you."

"I'll miss you too, Miss Pru. See you in a week or two?"

"That rhymed," she said, giggling. "I'll bring back some shells."

"Perfect. We'll make necklaces, and you'll tell me all about the beach."

The girl kissed Griselda's cheek and hurried after her father.

"Well," said Sabrina, "take care of things while we're gone?"

"You know I will," said Griselda, embracing her employer, then stepping back against Holden.

"You look good together. You look . . . *right*." Sabrina tilted her head to the side, giving them a saucy look. "Just don't, ah, burn the place down, huh?"

Griselda's face turned as red as a tomato, but Holden chuckled as they waved good-bye before heading back into the quiet, empty house together.

***

Lord, she felt nervous.

Wasn't that a strange development? That she should feel nervous with Holden, of all people, made zero sense. But she did. They hadn't been together—*in bed*—since the cabin, and that was almost two months ago.

She felt his eyes on her as he followed her through the entryway, into the kitchen. She walked around the center island, resting her elbows on the counter and looking up at him.

Squelching the impulse to whimper in pleasure, she bit her bottom lip, feeling her cheeks flush. He was so handsome, her breath caught. For the first time since being reunited, his face wasn't black and blue with cuts and bruises, and her tummy fluttered, flipping over just from looking at him.

He pulled up a stool across from her and placed his elbows on the counter, like her.

"Hi," he said.

"Hi," she breathed, her heart quickening. She felt her nipples harden against her T-shirt, and she squirmed a little as the walls of her sex clenched, then relaxed.

His eyes dropped to her chest for a moment, then darkened as he licked his lips. "I hated being away from you."

She swallowed. "Me too."

"I missed the way you say my name," he said, his eyes intense as they stared back at her. "The way your skin feels under my fingertips."

She shifted her hips beneath the counter, her breath hitching as she listened to his warm, low voice.

"I missed the way your eyes get dark when you want me."

Then they must be black as coal right now.

"And the sounds you make in the back of your throat when you're about to come."

He slid off his stool and stood up, slowly circling the counter.

"I missed the feeling of your ankles around my waist."

She'd been breathing deeply again for weeks, but now she couldn't seem to get enough air.

"And the way you say 'I love you.'"

He stood next to her at the counter, and she turned to face him.

"I love you," she whispered.

His mouth came down so hard and fast over hers, their teeth clashed together and it hurt, but she stayed pressed against him. Her hands slid up his T-shirt, fanning out along his jaw as he conquered her mouth, his hot, velvet tongue sliding against hers again and again. His hands slipped to her hips, and suddenly she was on the countertop with Holden between her legs, and those ankles he'd just spoken of were locked around his back.

He was hard against her chest and hard between her legs and hard where his arms encircled her, tightly holding her against him like he'd never let her go. She let her soft mouth be taken. She let her soft body be held, and moments from now she'd let him thrust deep inside her soft, wet sex, which pulsed for him with urgency, aching to be filled by him again.

"Downstairs," she whimpered into his ear, wrapping her arms around his neck.

"Where? How?" he asked, putting his hands under her backside and lifting her off the counter.

"The door behind you."

He took two steps, fumbling with the doorknob for a moment before it turned, then took the stairs quickly. At the bottom she whispered, "Left," and he pushed open the French doors that led to her studio apartment, complete with a plush, queen-size bed straight ahead. Stopping at the foot of the bed, he lowered her gently. He covered her with his body and kissed her again.

Dizzy from him stealing her breath, she moaned and arched against him. "I need you."

His hands skimmed under her T-shirt and bra, pushing both to her shoulders, and as she wiggled out of them, he stood up, quickly pulling off his shirt, unzipping his pants, and pushing them down. Her mouth watered as she stared at his naked body, and she unbuttoned her shorts with trembling fingers and shimmied them down her legs. Holden reached for her panties, pressing the foot of his palm against her sex, and let out a low groan.

"Jesus, Gris. You're soaked."

His eyes cut to hers, dark and intense, as her most sensitive skin throbbed under his hand, aching for the touch of his mouth. As though reading her mind, he yanked her panties down her legs and leaned forward, pulling her hips to the edge of the bed.

"What do you need?"

"You," she whispered, her face hot as she panted the word.

"Like this?"

In one smooth motion, he dropped to his knees and placed her legs over his shoulders. Leaning forward, he gently spread her lips with his fingers and lowered his mouth to her clit. Her fingers twisted in the comforter, her neck bending back as she cried out. His tongue licked her, slow, lapping caresses that made her hips buck off the bed and press closer to his mouth. He sucked gently then increased the speed and pressure of his tongue, and her body started shaking. She opened her eyes to look down at him, only to find him staring up at her, a sight so erotic she lost it. Her muscles convulsed, clenching and releasing, pulsing endlessly as he lifted his mouth and carefully flipped her over so she was facedown on the bed. He pulled her hips to his pelvis and the thick head of his penis pushed slowly into her waiting sheath. The walls of her sex, still throbbing from her orgasm, sucked him forward until she was fully impaled. He leaned forward, his arm under her breasts elevating her off the bed until the angel on his chest met the skin of her back.

"Is this okay?" he groaned close to her ear.

She leaned her neck to the side, and he ran his lips over the damp skin as she sighed, "Yes. You're so . . . deep. Holden. We're . . . one."

"I've dreamed of having you like this," he panted, staying still, letting her get used to him.

"Then have me," she said, pushing her hips back against his.

"I love you, angel," he whispered, his lips touching down lightly against her throat as his hips thrust forward. "I'll never get enough of you."

She covered his hand with hers, locking their fingers together under her breasts as he continued to pump into her from behind, his pants quicker as deep moans rose up from the back of his throat. The swirling that had just consumed her started building again, more intense with every thrust, with every whispered word of love, until she felt his teeth bite the lobe of her ear, and she screamed his name as her body shattered into a million pieces of pleasure. Holden's voice growled, "Griselda" close to her ear, then he cried out, his body emptying its tribute into hers.

***

"I missed you like crazy. I love you forever," murmured Holden. He rested his forehead against the back of her neck, his body limp and loose and entirely sated, though his dick twitched against her ass, suggesting it wouldn't take much to start round two.

Griselda turned in his arms, her face flushed and glistening with sweat and arousal. His gaze dropped to the pink tips of her breasts that brushed against his angel, and his blood sluiced south.

"Eyes up here," she said.

She was grinning when he looked up, though he knew her well and he saw the uncertainty behind her eyes.

"Tell me about Gemma . . . and your . . ."

"Daughter," said Holden, watching the way Gris's pink lips parted in surprise. "Hannah. We decided to name her Hannah."

"Hannah," she said, her eyes welling with tears. "Hannah."

Holden nodded, his body calming down as he talked about his daughter, and pulled Griselda tenderly into his arms. "I saw her last week on an ultrasound. She was perfect, Gris. Ten fingers. Ten toes. She belched once or twice while we were watching. Little bubbles floating around in there with her. Probably my genes. It was like a miracle to see her."

"I bet."

"And I heard her heartbeat. It was really strong. Like a race horse. Pretty amazing. She should be here around Christmas."

Griselda's smile faded a touch, then, as though she realized it, got broader but more forced. "And . . . Gemma?"

"She's doing really well. We had to make peace, you know? For Hannah's sake."

"Oh," said Griselda, searching his face, struggling to hold on to her smile. "Of course."

Holden's eyes narrowed. "Gris? What's going on in your head?"

"Peace." She took a deep breath, dropping his eyes. "So you're . . ."

"What?" he asked, tipping her chin up and wincing from the tears brimming in her eyes. "What, angel?"

"Are you back together? Are you . . . going to, you know, try to be a family?"

"W-what?" he said. "What are you talking about? W-we just—"

"I know," she said quickly. "But I . . ."

His anger was rising fast, so fast it made his heart thrum uncomfortably. "I love *you*! We just made love. I . . . G-Griselda, are you actually asking me if I got back together with Gemma, then came here to f-fuck you once before boot camp?"

She blinked at him, licking her lips nervously.

He reached for her face, cradled her cheeks, and reminded himself to be gentle despite his fury. "G-Gris, tell me that you know I'm all in. I'm yours. I love you. I b-belong to you. No one else."

She swallowed, looking down for several seconds before looking up again. "I want to believe that."

It felt like she'd smacked him. "W-why w-wouldn't you?"

"You're having a baby with Gemma," she said in a rush. "And you always wanted a family and to be a good dad—"

"I *will* be a good dad to Hannah, but I'll have a *family* with *you*, d-damn it."

She continued like she hadn't heard him. "—and so I didn't know if you'd reconsider being with Gemma, and there are so many tally marks on your arm, and—"

"G-Griselda!" He was so angry he was afraid of hurting her, so he dropped his hands from her cheeks and rolled onto his back, putting a little distance between them. His heart twisted with hurt, and he tried to catch his breath. He didn't want to yell at her or frighten her, but he was furious . . . and hurt. "You d-don't trust me."

She rolled onto her back beside him, both of them staring up at the ceiling in misery.

"I trust you as much as I can trust anyone," she said softly.

"That ain't sayin' much," he retorted, his eyes burning.

She leaned onto her side to face him. "Holden, please don't be mad at me. I love you more than anyone. I want this . . . I want you . . . I just . . ."

"Every one of the marks on my arm . . . is you," he confessed.

"What?"

He turned his neck to look at her, feeling the heaviness of his heart as he revealed himself to her—his true colors, infused with guilt, regret, and shame. "Every single mark, every single one, b-belongs to you."

"What does that even mean?"

His eyes burned with tears, and he blinked them back, focusing on her face. "It didn't matter who it was, who I was with. It didn't matter that you were d-dead. I'd close my eyes in that moment, and I'd see *your* face. Always. Even with Gemma."

"Holden," she said, a sound of disbelief and pain.

"I know it's sick. You were only thirteen the last time I saw you." His voice trailed off, as he searched her face, hoping she would understand. "B-but I was already in love with you. The way you'd lie down next to me in that shitty little dirty bed made me feel . . . *alive*. My whole life, you were what I missed, what I wanted, what I longed for. I . . . I didn't want anyone else. For all my life—*all* my life—you have been my beating heart, the woman of my dreams." He raised his arm, looking at the marks, running a finger over the blue and black lines. "This was me trying to replace you. This was me failing every time."

Her face was devastated, but something desperate inside him made him press on.

"My body is marked with you. My arms. My chest. My eyes. My head. My heart." Tears rolled down her cheeks. "I can't erase you. I'd have to die to be free of you. D-don't you see that, Gris? C-can't you see? There is only *you* for me."

"I see," she sobbed in a whisper, opening her arms and reaching for him.

He rolled into her, dropping his forehead to her shoulder as fresh pain assaulted him—the pain of losing her on the Shenandoah, of learning of her death, of being forced to live with Caleb, who'd killed her. The open wound that had been Griselda for so long was still healing inside, and he suddenly remembered, in fresh, visceral pain, how it had felt to believe her dead.

Go to the ends of the earth for you . . . to make you feel my love.

"I *c-can't* lose you again," he said, wrapping his arms around her, his voice husky and eyes burning with unshed tears.

"You won't," she promised, her hands stroking his hair. "Never."

"You mad about the other w-women? Or freaked-out that I'd think of you while I was with—?"

"No," she said gently. "No. I understand now." She stroked

his hair, cradling him against the soft warmth of her body. "I'm not mad. I'm just sad you couldn't find a second of happiness with anyone else. You must have been so lonely, Holden. That hurts my heart more than anything."

"I *was* lonely. I was damn near dead on the inside, Gris. But I don't want to be dead anymore. I want to be strong. I want to offer you something good." He clenched his eyes shut. "But I c-can't lose you. Not now. Not when I've held you and loved you and known what it is to feel happiness again in my shithole of a life. I'll do whatever I have to do to prove that you can trust me, angel."

"You *won't* lose me, Holden," she promised again, her voice resolute, close to his ear. "It's just that *I* lose everyone I love too: my mother, my grandmother, you. At the cabin, just as I started to believe that we could be together, you found out about Hannah, and I lost you *again*. So it's hard for me to trust. I want to, but it's so hard for me not to have doubts. I've been protecting myself for so long . . ."

"I know," he murmured, pressing his lips to the skin of her shoulder. "I know, angel. But you can't live like that forever, and you've got to start somewhere. Why not start with me?"

***

Her eyes widened as she stared back at him because his words were an echo of Maya's when Griselda was in the hospital:

You are strong and you are smart, Zelda, but you gotta start letting people in. You gotta trust that they're not all gonna let you down. I'm not gonna let you down. Sabrina's not gonna let you down.

And somehow she had to find the strength to believe that Holden—whom she loved more than anyone else in her life, whom she kept losing yet somehow finding—wasn't going to let her down either.

CHAPTER 35

August 20

    Dear Gris,

    Well, I did it. I passed my MEPS with flying colors, took an oath to support and defend the Constitution of the United States, and now here I am on a plane to Parris Island, South Carolina. A PLANE, Gris. My first plane ride. Damn, but I wish you were sitting next to me.

    Thanks for the notebook you lent me. I'll use it to write your letters until the paper runs out. Then I'll probably keep it anyway because you gave it to me in the first place.

    Saying good-bye to you today was just about the hardest thing I've ever had to do. But here's what I know: we keep losing each other, but we keep finding each other too, which pretty much means we're meant to be. Think about how much we've already been through, Gris, and we survived it all.

    But I know you still have doubts, so here's the deal. While I'm away, I'm going to write you a letter every day. Every day, Gris. And that'll be me proving to you what I already know: I love you and I choose you, and from now until forever, that's how it's going to be. And when boot is over, I'm coming back for you, angel. That's a promise.

    IMYLCILYF

    Recruit Holden Croft

***

August 21

> *Dear Holden,*
>
> *I keep thinking that my stupid worries about you and Gemma ruined the last of our time together. God, I hope not. I promise that while you're away, I am going to work on trusting you and trusting everything that's between us. It's taken me long enough, huh?*
>
> *It was so strange to get your phone call last night. I knew you were reading from the script they gave you, but I was so glad to hear your voice, I didn't care.. Did you hear me when I told you I loved you? I know you couldn't say it back, but I had to say it.*
>
> *Thank you for telling me to call Lieutenant Jones for your address. He gave it to me right away, and now I can write to you even if you can't write to me yet.*
>
> *I went to UDC to register for classes today and got totally weirded out by a class I wanted taught by a Professor Foster. I swear, if this was a year ago, it would have been enough to send me running for the hills, but I took a deep breath, thought of your face, and enrolled in the class. It's called the Structure of English. I also registered for British Lit, American Lit, and Intro to Critical Writing. Sounds like a lot of reading and writing, huh? What's kind of cool is that all of my classes are on Mondays, Wednesday, and Fridays, so I'll be able to work for Sabrina at Nannies on Ninth two days a week.*
>
> *We didn't get a chance to talk about Hannah again, and I didn't feel like I got a chance to tell you how happy I am for you. Truly happy, not fucked-up happy. I could see the wonder on your face when you were telling me about her, and I ruined that moment for you with my worries about Gemma. Oh God. Please be patient with me.*
>
> *I'm relieved you got a chance to text me on your way to Parris Island. What I can't believe is that you texted me on the*

way to the <u>airport</u>. *You better remember to tell me what it was like to fly.*

I'm so proud of you, Holden. My heart is almost bursting from it.

IMYLCILYF

Gris

***

August 21

Dear Gris,

I won't be able to mail these letters for a while, and I hate that, but I'm still writing them. One a day. Every day. No matter what. Because nothing in the world is more important than you. I just hope you're working on the trust thing and that not hearing from me doesn't fuck that up.

Let me tell you about boot. I don't know what I was expecting, and I'm not complaining, but man!

Bus picked us up at the airport yesterday around six in the evening and took us to PI. We get here and they're yelling orders at us right when we step off the bus. Like, yelling like crazy. And there's all this paperwork, and you pee in a cup, and I swear, we didn't hit the showers until almost 2 a.m. Then we're in these temporary barracks, but you're so hopped up on adrenaline, nobody sleeps. At 4 a.m. they come wake you up by banging on a garbage can, yelling, "Get on the line!" And you don't know what the hell is going on, but they're barking orders, and suddenly we're all on the ground doing fifty push-ups.

We marched around all day—to breakfast, to get our heads shaved, measured for uniforms, and other stuff. And they make you count everything you're given, and you're so tired, and this guy next to me, Jimmy, kept fucking up his count and every time he'd get ten sit-ups and then have to do it again.

I'm so tired tonight, I can barely keep my eyes open, but you're the last thought of my day, angel, and I'm glad to be here because we're going to have a good life together. I promise you that.

> *I can hear taps.*
> *Oo-rah!*
> *IMYLCILYF*
> *H.C.*

***

August 22

> *Dear Gris,*
> *I'm so beat, I can't see straight.*
> *So today's letter will be short, but I promised to write every day, and a promise is a promise, especially on the days when it's toughest to keep.*
> *IMYLCILYF*
> *H*

***

August 23

> *Dear Gris,*
> *IMYLCILYF*
> *Holden*

***

August 25

> *Dear Holden,*
> *I'm trying to be strong and trust you and trust us. I promise you I'm working on it every day, and by the time you come home, I'm not going to be scared anymore. Well, I probably will be, but I'm not going to let that hold me back from us being happy.*
> *I think a lot about our life so far—at Caleb Foster's, especially. That dingy cellar and the panel in the wall. The garden where we grew so many things. Boiling the vegetables in the barn so you could can them. I think about that day on the Shenandoah and how we were apart for so long, and then how I found you again in June. I think about the cabin. I think about you coming to the hospital when I was hurt. I think about*

opening the McClellans' door to find you standing there (and everything we did in my bed last Monday morning before you had to go). I haven't changed the sheets yet because I can still smell you.

We've walked a long road together, you and me.

And here I am, missing you again. Sometimes I feel like so much of my life has been spent missing you, but maybe I've been looking at things the wrong way. Because it's weird, but I sort of feel like even when we were apart, we were still sort of together the whole time. Does that make sense?

School starts tomorrow, and I am scared.

But then I think of you and where you are, and everything we went through...I think to myself, I can do this.

You give me that strength, Holden

I feel like you're with me all the time even though you're far away.

Keep your fingers over the letters.

IMYLCILYF

Gris

xo

***

August 26

Dear Holden,

I did it.

I had my first day at college.

You're in love with a college girl, Marine.

IMYLCILYF

Gris

***

August 29

Dear Holden,

The phones are so quiet here today, so I thought I'd write you another letter. You're going to get a lot of letters from me. I hope that's okay because they're mostly just rambling and probably not that interesting. Sorry. I'll try harder.

I've been reading online about boot camp, and it sounds bad with all the yelling and mind games. And then I had a weird thought, but I think you'll understand what I'm saying. Remember at Caleb Foster's? We got yelled at all the time—and beat up—and we never knew when he was going to start in on us. Those boots would start coming down the stairs, and I didn't know if we'd be listening to a sermon, scrubbing the floor, or getting our backs belted. And then I was thinking that maybe boot camp isn't as much of a shock for you as it is for the other recruits because in a weird way you've already been, only you were little and we were all alone. And now you're big and strong, and being there is a choice, not a prison.

Is that a sick thought? Maybe it is. But you know? I don't think you can have a childhood like ours and come out of it totally normal.

Maya found this support group for kids who grew up in foster care, and I've been going. I've mostly been quiet. I definitely haven't talked about Caleb Foster. Not ready. I'm trying to open up, though, and trust that I can tell people things without getting hurt. The group leader is always saying, "It's a process." I kind of like that. I'm a process too.

I heard from the detective who worked on Jonah's assault case that it went to trial and he was sentenced to eight years. I was probably a coward for refusing to testify, but I felt like the pictures and evidence were enough to convict him. I never want to see his face again. Never, ever. I'm so relieved that chapter of my life is finally over.

I got your postcard yesterday, and even though it didn't have anything but your address, I knew your hand had touched it, so I slept with it under my pillow. I read that recruits like to get pictures from their girlfriends. You've got me on your arm, but here's another just in case.

I'm smiling because I'm thinking of you.

IMYLCILYF
Gris

***

September 2
    Dear Gris,
    It's Sunday. Oo-rah!
    I finally got all thirteen of your letters mailed out, and I get a little bit of free time today to write you a nice long letter before shining my shoes and ironing my clothes. I figure this is me spending time with you, angel, so I am going to enjoy it.
    First, I have to tell you that I'm staring at your picture, and you're the most beautiful woman that God ever made, but you already know that.
    Second, you've got no idea what your letters mean to me. They're not boring. They're amazing. Please keep them coming.
    Gris, just hearing from you makes me feel weak, then strong. I picture your face, and I see your lips moving as I read your words. Sometimes I miss you so much it feels like I'm going crazy, but I reread your letters and I feel better. I swear I have all of them memorized within a day of receiving them.
    Going back to your first letter: you didn't ruin anything when I visited you in Georgetown. That morning was heaven, and I loved every second, even when we were knocking heads. I know you have trouble trusting, but it means a lot to me that you're trying. I know it's hard, Gris. Remember, I was there, right where you were. I know what you lost. I know what you endured. Not because you told me, but because I remember. And when I get tired or frustrated here, just like you said, I remember our time at Caleb Foster's place, but I don't think about me. I think about you, a little girl with amber braids who made those days bearable when they shouldn't have been. I think of you and I keep moving forward because we deserve a chance to be happy, but we have to make it happen for ourselves.
    When I have quiet moment here, which isn't often, just like

you, I feel myself going over a lot of ground, and the thing my whole history seems to have in common is you. You weren't there with me and my parents when I was growing up, but the dream of you was. I wanted someone in my life like my father had my mother. I wanted to love a woman and treat her special and stop by a department store for perfume samples to make her smile when I got home at night. And that's the kind of husband I'll be for you one day, Gris. The kind who tries to make you happy however he can. Now, I'm not proposing or anything, so don't get all freaked out. I'm just sayin', even when I didn't know you, I already did.

And now you're a college girl and it's my turn to be proud, Griselda Schroeder. But I have one gripe: Where are my stories? Did you forget to send me some?

Tell me about your classes and what you're reading. I want to know everything. And how's Prudence? Tell her the Sun King's head is as bald as a yellow billiard ball.

I'm glad you're in that support group with Maya. Keep going. Try to open up if you can. You are a process, Gris. We all are.

Flying was amazing and ridiculous. You're up in the air in a ten-ton metal capsule! We'll have to do it together sometime. I promise we will.

I know you're happy for me about Hannah. I got a letter from Clinton that he is helping Gemma with her birthing class. I told him to make any move on her that feels right, and I think there's a future for those two, but don't tell them I told you. Wink, wink.

I'm sorry the letters you'll get from the last two weeks were only a couple of lines, but you'll get them all at the same time, and this one should explain why those are so brief. I sneak in those lines in the dark after taps. I do it because I love you and because I promised.

This is a tough place, Gris. Tough like I never even

imagined. I see some guys who aren't in as good shape as me, and man, they're struggling. It's insane here, but if you can believe it, I'm actually having fun. I like all the physical stuff—the drills and marching and training. But there's a lot of studying too. Way more than I thought.

We can't talk at any time for any reason, and damn, it makes me mad when some of the guys talk and then we all have to drop and pay for it. One guy ran off—just left in the middle of the night—because he couldn't hack it.

I dream about graduation.
I dream about November.
I dream about you, angel.
Keep your fingers over the letters.
And send me a story.
IMYLCILYF
Your,
Holden

***

September 6
Dear Holden,
I GOT YOUR LETTERS TODAY! All of them! All thirteen!
I loved reading about your plane trip and your first day. I even loved the letters that only said "IMYLCILYF" because it meant you were thinking about me.

Boot camp sounds really hard, but I'm so proud of you, Holden—every minute of every day. On Saturday I was at the post office, and a Marine walked in. He was in his full dress uniform (probably for the Labor Day festivities), and all I could think was how handsome Holden will be in his. When I think of us scratching in the dirt at Caleb Foster's farm, I could just die of pride. We didn't just survive, Holden. We didn't just survive. (I learned that in my support group. Some kids survive foster care, some thrive and go on to live meaningful lives. We didn't just survive foster care—we also survived Foster, and now we're going to thrive.)

Speaking of Foster, something incredibly weird happened yesterday, and I can't stop thinking about it. A woman met Professor Foster after class, and he hugged her to him and called her Ruth. I swear to God he did, and I'm not just imagining it. I asked the TA who was sitting next to me who the woman was, and she told me it was Prof. Foster's wife. Now, yes, of course, it occurs to me that Foster was this Ruth's married name (and her childhood name was probably Ruth Smith or something), but it still threw me for a loop. Just in case you're wondering, Professor Foster's name is Bill. Which means I'm obsessing about nothing.

I'm studying a book called The Canterbury Tales by Geoffrey Chaucer, and it's hard reading. I have to constantly try to figure out what it means. I read a line last night: "Alas, alas, that ever love was sin!" and I started thinking about Seth and Ruth, and you and me, and how they loved each other and we loved each other, and Caleb Foster was so sure we were all sinning. And we weren't, and they weren't, and the only one sinning was him. If I ever met the real Seth and Ruth, I feel like I'd understand them and they'd understand us. It's crazy because they died in that barn fire so long ago, but sometimes I dream that they didn't.

Do you still dream of Foster's farm? When you do, does it frighten you? Since I found you again, my bad dreams have mostly gone away, Holden. Mostly, I dream of you. Of your arms around me and your angel pressed to my chest and your heart beating against mine.

Stay strong.

Keep your fingers over the letters.

I

Miss

You

Like

Crazy
I
Love
You
Forever

Gris
xo

CHAPTER 36

October was going to be a bitch.

Although Holden was mostly used to boot camp now, like everyone else around him, he was homesick as hell—*home* being defined purely and simply as Griselda—and the Crucible was coming up at the end of the month. He wasn't scared of the Crucible—the fifty-four-hour grueling exercise meant to break, build, and teach—but it represented the pinnacle of boot camp, with graduation following a few weeks later.

After graduation and his ten-day leave, he'd have another three weeks of training at Camp Lejeune in North Carolina before heading to Fort Sill in Oklahoma for fire support man training. After a month at Sill, he'd head to California for another month of EWTGPAC training, followed by his assignment to a Permanent Duty Station. And because he had opted for Artillery, there was a ninety percent chance he'd be assigned to Twentynine Palms or Camp Pendleton, both in California.

California.

Not Georgetown, where Griselda had built a life for herself, complete with a place to live, friends, a job, and, most important, college, but *California*, all the damn way across the country.

He hadn't shared with her yet that his life would almost

certainly be taking him to the West Coast, because she was doing so well. She'd finally started sending him stories again, and she loved college. She was helping mentor some of the girls sent to Nannies on Ninth and still attended the foster care survivors' support group with Maya. He could tell from her letters that she was getting stronger and more confident, believing more in herself and in them as a couple. He was desperate not to upset that progress.

But on the flip side, he didn't want to wait anymore for them to be together, and his ten days of leave was the only free time he'd have until he was assigned to his PDS, which meant that if he wanted to solidify their relationship—and he did, more than anything—he needed to do it when he saw her in November.

In other words, he was planning to propose. And if she said yes, he wanted to leave for the School of Infantry a married man and meet Gris at his PDS in March, not as his girlfriend, but as his wife.

He knew what this meant, what he was asking of her, and it troubled him. He was asking her to make a decision over the course of ten days that would affect the rest of her life, and to commit her life to him. He was asking her to uproot her whole life and move to California. He was asking her to leave her home, her friends, her job, and her studies, and choose a life with him instead.

Not that she couldn't enroll in college in California. She could. She *would,* if Holden had anything to say about it, and he would support her in finding a job, if that's what she wanted. And heck, the Marines would give them housing and all the other benefits that came with life on base.

But would she choose him?

Would she give up everything she knew and choose him?

He didn't know. He didn't know if she was strong enough to leave her life behind when all she got in return was him.

Lately it kept him up nights, but he didn't see another way. He could take leave in the spring or over the summer if he applied for it and hadn't yet been deployed for his first six-month trip to the Sandbox, aka the Middle East. But if he was honest—and yeah, a little selfish—he wanted her with him as soon as possible. He wanted her to start this whole new adventure with him. He wanted her there, wherever he was stationed, every night when he got back from training, and in the inside loop with other military wives while he was away. He'd lived half his life *without* her. He wanted to live the rest of his life *with* her.

"Hey, Postal," said one of his bunkmates, Tex, as Holden walked back into their barracks on Sunday afternoon, "sending another fucking letter to your girl?"

Because of the volume of letters he both wrote and received (and probably also because of his fierce, crazy-eyed fighting skills when he was "in the zone"), his drill instructor had started calling him Private Postal, and the nickname stuck. He didn't mind. It was sort of perfect, actually, because it constantly reminded him of his commitment to Gris and their future together.

"No," said Holden, "I was sending it to your mom because I saw her checking out my ass when she dropped you off."

"Oooo, burn," said his friend Graham, setting the iron on the ironing board and offering Holden a high five as he walked by.

"You're a wiseass, Croft."

"Team Week's coming up," tossed Holden over his shoulder in Tex's direction. "Heard they want you on laundry, grunt."

And of course Tex walked right into it. "Why's that?"

"They heard you're real good at getting skid marks out of your tighty-whities."

"Fuck you, Croft," said Tex, giving Holden the finger before heading out of the barracks in a huff.

"He's gonna clock you one of these days," said Graham, carefully folding his ironed pants.

"D-don't like it when he makes comments about my girl," said Holden, lying down on the bottom bunk and looking up at the picture of Griselda sandwiched between the bars of the metal bunk frame. "Screw him."

"You talk to her about it all yet? Getting married? Moving out to Cali?"

Graham, who was planning to marry his high school girlfriend, Claire, once he was assigned to his first PDS, was also headed into the artillery, though he'd opted to be a cannon crewman instead. Chances were decent they'd be stationed together, or at least close by.

Holden shook his head. "Not yet."

"Claire could be a friend to her to her," said Graham, leaning on Holden's bunk. "She's from Indiana and doesn't know a soul in California. They're kind of in the same boat. I mean, if Griselda says yes. They'd both be picking up stakes and heading west to marry a Marine."

Holden nodded. "Yeah. I'll . . . I'll let you know after I talk to her. Hey, I appreciate it, man."

He watched as Graham turned away, heading to his bunk, no doubt to write Claire another letter or study for their final written exam, coming up in a few weeks.

Holden stared up at Griselda's bright blue eyes, his heart clenching as he wondered, *Will you say yes, sweet girl? Will you say yes to me?*

***

Griselda loved college.

She loved it so much more than she'd imagined she would. She loved the assigned reading, challenging though it was, and the exchange of ideas, the new ways of thinking. Though her British and American lit classes were, far and away, her favorites, she also appreciated the solid knowledge she was getting in her Critical Writing and Structure of English classes too. Though she had to admit, there was something about Professor Foster that still bothered her.

He didn't look especially familiar.

His name wasn't Seth.

And yet occasionally, very occasionally, she picked up a slight twang in Professor Foster's cultured voice. It was so slight as to be almost imagined, but it was the way he said *your* like *yer* once or twice, and she was sure she'd heard him say *agin* rather than *again* at least once. The slight accent had pinged in her brain, and both times she'd had to calm her heart and convince herself that the name Foster was screwing with her head, and nothing else.

Lost in her thoughts about Professor Foster, she didn't hear the door to her room open, but suddenly Prudence's wide smile was staring at her from the foot of her bed.

"Pru!" exclaimed Griselda. "You scared me!"

"Just got home from school. Mama's making me a snack."

Griselda sat up, pushed her books and notebook aside, and patted the bed. "How was school today?"

Prudence sat down and shrugged, and the collar of her crisp, white long-sleeved dress shirt grazed her ears. "Okay, I guess."

"Not letting Sybil Lewis get under your skin, right?"

Sybil was the difficult child of a well-known congressman, and Prudence's key rival at the expensive private school she attended.

"Nope. But it was hard not to laugh when she felled down and skinned her knee at recess."

"I hope you managed not to," said Griselda.

Prudence shrugged. "Will you tell me another story after my snack?"

"Sorry, baby," Griselda said. "I got an extension on this paper for my class and need to drop it off at my professor's office by five.

"What's a professor?"

"A teacher."

"Like Mrs. Simmons?"

"Sort of. Go have a snack. If I'm back in time, I'll come tell you a story before bed, okay?"

"Okay!" Prudence ran from the room, closing the French doors behind her.

Griselda rolled onto her back, glancing at the framed picture on her bedside table: Holden in his uniform, his handsome face grim. She smiled as she reached for the photo and pressed her lips to the glass before rolling onto her stomach and staring at him.

"I miss you like crazy," she whispered, tracing his lips. "I love you forever."

She kept waiting for Holden to talk to her about what came next for them, but she didn't want to distract him from boot camp, or put pressure on him to build a future with her when Gemma hadn't had the baby yet. He hadn't even been stationed yet. He couldn't very well invite her to go somewhere if he didn't know where he was going.

Sometimes her doubts encroached—she no longer wondered if he'd leave her for Gemma, but maybe he'd decide that his life in the Marines was more exciting for one, and choose not to be tied down so soon. For her part, all she wanted was to be tied to him. For life. Forever. Even if it meant leaving Georgetown, the McClellans, and Maya behind. Even if it meant leaving college behind. Even if it meant that all she got in return was a life with Holden because truly that's all she'd ever really wanted.

She kissed his face again, replacing the frame and picking up the paper she'd been proofreading, when Prudence came down to visit. She checked her watch. It was four o'clock. She'd have just enough time to get to Professor Foster's office if she left now.

Pulling on her jacket, she slipped the paper in a manila envelope, picked up her keys, and headed out the door.

***

Forty-five minutes later, Griselda walked up the steps of the Arts and Sciences building, following a middle-aged woman into the building.

On the bus ride over, she'd opened and read Holden's latest letter.

October 10
Dear Gris,

I miss you. I miss you so bad it feels like we've been apart for years, not months. I know you want to come to graduation, and I love you for it, angel, but don't spend the money or miss your classes. I'll leave for D.C. first thing after the ceremony and text you when I'm on the way. Not that I don't like Sabrina, Roy, and Pru, but I'm kind of relieved that they'll be in Rhode Island for Thanksgiving. Call me a selfish asshole, but I love the thought of having you all to myself. Get a lot of sleep now, Gris. I promise we won't be getting much once I'm home.

Can you believe that the Crucible is in three weeks? I admit it, I'm a little nervous. From what I can gather, this is the worst part of boot camp, and some Marines don't even make it. It takes place over three days and includes forty-five miles of marching, combat assault courses, and warrior exercises. Almost no sleep. We've got to work together. We've got to be a team. Pray that I don't break any bones, because even if I do, I'll keep going, but damn, it would hurt. Sort of glad for all those fights I had now. Never quit one, even when I was hurting like hell. I know I can make it

*through this. I'll be thinking of you, angel. I know, in a
weird way, you'll be with me.*

*I loved your latest story. Sounds like the Sun King
and Lady Starlight are going to get their happily-ever-
after pretty soon. What about us, Gris? Think we'll get
ours? All I want out of life is you beside me. Is that
what you want too?*

*Write to me soon, angel. Your letters keep me
going.*

*IMYLCILYF
Holden*

She had reread the letter three times on the bus, touching
the words with her fingertips. Her breath quickened when she
read the part about not getting any sleep, and her eyes brimmed
when she read about him wanting her beside him for the rest of
his life.

But why hadn't they come up with a solid plan for the
future yet? He couldn't possibly doubt her feelings for him, and
she didn't doubt his for her. Their time apart had strengthened
their bond and, for Griselda, built her trust in a future with
Holden. She trusted that their feelings were strong and true, but
action was required to make life changes happen, and neither of
them had initiated that particular conversation. She took a deep
breath as she walked behind the woman who'd preceded her into
the building, and told herself to be patient. He'd be home in five
weeks. They'd have time to talk about everything then.

The woman in front of her stopped at Professor Foster's
office and turned the doorknob. Finding it locked, she knocked
lightly, then turned to Griselda. It was Ruth, the professor's
wife, whom Griselda had seen after class once or twice.

"Hello, dear. Are you looking for Professor Foster too?
Don't tell anyone, but when it's locked, he's napping."

Griselda realized that she was scanning the woman's face

for similarities to Caleb Foster's, and, finding none whatsoever, she said, "I have a paper to drop off."

"Shall I give it to him? Oh! Here he is now."

The door opened, and Professor Foster stuck his head out just enough to see his wife. "You're early, love."

She shrugged, grinning up at her husband. "I was in the neighborhood, Seth. I thought we'd walk home together."

Griselda didn't feel the envelope slip from her fingers, but she felt her lungs close up as she sucked in a ragged breath and held it. Her whole body trembled, and it felt like the world was spinning, faster and faster—so fast she was barely able to see anything. Her hand reached out and touched the slick, painted cinder block of the wall beside the office door, and she shuffled closer to it, flattening her palm against the cool stone and finally dragging in a gasping breath.

"Dear? Dear, are you all right?"

The woman's voice was distorted and far away.

"Seth, I think she's sick. Help me get her to a chair."

Her professor took her other arm, and together Seth and Ruth led her into the office, closing the door behind her.

CHAPTER 37

She was carefully maneuvered onto a couch in the professor's office, and a moment later a glass of water was placed in her hand.

"Are you ill, dear? Do you need a doctor?"

Griselda sipped the water, and the world finally stopped spinning.

Ruth Foster was sitting beside her, and Professor—Seth? William?—Foster was standing in front of her. She looked up at him, searching for similarities between him and Caleb Foster, but she didn't see any in his face either. Professor Foster was clean-shaven, with kind eyes and neat gray hair. His face was only slightly wrinkled and still very handsome, and his body wasn't as large and terrifying as his older brother's had seemed to little Griselda so long ago.

She looked down and swallowed another gulp of water, trying to get her head around what her heart already knew, what her heart had somehow known since the day Professor Foster called his wife Ruth after class: Seth and Ruth hadn't died in that fire so long ago—they'd merely used it as a way to escape. And now? They were here, in the same room as Griselda.

"You're name is Seth?" she panted.

Professor Foster nodded. "My middle name. William Seth Foster."

"You didn't die in the fire," she said, taking a deep breath. She sat back on the couch and looked up at her professor for a moment, then at the woman beside her, who had turned as white as a ghost.

"What?" asked Ruth, sliding away from Griselda on the couch, her eyes wide as they flicked to Seth's. He looked at his wife evenly, then back at Griselda, his face carefully blank.

"What do you mean, Miss Shroder?" he asked, his voice tight.

"My full name isn't Zelda. It's *Griselda*," she said slowly, looking at Seth's eyes for a flicker of recognition. There was none. She turned to Ruth. Still none. They didn't know her name. They didn't know her story. "My foster brother and I were kidnapped in 2001 by a man named Caleb Foster and held captive for three years at his farmhouse in West Virginia."

Ruth gasped. Griselda raised her chin a touch, turning her gaze to Professor Foster. "I know you're them. His brother and sister. You're Seth and Ruth Foster."

Seth pulled his bottom lip into his mouth, his nostrils flaring.

"He's dead," she added softly, wondering if they knew. "Caleb Foster died in Oregon many years ago."

Seth's eyes fluttered closed in relief. When he opened them, they were glassy as he looked at Ruth. "He's dead."

Ruth nodded, taking a deep breath and sighing raggedly. "How did you know? How did you know who we were?"

"Caleb Foster called *me* Ruth. The boy, he called Seth. Hard to forget those names." Griselda looked at Ruth with sympathy. "I'm sorry for what you went through."

"For what *I* went through? My God, what happened to *you*?" asked Ruth.

"He abducted me and my foster brother, Holden, in July of 2001."

"Sweet Lord," gasped Ruth.

"In fairness, we got into his truck willingly. We thought he was a relation of our foster mother's. He didn't steal us, but he did hold us hostage. Forced us to work. Tried to . . . *reform* us. He thought we were you."

Professor Foster pulled up a chair, sitting across from Griselda and Ruth, his hands tented under his chin, his eyes grave. "I'm trying to get my head around this. You're saying that our older brother, Caleb, abducted you and kept you hostage as a child?"

"Yes," she said. "You can look it up." Griselda's eyes narrowed, thinking that at some point they should have read about the abduction, somehow found out about it. "How did you not know? You *never* looked him up? In all these years?"

"We turned our backs on Caleb the day we left West Virginia. We promised to never, ever look back. We promised each other not to look for him, or ever seek him out, or help him. We had to pretend he was dead. It was . . . safer," explained Seth, his gaze resting on Ruth tenderly.

Ruth spoke softly. "He was . . . *so crazy.*"

"He ranted a lot about you two. Constantly."

"Leviticus," murmured Ruth.

"Yes!" said Griselda. "Hellfire and damnation, the sins of the flesh, evil, wickedness."

"How did you get away?" asked Seth, drawing her attention from Ruth, who was still pale and trembling.

"We ran," said Griselda, her eyes tearing. "While he was at church one Sunday morning, we ran away. But Holden . . ." She swallowed the painful lump in her throat. "Holden didn't make it. Only I was able to escape. Holden stayed with him until Caleb died."

"And Caleb thought Holden was me? Seth?"

Griselda nodded.

"Did Holden . . . did he . . . survive?" asked Ruth, her eyes worried.

"Yes," said Griselda, wiping her tears away and allowing a small smile. "He did."

They were all silent for a moment before Seth cleared his throat. "I'm so sorry, Griselda. I'm so very, very sorry for what you went through."

"Me too," said Ruth, reaching for one of Griselda's hands. "Did he . . ."

"Hurt us? Yes. He beat us. He kept us in the cellar. He had a strict set of rules we had to figure out and obey. He made us work long hours. We were frightened all the time, often hungry, almost always hopeless."

"How did you survive?" asked Seth, taking off his glasses and wiping his eyes.

"We had each other," said Griselda, squeezing Ruth's hand once before releasing it.

Ruth looked up at Seth, and Griselda read the meaning in the older woman's eyes: love, understanding.

"You're brother and sister," said Griselda, looking back and forth between them, trying to keep her voice even and nonjudgmental. Some part of her had always wondered—or hoped?—that they weren't.

"Not by blood," said Seth quickly, dropping Ruth's eyes.

Griselda's eyes widened. "What? What do you mean? You're twins."

Seth shook his head. "No. We were born on the same day, but Ruth was adopted. Her mother died in childbirth in the same hospital where my mother was giving birth. It was such a small, rural town, and Ruth's mother was a young girl, a runaway. They didn't know how to track down her family, so they asked my parents if they had room for both of us."

"You're not related?" clarified Griselda.

"No," said Ruth, "though we *were* raised together, and our parents never told us the truth. We *believed* we were brother and sister. But Seth and I had feelings for each other that started

441

when we were—what?" She looked at her husband, and he nodded. "Twelve? Thirteen? We knew it was wrong on one level, but it felt so right on another. We couldn't help it. We tried to keep it a secret, but the bigger the secret, the closer we became. And then Caleb caught us."

Griselda nodded. "We figured that out."

"And he started falling apart. We were a Bible-reading family. Very strict."

"Plus, Caleb was kicked in the head by a breeding mare when he was little," offered Seth. "He'd never been *right*, but after he caught us, he unraveled."

"How'd you find out? That you weren't related?"

"When our mother died. I found my birth certificate in her things," said Ruth. "Different mother. Father unknown. Different time of birth by several hours."

"Caleb had become very dangerous, especially to Ruth," said Seth, reaching out his hand, which Ruth took, lacing her fingers through his. "He didn't believe us, even when we showed him Ruth's birth certificate. He blamed her for leading me astray. He ranted and raved, following me around and reading Bible verses. He tried to hurt her several times, beating her with his belt and hitting her hard in the face. He finally drugged our dinner one night, and we woke up locked on separate sides of the cellar. He told us we couldn't come out until we repented."

"How'd you get away?"

"He was scattered. Got drunk and forgot to lock the kitchen door one night before heading to Rosie's," said Ruth. "Seth managed to loosen one of the panels in the wall between our rooms, and we decided we had to run away because Caleb was our legal guardian for two more years."

"There's no way Ruth would have survived," said Seth softly.

"So we walked out of that house, I took off my sweet-sixteen silver bracelet and threw it in the barn, and then Seth set it on fire."

"That's how you escaped."

Ruth nodded. "We never looked back. I had a little money that Mother left us. We walked all the way into Charles Town in the dark, got on a bus to Florida, and never looked back."

"You were just kids," said Griselda, marveling at their strength. "How'd you live?"

Seth gazed at Ruth. "Not easily. We worked awful jobs and lived in homeless shelters. We'd chosen a warm place, and we stretched Mother's money as far as it would go. We eventually got our GEDs and kept working. Ruth put me through college managing a Denny's, and I put her through college once I got a job."

"We made it," she said proudly.

"Because we stayed together," he said.

"Three years ago," said Ruth, squeezing her husband's hand, "Seth was offered a professorship here in D.C. We weren't sure about coming back north, but we hired someone to check and see if Caleb had paid taxes or still owned property in Charles Town. We didn't want any other information about him. Just that. When we learned he didn't pay taxes or own property in West Virginia anymore, we assumed he was dead or gone."

"And Ruth always missed her white Christmases."

"So we came back up north."

"And here we are," said Seth. He searched Griselda's face, his own filled with sorrow and remorse. "I am . . . oh, my dear, I am *profoundly* sorry for what you went through."

Ruth's face was wet with tears, lined with sorrow, when she looked at Griselda. "I don't know how you survived as . . . *me*. He hated me so terribly."

"Holden protected me. We learned what to do—and what not to do—to make things bearable. I think he would have killed us, though. If we'd stayed much longer."

"He certainly would've killed *me*," whispered Ruth.

"I don't know what else to say," said Seth, letting go of Ruth's hand and sitting back in his chair. He searched Griselda's eyes. "This is a lot to take in. Can we do anything to help you? Can I . . .? Can we . . .? Do you *need* anything?"

"No, but I'm glad you're alive. I'm glad you survived. I'm glad you thrived." She chuckled as tears streaked down her face. "That sounded ridiculous."

"It wasn't Shakespeare," said Professor Foster, raising an eyebrow.

"Seth!"

He smiled at Griselda kindly, his eyes rimmed with deep sorrow. "You know, he wasn't always like that, Caleb. He wasn't *right*, but before he found out about us, he was . . . kind to me. In his own way, I think he loved me."

Griselda thought about Holden's conflicting feelings for Caleb Foster, how he hated him even as he felt gratitude for Caleb's saving his life.

"I know this will sound unbelievable," said Griselda, who had embarked on a journey of healing the day she was reunited with Holden, and was anxious to leave the horrors of Caleb Foster's basement behind and finally move toward the future. "But I don't think he was all bad. Holden calls him a principled monster. There's some truth in that. He was trying to save Seth, I think. And I think that yearning to save could have been born from love."

"You're incredibly forgiving," said Ruth.

Griselda swallowed, her face hardening. "I *don't* forgive him. I'll *never* forgive him."

"Of course," said Ruth softly. "What a stupid thing to say."

"Do you still know him? This . . . Holden?" asked Professor Foster.

Griselda nodded. "Yes. He's at boot camp. He's going to be a Marine."

"And you love him," said Ruth.

"More than anything."

Seth grinned at Ruth, shaking his head. "It's a hell of an irony, isn't it? That Caleb would try his damnedest to keep two couples apart for the wrong reasons and end up pushing them both together for the right ones?"

Ruth gave Seth a look. "I doubt Griselda is ready to laugh about any of this yet, dear."

"I mean no disrespect," said Seth quickly. "I just mean that—for me, at least—Caleb's fierce disapproval made me fight harder for what I wanted. For Ruth. We left that farm at sixteen years old, barely schooled, with a couple hundred dollars. And now here we are. Married for over thirty years. Attached to each other as fiercely as Caleb's disapproval would have separated us. We fought so hard, so early, we never really had to fight for each other again."

"When you make sacrifices like we did," said Ruth, "the rest is easy somehow. Life will always throw curveballs. No money. Losing a pregnancy and finding out no more will be possible. Getting laid off. A storm that levels your home. Sickness." She looked up at Seth with tears brightening her eyes. "Our life together wasn't *easy*. We had plenty of heartbreak, plenty of sorrow. But we also had each other. We'd *fought* to have each other. The rest? Well, as long as we had each other, anything was bearable. Anything was possible. The biggest battle had already been waged and won. We belonged to each other."

Tears streamed down Griselda's face as Ruth finished this elegant speech, all while looking at Seth with such profound love that Griselda almost felt as if she should slip quietly away and leave them to their memories. But Ruth turned to her and asked, "Is that the kind of love you and Holden have?"

"Yes," said Griselda, realizing in her heart, in her very *soul*, that it was true.

Nothing, *nothing*, would ever come between her and Holden, despite their absences and separations from each other, now and in the future, despite trials and tribulations, good and bad times, sickness and health, plenty and want. Like Seth and Ruth, they'd already waged and won the biggest battle of all. Oh, she would always have some trouble trusting the situations and people in her life, but in that moment she decided once and for all to exclude Holden from that list. She trusted him. She trusted *them*. She was all in. And all that lay ahead was forever.

They talked for a few more minutes, and Griselda turned in her paper. She promised she would bring Holden to meet them when he was on leave, and they made her promise to ask them if she ever needed anything at all.

Then she embraced them both—these mythical people, Seth and Ruth, who had somehow turned out to be real—and as she left the office, she looked back just in time to see them reach for each other's hands and lace them tightly together.

***

October 21

Dear Gris,

I was so stunned by what you told me in your latest letter, I had to read it three times. Seth and Ruth are not just alive, but happy and safe and in love? Married for thirty years? I just don't even know what to say.

Is it weird that I'm a little mad? I mean, they knew he was crazy (he fucking locked them up, Gris, and from what you said, he was on a path to kill Ruth), and they didn't call anyone or report him? Could have saved our lives a lot of terror and grief.

Then again, if I go down that wormhole and start rewriting history . . . It always could have been worse. What if Miz F had turned her eyes to me and started molesting me? Or what if you or I had been transferred to another placement before we got to know each other? If I rewrite one thing, I could ruin it all, the entire journey, right up to the moment you showed up at that fight in June. So, I guess I wouldn't trade it. Any of it. Because I also wouldn't trade our time at Quint's cabin. I fucking hate Jonah, but I wouldn't even trade that time we had in the hospital, since you turned out okay. And I sure as fuck wouldn't trade that morning we spent in your bed in Georgetown. I wouldn't trade that I'm in the military now and you're in college. So, okay. Everything happened a certain way, and a lot of it sucked, but here we are today. And I like where we are today. So, okay.

I heard from Gemma, and I hope that doesn't make you paranoid. (It shouldn't. I don't love her. I love YOU.) She just wrote to me to tell me how good she and Hannah are doing. Hannah is kicking up a storm, and Gemma said that she was always out of breath climbing up the stairs to my apartment, so she moved in with Quint, Maudie, and Clinton. She said that Maudie won't let her lift a finger and asked me how I'd feel about Hannah growing up with Clinton as a stepdaddy. I wrote back and told her I couldn't think of anyone I'd rather have around my little girl. Hannah's going to have a lot of love, Gris. All of them. You and me. So much love. That's all that matters.

Only four more weeks until graduation. Only two more until the fucking Crucible, which makes my head spin. This week is basic combat: marksmanship skills, land navigation, and how to maneuver under enemy fire. I'm getting to be a good shot, Gris. My DI said I have aptitude with a gun and told me to consider a transfer to infantry if artillery isn't my thing. Maybe scout sniper. Something to think about. I was proud as hell when he said it.

We haven't talked a lot about what comes next, Gris, but I'm hoping we can talk when I come see you in November. I have to tell you, it looks like my PDS will be out in California. Slight chance of North Carolina, but almost certainly Cali. I know that's a long way from home for you. It's a long way from college and the McClellans and Maya. But the weather looks

real nice. And a friend of mine named Graham? His girlfriend is
moving out there too, and he said he could hook you up with
Claire. I'm not asking you anything. I just wanted you to chew
on it a little. We'll talk more when I'm home, okay?

> *A month from today I'll be with you.*
> *I can barely believe it's true, but it is.*
> *Please keep writing. I need every letter.*
> *I miss you like crazy.*
> *I love you forever, angel.*
> *Holden*

Griselda read the letter once, then twice, then a third time,
as usual, loving the feeling that Holden was here with her,
talking to her. She ran her fingers over his neat handwriting,
grinning and crying a little, and missing him, and proud of him
at turns.

But in the end, two things made her lips tighten:

His girlfriend is moving out there too . . . I'm not asking
you anything.

She reread the letter, but instead of having the warm,
wonderful feeling she usually had when she read one of
Holden's letters, her eyes skated back up to those lines again.

Griselda did not play games, and she had not demanded
anything of Holden, but she knew two things in the deepest
reaches of her heart: she didn't want to be Holden's girlfriend,
and there was a very specific question she definitely wanted him
to ask her.

He'd alluded to marriage before, but not for many weeks,
and now in this letter—the only recent letter that mentioned the
future in any solid way—he referred to someone else's girlfriend
and her in the same breath, and then said he wasn't asking for
anything. Hmm.

She folded up the letter and placed it carefully under his
picture, lying back down on the bed and staring up at the ceiling,

annoyed with herself.

She didn't want to read into it. She didn't want to jump to conclusions or get her panties in a wad because he wasn't proposing by letter, which, hell, wasn't what she would want anyway. And honestly it was encouraging that he wanted her to consider moving to California with him. It was. Because she wanted to be with him more than anything else in the world. And if he asked her to go without a ring, chances were she'd say yes. But the truth? The God's honest truth? She had only recently started daring to dream of her life the way she wanted it, and the way she *wanted* to move to California with Holden was with a ring on her finger and with the name Griselda Croft.

CHAPTER 38

Griselda's little apartment at the McClellans' house wasn't Holden's home, but it was where Griselda lived, which meant it was the closest thing to a home that he had.

Instead of flying north, he'd opted to take a bus because it saved him enough money to slip into Kay Jewelers in Beaufort and buy a ring. It was only a tenth of a karat, but he'd selected it right away because the ring was a silver color and the setting was copper-colored gold in the shape of a heart, and something about it just felt perfect for Gris. It had cost almost four hundred dollars, and in the whole of Holden's life, he'd never made such an extravagant purchase, which is why he kept patting his breast pocket and refused to close his eyes to sleep on the fifteen-hour trip from South Carolina to Washington, D.C. He couldn't risk someone trying to lift it. He'd never be able to replace it in any sort of timely manner, and for all that it was small, it held the fate of his world in its shiny depths.

He'd boarded the bus at ten o'clock last night. It was eleven o'clock in the morning now, and they were almost there. He scrubbed his hand over the bristles of hair left after the fresh buzz cut before graduation yesterday, and smiled at his reflection in the bus window. It looked like a warm, beautiful November day outside, which was exactly what he'd hoped for.

On Thursday, the day before graduation, when most of his

fellow recruits were entertaining their visiting families, Holden had spent the afternoon on the Internet, planning a special day for Griselda. He'd looked up the twenty-five most romantic places in D.C. and Georgetown, and his plan was to visit five of them with her today. They'd start at the small, often overlooked D.C. War Memorial, a white marble gazebo-like building near the National Mall, then take a hand-in-hand stroll along the Tidal Basin. And if her feet got tired, they could relax a spell on the lawn of the Mall. As the late afternoon set in, they'd cab it over to Georgetown and follow the pretty path along the C&O Canal, and as the sun started to set, he wanted to end up near the Key Bridge, where he'd take her hand, drop to one knee, and ask her to be his wife.

For whatever reason, it was symbolically important to Holden to propose to Gris near the river—maybe because he wanted to replace their memory of the Shenandoah with a happier one, of officially starting their lives together.

He breathed deeply and patted the ring again. As he checked his watch, his heart kicked into a gallop. He'd be arriving at Union Station in forty minutes, and then it was a quick ten-minute ride to Griselda's apartment, where he'd drop off his bags and open his aching arms to his love.

***

Griselda blow-dried her strawberry hair, trying not to be nervous, but she was. Dang it, but she was.

She'd said good-bye to the McClellans, who traditionally spent Thanksgiving week with Sabrina's parents in Rhode Island, this morning. They'd be home next Sunday, and Sabrina had already asked Griselda if she and Holden would join them for dinner that evening. She'd accepted her boss's well-intentioned invitation, though inwardly she groaned. Holden left for Fort Sill, Oklahoma, next Monday afternoon, and the last thing Griselda wanted to do on their final night together was share him with anyone.

She had bought a new pair of soft, off-white corduroy jeans from Old Navy, and a new pair of brown leather-looking boots from Payless. She'd splurged a little on a tan turtleneck sweater that was supersoft and hit right about where her jeans rested on her hips. If she moved just so, he'd see a little of her flat tummy, and she delighted in the idea of teasing him.

She did a careful job on her makeup, keeping it natural but pretty, making her blue eyes pop with bronze eye shadow and darkening her pale lashes with a deep brown mascara. Tracing her lips with a rose-pink lip pencil, she filled them in with pink lip gloss that tasted like pineapple, then leaned back to check her work.

And smiled.

She didn't look like a foster kid or some kidnapped waif who'd ended up back in the system. She didn't look like an abused girlfriend or someone's nanny. She looked fresh and young—like the college girls she saw on campus at UDC. She could pass for any of them today in her new clothes. But it was more than that, and Griselda knew it: she'd changed in the months since finding Holden again. She'd become more confident, less introverted; more hopeful, less frightened. She had started to determine her worth in the world, based on the power of his love for her, and found herself not undeserving. Her past was checkered with terrible things, but she was more whole every day.

Ask me if I'm whole or broken, Holden. Just ask me today. I'll tell you I'm almost whole. I'll tell you that, for the first time in my life, I'm almost whole.

She flicked off the light in her bathroom and checked the clock by her bedside. It was twenty past eleven, and though he'd told her not to meet his bus, there was simply nowhere else on earth that she wanted to be than in his arms. She grabbed her keys and headed out the door.

***

Holden was minutes from Union Station when his phone rang, and a grin broke out across his face because he assumed it was Gris checking on his ETA. They'd decided not to talk on the phone after graduation, building the anticipation of finally seeing each other when he got to her apartment, but it made him happy to think she couldn't wait. Truth told, he couldn't either.

But when he looked at the phone, it wasn't Griselda's 202 area code that greeted him. It was a 304 number. It was Clinton.

"Hey, Clinton! How's it—"

"Seth, you gotta come," said Clinton, his voice abrupt and tight. The hairs on Holden's arm stood at attention.

"W-what's going on?"

"Oh God," sobbed Clinton. "I don't know. Gem was complainin' about headaches yesterday and had this pain in her right side, but we just thought, you know, she's big and uncomfortable. She's getting closer. But she . . . God, she had a seizure this morning."

"A seizure? Jesus, Clinton. Is she okay? Is Hannah—?"

"I don't know. She fell off her seat at the kitchen table, and her whole body was shakin' on the floor, and my mama called the ambulance. They came and took Gem away, and now I'm here at the hospital, but I'm not the father and we're not married yet and her fucking mother's on a bender, so she ain't got no immediate family in there with her. You gotta come, Seth."

Holden nodded as the bus pulled into the depot at Union Station. "Of course. Of course, I'll . . . I'll c-come right now. I just . . . I'm in D.C. I g-gotta figure out a way to . . ."

"She's only thirty-four weeks, Seth! It's too fucking early!"

"I know, man. I know. Listen, I'm on my way. I'll be there just . . . just as soon as I can. Tell Gem to hang in there."

"Can't fucking see her, Seth. Can't tell her nothin'! *You* gotta come."

"I'll be there. Hold it together, C-Clinton. I'm c-coming."

His heart thundered with worry. So much worry that when he glanced out the bus window and saw the prettiest girl in the world waving at him after three months apart from her, he could barely wave back.

***

Griselda saw it on Holden's face immediately, reading his expression just as easily as she'd always been able to.

"What happened?" she asked, scanning his worried face as he stepped off the bus.

"Gemma went into labor this morning."

Griselda grimaced. "Oh no! She's not due for six weeks."

"I know. Clinton's a mess. Something's wrong." He stopped talking for a second and looked at her face—her beautiful face and soft hair, her amazing body in new clothes. His bags fell from his shoulders, and he pulled her roughly into his arms. "You look beautiful. I missed you like crazy."

"I love you forever," she sighed against his neck, her arms coming around his waist as she stepped closer, so that her breasts pushed against his chest.

"You were with me every second at boot, Gris. Your letters. They were . . ."

"So were yours," she said, leaning back to look into his eyes. "It was like one long conversation. Something new every day. I missed you so much, but I don't feel like I *missed* too much. Does that make sense?"

"It does. I feel exactly the same way," he said, leaning down to press his lips to hers. He kissed her gently, but there was a heavy and immediate matter that needed his attention. And as disappointed as she was to miss out on some of their time together, she knew she had to let him go. She stepped back, and he loosened his arms.

"Well," she said, "at least we had this. I guess I'll see you when—"

"No way," he said, his face wiped clean of softness, his

hard jaw square as he stared back at her. "You're c-coming with me. No more separation. No more. I'm spending every second of these ten days with you, Griselda. You hear me? I had a whole day planned for us today, but, well, it'll have to wait . . . but—"

"You want me to go with you?" she asked, reaching up to cup his cheek with her palm.

"Yes! I'm not letting you out of my sight." His face fell, lines of worry deep between his eyes. "F-fuck, Gris, I'm going to *need* you by me if that b-b-baby—"

"No!" said Griselda. She shook her head. "No, don't go there. Holden, we've had enough fear and doubt for a lifetime— we don't need to borrow any more. Until we know different, we're gonna stay hopeful. She's gonna be okay. Hannah's gonna be okay."

He grabbed her roughly, pulling her back against his body and dropping his forehead to her shoulder. His voice was barely audible by her ear: "I love you, I love you, I love you. I love you so good and so much it hurts."

Her eyes welled with tears, but she wasn't crying today. No. Today they were together again, and today Hannah Croft was going to be born small but healthy. She knew it. She just knew it.

"I love you too." She cupped the back of his head, her fingers stroking the soft bristles. "Your hair's all gone."

"That okay?" he asked, his voice gruff and emotional.

"Of course it is," she said tenderly. "It's you."

He reached up and took her right wrist gently, pulling it down to look at it. He clenched his jaw once, shaking his head before pressing his lips to the small tattoo he found there. "The letters."

"I fall asleep with my fingers over them every night."

He swallowed, searching her face with tenderness, which segued to a mix of frustration and regret. "I'm so sorry this happened today. The timing . . ."

She heard Ruth Foster's voice in her head: *Our life together wasn't easy. We had plenty of heartbreak, plenty of sorrow. But we also had each other. We'd fought to have each other . . . as long as we had each other, anything was bearable. Anything was possible.*

"That's life, Holden. It isn't nice and neat," she said. "All that matters is that we're together again."

He looked back at her with wonder. "You're . . . different."

"I trust us," she said simply. "I'm strong."

"You were *always* strong."

Only you *would remember that,* she thought. *You're the only person alive who remembers what I was like as a little girl. And yes, I lost my way for a while. But I found it again when I found you.*

She leaned up and kissed him, gratitude making her eyes water. "We can talk more on the drive. I think we better get going."

***

Once back at the McClellans', Holden changed quickly into civilian clothes, and Griselda sat on her bed and sent a text to Sabrina, asking permission to use their car to drive to West Virginia.

"I'm allowed to drive Prudence to appointments and such, but I don't feel right taking it across state lines without permission."

He peeked at her from the bathroom doorway, jeans on, shirt in hand, and watched as her eyes widened and darkened, staring at his bare chest like it was Christmas morning.

"Angel, if you don't stop staring at me like that, I'm going to lose my mind."

She took a deep ragged breath, and her face flushed as she stood up.

Her voice was slightly breathless. "I'll go track down the keys. I'm sure she'll say yes."

He knew she was leaving the room to take the temptation of her body away from him, and he tightened his jaw, his head a battleground of emotion: fear for Gemma's and Hannah's safety; disappointment that he'd planned the perfect proposal for Griselda and it would have to wait; crazy amounts of love for her kindness, understanding, and compassion; and south of his belt, which had been neglected for weeks, waiting to be reunited with her again, frustration. Extreme frustration.

He took a deep breath and released it slowly, willing his body to calm down and focusing on Clinton's call. It would hurt like hell if little Hannah didn't pull through this. And Gemma. For all that she'd trapped him into parenthood, he still cared for her welfare. He buttoned up his shirt and tucked it in, offering up a quick prayer for their safety, but knowing better than anyone that prayers often went unanswered.

Shrugging into his jacket, he checked his bag to be sure he had everything he needed for the next two days, and found the small black velvet ring box tucked into the duffel pocket where he'd hid it while Griselda texted Sabrina. Casting his eyes quickly at the stairs that led to the kitchen, he pulled it out and flipped open the small box, then closed it, shoved it into his jacket pocket and met Gris upstairs.

"She said we could use the car," she said, grabbing two Diet Cokes from the refrigerator.

Worry crashed over him like a wave, and he thought about the ultrasound picture of his tiny daughter. He froze in the McClellans' kitchen and searched Griselda's bluer-than-blue eyes for comfort. "Gris, you think she'll be okay?"

"I do," she said confidently, holding open the door for him and locking it behind them.

***

Holden filled her in on Family Day and graduation, answering her questions about the Crucible and the friends he'd made at boot, but Griselda could tell that his heart wasn't into the conversation. He was preoccupied and worried, his body more and more tense the closer they got to West Virginia, and she respected his need for quiet by looking out the window and remembering the last time they'd crossed the border into West Virginia together:

Ten years old, their shoulders stuck with sweat to the vinyl backseat of the Fillmans' old station wagon and each other.

Looking straight ahead out the window, she saw the large blue, green, and yellow sign: "Welcome to West Virginia."

"I know you're thinking about it," he said. "The last time we were in a car together headed for West Virginia."

"You know me well."

He reached over and placed his hand on her thigh, flattening his palm against the soft corduroy. "C-come with me to California, Gris."

"I will," she answered without thinking, just as she knew she would.

"We'll find you a college so you can continue your studies. A job. Whatever you need."

"I just need *you*," she said softly, her heart hurting a little that he hadn't mentioned marriage.

He was talking about a place called Coronado, where he'd be finishing some training, and a base called Pendleton, where he thought he might be stationed. Her mind drifted.

Maybe we'll be unconventional, she thought. *Maybe we'll be one of those couples that live together their whole life, and everyone just assumes they're married, but they never actually said the words or did the deed. We'll still have a home and kids, and when enough years go by, we'll say "What's the point?" because a piece of paper couldn't make us love each other any more than we already do.*

She took a deep breath and sighed, wishing her little internal pep talk had eased her worries. It hadn't. But she'd fake it till she made it. The important thing was for them to be together.

"So you will? You'll come with me? For sure?"

"Of course," she said, her voice a little flat, but she knew Holden. He'd blame her lack of enthusiasm on their present circumstance.

"I'll hook you up with Graham's girlfriend, Claire, online. You two can touch base through e-mail, and then you'll know someone out there."

Great, thought Griselda. *The girlfriend. Maybe we can drive over to the base together and peek our noses through the chain-link fence, watching all those military wives swiping their cards at the PX.*

"Thanks," she said.

If she was so damn strong, as she'd boasted to him an hour ago, she should just find the courage to tell him how she felt. Right? Right. She glanced over at him—at the worry lines on his face. Nothing had gone the right way today. Nothing. They were supposed to have this wonderful romantic day to reconnect, and instead his child's life was in jeopardy, and they were talking about her moving to California as a way to comfort themselves instead of as a solid plan for their future. She felt all of this inside, and she even felt compelled to say something, but damn it, now was *not* the time.

"We can talk more about it later, Holden. Okay?"

"But you'll c-come?" he asked quickly, turning his head, his bleak gray eyes skewering her blue.

She stared back at him for a moment before refocusing on the straight stretch of highway up ahead and said the only thing that made sense.

"You jump, I jump," she said, placing her palm over his hand and squeezing.

CHAPTER 39

They were greeted at the hospital by a white-faced, perspiring Clinton, who rushed Holden to the information desk. Once Holden explained that he was the biological father of Gemma's child, he was whisked away to see her, leaving Griselda and Clinton in the waiting room with Quint and Maudie.

After she'd exchanged concerned greetings, Griselda was informed that Gemma had quickly gone from preeclampsia to eclampsia, and the seizure this morning had been their only real warning sign of danger besides the regular aches and pains they'd all chalked up to the pregnancy. As far as they knew— they heard this from a nurse who'd taken pity on their worried faces and shared what she could—the baby seemed to be okay, but she'd need to be delivered today. Gemma's body simply wasn't able to carry her any longer.

"She's so little," said Clinton, looking up at Griselda with red-rimmed eyes.

She sat beside him, putting her arm around his shoulders. "Thirty-four weeks is real close to term, and this looks like a good hospital. I bet they're going to be just fine. Both of them."

Offering to grab some coffee for the worried trio, she headed to the vending machines in the hallway and purchased four cups, then sat down with them to wait. It didn't take long. Holden returned about an hour later.

And she knew.

She knew from his eyes that she'd been right.

He pulled the surgical mask from over his mouth, his grin lighting up the whole room. "They're both going to be okay! Hannah was just born, and they're sewing up Gemma now. She's here. She's okay!"

Clinton hung his head, sinking down into a plastic chair, his shoulders trembling with relief and thanks, and Maudie rushed to comfort him while Quint stood up and offered his hand to Holden. "Congratulations, Papa."

"Thanks, Quint."

Griselda hung back a little, uncertain of her place until Holden swept her into his arms, spinning her around. His face was flushed and excited as he gushed, "She's f-fine, Gris. She's little, but f-fine. She weighed five pounds, and she cried real loud and strong. She got a seven on her Apgar test, and then a nine. She's got d-dark hair like Gem's, and blue eyes . . . sorta like mine."

Griselda's eyes watered instantly, and she cupped Holden's cheeks, kissing him joyfully. "Congratulations, Papa," she said, stealing Quint's line.

"P-papa," he sighed. "I'm a father, G-Gris. Somebody's related to me."

"Yes, you are," she said, nodding at him, her tears mixing with her smile. "And yes, she is."

Looking over her shoulder, Holden's expression of joy dimmed. "Gimme a sec."

He released her and headed over to Clinton, sitting down beside his friend.

"Gemma's gonna be okay, Clinton. She's gonna be real good. Just fine."

"I heard you say that," said Clinton, taking a deep breath and sniffling. "Very glad to hear it. Got a little worried there."

"You love her a lot."

"I love 'em both. I love 'em both so much, if anything

happened to 'em, I would've . . ." He paused, swiping at his eyes. "Well, I would've just about wanted to die."

"I know," said Holden, putting his hand on his friend's knee. "I know that. W-which is why Hannah's birth certificate says her daddy's name is Clinton Davis."

Clinton's neck jerked up, his face confused. "Se—Holden. What?"

Holden nodded. "She's yours."

"No! No, Holden. You don't have to do . . . She's . . . she's *yours*."

Holden shook his head slowly. "I won't be here for her. I'll be in C-California. I'll be in Hawaii. I'll be in Afghanistan. I'll always love her, and I'll try to get back here to see her when I c-can. And when I do, I'd like for her to know that it was me that gave her life. But it was you that gave her *a* life. You're the one that loves her mama. You're the one who's gonna love *her*. Right?"

"Already do." Clinton swallowed, blinking furiously as he dropped his embarrassed gaze to his lap. "I'll do right by her. I swear to God, I will love that child and protect her and give her the best life I can. And you'll *always* be welcome to come see her, Holden. Always. We're family now."

Holden blinked too, taking a jagged breath and slapping Clinton's knee twice before standing up. "Well, Daddy. Why don't you go b-back there and see your girls?"

Clinton stood up, giving his parents a proud smile before clapping his arms around Holden. "Thank you. I just . . . Thank you."

Griselda watched Holden clench his jaw tightly as he nodded, and he didn't turn around as Clinton rushed to Gemma's side.

***

Holden had had a lot of time to think about Hannah in boot camp, and while he'd always love her and she'd always be his biological child, he wouldn't be able to be a proper father to her. He didn't love her mother. He wouldn't be living in West Virginia. And getting to her from California between deployments? He simply couldn't guarantee that it would happen with any regularity. Sure, he'd visit her once or twice a year and send her pretty things on her birthday and at Christmas. But that wasn't a father. That wasn't the sort of daddy he wanted for Hannah.

Clinton Davis was the best friend Holden had ever had, and Quint was the closest thing to a father after his own. He knew the Davis family and trusted them. Truth be told? He trusted them more than he trusted Gemma. If he wanted Hannah to have the best possible life? He needed to make damn sure that Clinton had legal rights over his daughter. It was the best way to ensure her safety and her future.

It had ached to write in Clinton's name, denying his own. But he'd learned his first lesson about being a parent on Hannah's birth day. He'd learned that being a parent was about putting yourself second and your child first. And that's exactly what he'd done.

He turned to Quint, who looked at him with wonder and pride. "Welcome home, Marine. I couldn't be prouder if you were my own son. And since your baby girl just became my granddaughter, you'll forgive me if I hug you like you *are* my own."

Pulling Holden into his arms, Quint held him tightly. Holden's chest swelled with the rightness of his decision, and he felt a surge of peace break through his sorrow.

"Thanks, Quint," he said, finally pulling away. He caught sight of Gris over Quint's shoulder, tears running down her face faster than she could swipe them away, her eyes so full of love, he wondered if he could be blinded by it.

"Holden," said Maudie, clasping Holden against her massive bosom. "You didn't have to do that."

He leaned back. "I know y'all will love her, Maudie. You'll be an amazing family to her. B-better than anything I could offer."

Maudie pulled him back, rubbing his back and speaking excitedly. "Yes, we will. And I will send you pictures and footprints, and I will record her little voice saying 'Papa Holden' when she's ready, and she'll always know she had a daddy before Clinton who loved her enough to give her the family he wanted her to have. And when you come visit, she'll know you, Holden. She'll know you, and she'll already love you. I can promise you that, son. Now tell me what you and that sweet gal are doing for Thanksgiving on Thursday because I . . ."

Maudie kept talking a mile a minute, but Holden's eyes caught Griselda's over her shoulder.

He watched her mouth the words "I love you" before sucking her bottom lip into her mouth and placing the tattoo of their initials over her heart.

***

In those dark days in the cellar, Griselda had learned of Holden's selflessness and courage—the countless times he'd sassed Caleb intentionally to distract him from Griselda and take a beating in her place, or the times he'd simply demanded to take it for her because he couldn't bear to see her harmed. His deeply protective nature was a hallmark of his character, and the main reason that military service was such a wise and organic choice for him. He was selfless, courageous, and protective—values that would be put to excellent use in his career of choice.

But until the moment that Holden signed over his parental rights to his best friend, Griselda hadn't realized that the well of Holden's goodness was actually bottomless.

People were fond of saying things like, "I consider myself to be understanding, but even *I* have limits." Or, "I think of myself as a kind person, but I couldn't let *that* slide." People inherently had limits to their virtues, and as disappointing as that fact was, it was a part of life that we all came to understand as we matured, as we learned that life isn't black and white, but a million shades of gray.

The miraculous thing Griselda realized about Holden, standing in that hospital waiting room as he gave his daughter away, was that there was *no* limit to his virtue. His selflessness, courage, and protectiveness knew *no* bounds, *no* tether, *no* limits or conditions. In short, his love knew no end.

And her ridiculous worries about being married or not being married floated away like dust in a windstorm, like they'd never even existed. Because before her was the man of every woman's dreams, and she knew in her heart that God broke the mold after Holden Croft was born. And she knew something else:

Despite the terrible misfortunes of her life, the scales were balanced now because Holden belonged to her.

"That was amazing," she said, as she drove them from the hospital to his apartment on Main Street. "What you did, Holden, was *amazing*."

He took a deep breath. "What I did was *necessary*. I mean, what kind of an asshole f-father would retain his parental rights if he knew that, for the foreseeable future, he wouldn't see his child more than once or twice a year?"

Most, she thought. *Out of pride. Or selfishness. Or fear. Or misguided love.*

He continued, "You know, I'm no saint, Gris. I lucked out. I'm lucky because Gemma chose Clinton, and I *know* Clinton and I *trust* him. If it was some other guy? I can't say I w-would've made the same choice. But I was lucky, Gris. For once in my life, I was lucky."

Her lips turned up a touch as she glanced at him.

"Wait. Back up," he said, placing his hand on her thigh and smiling at her with love in his deep gray eyes. "Twice. Twice in my life I was lucky. The f-first time was when I got moved to the Fillmans'."

"The Fillmans were terrible people," said Griselda as she turned into the alleyway where she remembered him parking his truck.

"Yep," he said.

"And Caleb Foster? He was a monster."

"Yep."

"And we got separated for ten years," she said, cutting the engine.

"Yep."

"And you thought I was dead."

"Yes, I d-did."

"And then your girlfriend got pregnant."

"Yep."

"And your other girlfriend got beat up."

He flinched. "I'm so sorry about that."

"You know what, Holden Croft?" she asked in a saucy voice, ignoring his unnecessary apology and unbuckling her seat belt to lean over the supple leather bolster between the two front seats of the McClellans' Mercedes-Benz.

"Nope," he said, leaning so close that she felt his breath kiss her lips.

"It was about time you had a little more good luck."

And then it wasn't his breath. It was his lips. And he was kissing her madly, deeply, like he was the desert and she was the rain and he couldn't possibly quench his thirst for her in a million lifetimes. His hands reached up to cup her cheeks, his mouth slanting over hers again and again, the hot slide of his tongue against hers driving her out of her mind, and the bolster keeping him way too far away.

"Upstairs," she gasped, drawing back from him, her breasts heaving. "Please."

He scrubbed his hands over his hair, panting as hard as her. He got out of the car, slammed his door, and walked around to open hers. She took his hand, and he set off at a run without looking back at her, down the alley, around the corner of the building, onto the sidewalk, fumbling in his pocket for his keys, then turning the lock as quickly as he could.

Still clutching her hand in his, he took the stairs two at a time, with Griselda practically flying behind him. She was breathless and dizzy by the time he unlocked his apartment door and pulled her inside, backing her against the door and pulling her sweater over her head. There was an urgency between them borne of an intense three-month absence, and neither was prepared to wait another minute to be together.

"Naked. Now," he said, dropping his lips to hers and kissing her savagely as he unhooked her bra behind her back. Griselda let it slip down her arms, freeing her breasts and reaching for the buttons of his shirt. Sucking his tongue into her mouth and loving his low, hot groan, she pushed the material over his broad shoulders, and it fell to the floor. He crushed her against his body, the tight points of her breasts pushing into his hard muscle, made even harder by weeks of boot camp. She could feel the difference in his body, and it made her hotter and wetter to think of lying beneath him as all that strength and power drove into her.

His fingers trailed down her back to the waistband of her pants, skating around to the front. He unbuttoned and unzipped them quickly, slipping his thumbs into the elastic of her new, white, lace panties and yanking them down. Reaching up to hold his face, she kissed him deeply as she struggled out of her boots, then stepped on her pants to free her legs.

Completely naked, she reached for his jeans, unbuttoning and unzipping them as he pressed his lips to her throat, her neck, gently biting her earlobe and making her shiver and whimper. She slid her hand into his boxers, curling her fingers around his thick, satiny penis, which pointed straight up and pulsed against her palm. He gasped, pushing his remaining clothes over his hips and kicking off his shoes.

Holden took a step away from Griselda, and she took a step back from him, panting as she leaned against the door behind her. His chest, cut from stone, with its hard angles and ripples, heaved with every breath as he traced her body with his eyes: her hair, her eyes, her lips, resting on her breasts, sliding down her flat tummy to the tidy curls that concealed her throbbing sex, before dropping to her long legs and feet. Her feet, which, for as long as she lived, would be crisscrossed with the barely visible thin white scars, reminding them both of the sharp, dry corn husks that had sliced her skin.

Slowly, deliberately, Holden's eyes traveled back up her body, pausing at the apex of her thighs, his breath hitching at her breasts, finally resting again on her eyes.

"You're fucking beautiful," he murmured, dropping to his knees before her and reaching for her hips. His head fell forward, the close-cropped hair on the top of his head tickling her belly. She dropped her hands to his head, sliding her palms to his cheeks and tilting his face back so she could look down at him. His gaze was bewildered, worshipful, waiting for her permission to continue.

"Love me," she whispered.

"Do you trust me, angel?" he asked, his gray eyes smoldering as he stared up at her.

"Completely."

He leaned forward to push her back against the door, then grabbed her thighs and lifted them onto his shoulders so that his mouth was level with her sex. Still holding her eyes, his tongue dipped forward to find its mark—the tight bundle of nerves hidden behind soft, wet folds. Her shredded whimper made him groan as he stroked her more urgently, his tongue circling, then lapping, her heels pushing into his back. He looked up, and she managed to smile before letting her head fall back against the door, her breath coming in sharp pants. Her thighs tightened.

Her fingers curled into his scalp. And from the back of her throat burst a sound of pure pleasure as her body went rigid then limp, trembling against him in waves as she laughed quietly above him.

"Oh my God," she panted. "That was . . ."

He placed a palm on her tummy to hold her up as he disengaged her legs from his shoulders and stood up. Just as her knees buckled, he swept her into his arms, walked quickly through the living room and down the hallway to his bedroom, where he set her gently on the bed.

Covering her with his body, he kissed her with glistening lips that tasted of her essence, salty and sweet, a reminder of his tenderness: that her pleasure came first. Overcome with love for him, she opened her legs, running her ankles along the backs of his calves . . . thighs . . . finally resting lightly on his backside as he positioned himself to enter her.

"Holden," she said as he leaned over her, his arms taut, his eyes dark and desperate. "I meant it. I trust you completely. I trust *us* completely."

***

Her words mended whatever was left of Holden's once-shattered heart, giving him the only thing he still longed for between them: trust.

Holden's eyes clenched shut, and he slid forward into the tight, wet heat of her body, her quivering muscles pulling him forward until he was lodged as deep as possible, his pelvis flush against hers, one being, no room for breath between them.

He throbbed inside her, forcing himself to stay still as she accepted his length and thickness, the walls of her sex adjusting to embrace him. He reached for her face, framing it, cradling it, treasuring it, after such a long and aching absence.

"That means everything to me," he said.

Her lips tilted up, and she leaned her head back as she arched her hips into his, an unspoken request that he move within her, and he answered her plea, finding a rhythm that was new but familiar, immediate but eternal, the good and the right and the reward and the gift, and as the wave of perfection built steadily inside him, he rocked into her faster and faster.

"I love you. I love you . . . forever," he said, his voice strained and rough.

She opened her eyes, dark, dark, and wide blue that were the windows to the only soul he would ever want or ever love, and they locked on his without mercy.

"I jump, you jump," she murmured.

"Now!" he bellowed, sliding his arms beneath Griselda and clasping her to his chest.

Their bodies exploded together, shattering into a million mixed pieces of forever, and two people who had always been one—from the very beginning—were finally free.

Hours later, as the sun set and the sounds of American life funneled up from the sidewalk below, Holden sat against the headboard of his bed and laughed, shaking his head as Griselda lay naked beside him, her head propped up on one bent elbow.

"I swear," she said earnestly.

"I don't believe you," he said, marveling that he was here and she was here, and they were finally free: free of the Fillmans, of Caleb Foster, of Gemma, of fear, of longing, of loneliness. Free of mistrust and doubt. Free to love. Free to be together. Free to chase down their forever.

He'd left his jacket—and the ring—in the car, but it had occurred to him at least five times to get dressed and run downstairs. But was this how he wanted to propose? Lying in bed in his crappy apartment?

She was so beautiful with the dying sun backlighting her blonde hair like a halo, and he chuckled again as she held up three fingers in Scout's honor.

"I promise. I didn't do it—*not once*—until I was almost eighteen."

He slid down until he was lying level with her, his head propped on an elbow in a mirror image of her.

"That's impossible. You're so gorgeous. How did you keep the boys away?"

She looked down at the sheets, then back up at him, a rosy blush coloring her cheeks. "I didn't want any of them."

"Who'd you want?"

She gave him a saucy look through lowered lashes. "Billy. I was holding out for Billy, because he—ah!"

Holden's fingers slipped under her arms and started tickling, and she rolled onto her back, giggling like crazy, trying to escape him, but he followed her, lying partially across her chest. He took her wrists, holding them over her head, and then stared down at her with a teasing grin.

"Answer me now. Who'd you want, Miss Griselda?"

She took a deep breath, her breasts pushing against his chest on purpose. He knew from the sassy gleam in her eyes. "Hmm. Okay. I'll come clean." She sighed like she'd been found out. "Mr. Fillman. Those black socks he used to wear at the beach . . ."

He pushed her wrists together and held them with one hand, the other reaching for her armpit again.

"No!" she squealed. "Don't tickle me! You! *You*! I wanted you. I always wanted you."

He stared down at her, taking in the flush of her skin, the redness of her lips from so much kissing. "And I wanted you."

Though she was veritably trapped beneath him, she smiled so tenderly, so serenely, with such trust and love, it made his heart swell.

"You aren't mean," she whispered. "And you're real pretty."

He searched her eyes, remembering their perilous walk to a general store years and years ago, and the words he'd chosen to tell her how much he liked her. "It's as true now as it was then."

He let go of her wrists and dipped his head to kiss her, tangling his tongue with hers, and his erection grew thick and hard against her thigh, telling her he wanted her again.

"What comes next?" she asked.

"Hopefully you."

She looked surprised, then smiled, raising her eyebrows. "And you."

"Hell, yes," he said, rubbing against her.

"Then what?" she asked, winding her arms around his neck.

He glanced at the door to his bedroom. "I could use some help packing up here. Furniture stays, but I'll take my clothes and towels. The Xbox. We'll take what's mine. I'll leave a check for two months' rent and the key on the kitchen table."

"I'm happy to help. What's after that?"

"Sleep?"

"Unlikely." She licked her lips and raised her hips just a touch, teasing him. "And then?"

He shook his head at her minxy ways. "Visit Hannah tomorrow morning before we go?"

"I'd love to meet her." She gazed up at him, her fingers tickling the hairs on the back of his neck. "Before we go where?"

"Home."

"*My* home?"

He shrugged. "For this week, it's *our* home, angel."

"And when we get there?" she asked, her eyes expectant.

His mind flashed to the ring waiting for her in the car. Is that what she was asking him? Was she asking him about this week or about forever? He knew her so well, but there were moments that adult Gris threw him and he just wasn't sure. More than anything, he wanted the moment to be perfect for her when he asked. It was important to him. She deserved that.

Will you say yes to me, sweet angel?

"I guess you'll just have to wait and see," he said, claiming her mouth with his mouth and her body with his.

CHAPTER 40

After breakfast, Holden and Griselda stopped by the hospital to visit Hannah, and Holden's heart swelled when Gemma invited Griselda to hold his daughter.

Seeing Gris, so young and beautiful, holding his baby made all sorts of ideas swim around in his head, all ending in how fucking badly he wanted to be married to her and have babies with her and be allowed the privilege of calling her his wife. He kissed his tiny daughter on the forehead, whispering that he loved her, before gently handing her back to Clinton, who beamed down at the child's face like no baby had ever been more precious. And again Holden knew the rightness of his decision to relinquish his paternal rights. He would find his place in Hannah's life, but Clinton had been her real daddy right from the start.

After packing up the McClellans' trunk with Holden's meager belongings, they stopped by Quint and Maudie's to say good-bye, and Maudie made them promise to come back on Thursday for Thanksgiving. It was Griselda who accepted Maudie's invitation with tearful thanks, surprising him when she suddenly embraced the older woman, and Holden realized how much Griselda needed and wanted to be included in his life with the Davises. And he loved her for it because it meant that she had opened a room in her heart for his daughter, ex-girlfriend, best friend, and surrogate parents. It meant that Griselda wanted them in her life too.

As they drove out of town, Holden turned to her, the ring still burning a hole in his pocket, and asked, "M-mind if we make one more stop?"

She turned to him with bright eyes and shrugged. "Sure. Where?"

"You trust me?"

"With all my heart."

"There's just somewhere I need to see."

It was hard to find the spot where they'd tried to cross the Shenandoah so many years ago, with Caleb Foster and Cutter chasing them down, so in the end he'd had to approximate the location. He parked on the side of the road, as close as he could get, and turned to Griselda. "I want to see it."

She stiffened in her seat, staring out her window at the woods.

"I don't," she finally whispered, her eyes sad and heavy as she turned to face him. "I don't want to see the place where I left you."

"The place where we were *separated*."

"The place where I escaped."

"The place where we *survived*." He paused a moment, looking deeply into her eyes. "Come with me. We need to face it together, Gris. It'll haunt us if we d-don't."

"I can't," she sobbed.

"You *c-can*, angel. I'll be right next to you."

She tugged her bottom lip into her mouth, looked out the window, then took a deep, ragged breath. "Okay."

He stepped out of the car and walked around to open her door. Her fingers trembled as she took his offered hand. She stood up, looking at the woods with cautious eyes, before turning to him.

"It was a long time ago," he said, lacing his fingers through hers. "We were just kids trying to survive something terrible.

We were b-brave, Gris. We were strong. We had hope."

"We gave each other hope," she said, her voice breaking on the word "hope."

He tugged on her hand, leading her over the gravel at the side of the highway and into the woods, where they could hear the faint, faraway sound of the rushing Shenandoah through the trees. Griselda didn't say a word, her head down, as she walked quietly behind him.

It was a long walk, and Holden's memories rushed back—*I know you hurt, Holden. I hurt too, but don't stop!*—in jagged, painful flashbacks,—*Through the cornfields and across the river*—blinding him with snapshots—*Don't look back, no matter what*—that made his head ache—*You still with me, Holden?*—and heart clench—*You leave him be! Let him go!*

But he soldiered on, for a good half hour or so, pulling Griselda silently behind him. Stepping over fallen trees and around boulders, they drew closer and closer, until he looked up and there it was: the Shenandoah River, water rushing white over the exposed rocks, loud and ominous and . . . beautiful.

It was beautiful.

Through any eyes, by any yardstick, it was proof of nature's bounty, of God's mastery over His earth, and it was not responsible for the actions of Caleb Foster so long ago. It was a beautiful place that had been tainted by evil, but here and now Holden could see clearly: it was stunning.

The clear, fresh water.

The bright green trees flanking the shore.

The rolling hills.

The dazzling blue sky.

Finishing their walk to the shore line, he realized that he wasn't pulling Griselda anymore; she was walking along beside him, as much in awe of this magnificent place as he.

As he gazed down at her, she stared out at the river with wonder for a long time, finally looking up at him with tears in her eyes. And he saw it as much as he felt it: the lightness that comes when you settle old scores. The Shenandoah was just a river, and they were no longer the helpless children it had so cruelly separated.

"We're on the other side."

He nodded, just able to catch sight of the cornfields across and downriver in the distance. "That's right."

"We're on the other side," she said again, her voice soft and amazed.

"Together, Gris." He squeezed her hand, his eyes burning as he smiled down at her. "We finally made it across."

He wasn't just talking about that terrible day so long ago. He was talking about finding each other, and loving each other, and—hopefully, soon—choosing each other. Holden stepped behind Griselda and put his arms around her, pulling her tightly against his chest as the sun shone down on their faces and the river rushed before them.

Something terrible had happened here once upon a time, but now they stood victorious in the very place of their defeat, and their happily ever after was just within reach. At some point Gris reached up and covered Holden's hands with hers, and he thought to himself, *Right here. Right now. Me holding onto her and her holding onto me . . . this is as close to heaven as a man can get on earth.*

And then, *What in the world are you waiting for?*

He leaned down, settling his chin on her shoulder.

"Gris?" he said softly by her ear, his arms still tight around her.

"Mmm?"

"Gris, I gotta ask you something."

"Whatever it is," she said, her voice soft, full of trust and love. "The answer's yes."

He laughed softly, his chest rumbling behind her, joy making him smile and press his lips to the warn skin of her neck.

"No, angel. I gotta *ask* you."

Her breath caught—he felt her chest under his hands—and suddenly her fingers tightened.

"Holden . . .," she started.

He let his arms slip from around her and stepped in front of her, lowering himself to one knee. He heard her surprised gasp and when he looked up, her eyes were wide and glistening.

"What are you doing?" she asked, her voice nervous, breathless.

"You know exactly what I'm doing," he said, as she covered her mouth with trembling fingers.

Holden reached out for her free hand and held it, sweeping his gaze over her lovely face before focusing on her eyes.

"I fell in love with you when I was ten years old because you were pretty and you weren't mean. And I would've died so many times in this life if it hadn't been for you . . . my angel, my friend, my family, my hope, my joy, my love.

"Every time I said the words 'protect and serve' in boot camp, I'd think, 'protect Gris, serve Gris,' and then I'd add on every other word I could think of: talk to Gris, write to Gris, make babies with Gris, grow old with Gris. Love Gris. Loving you is like breathing for me. I can't live without it.

"And I know we're g-going to have to say g-good-bye a hundred times in this life, but I figure we're pretty good at holding on, aren't we? And we're pretty good at finding each other again. N-no matter what."

She nodded, her lips trembling as she swiped her tears away. He flipped her hand over then dropped his head, pressing his lips over the letters "H+G."

"You turned my life around, Griselda. You gave me my life back. You made me want to live again . . . and live well. You are the breath that I take and the beat of my heart, and no matter where I am, you are always beside me, so we will never be separated again. But I want one more thing from you. You ready?" he asked, blinking his eyes with emotion, but managing a lopsided grin that she lopsidedly returned with a small nod. "Griselda Schroeder, I will love you and protect you and serve you and honor you, angel, until the day I die. I jump, you jump. And you already said yes a few minutes ago, but I figure I should ask you again . . . W-will you marry me? W-will you be my wife?"

***

"Yes!" she exclaimed, still holding out her hand and trying, unsuccessfully, to keep it steady.

Holden leaned down to press his lips to her fingertips before reaching into his pocket to take out the little black velvet box. He flipped it open, taking out the ring and slipping it onto her finger. She leaned down and reached for his cheeks, cradling them tenderly and urging him to stand. Once he did, she pulled his face down to hers.

"I love you," she said. "I have *always* loved you. I *will* always love you, Holden Croft. I can't wait to be your wife."

"My wife," he murmured.

"You taught me how to love again, how to hope, and how to trust. I wasn't alive until the day you walked back into my life, and now nothing matters but you. You and me. Together," she finished, her voice breaking with emotion.

When she'd exited the McClellan's car an hour ago, Griselda never imagined she could feel a peace as profound as that she'd felt standing at the banks of the dreaded Shenandoah with Holden's arms around her. No, they could never go back to that catastrophic day so many years ago, but life had given them a second chance to cross to the other side together, and this morning all of her dreams had come true.

"I love you forever," she whispered.

His lips descended swiftly, the weight of his body crashing into hers as she kissed him back.

By now, it felt like she'd kissed Holden a thousand times,

certain in the knowledge that their hearts and souls and minds were bound on an otherworldly level, and yet this kiss was new because the ring on her finger would join her life to his in the last remaining—very worldly—way: in marriage. She had been Griselda Schroeder and Zelda Shroder. But becoming Griselda Croft—a name written on her heart more than a decade ago—would be her dearest, most longed- for dream come true.

Holden drew back, smiling down at her. "You said yes."

"Twice."

"There's more."

Worry crept into her joyful heart. "What?"

"I want us to get married now."

"Today?"

"No. Well, sure, if that's what you want. I mean *now*, before I go to Fort Sill a week from Monday. Once we're married, we can apply for base housing at my PDS, which will almost definitely be Camp Pendleton. I want you to meet me out in California in a few weeks, and we can move into our first house, Gris."

"Our first home," she said, sniffling from tears, her heart overflowing with love for him and excitement for her life with him.

"*You* were my first home," he answered softly, kissing her again.

Her fingers spanned his scalp as she slipped her tongue into his mouth, swallowing his groan. Running her hands down the strong arms that had held her as a child, and now held her as a woman, she acknowledged the profound depth of her gratitude and the eternal well of her love for him.

"I want you, fiancée," he growled, the words tickling her ear.

"We have wedding plans to make," she said, arching her back to tease him, "as soon as we get home."

"That'll have to wait," he said, the low rumble of his

chuckle making her toes curl with happiness. "I've got other business with you first."

"Okay, Holden Croft, you win." She leaned back to look up at him and knew that her eyes were shining with more joy than she ever imagined she could possibly deserve. "But you better not tire me out *too* much. I've got a wedding to plan."

***

Holden quickly learned that when you ask a girl to marry you and tell her she has nine days to make it happen, she doesn't waste a minute.

After a call to Sabrina, who insisted they get married at their house in Georgetown on Sunday night—Roy would take care of the license and officiant—Griselda called Maya to ask her to be her maid of honor, and Holden called Quint to be his best man, since Clinton needed to stay close to Gemma and Hannah. Maudie made Quint wrangle another promise from them to come back for Thanksgiving on Thursday, and while there, Maudie offered Griselda her wedding dress, which had been lovingly preserved in a box of tissue paper for twenty-five years and fit Griselda like a glove.

On Friday they stopped in to see Professor and Mrs. Foster, sharing their good news, and Professor Foster handed them a check, calling it a wedding gift, and Ruth asked them to please keep in touch. When they opened the envelope outside and found out the check was for five thousand dollars, they raced back inside to return it. But Seth and Ruth, hands interlaced, eyes kind, insisted that the amount was right, and asked that they keep the money to start a good life and take a little of the sting away from the name Foster.

Sabrina arranged for the wedding dinner and cake, Maya picked out a bridesmaid dress for herself and a flower girl dress for Prudence, and on Sunday night, Holden stood next to the fireplace in the McClellans' living room and smiled as the woman of his dreams took her place by his side and promised to be his wife.

The officiant, a judge who was a friend of Roy's, smiled at the couple and said, "We are gathered together here in the sight of God, and in the face of these friends and loved ones, to join together Holden Croft and Griselda Schroeder in holy matrimony, instituted by God since the first man and first woman walked the earth. Therefore, it is not to be entered into unadvisedly, or lightly, but reverently and soberly. Into this holy estate these two persons present come now to be joined."

Holden looked into Griselda's blue eyes, focusing on her unspeakably beautiful face, remembering her as a child, a teenager, an adult woman climbing the stairs to his apartment, his love, his life, his angel.

"Do you, Holden, take Griselda to be your lawfully wedded wife, to have and to hold, in sickness and in health, to love, honor, and cherish, in good times and bad, for richer or poorer, keeping yourself solely unto her for as long as you both shall live?"

"I do," he said, squeezing her hand.

"Do you, Griselda, take Holden to be your lawfully wedded husband, to have and to hold, in sickness and in health, to love, honor, and cherish, in good times and bad, for richer or poorer, keeping yourself solely unto him for as long as you both shall live?"

"I do," she said, her smile brilliant and strong.

"Who has the rings?" asked the judge, and Quint stepped up, winking at Holden and handing them each a simple gold band.

The officiant nodded, and Holden took a deep breath as he slipped the wedding band onto Griselda's finger.

"I give you this ring as a symbol of my love. As it encircles your finger, may it remind you always that you are surrounded by my enduring love. I give you this ring as a symbol of my faithfulness. As I place it on your finger, I commit my heart and soul to you. I give you this ring because no matter where I am on this earth, I b-belong to you and only you until the d-day I die."

***

She couldn't hold back the tears as Holden pledged his eternal love and fidelity to her, but she took a deep breath and smiled for him, trying not to tremble as he held out his hand and she slipped a matching gold band onto his ring finger.

"I give you this ring because I have already given you my heart, my soul, and my life. As it encircles your finger, may it remind you always that you are surrounded by my enduring love. I give you this ring as a symbol of my trust. As I place it on your finger, I join my life and my destiny with yours. I give you this ring because no matter how far apart we are, I belong to you and only you until the day I die."

Holden nodded once, blinking furiously and taking her hands in his once again, before looking back at the judge, who intoned, "Love is patient, love is kind. It does not envy, it does not boast, it is not proud. It does not dishonor others, it is not self-seeking, it is not easily angered, it keeps no record of wrongs. Love does not delight in evil but rejoices with the truth. It always protects, always trusts, always hopes, always perseveres."

At first, Griselda had hesitated to add a Bible verse to their wedding ceremony since Old Testament verses accompanied some of her worst memories. But when the judge suggested this *New* Testament reading, it had felt so right, described their love so perfectly, she had quickly consented. And now she looked up at Holden as the words were said.

Patience. Kindness. Protection. Trust. Hope. Perseverance. It was perfect. It was them.

She nodded at him, and he grinned at her in return.

"Holden and Griselda, may the blessings of life, the joy of love, the peace of truth, and the wisdom and strength of spirit, be your constant companions, now and always. I now pronounce you husband and wife." He turned to Holden. "You may kiss the bride!"

As their friends and family cheered, Holden placed his palms on her cheeks, and Griselda looked up into his eyes as they cemented their formal vows with words of their own:

"I jump," she whispered.

"You jump."

"Never let me go."

"I promise."

"I love you forever, Holden," she said.

"I love you forever, angel."

Gray eyes met blue, fingers intertwined, hearts pressed together, and Holden and Griselda, who'd been lost then found, apart then together, unloved then cherished, pressed their lips together and finally crossed over the river into forever.

EPILOGUE

"Gris!" exclaimed Claire, waving from a bench that looked out on the base parking lot. "I saved you a spot."

Griselda made her way through the crowd, grinning at her very pregnant friend. "Baby ended up waiting for daddy to get home, huh?"

"And just in the nick of time," said Claire, pointing at her massive belly. "*This* is happening any minute."

"All this excitement? I bet your water breaks when he kisses you hello," teased Griselda, taking a seat.

Claire sighed. "Did this tour feel longer than six months? Or is that just me?"

It always feels longer, thought Griselda, remembering the spring day, half a year ago, when she kissed Holden good-bye and watched him step onto the bus for his second tour to Afghanistan.

"Oh, I don't know," she said. "At least they're home for Thanksgiving this time."

"You two going East?" asked Claire. "To see family?"

Griselda nodded. "That's the plan. Hannah's turning three. Can you believe it?"

They'd missed Thanksgiving and Hannah's first birthday due to Holden's first deployment, but they'd managed to make it last year, and Griselda was overjoyed that they'd be there again this year. Hannah Croft Davis was a delightful, smart, beloved little girl who was still learning how to be nice to her brand-new little brother, according to Maudie's most recent letter.

"I'm surprised the doc's letting you fly," said Claire, looking pointedly at Griselda's tummy, which wasn't quite as round as her friend's yet.

Griselda placed her palms protectively over the swell under her red baby-doll top. "I'm not even seven months yet! Don't rush me."

"Oh, yeah," said Claire with a tired sigh. "I guess I was thinking of me. Not allowed to fly until after she comes." Claire nudged Griselda in the side. "Does Holden know yet? That you're having a boy?"

Griselda shook her head. "No. But he's going to find out today."

"Oh!" said Claire, shifting to the side to pull something out of her purse. "I almost forgot! I wanted you to sign this before the baby gets here. I bought it off Amazon."

Griselda looked down at the familiar, colorful cover of her first book of children's fairy tales. "Claire! You didn't have to do that! I would have given you one for free."

"Nuh-uh," she answered. "I'm a paying customer!"

Griselda took the proffered pen, signing her name and writing a message to Claire and Graham's first child, a girl they planned to name Grace, before handing the book back to Claire.

"'Dear Grace,'" Claire read. "'May you find your Sun King too. Love, Lady Starlight.' What does it mean?"

"It means I wish her happiness," said Gris softly.

Their conversation was interrupted by a sudden chattering among the other family members around them. Mothers, fathers, sisters and brothers, wives like Griselda and Claire, and their children stood up from the bleachers as the big white truck pulled into the parking lot bearing the luggage of the returning platoon.

"They're almost here!" exclaimed Griselda, leaping up and helping Claire to her feet.

First the white truck, then the white school buses, she thought, her heart leaping with excitement to see her husband again. Holding Claire's hand, she strained up on tiptoes to see if the buses were coming around the corner yet.

"Any minute!" said Claire, squeezing her friend's hand.

A moment later, the joyful whooping and clapping started, and Griselda looked up to see three white buses approaching the empty parking lot. The buses pulled in and parked as the roar of the crowd grew louder. Her eyes started to water with anticipation, and she scanned the buses, wondering which one held Holden.

"They're here!"

Cameras clicked and flags waved. Little children in their patriotic best asked, "Where's Daddy?!" while holding homemade welcome signs, and the whole crowd laughed and smiled, whooping and clapping.

As the buses parked, the crowd surged forward for their reunions, and Griselda gave Claire a careful hug before dropping her friend's hand. Khaki-covered Marines started filtering through the crowd as they exited the buses, looking for loved ones with big smiles and glistening eyes.

Griselda's heart thumped like crazy as she searched their tan faces, recognizing some, but looking for the one she loved, and then . . . there he was, just a few feet away, sliding his hat off his shaved head with wonder, and beaming as his eyes caught hers. She laughed, tears streaming down her face as he closed the distance between them. His eyes dropped, just for a second, to her belly, before sliding back up to her face.

"Gris," he said, pulling her into his arms and dropping his lips to hers.

He kissed her tenderly, their tears mixing together as she instantly remembered how he felt, how he tasted, how he loved her more and better than anyone ever would or could.

Breathless, she dropped her forehead to his shoulder, and he held her tightly as he whispered, "I missed you like crazy," close to her ear as they rocked back and forth together.

She leaned back to kiss him again, smiling and laughing and crying as she answered, "I love you forever."

"You feeling okay, Mrs. Croft?" he asked, stepping back and letting his eyes drop to her swollen tummy.

"I'm feeling pregnant," she said, smoothing her hands over the bump. "And I missed you." She grinned up at him. "And so did our son."

"Our . . .?" He sucked in a deep breath, his eyes wide.

"Our son." She nodded, cupping his cheeks and giggling through her tears. "We're having a boy, Holden."

"G-Gris," he murmured, blinking his eyes, his lips trembling, overcome.

He clutched her against him again, resting his forehead on her shoulder as she laced her fingers on the back of his neck, savoring the feeling of his strong arms around her. And her heart sang, for this was Holden: her best friend, her confidant, her lifelong protector, the keeper of her memories, the father of her child, the love of her life, her beginning and her end—Holden, whom she loved, whom she trusted, who belonged to her, was beside her once again.

I jump, you jump, she thought, resting her head in the curve of his neck and breathing in the scent of his sweet-smelling skin. *We did it. We're on the other side, my love.*

"Ask me if I'm whole or broken, Griselda Croft," he said, leaning back to tenderly place his palm on her belly before looking up at her with tears in his beloved gray eyes.

"Are you whole or broken, Holden Croft?"

"I'm whole, angel," he said, staring down at her face before drawing her back into the heaven of his arms. "I'm finally home."

THE END

A LETTER TO MY READERS

Dear Reader,

Thank you so much for reading *Never Let You Go*. I hope you enjoyed Holden and Griselda's love story.

As I wrote this book, I was very much inspired by the real-life story of Elizabeth Smart, who was kidnapped from her home at fourteen years old and reunited with her family nine months later, after enduring unthinkable abuse, including rape and brainwashing. With the love and support of her church and family, Elizabeth managed to "come back" from her nightmare and build an amazing life for herself: she married a wonderful man, published a book, started a foundation, and she gives hope to the survivors of abduction and abuse with her story every day.

I wondered if I could write a story in which the hero and heroine were abducted and endured abuse but somehow managed to survive, to find each other again, and to build a life for themselves. After losing a beloved pet named Gretl and rereading the fairy tale *Hansel and Gretel*, *Never Let You Go* was born.

In the Grimm brothers' *Hansel and Gretel*, the brother and sister held captive by the witch leave a trail of bread crumbs to find their way home. Well, there are no literal bread crumbs in this story, but the figurative ones are clear. They are love, faith, trust, and the strength to hold on when all hope seems lost. *Those* are the bread crumbs that matter in all of our lives, and the very ones that lead

Holden and Griselda back into each other's arms.

In honor of the inspiration Elizabeth Smart's story gave me in the writing of this book, **I am pleased to give back 25% of my gross royalties for June and July 2015 to the Elizabeth Smart Foundation,** which aims, among other things, to support the **Internet Crimes Against Children** Task Force and to educate children about violent and sexual crime. For more information, go here: elizabethsmartfoundation.org

Love,
Katy

Never Let You Go
Writer Playlist

"Always You," Ingrid Michaelson
"At This Moment," Billy Vera & the Beaters
"Before It Breaks," Brandi Carlile
"Can't Take My Eyes Off Of You," Lauryn Hill
"Falling Slowly," Elenowen
"Gold In The Air," Jesse Woods
"Hero," Family of the Year
"I See the Light" (from the *Tangled* sound track), Mandy Moore and Zachary Levi
"Look So Tired," Landon Pigg
"Make You Feel My Love,"* *Glee* cast
"No One Will Ever Love You," *Nashville* cast, featuring Connie Britton and Charles Esten
"The Very Thought Of You,"* Ray Noble
"Through My Prayers," The Avett Brothers
"We Might Be Dead By Tomorrow," Soko

*Mentioned in the book

ACKNOWLEDGMENTS

To all of my friends on Twitter, Pinterest, Goodreads, and Facebook, I am so excited to share *Never Let You Go* with you! Thanks for your daily support and encouragement. I have the best fans ever!

A special shout-out to Katy's Ladies, the kindest, most amazing street team an author could ever ask for. I am grateful for every one of you.

To Mia Sheridan, who answered a ton of questions for me about whether to split this book in half (like *Becoming Calder* and *Finding Eden*) or go ahead and publish a behemoth! I am grateful for your counsel, sweet Mia.

To Marianne Nowicki for my gorgeous cover. You are the best at what you do and the easiest to work with. That you're a perfectionist too is just the cherry on the sundae.

To Tessa for her superhelpful developmental edit, and to Cassie Mae for her fabulous formatting. I'd be lost without you two!

To Chris Belden and Melissa DeMeo, my editors, who don't let me get away with anything. That's the way I want it. That's the way I need it. Your insight, notes, and advice make my writing the best it can be. I am so thankful to work with a team like you.

To my parents, who never fail to encourage and inspire. Your support means the world to me. Always has, always will. Thank you from the bottom of my heart for your love.

And finally, to George, Henry, and Callie, my dearly beloved. The most important thing is kindness, and I love you all the much.

ABOUT THE AUTHOR

Award-winning and Amazon bestselling author Katy Regnery started her writing career by enrolling in a short story class in January 2012. One year later, she signed her first contract for a winter romance entitled *By Proxy*.

Now a hybrid author who publishes both independently and traditionally, Katy claims authorship of the six-book *Heart of Montana* series, the six-book *English Brothers* series, and a Kindle Worlds novella entitled *Four Weddings and a Fiasco: The Wedding Date*. Katy's short story "The Long Way Home" appears in the first Romance Writers of America anthology, *Premiere*, and she has published two stand-alone novels, *Playing for Love at Deep Haven* and the Amazon bestseller *The Vixen and the Vet*, which is book one in Katy's a m o d e r n f a i r y t a l e collection. *The Vixen and the Vet* was nominated for a RITA® Award in 2015.

Katy lives in the relative wilds of northern Fairfield County, Connecticut, where her writing room looks out at the woods, and her husband, two young children, and two dogs create just enough cheerful chaos to remind her that the very best love stories begin at home.

Upcoming (2015) Projects:

The Winslow Brothers (Books #1-4)
Ginger's Heart, a modern fairytale

Sign up for Katy's newsletter today:
http://www.katyregnery.com**!**

Katy Regnery loves to hear from her fans!
Connect with her on **www.facebook.com/KatyRegnery**

CPSIA information can be obtained
at www.ICGtesting.com
Printed in the USA
FSOW04n2055070416
18975FS